Tawny-Lynn leaned into Chaz, her body trembling. Ever since that awful accident, she'd felt alone.

She'd learned to deal with it and to stand on her own, but for just a moment, she allowed herself the comfort of Chaz's arms.

Tension slowly seeped from her tightly wound muscles. She felt the warmth of his arms encircling her, the soft rise and fall of his chest against her cheek, the whisper of his breath against her ear.

But the safety felt too wonderful for her to fantasize that it would last.

Finally she raised her gaze to his. His eyes darkened with concern and other emotions that made her want to reach up and touch his cheek.

Kiss his lips.

D0318645

COLD CASE AT CAMDEN CROSSING

BY
RITA HERRON

MILLS & BOON

First published in Great Britain 2013
by Mills & Boon, an imprint of Harlequin (UK) Limited,
Eton House, 18-24 Paradise Road, Richmond, Surrey TW9 1SR

© Rita B. Herron 2013

ISBN: 978 0 263 90384 3

46-1213

Harlequin (UK) policy is to use papers that are natural, renewable and recyclable products and made from wood grown in sustainable forests. The logging and manufacturing processes conform to the legal environmental regulations of the country of origin.

Printed and bound in Spain
by Blackprint CPI, Barcelona

Award-winning author **Rita Herron** wrote her first book when she was twelve, but didn't think real people grew up to be writers. Now she writes so she doesn't have to get a *real* job. A former kindergarten teacher and workshop leader, she traded storytelling to kids for writing romance, and now she writes romantic comedies and romantic suspense. She lives in Georgia with her own romance hero and three kids. She loves to hear from readers, so please write her at PO Box 921225, Norcross, GA 30092-1225, USA, or visit her website, www.ritaherron.com.

To Dana for her support and help on this book!

Prologue

Sixteen-year-old Tawny-Lynn Boulder gripped the edge of the seat as something slammed into the back of the bus and sent it careening to the right, skimming the guardrail.

Tires squealed, the driver lost control and sparks spewed from the sides as they swerved back and forth. Screams from the other girls on the softball team echoed around her. Glass shattered.

She glanced sideways as she struggled to keep from pitching into the aisle. The ravine loomed only a few feet away.

Her body bounced against the seat as the bus rolled. Her sister, Peyton, cried out as her head hit the roof of the bus. Someone's shoe sailed over the seat. A gym bag clumped down the aisle.

Peyton's best friend, Ruth, clawed at her with bloody hands.

Then the bus was sliding, skidding, skating toward the edge of the ravine. Metal screeched and gears ground as they broke through the railing. For a terrifying second, the bus was suspended, teetering on the edge of the cliff.

More screams and blood flying. Then the vehicle crashed over the edge of the embankment, plunging downward into the ravine below.

"Peyton!" Tawny-Lynn cried.

The force threw Peyton over the seat. More glass rained inside as the bus slammed into a boulder.

Her head hit something, her shoulder ramming into the opposite side of the bus. For a moment, she lost consciousness.

Seconds or maybe minutes later, she stirred, her body aching, her leg twisted beneath a gnarled metal seat edge. She searched for Peyton, terrified she was dead.

They'd had a fight earlier. Stupid sister stuff.

She wanted to make up.

Suddenly smoke began to fill the bus. She struggled to free her leg, but she was trapped.

Someone was crying in the back. But the other screams had subsided.

She managed to raise herself and look into the aisle.

God, no… One of the girls wasn't moving.

And Peyton and Ruth, where were they?

The bus rocked back and forth as if hanging on to a boulder. The smoke grew thicker. Somewhere through the gray haze, she saw flames shooting up toward the night sky.

She coughed and choked, then everything went dark.

Chapter One

Seven years later

"Your daddy is dead."

Tawny-Lynn gripped the phone with sweaty palms, then sank onto the bench in her garden. The roses that she'd groomed and loved so much suddenly smelled sickly sweet.

"Did you hear me, Tawny-Lynn?"

She nodded numbly, fighting the bitter memories assaulting her, then realized her father's lawyer Bentley Bannister couldn't see her, so she muttered a quiet yes.

But the memories crashed back. The bus accident. The fire. The screams. Then half the team was dead.

Somehow she'd survived, although she had no idea how. She'd lost time when she'd blacked out. Couldn't remember what had happened after the fire broke out.

But when she'd woken up, her sister and her friend Ruth were gone.

She'd been terrified they were dead. But the police had never found their bodies.

They had escaped somehow. Although half of Camden Crossing thought they'd fallen to foul play, that the accident hadn't been an accident. That a predator had caused the crash, then abducted Peyton and Ruth.

Just like a predator had taken two girls a year before that from a neighboring town.

Bannister cleared his throat, his voice gruff. "He was sick for a while, but I guess you knew that already."

No, she didn't. But then again, she wasn't surprised. His drinking and the two-pack-a-day cigarette habit had to have caught up with him at some point.

"Anyway, I suppose you'll want to be here to oversee the memorial service."

"No, go ahead with that," Tawny-Lynn said. Her father wouldn't have wanted her to come.

Wouldn't have wanted her near him.

Like everyone else in town, he'd blamed her. If she'd remembered more, seen what had happened, they might have been able to find Peyton and Ruth.

"Are you sure? He was your father, Tawny-Lynn."

"My father hated me after Peyton went missing," Tawny-Lynn said bluntly.

"Sugar, he was upset—"

"Don't defend him," she said. "I left Camden Crossing and him behind years ago." Although the crash and screams had followed her, still haunted her in her dreams.

A tense heartbeat passed. "All right. But the ranch... Well, White Forks is yours now."

The ranch. God... She bowed her head and inhaled deep breaths. The familiar panic attack was threatening. She had to ward it off.

"You will come back and take care of the ranch, won't you?"

Take care of it as in *live* there? No way.

She massaged her temple, a migraine threatening. Just the thought of returning to the town that hated her made her feel ill.

"Tawny-Lynn?"

"Just hang a for-sale sign in the yard."

His breath wheezed out, reminding her that he was a heavy smoker, too. "About the ranch. Your father let it go the last few years. I don't think you'll get anything for it unless you do some upkeep."

Tawny-Lynn glanced around her small, cozy apartment. It was nestled in Austin, a city big enough to support businesses. A city where no one knew her and where she could get lost in the crowd.

Where no one hated her for the past.

The last thing she wanted to do was have to revisit the house where her life had fallen apart.

But her conversation with her accountant about her new landscape business echoed in her head, and she realized that selling the property could provide the money she needed to make her business a success.

She had to go back and clean up the ranch, then sell it.

Then she'd finally be done with Camden Crossing and the people in it for good.

SHERIFF CHAZ CAMDEN glanced at the missing-persons report that had just come in over the fax. Another young girl, barely eighteen.

Gone.

Vanished from a town in New Mexico in the middle of the night. A runaway or a kidnapping?

He studied the picture, his gut knotting. She was a brunette like his sister, Ruth, had been. Same innocent smile. Her life ahead of her.

And according to her parents, a happy well-adjusted teenager who planned to attend college. A girl who never came home after her curfew.

They thought someone had kidnapped her just as he'd suspected someone had abducted Ruth and Peyton after that horrendous bus crash.

Not that New Mexico was close enough to Camden Crossing, Texas, that he thought it was the same sicko.

But close enough to remind him of the tragedy that had torn his family apart.

The door to the sheriff's office burst open, and he frowned as his father walked in. Gerome Camden, a banker and astute businessman, owned half the town and had raised him with an iron fist. The two of them had tangled when he was growing up, but Ruth had been his father's pet, and it had nearly killed him when she'd disappeared.

"We need to talk," his dad said without preamble.

Chaz shoved the flier about the missing girl beneath a stack of folders, knowing it would trigger one of his father's tirades. Although judging from the scowl on his aging face, he was already upset about something.

Chaz leaned back in his chair. "What is it, Dad?"

"Tawny-Lynn Boulder is back in town."

Chaz stifled a reaction. "Really? I heard she didn't want a memorial service for her father."

The gray streaks in his father's hair glinted in the sunlight streaming through the window. "Who could blame her? Eugene Boulder was a common drunk."

"Guess that's how he dealt with Peyton going missing."

Unlike his father who'd just turned plain mean. Although he'd heard Boulder *had* been a mean drunk.

"Don't make excuses for that bastard. If Tawny-Lynn hadn't faked that amnesia, we might have found Ruth a long time ago."

Chaz started to point out for the hundredth time that the doctors said the amnesia was real, but his father didn't give him time.

"Bannister handled the will. The ranch is hers."

Chaz sighed and tapped his foot under the desk. "That's no surprise. Tawny-Lynn was his only living relative. It makes sense he'd leave her White Forks."

His father's cheeks reddened as he leaned forward on the desk, his anger gaining steam. "You need to make sure she doesn't stay. This town barely survived that girl years ago. We don't need her here as a reminder of the worst thing that ever happened in Camden Crossing."

Chaz had heard enough. He stood slowly, determined to control the anger building inside him. Just because his father was a big shot in Camden Crossing, he refused to let him push him around.

"Dad, I'm the sheriff, not your personal peon." His father opened his mouth, his hands balling into fists, but Chaz motioned him to hear him out. "My job is to protect the citizens of this town."

"That's what I'm saying—"

"No, it's not. You all ran roughshod over a sixteen-year-old girl who was traumatized and confused. And now you want me to make her leave town?" He slammed his own fist on the desk. "For God's sake, Tawny-Lynn lost her sister that day. She was suffering, too."

She'd been injured, although someone had pulled her free from the fire just before the bus had exploded, taking the driver and three other classmates' lives. The other teammates would have probably died, too, if they'd ridden the bus.

At least they'd speculated that someone had rescued Tawny-Lynn. But no one knew who'd saved her.

And no one else had survived. So how had she escaped?

"She knew more than she was telling," his father bellowed. "And no one wants her here now."

An image of a skinny, teenage girl with wheat-colored hair and enormous green eyes taunted him. Tawny-Lynn had lost her mother when she was three, had adored her sister, Peyton, and suffered her father's abuse.

"You don't know that she even wants to stay. She probably has a life somewhere else. But if she does decide to live at White Forks, that's her right."

"She doesn't give a flying fig about that property or this town. Else she wouldn't have run the way she did."

"She went to college, Dad. Besides, you could hardly blame her for leaving," Chaz said. "No one here seemed to care about her."

"You listen to me, Chaz," his father said as if Chaz were still twelve years old. "I'm not just speaking for myself. I've discussed this with the town council."

Two of the members who'd also lost girls that day served on the council now.

"That ranch is run-down," his father continued. "Just pay her a visit and tell her to sell it. Hell, I'll buy the damn property from her just to force her out."

Chaz couldn't believe that his father was so bitter. That bitterness had festered inside and turned him into a different man.

And not in a good way.

"You want me to go see her and write her a check myself?"

Chaz gritted his teeth. "No, I'll talk to her. But—" He gave his father a stern look. "I'm not going to run her off. I'll just ask her what her plans are. For all we know, she's here to hang a for-sale sign and you're in an uproar for nothing."

His father wiped a bead of perspiration from his neck. "Let me know." He strode to the door, but paused with one hand on the doorknob. "And remember what I said. If you don't get rid of her, I will."

Chaz narrowed his eyes. "That sounds like a threat, Dad."

His father shrugged. "Just thinking about the town."

He couldn't believe his father had held on to his anger for so long. "Well, don't. Leave her alone and let me do my job."

In fact, he would pay Tawny-Lynn a visit. Not to harass her, but to find out if she'd remembered anything else about the day of the crash.

Something that might help him find out what happened to their sisters.

TAWNY-LYNN SHIVERED as she climbed from her SUV and surveyed White Forks. The ranch consisted of fifty acres, just a small parcel of the original two hundred acres that had been used to breed livestock.

But her father had sold it off to make ends meet long ago, and now the barns and stables were broken down and rotting. The chicken coop had been ripped apart in a storm. The roof needed new shingles, and the grass had withered and died—only tiny patches of green poking through the dry ground.

Spring was fading into summer, the weeds choking the yard and climbing near the front porch. The big white farmhouse that she'd loved as a little girl needed painting, the porch was sagging and the shutters hung askew as if a storm had tried to rip them from the frame of the house.

As though the life had been ripped from it the day Peyton had gone missing.

Maybe before—when her mother had died. Although she hardly remembered her. She was three, Peyton five.

Their father's depression and drinking had started then and had grown worse over the years.

Somewhere she heard a dog barking, and figured it had to be a stray

A breeze stirred the leaves on the trees, echoing with voices from the past, and sending the tire swing swaying. Images of her and Peyton playing in the swing, laughing and squealing, flashed back. Snippets of other memories followed like a movie trailer—the two of them chasing the mutt they'd called Bitsy. Picking wildflowers and using them for bows in their hair.

Gathering fresh eggs from Barb and Jean, the two chickens they'd named after their favorite elementary school teachers.

Then her teenage years where she and Peyton had grown apart. Peyton and Ruth Camden had been the pretty girls, into boys, when she'd been a knobby-kneed, awkward shy tomboy.

She'd felt left out.

Then the bus crashed, and Peyton and Ruth were both gone. And her father and the entire town blamed her.

Willing away the anguish and guilt clawing at her, Tawny-Lynn started toward the house. But an engine rumbled from the dirt drive leading into the ranch, and she whipped her head around, alarmed as the sheriff's car rolled in and came to a stop.

Had the town already heard she was back and sent the sheriff to run her off?

They were pulling out all the punches before she even set foot in the house.

The sheriff cut the engine, then opened the door and a long, big body unfolded itself from the driver's side. Thick dark hair capped a tanned, chiseled face. Broad shoulders stretched tight in the man's uniform, and he removed sunglasses to reveal dark, piercing eyes beneath the brim of his Stetson.

Eyes that skated over her with a deep frown.

Her heart stuttered when she realized who the man was.

Chaz Camden.

Ruth's brother and the boy she'd had a crush on seven years ago. The boy whose family had despised her and blamed her for their loss.

The boy who'd visited her in the hospital and tried to push her to remember like everyone else.

CHAZ HADN'T BEEN to White Forks in years and was shocked at its dilapidated condition.

He was even more stunned at how much Tawny-Lynn had changed.

The wheat-colored hair was still the same, although longer and wavier than he remembered. And those grass-green eyes were just as vivid and haunted.

But the skinny teenager had developed some womanly curves that would make a man's mouth water.

"Hello, Tawny-Lynn." Damn, his voice sounded hoarse. Rough with desire. Something he hadn't felt in way too long.

And something he'd never felt for this girl…er…woman.

She shaded her eyes with her hand. "You're sheriff now?"

He gave a clipped nod. He hadn't planned on law enforcement work, but his sister's disappearance had triggered his interest. He'd wanted to find her, and it seemed the best way.

"So the town sent you to run me off?"

She had no idea how close to the truth she was.

"I just heard you were here. I'm sorry for your loss."

"Don't pretend that your family and mine were friends, Chaz. I know how the town and the Camdens feel about me." She gestured to his car. "So you can go back and report that I'm here only to clean up this place so I can put it on the market. I don't intend to stick around."

Chaz heard the anger and hurt in her voice and also recognized underlying guilt. God knows, he'd blamed himself enough.

He was Ruth's big brother. He should have been able to keep her safe.

If only he'd been closer to his sister, known what was going on in her head. Some folks thought she and Peyton had run off together, maybe with boys they'd met some-where.

But others believed they'd been kidnapped.

Tawny-Lynn turned to her SUV, raised the trunk door and reached for her suitcase. He automatically reached for it himself, and their hands touched. A frisson of something sparked between them, taking him off guard.

She must have felt it, too, because her eyes widened in alarm. "I can handle it, Chaz."

"Tawny-Lynn," he said, his voice gruff.

Her shoulders tensed. "What?"

What could he say? "I'm sorry for the way things went down back then."

Anguish flickered on her face before she masked it. "Everyone was hurting, Chaz. Grieving. In shock."

The fact that she was making excuses for the way peo-ple treated her proved she was compassionate. Still, she'd been wronged, and obviously hadn't overcome that pain.

"Did you ever remember anything else?" he asked, then immediately regretted pushing her when she dropped the suitcase and grabbed the handle.

"No. If I did, don't you think I would have told some-one?"

That was the question that plagued him. Some specu-lated that she'd helped Ruth and Peyton run away, while others believed she'd seen the kidnapper and kept quiet out of fear.

Of course, Dr. Riggins said she had amnesia caused from the accident.

So if she had seen the kidnapper, the memory was locked in her head.

HE PULLED THE file with the photos from the bus crash from his locked desk and flipped through the pictures from the newspaper. The bus driver, fifty-nine-year-old Trevor

Jergins, had died instantly when he'd crashed through the front window as the bus had careened over the ridge.

The pictures of the team were there, too. Seventeen-year-old Joan Marx, fifteen-year-old Cassie Truman and sixteen-year-old Aubrey Pullman. All players on the high school softball team.

All girls who died in that crash.

Then there was Ruth and Peyton…

And Tawny-Lynn.

She'd had a concussion and hadn't remembered anything about the accident seven years ago. Had she remembered something since?

Now that she was back in town, would she expose him for what he'd done?

No…he couldn't let that happen. If she started to cause trouble, he'd have to get rid of her.

He'd made it this long without anyone knowing. He didn't intend to go to jail now.

Chapter Two

Tawny-Lynn bounced her suitcase up the rickety porch steps, her pulse clamoring. Good heavens. She'd had a crush on Chaz Camden when she was sixteen, but she thought she'd buried those feelings long ago.

He was even more good-looking now. Those teenage muscles had developed into a powerful masculine body that had thrown her completely off guard.

He looked good in a uniform, too.

Don't go there. You have to clean this wreck of a place up and get the hell out of town.

The door screeched when she jammed the metal key in the lock and pushed it open. Dust motes rose and swirled in the hazy light streaming in through the windows, which looked like they hadn't been cleaned in a decade.

But the clutter inside was even worse. Newspapers, magazines, mail and bills overflowed the scarred oak coffee table and kitchen table. Her father had always been messy and had liked to collect junk, even to the point of buying grab bags at the salvage store, but his habit had turned into hoarding. Every conceivable space on the counter was loaded down with canned goods, boxes of assorted junk, beer cans, liquor bottles and, of all things, oversize spice containers.

Odd for a man who never cooked.

Junk boxes of nuts and bolts and screws were piled in

one corner, dirty clothes had been dumped on the faded-plaid sofa, several pairs of tattered shoes were strewn about and discarded take-out containers lay haphazardly around the kitchen and den.

The sound of mice skittering somewhere in the kitchen sent a shudder through her. If the main area looked like this, she dreaded seeing the other rooms.

The stench of stale beer and liquor mingled with moldy towels and smoke.

Tawny-Lynn heaved a frustrated breath, half tempted to light a match, toss it into the pile and burn the whole place down.

But knowing her luck, she'd end up in prison for arson and the town would throw a party to celebrate her incarceration.

She refused to give them the pleasure.

But she was going to need cleaning supplies. A lot of them. Then she'd handle what repairs she could on her own, but she'd have to hire someone to take care of the major problems.

She left her suitcase in the den while she walked to the master bedroom on the main floor, glanced inside and shook her head. Her father's room was as messy as the other two rooms. More liquor bottles, papers, clothes, towels that had soured and would need to be thrown away.

Had he lived like this?

He was probably so inebriated that he didn't care.

Deciding she'd check out the upstairs before she headed into town to pick up supplies, she stepped over a muddy pair of work boots and made it to the stairwell. Cool air drifted through the eaves of the old house as she clenched the bannister. At one time her mother had kept a runner on the wooden steps, but apparently her father had ripped it out so the floors were bare now, scarred and crusted with dirt.

Bracing herself for a blast from the past, she paused at the first bedroom on the right. Peyton's room. The frilly, once bright pink, ruffled curtains still hung on the windows although they'd faded to a dull shade. But everything else in the room remained untouched. Posters from rock bands, a team banner and photographs of the team and Peyton and Ruth were still thumbtacked on the bulletin board above the white, four-poster bed. The stuffed animals and dolls she'd played with as a child stood like a shrine on the corner bookcase.

Memories of her sister pummeled her, making it difficult to breathe. She could still see the two of them playing dolls on the floor. Peyton braiding her hair in front of the antique mirror, using one of their mother's fancy pearl combs at the crown to dress up the look.

Peyton slamming the door and shutting her out, when she and Ruth wanted to be alone.

Cleaning this room would be the hardest, but it would have to be done. Although she'd feared the worst had happened to her sister over the years, that she was dead or being held hostage by some crazed maniac rapist, it still seemed wrong to discard her things, almost as if she were erasing Peyton from her life.

Or accepting that she was gone and never coming back.

Dragging herself back to the task at hand, she walked next door to her room. Her breath caught when she looked inside.

Her room had not been preserved, as Peyton's had.

In fact, someone had tossed the drawers and dresser. And on the mirror, hate words had been written in red.

Blood or lipstick, she wasn't sure.

But the message was clear just the same.

The girls' blood is on your head.

CHAZ COULDN'T ERASE the image of Tawny-Lynn from his mind as he made rounds in the small town. He hadn't paid much attention to her when she'd tagged after his sister years ago. Had thought she had a crush on him and hadn't wanted to encourage it.

He'd been in love with Sonya Wilkerson and, that last year when Ruth had been a senior, he'd played baseball for the junior college on a scholarship that he'd planned to use to earn a forestry degree.

Then Ruth and Peyton went missing and he'd decided to pursue law enforcement and get the answers his family wanted.

Only so far he'd failed.

Maybe Tawny-Lynn would remember something now that she was back.

His phone beeped as he parked at Donna's Diner on the corner of Main Street, and he noticed the high school softball coach, Jim Wake, chatting with Mrs. Calvin. He'd kept up with the local games enough to know her daughter played for the team. The woman looked annoyed, but the coach patted her arm, using the charm he'd always used to soothe meddling, pushy parents. Everyone wanted their kid to get more play time, to be the star of the team.

If he remembered correctly, Tawny-Lynn had been damn good. Much better than her sister, although Peyton had been prettier and more of a flirt. She'd danced through dating the football team one at a time, then when spring rolled around, she'd moved on to the baseball players.

But he'd stayed clear. Peyton was his sister's best friend. Off-limits.

He parked and went inside, his stomach growling. One day he'd learn to cook, but for now Donna supplied great homemade meals at a decent price, and today's special was her famous meat loaf. She refused to give anyone the recipe or reveal her secret ingredient.

A late-spring storm was brewing, the skies darkening as the day progressed. Wind tossed dust and leaves across the asphalt, the scent of coffee, barbecue and apple pie greeting him as he entered.

The dinner crowd had already arrived, and he waved to Billy Dean and Leroy in the far corner, then noted that the parents of the three girls who'd died in the crash were sitting in a booth together, deep in conversation.

Mayor Theodore Truman, Cassie's father, seemed to be leading the discussion. The Marx couple and Aubrey Pullman's mother listened intently. Sadly, Aubrey's father had killed himself two years after the accident without even leaving a note. Rumor was that he'd grieved himself to death.

He had to walk past them to reach the only empty booth, and Mayor Truman looked up, saw him and gestured for him to stop.

"Hello, Mayor." He tipped his hat to Mr. and Mrs. Marx and Judy Pullman in greeting.

"Is it true? Tawny-Lynn Boulder is back?" Mayor Truman asked.

Chaz tensed, hating the way the man said her name as if she'd committed some heinous crime. "She's here to take care of her father's estate."

Mr. Marx stood, his anger palpable as he adjusted his suit jacket. "Your father said he talked to you."

Chaz hated small-town politics. He hated even more that his father thought he ran the town just because he had money. "Yes, he voiced his concerns."

"What are you going to do about that *woman?*" Mayor Truman asked.

Chaz planted both hands on his hips. "Ms. Boulder has every right to be here. You might show a little sympathy toward her. After all, she lost her father and, seven years ago, her sister, too."

The mayor's bushy eyebrows rose. He obviously didn't like to be put in his place. But Chaz was his own man.

He started to leave, but Judy Pullman stood and touched his hand, then leaned toward him, speaking quietly. "Sheriff, does she...remember anything about that day?"

Chaz squeezed her hand, understanding the questions still plaguing her. For God's sake, they dogged him, too. Like who had caused that freak accident.

Or had it been an accident?

They needed closure, but unfortunately their hopes lay in Tawny-Lynn's hands. A lot of pressure for her.

"No, ma'am. I know we all want answers, and if she does remember something, trust me, I'll let everyone know."

"Is she...here to stay?"

He shook his head, thinking about how lost she looked facing that crumbling farmhouse. There had to be ghosts inside waiting for her.

"She said she's just going to clean up the ranch and put it on the market."

Mrs. Pullman stared at him for a long minute, then gave him a pained smile. "I guess I can't blame her for running."

Neither could he.

But if others still harbored as much animosity as the mayor and his father, he'd have to keep an eye out for her.

TAWNY-LYNN TUCKED the laundry list of supplies she needed into her purse and drove toward town. The road was lonely and deserted, the countryside filled with small houses interspersed between flat farmland.

A mile from town she passed the trailer park where Patti Mercer, the pitcher on her old team, used to live. Patti had dodged a bullet because of a stomach bug that day. Unlike her sister, Joy, who'd gotten pregnant at eighteen and still lived in the trailer where she'd grown up, Patti had earned a softball scholarship and had left Camden Crossing. Tawny-Lynn wondered what she was doing now.

The road curved to the right, and she wove around a

deserted tractor. The town square hadn't changed except they'd refurbished the playground in the park, and the store-fronts had been redesigned to resemble an old Western town. The tack shop had expanded, a fabric store had been added near the florist, the library now adjoined city hall and the sheriff's office had been painted and bore a new sign.

She passed the sheriff's office and the diner, then saw the general store and decided they'd probably have every-thing she needed. If not, Hank's Hardware would. But she wasn't ready to tackle repairs. She had to start by scraping off the layers of dirt and grime.

She pulled into a parking spot, noting that the diner was crowded. A couple who looked familiar, but one she couldn't quite place, exited the general store as she entered.

She grabbed a cart, then strolled the aisles, filling it with industrial-size cleaner, Pine-Sol, scrub brushes, dish soap, laundry detergent, dusting spray and polish, glass cleaner, then threw in a new broom and mop along with buckets, sponges and a duster with an extended handle so she could reach the corners.

Thankfully she'd checked her father's supply shed and had been surprised to find buckets and boxes full of tools of every kind. Apparently tools were another aspect of his hoarding. He could have opened his own hardware busi-ness from the shed out back.

A couple with a toddler walked by, the baby babbling as he rode on his father's back. She frowned, her heart tugging a little. She hadn't thought about having her own family, hadn't been able to let any man in her life.

But this guy looked familiar. Maybe he'd been in her class?

She continued past them with her head averted. She didn't intend to be here long enough to renew friendships or start new ones.

The locals probably wouldn't welcome her anyway.

She bent to choose some oven cleaner, then added it to the cart, but as she stood, she bumped into a body. She twisted to apologize then looked up to see an older woman with thinning gray hair staring at her.

She frowned, trying to place her.

"Are you Tawny-Lynn Boulder?" the woman asked.

Tawny-Lynn swallowed. "Yes."

"You probably don't know me but my name is Evelyn Jergins. My husband drove the bus for the softball team. He died that day in the crash."

Tawny-Lynn's heart clenched. "Oh, I'm sorry."

The woman narrowed her eyes. "You— They said you might know what made him wreck."

The urge to run slammed into Tawny-Lynn. "No.... I'm so sorry, but I still don't remember much about that day."

"Well, that's too bad. Trevor was a good man. I miss him every day."

"I miss my sister, too," Tawny-Lynn said.

"I heard about your daddy. That's too bad."

Tawny-Lynn shrugged, touched by the woman's sincerity. "I came back to clean up the ranch and sell it."

"Then you're not moving back?"

She shook her head. "No, I live in Austin."

She arched her brows. "Really? Are you married?"

"No." God, no. She hadn't been involved with anyone since her freshmen year in college when she'd found her boyfriend cheating on her. He'd blamed her. Said she wouldn't really let him in. That she was closed off emotionally.

Maybe she was. The nightmares of the past tormented her at night.

She quickly said goodbye, grabbed her cart and headed to the front. A silver-haired woman with tortoiseshell glasses was working the checkout counter and smiled as Tawny-Lynn unloaded the cart.

"Looks like you got a job ahead of you, hon."

Tawny-Lynn forced a smile, although she dreaded the backbreaking job. "Yes, I do."

She didn't offer more information, and thankfully another customer came up behind her and the woman tallied her items quickly. Tawny-Lynn paid with her debit card and headed outside, but as she loaded the items into her trunk, she sensed someone watching her, and anxiety tightened her shoulders.

When she turned, Cassie Truman's father was standing behind her. Age lines fanned his face, his hair had streaks of gray, but he still carried himself as if he were superior to everyone else.

"Mr. Truman," she said, remembering the way he'd banned her from his daughter's funeral.

"I'm the mayor now."

So he and Chaz's father must be buddy-buddy, both in control of the town.

She reached to close the trunk of her SUV. "Excuse me, I need to leave."

"*Are* you leaving?" he said.

Anger shot through her at his tone. The Camdens and the parents of the girls who'd died blamed her for not remembering details of that day, but she couldn't help it.

It was like a black hole had swallowed her memory of that day. She wanted the memories back, wanted to know how she'd escaped the bus with a broken leg and where Ruth and Peyton were.

But no amount of pushing or counseling had helped. She'd even tried hypnosis, but that had failed as well.

"As soon as I put the ranch up for sale," she said, a trace of bitterness in her tone.

"You still aren't going to tell us what happened back then?"

Pain, sharp and raw, splintered her. "Believe me, *Mayor* Truman, if I ever remember, the town will know."

Battling tears, she brushed past him, jumped in the SUV and backed away.

Her hands were shaking, her heart racing. Damn him. Damn her.

She wanted to remember and put the story to rest.

She slapped the steering wheel and brushed away tears. She had lost her sister that day, too.

Night had set in, the Friday-night diner crowd filing outside to their cars and heading home. She wondered if they still played bingo at the church and had monthly dances at the rec.

Not that she would be attending any. She meant what she'd said. She'd clean up White Forks and get the hell out before the town destroyed her again.

Her SUV hit a pothole, and she braked, then slowed as she drove the country road. Seconds later, lights appeared behind her, and she checked her rearview mirror, anxious as the car sped up and rode her bumper.

Irritated, she braked again, hoping the driver would pass her, but the jerk slowed slightly, then continued to ride her as she left town. The curve caught her off guard, and she skimmed the edge of the road, then the car passed, forcing her toward the ditch.

Sweat beaded on her hands as she clenched the steering wheel and tried to maintain control, but her tires hit another pothole, and the Jeep skidded off the road.

Her body slammed against the steering wheel as the SUV pitched forward, the front bumper ramming into the ditch.

The impact jerked her neck, her head hit the back of the seat and the world went dark.

Chapter Three

Chaz paid his bill at the diner, then checked in with his deputy, Ned Lemone, a young, restless guy who'd taken the job but made it clear he wanted to move to a big city and make detective. Not enough action around Camden Crossing.

At least he didn't mind the night shift.

"Anything I need to know about?" Chaz asked.

Deputy Lemone shook his head. "A domestic out at the Cooter farm."

"Wally and Inez at it again?"

His deputy nodded. "She threw a cast-iron skillet at him. Broke his big toe."

Chaz shook his head. The couple fought like cats and dogs, but refused to separate. He'd been out there a half dozen times himself.

Chaz walked to the door. "Call me if anything comes up."

Deputy Lemone nodded, and Chaz strode outside, went to his car and drove toward his cabin a couple of miles outside town on a creek, only three miles from White Forks.

And on the opposite side of town from his folks. Maybe *he* should relocate even farther away from them.

But he'd stayed, hoping being close might lead him to a clue about Ruth's disappearance.

He wound around the curve on the deserted road, fighting thoughts of Tawny-Lynn when he noticed a battered, blue SUV had nose-dived into the ditch.

Tawny-Lynn's SUV.

Dammit.

He swerved to the side of the road, threw the cruiser into Park and jogged over to her Jeep. His boots skidded on gravel as he rushed down the incline.

He glanced inside the driver's side and saw Tawny-Lynn raise her head and look up at him. Blood dotted her forehead, and she seemed dazed and confused.

He pulled the door open. "Tawny-Lynn, are you all right?"

She nodded, then touched her forehead. He did a quick assessment. Her seat belt must have kept her from serious harm, but the Jeep was so old it didn't have air bags.

"What happened?" Chaz asked as he lifted her chin to examine her for other injuries. The cut was small, and he didn't think it needed stitches, but she could have a concussion.

"I… A car came up behind me," she said, her voice hoarse. "I slowed to let him go past but he kept riding my bumper. And when he passed me, he was so close I ran off the road."

"Did the driver stop?"

She shook her head. "No, he raced on by. He seemed like he was in real hurry."

"Did you see who was driving?"

"No."

"But you said 'he.' You're sure it was a man?"

She dropped her hands to her lap. "No. The car had tinted windows."

"What kind of car was it?"

Tawny-Lynn shrugged. "I don't know, Chaz. It was dark and the lights nearly blinded me." She reached for her keys. "Do you think you can help me get out of here?"

"Sure. But I'm going to call a medic to check you out. You might have a concussion."

"I'm fine," Tawny-Lynn said. "I just want to go back to the ranch."

He grabbed the keys from her. "You're not driving until you're examined by a professional."

She glared at him. "Chaz, please—"

"It would be irresponsible of me to let you drive when you might have a head injury." He grabbed his phone from his belt and made the call.

"Racine, there was an accident on White Forks Road. Send the medics out here now." A pause. "Yeah, thanks." He disconnected then punched the number for Henry's Auto Repair. "Henry, can you send a tow truck out to White Forks Road? A car accident, Jeep in a ditch that needs pulling out."

"Sure. I'm on my way," Henry said.

Chaz disconnected, his chest tightening as he glanced down at Tawny-Lynn. Her face looked pale in the moonlight, and she was rubbing her chest as if she might have cracked a rib.

He didn't like the fact that she'd had an accident the very day she'd come to town. Or the fact that the driver had left her in the ditch.

Had it been an accident or had someone intentionally run her off the road?

TAWNY-LYNN STRUGGLED to remember details about the car. The driver was probably some joyriding teenager, or maybe a drunk driver.

But the message on her mirror at home taunted her.

Someone didn't want her here. Actually a lot of people didn't want her here. Had one of them run her into that ditch to get rid of her?

She unfastened her seat belt and started to climb from

the car, but Chaz took her arm and helped her out. For a moment she was dizzy, but he steadied her and the world righted itself.

"You are hurt," he said in a gruff voice.

"I've been through worse," she said, then immediately regretted her comment when his gaze locked with hers. They both knew she'd barely survived that crash. Although no one knew how she'd escaped the burning vehicle.

Chaz started to say something, but the sound of a siren wailing rent the air, and red lights twirled in the night sky as the ambulance approached. A second later, the tow truck rolled in on its heels, and Tawny-Lynn had to succumb to an exam by the paramedics.

Meanwhile, Chaz spoke with Henry, the fiftysomething owner of the auto repair shop, and supervised as the man towed her Jeep from the ditch.

"Your blood pressure's a little high, miss," the blond medic said.

"Wouldn't you think that's normal after an accident?" she said wryly.

He nodded, then listened to her heart while the other medic cleaned her forehead and applied a small butterfly bandage.

"Heart sounds okay," the medic said. He used a penlight and examined her eyes, instructing her to follow the light.

"I'm really fine," Tawny-Lynn said. "I was wearing my seat belt so I didn't hit the windshield."

"How about the steering wheel?"

She nodded. "My chest did, but nothing is broken." She had suffered broken ribs in the bus accident and knew that kind of breath-robbing pain.

"We should take you in for X-rays."

Tawny-Lynn shook her head. "No need. I told you, I'm fine."

The medics exchanged looks as Chaz approached. "If you won't go in, you need to sign a waiver, miss."

"Then let me sign it. I just want to go home." Not that she considered White Forks home anymore. But she didn't like people hovering over her.

She'd had too much of that after the bus wreck. Of course, the hovering had been people demanding that she remember, pressuring her, wanting answers that she couldn't give.

"Maybe you should go to the hospital for observation," Chaz suggested.

She'd been taking care of herself far too long to welcome attention, especially from Chaz Camden.

"I don't need a hospital," she said. "It was just a little accident."

The medic handed her a form attached to a clipboard, and she gave them her autograph.

They packed up and left just as Henry finished dragging her SUV from the ditch. The thing was old and beat up, so a bent fender with a little body damage didn't faze her. Not as long as the car would run.

"You shouldn't drive it until I check it out," Henry said. "Front end probably needs realignment. And that back tire is as bald as a baby's butt."

"How long will it take to replace the tire and check the alignment?"

"Day or two. I can call you when I'm done."

Tawny-Lynn hedged. She didn't have a lot of money, but she also didn't want to get stranded on her way back to Austin. And her father's old pickup was at the ranch, so she'd have transportation. "All right."

"I'll give you a lift home," Chaz offered.

She didn't want to be in the same car with Chaz—to share the same air—because he smelled too good, too darn masculine.

Sexy.

And whether or not she wanted to admit it, she was shaken by the accident and would love to lean on him.

But she couldn't allow herself to do that.

She grabbed her purse from the Jeep, then removed one of her business cards with her phone number on it. "Call me when you have it ready."

By the time she finished talking to Henry, Chaz had unloaded her supplies and stowed them in the trunk of his squad car.

Henry waved to her, then jumped in the tow truck and chugged away, pulling her Jeep behind him, the clank of metal echoing as he disappeared from sight.

"He'll give you a fair price," Chaz said as if he sensed her concerns about money.

She didn't comment. Instead she walked around to the passenger side of his car and climbed in. The world was spinning again, the seconds before she'd slammed into the ditch taking her back seven years.

She massaged her temple, but the sound of screams and crying reverberated in her head.

"Tawny-Lynn," Chaz said softly. "Are you sure you're all right?" He closed his hand over hers, and her fingers tingled with awareness, unsettling her even more. She desperately wanted to hold on to him. To have someone assure her that things would be all right.

"Yes, I'm fine," she said.

BUT NOTHING WAS all right. She was all alone. Everyone in Camden Crossing hated her, and the only way to fix that was to remember what had happened that day.

Chaz gave her a sympathetic look, then started the car and drove to White Forks. The woods backing up to the ranch seemed darker and more ominous tonight. Chaz maneuvered the dirt drive, avoiding the worst potholes, then parked in front of the house.

Somewhere in the distance, she heard an animal rustling in dry leaves as she climbed out. Then the howl of a coyote as if it was close by.

Chaz opened the trunk and lifted one of the boxes, and she grabbed two bags of supplies and led the way up the steps. But when she touched the doorknob to unlock the door, it swung open.

Chaz immediately pressed a hand across her chest to stop her from entering. "Did you lock it when you left?"

She nodded, remembering the bloody message on her mirror.

Was someone inside now?

CHAZ'S INSTINCTS SNAPPED to full alert. He set the box on the porch, removed his weapon and scanned the front of the property. He hadn't seen anyone pulling up, and there were no cars in sight.

Still, the door was unlocked, and on the heels of Tawny-Lynn's so-called accident, that raised his suspicions.

"Chaz?"

He pressed a finger to his lips to shush her, then motioned for her to stay behind him. He inched inside, looking left then right, shocked at the stacks of papers and junk filling every nook and cranny of the living room and kitchen.

The stench of stale beer and liquor mingled with mold, and gave him an understanding of the mammoth amount of trash bags and cleaning supplies Tawny-Lynn had bought.

It had been years since he'd been in the house and tried to remember the layout. The master bedroom was on the main floor, the girls' rooms upstairs.

The floor creaked as Tawny-Lynn followed behind him, and he veered to the left into the master suite. It was just as nasty and cluttered as the front rooms.

But no one was inside.

"I don't hear anything," Tawny-Lynn whispered.

Neither did he, but a predator could be hiding in a closet or upstairs, ready to attack. He slowly closed his hand around the bedroom closet doorknob and yanked it open, his gun raised. It was empty except for the stacks of old shoes, hats and clothing.

"Stay here while I check the upstairs."

"No, I'm going with you," Tawny-Lynn whispered.

He gave her a sharp look, then decided maybe it was best if she did follow him, in case the intruder was hiding in the storage shed outside. He didn't want to leave her alone.

They crossed back through the room, then he tiptoed up the steps, but the wooden boards creaked beneath his weight. The first room was Peyton's, still decorated like it had been years ago. For a moment, grief hit him as an image of Ruth sitting cross-legged on Peyton's bed flashed in front of his eyes.

Heaving a breath to refocus, he yanked open the closet door, but all he found were Peyton's clothes. Jeans and T-shirts, a prom dress.

The softball cleats gave him another pain in his chest. No wonder the parents of the three girls who'd died couldn't forget.

No one should have to bury a child.

He kept his gun poised as he pivoted, Tawny-Lynn's choppy breathing echoing behind him as he entered the hall and inched to her room.

He paused at the doorway, anger bolting through him at the sight of the mirror.

"What the hell?"

"That was there when I first arrived," Tawny-Lynn whispered.

He swung around to her. "What? Why didn't you tell me?"

Tawny-Lynn shrugged. "I had no idea how long it had been there."

Chaz cursed, then strode forward to examine it. He studied the writing, then took a sniff. "Looks like blood but it's dry, so no smell. I'll take samples and send to the crime lab."

Tawny-Lynn nodded, then he stepped inside the bathroom and cursed again. "Was this here, too?"

Her eyes widened in shock as she entered. Then she shook her head in denial.

Chaz was disgusted at the sight.

The walls were covered in more blood. Fresh blood.

Whoever had broken in had written another message on the walls.

We don't want you here.
Leave or die.

THE SHERIFF WAS inside Boulder's house with the girl. Dammit to hell and back.

Chaz asked too many questions. He just wouldn't give up investigating his sister's disappearance and the bus wreck that had taken those girls' lives.

Why couldn't he let it go?

It was over. Years ago.

But now Tawny-Lynn was back.

What if she remembered something while she was in town? What if she remembered *him?*

His *face?* That he'd been there?

No, Tawny-Lynn had sustained a head injury that had robbed those memories, wiped them out and given her a clean slate. She couldn't remember now.

If she did, she'd have to die.

Chapter Four

Chaz studied the bathroom, his anger mounting. Tawny-Lynn hadn't done anything to earn this kind of abusive treatment. Not certain he believed her earlier statement about the message, he pressed her again. "Why didn't you call when you found that first message?"

Tawny-Lynn shrugged. "I know you and your family hate me."

"I'm not my family," Chaz said. "I'm the law, and no one is harassed or threatened on my watch without me taking it seriously."

Tawny-Lynn averted her eyes as if she didn't know how to respond.

"I'm going to take samples and look for prints."

"In here or all through the house?"

He grimaced as he considered the question. "I'll start in here."

"With all this dust and clutter, it would probably be a nightmare to do every room."

She was right. "I'll check the doors and major surfaces. But it'll take me a while. Let me grab my kit from the car."

"Okay. I'll bring in the rest of the cleaning supplies."

"I'll give you a hand. But I'd rather you not clean anything until I look around."

He followed her down the stairs, noting how fragile and tired she looked. No telling what time she'd gotten up this morning, and then she'd driven for hours and walked into this disaster.

It took them three trips to bring everything inside. Chaz retrieved his kit and decided to check the doors and kitchen first, so Tawny-Lynn could at least clean up the kitchen enough to prepare a meal or make coffee in the morning.

She watched him as he shined a flashlight along the doorway and kitchen counter and took a couple of prints on the back doorknob and screen. There was so much dust on the piles of newspapers and table that he didn't see any prints. Besides, there would have been no reason for the intruder to touch the empty liquor and beer bottles Boulder had thrown into the heap in the corner

"I'm done in here if you want to start cleaning this room while I'm upstairs."

"Thanks. I don't think I could eat anything in this house until it's fumigated."

He chuckled. "Your father obviously never threw anything away."

"Or took out the garbage." She grabbed a trash bag and began to sort the cans and bottles into one bag for recycling, while he headed to the stairs.

He yanked on gloves and set to work. On the chance that the intruder hadn't worn gloves and had touched the railing, he examined it, found a print and lifted it. Then he realized it was probably Tawny-Lynn's and asked for a sample of hers for elimination purposes when he sent the others to the lab.

Upstairs, he scraped off a sample of the blood on the dresser mirror and dusted the gilded frame, but found nothing. Then he moved to the bathroom and checked the sink's countertop, but if someone had touched it, they'd wiped it clean.

He took a generous sampling of the blood on the wall, hoping to learn something from it. Was it human blood?

He photographed the writing, then took pictures of the message on the mirror, as well. Maybe a handwriting expert could analyze it. And if he had a suspect, he could compare samples. The dot over the *i* in the world *Die* had a curly tip. The writing also slanted downward at an angle and looked as if someone had jabbed at the wall out of anger.

He paused in the bedroom, his mind ticking as he wondered how the intruder had known this room was Tawny-Lynn's. It was certainly not as frilly as Peyton's, and there were dozens of sports posters on the wall, but no nameplate or picture of Tawny-Lynn to give it away. A plain navy comforter covered the antique iron bed, a teddy bear and rag doll sat on the bookshelf above a sea of mystery books, and CDs were stacked in a CD holder by a scarred pine desk.

Which suggested that the intruder had known the family well enough to know which room belonged to her.

And that he or she might have been in the house before.

TAWNY-LYNN RAKED trash and old food off the kitchen counter and into the garbage bag. She'd already filled up three bags and was going to need a truck to haul away the junk once she finished with the house.

Exhaustion pulled at her shoulders, a headache pulsing behind her eyes. a result of the accident she assumed. Or maybe it was due to the mounds of dust in the house.

She'd have to stock up on her allergy medication.

Carrying that bag out the back door, her gaze scanned the woods beyond. Was the person who'd left her those vile messages hiding out now, watching her? Hoping she'd flee the town as she had seven years ago?

"I don't want to be in Camden Crossing any more than you want me here," she muttered.

"Who are you talking to?"

Tawny-Lynn startled and spun around. Chaz stood in the

kitchen doorway, his hand covering the gun at his waist. "Did you see someone out here?"

She shook her head, silently berating herself. "No, I was talking to myself."

His eyes darkened as he studied her. "Are you sure you don't have a concussion?"

"I'm just exhausted," she admitted. "But I'm not going to bed until this kitchen is clean, so you can go home if you're finished."

"Actually I came down for a bucket and bleach."

She frowned. "What for?"

"To clean the blood off your wall and mirror."

"That's not necessary, Chaz. You've done enough already." In fact, it felt too good to have him here. Made her feel safe. Secure. Needy.

She couldn't lean on him or anyone else.

"I'll do it once I finish with the kitchen."

"No way," he said gruffly. "I don't intend to leave you here with that disgusting threat in your room, especially after you were in an accident."

God, his voice sounded almost protective. Odd, when years ago he'd hated her just like everyone else.

He didn't wait for a reply. He rummaged through the boxes of supplies, grabbed a bucket, a container of bleach and a sponge and strode back toward the stairs.

Tawny-Lynn sighed shakily and rushed back inside, but the wind whistling through the trees unnerved her and she slammed the door. Maybe it was better if Chaz was here, acting as the sheriff, of course, just in case the intruder had stuck around.

Her adrenaline kicked in, and she finished scraping off the counters, chairs, table and floors of junk, carefully stowing any unpaid bills she located, and there were dozens, into a basket on the counter. Next, she tackled the refrigerator, not surprised to find it virtually empty except for condiments that had expired, something moldy growing in a jar, a jug of sour milk and a carton of outdated eggs.

Next she tossed a rusted can opener, a toaster that was so crusted with grime that she doubted she could ever clean it, then dish towels that were mildewed.

When she finished with that, she pulled out the bleach and industrial cleaner and scoured the sink, counter and the inside and outside of the refrigerator. The counters were worn, but after several layers of crud had been removed they were passable. Other things might need to be replaced.

That is, unless she just decided to sell the ranch as it was. Maybe that was best. She didn't have money to invest in the house. The property held the real value. Whoever bought the ranch could tear down the house and build a new one or remodel this one the way they chose.

By the time she finished and mopped the floor, her body was aching for sleep. Footsteps sounded, and Chaz appeared, his big body filling the doorway.

She was filthy, sweaty and covered in dirt, while he looked so handsome and strong that he stole the breath from her.

"You look like you're about to fall over," he said.

Tawny-Lynn leaned against the counter. At least it smelled better in this room. "It's been a long day. A good night's sleep will work wonders." Although truthfully, she hadn't had a good night's sleep in nearly a decade.

The nightmares dogged her every time she closed her eyes.

TAWNY-LYNN SWAYED, and Chaz caught her by the arm. "Exhausted? You're dizzy."

"It's just the cleaning fumes," she said, her voice strained. "I have allergies."

He nodded, unconvinced. "I'm going to send Jimmy

James out here tomorrow to install new locks on the house. Dead bolts, too."

"I can take care of it," Tawny-Lynn said.

"Don't argue." Chaz gestured toward the mess in the living room. "You have your hands full already."

She rubbed her forehead, then looked up at him warily. "Why are you helping me, Chaz? I thought you hated me just like your folks and the rest of the town."

Chaz's chest tightened at her directness. He wanted to tell her that he didn't hate her, that he regretted the way he'd treated her after Ruth had disappeared, that he'd shouldered his own share of guilt and had been desperate for answers to satisfy his father.

But there was no way he could get personal with her. Revealing the truth would make him vulnerable. And he had to focus.

One day he would find his sister. That was all that mattered.

So he kept the conversation on a professional level. "I'm the sheriff, I'm just doing my job."

Something akin to disappointment flared in her big green eyes. "Of course. Well, thanks for the ride home and for cleaning the walls."

He nodded. "I'll let you know if I find a hit on any of the prints or the blood samples."

Tawny-Lynn led him to the front door, but he hung there, hesitant to leave. She looked so small and fragile. Vulnerable.

She'd been here less than twenty-four hours and already had an accident, which could have been intentional, and an intruder in her house who'd left vile threats against her.

Tawny-Lynn held the door edge, and offered him a brave smile. "Well, even if you are just doing your job, I appreciate it, Chaz. I know how the locals feel about me. I...just wish I could give them what they want."

He narrowed his eyes, pained at the sorrow in her tone. "You suffered, too. You lost your sister. People should have been more sensitive to that."

She shrugged, but the effort didn't meet her eyes.

He had the sudden impulse to reach up and pull her against him. To hold her and assure her that everything would be all right. That she'd done all she could, just as he had.

But touching her would be wrong. Would make it more difficult to keep his distance and do his job.

And his job was to keep her safe and to find the person who'd threatened her.

So he handed her his business card, told her to call him if she needed anything, then headed to his car, determined to ignore the pull of attraction between them.

TAWNY-LYNN WATCHED Chaz leave with mixed feelings. As long as he'd been in the house, she could chase away the monsters.

But when she was left alone in the house, the ghosts seeped from the walls to haunt her.

For a moment she couldn't breathe. The familiar panic attacks she'd suffered after the bus accident threatened. Willing herself to be strong, she closed her eyes and took slow, even breaths.

It had been seven years. She was alive. She was safe.

Or was she?

Judging from the bloody message on her mirror and walls, someone didn't want her here.

A shudder coursed up her body and she locked the door, then shoved a chair in front of it. The chair wouldn't keep an intruder out, but at least if it fell over, it might wake her.

If she ever managed to fall asleep.

Dusty and grimy from the work she'd done and achy from the earlier nosedive into the ditch, she forced herself to leave the chaotic mess waiting in the living room, grabbed a bottle of cleaner for the shower and climbed the stairs. She'd tackle the den tomorrow.

Chaz had erased the message from the mirror, but the ugly words still taunted her. She stripped the sheets, found clean ones in the closet and put them on the bed. Then she retrieved her toiletry bag and walked into the bathroom.

The walls smelled of bleach, but the shower looked grungy, so she scrubbed it, then the toilet and sink. Then she turned on the water, stripped and climbed in the shower. The hot water felt heavenly on her aching muscles, and she soaped and washed her body and hair, then rinsed off. She wrapped a towel around her damp hair, then stepped from the shower and brushed her teeth twice to get rid of the dust in her mouth.

She towel dried her hair, slipped on a pair of pajamas, took a sleeping pill and fell into bed. Seconds later, she closed her eyes and drifted off.

But even as she faded into sleep, images of the bloody message flashed back.

If she didn't leave town, would the intruder come back and kill her?

Chapter Five

Chaz hesitated before driving away from White Forks, but he couldn't stay with Tawny-Lynn around the clock.

Could he?

If the threats continued, he'd have to.

He carried the blood samples and prints he'd collected to the sheriff's office. His deputy was on the phone when he walked in.

Judging from the goofy grin on his face, he was talking to his girlfriend, Sheila.

He looked up at Chaz and dropped his feet from the desk. "Listen, honey, I've gotta go. Call you later."

He hung up, then quirked his brows at Chaz. "I didn't expect you back tonight."

"There was some trouble out at White Forks."

"You mean that place where the Boulder broad lives?"

"She hasn't lived there in years, but yes, that's the one. She came back to town to get her old man's ranch ready to sell."

"I heard folks around here don't much like her."

Chaz scowled at his deputy. "Who've you been listening to, Ned?"

"No one in particular. Some old women were gossiping about her in the diner. Said if she'd spoken up about what happened that day, they might have tracked down your sister and Peyton Boulder." He scratched the back of his neck. "Hell, someone even said that she helped them run off."

Chaz silently cursed. Ned had come from a neighboring town and had formed his opinions based on rumors. "First of all, I don't think my sister just ran off. She wouldn't have done that. Second, Tawny-Lynn almost died in that crash herself. She was unconscious when the paramedics found her, had a broken leg and a concussion."

Ned made a clicking sound with his teeth. "The concussion caused her amnesia?"

"Yes, according to the doctor," Chaz said.

"But the accident— Didn't the sheriff think that was suspicious?"

Chaz nodded. "There were skid marks from another vehicle on the pavement, but it started raining and they couldn't get a good print."

"Why would someone run the bus off the road?"

"Good question. The bus was carrying the softball team. Could have been some teen following too close or—"

"Competitors from another team?"

"I don't think so. The sheriff looked into each of the girl's lives, but none of them had any serious enemies."

"So what's your theory?" Ned asked.

Chaz contemplated the file he had at home. How many times had he studied the damn thing for answers?

"I don't know. Two girls went missing from Sunset Mesa before the Camden incident and were never found. A lot of people think that a serial kidnapper took them. It's possible he was stalking one of the girls on the team and caused the accident, then kidnapped Ruth and Peyton."

"He'd have to be strong to wrestle both girls."

"Not if he had a gun, or if they were hurt in the crash."

His deputy studied his fingernails. "Do you have any idea who this guy is?"

Chaz shook his head. "No, and that's just a theory. No proof."

"But you all think that Tawny-Lynn Boulder saw this guy that day?"

"Some people think that. Like I said, she was unconscious when the medics arrived. But somehow she got out of the bus before it caught fire. Considering the fact that she had a broken leg and head injury, it's not likely she walked."

"Meaning someone dragged her to safety. But if it was the kidnapper, why not take her, too?"

"Maybe he was fixated on Ruth or Peyton. And like I said, Tawny-Lynn had a broken leg." He gritted his teeth. Depending on what the sick bastard's plans were, he probably hadn't wanted her with the injury.

"Anyway," Chaz continued. "Tonight someone left a bloody threat for Tawny-Lynn at White Forks. I took samples and managed to lift a few prints. Call the courier to pick it up, take it back to the lab and analyze it."

"Sure."

Chaz took a form from the desk and filled out the paperwork for chain of custody. "Tell the lab to call me as soon as they get the results."

The deputy narrowed his eyes as he examined the photograph of the bloody message. "Someone really wants her gone."

"It looks that way." Chaz headed back to the door. "But it's our job to protect her, Deputy. And to find out who made that threat."

TAWNY-LYNN GRIPPED *the bat with sweaty palms. It was the bottom of the ninth and the Camden Cats were one run behind. The team was depending on her.*

The pitcher threw a curve ball that came in low, and she barely managed to check her swing in time before the umpire called ball one.

Two more pitches and she'd tipped the ball twice. Her stomach felt jittery. Her chest hurt. She couldn't strike out now.

Another ball and it nearly hit her shoulder. She jumped back, the ball whizzing by her head. She stepped aside to steady herself, then ground the bat at the base and raised it, ready.

The pitcher wound up as the crowd and her teammates chanted her name. A second later, she swung at the ball. Metal connected with it, sending the ball flying, and she took off running as the ball soared over the fence. Her teammates screamed in excitement, the crowd roared and Peyton, who was on second base, sailed around the bases. Tawny-Lynn was faster than her sister and nearly caught her as they raced into home plate.

Her homerun sent the team one point ahead.

Roars and cheers from the crowd echoed in her ears as Ruth stepped up to bat. Three straight swings though and she struck out.

Still, the Cats had won. The girls rushed her, clapping and shouting and hugging. The coach pounded her on the back. "You're our hero today, T!"

She beamed a smile as they grabbed their gym bags and jogged toward the bus. More congratulations and pats as the girls clamored into their seats.

"I have to stop by the bank. Let's meet up at the pizza parlor to celebrate," Coach Wake announced. He made his way back to his car while the bus driver fired up the bus.

Tawny-Lynn settled into a seat by herself while Peyton jumped in beside Ruth, and they started whispering and giggling.

Peyton was boy crazy, and Ruth was interested in someone, but they were keeping it a secret, talking in hushed voices. Jealousy sparked her to glare at them, but her sister pulled Ruth closer and tucked their heads together to shut her out.

The bus chugged around a curve, but it was dark on the country road, a storm brewing, thunder rumbling. A car raced up behind the bus and rammed it, and the bus jolted forward. The driver shouted, then tires screeched and the bus swerved toward the embankment. The ridge loomed below, and fear shot through Tawny-Lynn.

She hated heights. Had always been scared on the switchbacks.

The bus jerked again, something scraped the side, then the bus went into a skid. One of the girls screamed, brakes squealed, then the bus flew out of control, slammed into the metal guardrail and careened over the ridge.

Backpacks and gym bags slid onto the floor, and she gripped the seat edge to keep from falling. Bodies fell into the aisle, blood was flying, and she was thrown against the metal seat top as the bus crashed into the ravine.

Sometime later, she roused. It was dark, so dark...pain throbbed through her chest and leg.

She couldn't move. It was deathly quiet.

Then she felt hands pulling at her, moving her. She tried to open her eyes, but the world was foggy.

Breathing rasped around her. She tried to see who was pulling her from the bus, but it was too dark. Then she heard crying again—another scream. Voices.

Was her sister all right?

She struggled to see, but...there was a man...his face... hidden in shadows. Who was he?

Tawny-Lynn jerked awake, panting for a breath. The dream...had been so real. A memory.

She had heard a voice. Seen a face.

A man's? A woman's? Peyton's maybe?

God help her, who was it?

CHAZ POPPED OPEN a cold beer when he made it home, his mind obsessing over Tawny-Lynn. Was she sleeping now? Or was she awake, terrified the person who'd left her that bloody message would return and make good on his threat?

Tension knotted his shoulders. He wanted to be back at White Forks watching out for her. Making sure she was safe.

Holding her…

Dammit, no. Tawny-Lynn was the last woman on earth he needed to be attracted to.

Why her?

Why now?

Life would be so much simpler if she cleaned that place up quickly, hung the for-sale sign, left town and never came back.

Then he wouldn't have to think about her being on that deserted run-down ranch by herself where God knew anyone could sneak up and attack her.

It wasn't as if she didn't have enemies. She had too many to count.

The people who'd lost family members in that crash despised her for not being able to give them closure by identifying the person who'd hit the bus and caused the crash.

Their family members, Coach Wake and half the town had also been questioned as suspects and resented it because Tawny-Lynn could have cleared their names.

Coach Wake has literally sobbed at the news of the crash, saying maybe if he'd been with the girls on the bus he could have done something to save them. Instead, he'd driven his own car, taken a side road, then stopped for cash and a surprise cake to take to the celebration dinner.

Tawny-Lynn's delicate face flashed in Chaz's head, and he grimaced, sipped his beer and headed to his home office. The cabin was small, but he'd carved a workspace in the second bedroom where he'd hung a gigantic whiteboard and laid out everything he knew about the missing girls from Sunset Mesa and Camden Crossing.

A smaller board held photos of other missing young women from various states for comparison purposes so he could look for connections.

Once again, he studied the pictures former sheriff Harold Simmons had taken of the accident. The bus was a mess, dented and crushed against a boulder in the ravine, flames shooting from all sides.

Keith Plumbing, a local handyman had driven up on the scene and called it in. His statement said he'd first seen smoke, then stopped and realized it was a bus and called 911. He'd run down the embankment to rescue the students trapped inside, but by the time he reached the bus, it burst into flames. He saw Tawny-Lynn lying in the dirt several feet away. But no one else was around.

Due to the fact that Keith called in the accident and had a history of drinking on the job, and he'd worked in Camden Crossing and Sunset Mesa, the sheriff questioned him as a person of interest. Plumbing could have caused the crash, then lied about the timing, dragged Tawny-Lynn out to safety but couldn't save the others.

Although he'd sworn he hadn't seen Peyton or Ruth. And if he'd hurt them or kidnapped them, where had he taken them? He hadn't had enough time between the time of the crash and when he'd called in the accident to dispose of a body.

Another photograph showed Tawny-Lynn unconscious on the stretcher, her leg twisted, blood streaking her face and hands. She looked so pale and fragile that he wondered how she'd survived.

Shaking off emotions he didn't want to feel for her, he glanced at the list of suspects the sheriff had considered. Plumbing had been one. He'd also questioned Barry Dothan, a young man with a mental disability that affected his learning and behavior.

Dothan liked to watch teenagers and took pictures of them on the track, swim team and softball field. But his mother swore that Barry was harmless, that he would never hurt a soul. The pictures of Ruth and Peyton posted on the corkboard above his bed were the only evidence that incriminated him. Some of the girls at school claimed they felt uncomfortable around him, but none of them had accused him of inappropriate behavior.

Chaz downed the rest of his beer and grabbed another, pacing to calm himself. God, his heart hurt just imagining what might have happened to his sister and Ruth.

He skimmed the former sheriff's notes. The investigators they'd called in from the county had found remains of three girls and the driver in the ashes left after the bus had exploded.

Ruth and Peyton were not among them.

So what the hell had happened to them?

Could Plumbing have had more time than they'd originally thought, time to kill the girls and dump their bodies somewhere?

They'd searched the man's truck. No girls, blood or forensics inside.

They'd also combed the area surrounding the crash site for bodies, a dead end as well.

Dothan didn't seem smart enough to abduct two girls and hide them.

But nobody else was there.

There had to be, though—or else how had Tawny-Lynn escaped the burning bus?

Peyton or Ruth could have dragged her out. But then what?

Frustrated, he slammed his fist on the desk, rattling paper clips and files.

He forced himself to look at the pictures of the two girls who'd gone missing from Sunset Mesa the year before. Almost the same time of year.

Avery Portland and Melanie Hoit. Avery grew up with a single mother, worked at the ice cream shop and was voted most likely to succeed in her class. She was popular, on the dance team at school, and class president.

Melanie was a cheerleader, pretty and aspired to be a model. Some of her classmates described her as the girl everyone wanted to be. A few others commented that she was a snob.

But so far everyone they'd questioned had alibis.

And neither girl had been found. No body. No ransom calls.

Nothing.

The parents wanted closure just as the residents in Camden Crossing did.

He slumped down in the chair and glanced back at the photo of Tawny-Lynn. No wonder his parents and the other family members of the victims had turned on her.

She might be the only lead they had.

He understood people's anger and frustration.

But why would someone want to hurt her? Then she'd never be able to tell them who else had been there that day.

The answer hit him like a fist in the gut.

Someone didn't want her to remember because there had been foul play.

And if she could identify the culprit, she could put him or her in jail....

HE WATCHED THE house where Tawny-Lynn slept.

The images of the girls who'd died tormented him. He hadn't meant to kill them all. He loved them too much to do them harm.

But things had gotten out of hand. Then everything had gone wrong.

His gut churned with memories of the screams of those girls in the fire. That had been…terrible. He had nightmares to this day. He would never have wanted any of them to suffer like that.

His heart was racing as he remembered the panic that had seized him when the bus had exploded.

Ah, sweet Peyton. So easy to love.

And Ruth… He'd wanted her so badly back then.

Another few months and maybe Tawny-Lynn would have appealed to him, too. She did now.

So sexy and athletic and that soft, blond hair… She'd turned out to be pretty after all.

Too bad she might have to die.

Chapter Six

Tawny-Lynn couldn't go back to sleep. She didn't even want to go back to sleep, and relive the same old nightmare.

If only she could recall the face of the person who'd rescued her.

She climbed from bed, threw on a pair of jeans and a T-shirt and yanked her hair back into a ponytail. The mammoth job of cleaning the rest of the house awaited her.

But she needed coffee and food, and now that the kitchen was clean, she needed some groceries to get by on until she could make the necessary repairs to the ranch.

She jogged down the stairs, but the sound of her sister's voice called to her as if she was begging her to find her.

She grabbed her purse and cell phone, then remembered her car was in the shop. She'd seen the keys to her father's pickup somewhere. If it was still running, she'd take it into town.

She glanced around the living room, daunted by the task she faced, then went back to the kitchen and remembered that she'd put the keys in the wicker basket with the bills that needed attention. Keys in hand, she jogged outside and found the truck parked beneath the makeshift carport her father had erected. The ancient truck was rusty and chugged and coughed as she tried to start it, as if it hadn't been cranked in ages. But her father had to have driven it to pick up his booze and the junk boxes he collected.

After three attempts, the battery finally charged to life, and she pulled from the carport. Remembering the intruder the night before, she scanned the property surrounding the ranch, but everything looked still and quiet.

Relieved, she barreled down the dirt drive and turned on the road to town. She passed the high school, pausing for a second to watch as the teenagers began to arrive. Students had gathered in the parking lot to hang out before going inside just as she and Ruth and Peyton used to do with the team. Softball season was almost over, and a sign out front congratulated the team for making it to the state finals. They were probably beginning play-offs now. Coach Wake was sure to be ecstatic.

She sped up, entered the town square and parked in front of the diner, desperate for coffee and breakfast. Thunderclouds darkened the sky, promising rain, and she pulled on her denim jacket and walked up the sidewalk to the diner. An old-fashioned hitching post and wagon wheel made the wooden structure look like a building from the past.

The delicious scent of bacon and coffee engulfed her when she entered, and her stomach growled. When had she eaten last?

She glanced around the room in search of an empty booth and suddenly felt tension charge the air. Voices quieted. Laughter died. A few whispers echoed through the diner.

Nerves climbed up her neck.

Suddenly Chaz appeared looking larger than life and so sexy that need spiraled through her.

"Good morning, Tawny-Lynn."

She wasn't so sure of that. "Maybe I should leave."

He shook his head. "No, sit down, have breakfast with me."

Did he know what he was doing? "I'm not sure that's a good idea."

He took her arm and ushered her into a booth to the left. "Well, I do. I'm sheriff. People had better take note."

Some emotion she couldn't define swelled inside her. She hadn't had anyone stand up for her in a long time.

She sank into the booth, exhausted already, and the day hadn't even begun. Chaz motioned for the waitress, and she appeared, a pencil jammed into her bouffant hairdo.

"Morning, Sheriff." She glanced down at Tawny-Lynn, her penciled-in eyebrows knit together. "Hey, sugar. You new to town?"

Tawny-Lynn fiddled with the paper napkin as she read the woman's name tag. Her name was Hilda. "I used to live here. I'm Tawny-Lynn Boulder."

"Oh, right, hon, I heard you were coming home. So sorry about your daddy." Hilda set two coffee cups on the gingham tablecloth and filled them with coffee from the pot on her tray. "He used to come in for coffee every now and then."

When he was sober? Tawny-Lynn couldn't imagine.

But she relaxed at the woman's friendly smile.

"What'll you two have?"

"The breakfast special for me." Chaz grinned at Tawny-Lynn. "They make the best biscuits in town."

She noted the chalkboard. The special was three eggs, sausage and pancakes. If she ate all that, she'd be too full to get any work done.

"I'll take the country breakfast. Scrambled eggs with cheese."

"Sausage or bacon?"

"Sausage."

Hilda smiled again, then called their order in and headed to the next table.

"Did you sleep any last night?" Chaz asked.

She fiddled with her napkin. "A little. But I dreamed about the crash."

He was watching her, his interest piqued, but he didn't push. "You dream about it a lot?"

She nodded. "All the time."

"What happens in the dream?"

She tucked a strand of hair that had escaped the ponytail holder behind her ear. "I'm at the ball game. We win, everyone's excited, cheering. Then we run to the bus. Coach says we'll meet for pizza." Goose bumps skated up her arms.

"Then?"

"Then we're in the bus and everyone's talking and then the bus jerks...like someone hit us, and the driver loses control."

Chaz sucked in a sharp breath. "That fits with our theory."

"You believe someone caused the accident?"

"Yes, but we don't know if it was an accident, or if someone intentionally slammed into the bus."

Tawny-Lynn's gaze met his. She'd never heard the authority's theories or if they had any suspects. The sheriff had expected her to have the answers.

"Any leads on the driver of the vehicle who hit us?"

He shook his head. "A small paint sample was taken, but it got lost in the mess that came afterward."

A strained silence fell over them as Hilda brought their food. Chaz poured syrup on his pancakes and wolfed them down, while she made a breakfast sandwich with the eggs, biscuit and sausage. He was right. The biscuit melted in her mouth.

"Any more trouble last night?"

"No, thank goodness."

He sipped his coffee. "How'd you get into town?"

"Daddy's truck. It's old but it made it." She stirred sweetener into her coffee. "Guess I'll need to sell it, too." She shrugged. "Or maybe I'll just give it away. I doubt it's worth anything."

She felt someone beside them, then looked up at Coach Wake who'd stopped by the table. "Tawny-Lynn, I was sorry about your father. Are you here to stay and run the ranch?"

Her stomach clenched. She'd once loved softball more than anything in her life. The coach had been her and Peyton and Ruth's idol.

Now he was a reminder of the worst day of her life, and softball was a sport she couldn't stand to watch.

CHAZ FELT TAWNY-LYNN shutting down before his eyes. She'd been devouring her breakfast, but dropped the biscuit onto her plate and sipped her water.

"No, I'm not staying," she said, her voice warbling. "The ranch hasn't been a working ranch in a long time."

Coach Wake glanced at Chaz, then at Tawny-Lynn as if he were trying to dissect their relationship.

"Then you're going to sell it?" the coach asked.

Tawny-Lynn nodded. "Just as soon as I clean it up."

Coach Wake shifted as someone else passed by. "If you need help, Keith Plumbing can use the work. He did some repairs around my house. My wife thought he was reliable and did a good job."

Tawny-Lynn twisted her napkin into shreds. "Thanks for the reference."

"No problem."

Two teenage girls brushed by, then stopped to speak to the coach, both of them giggling. "Hey, Coach, thought you said you were laying off Donna's gravy."

He patted his stomach. "I need the calories to keep up with you girls. We're doing sprints this afternoon."

The girls groaned, then the redheaded one checked her watch. "We gotta go. We're going to miss first bell."

They rushed off, and Coach Wake rubbed his stomach.

"Well, guess I'd better get to school. We have practice this afternoon. Did you know we made the play-offs?"

Tawny-Lynn took another sip of her coffee. "I saw the announcement on the marquis in front of the school on my way in to town. Congratulations."

The coach's smile broadened. "We've got a good team. But I haven't had a pitcher like you since you left. Stop by and watch the drills if you want. You could show the girls a thing or two."

"I don't think I'll have time, but thanks," she said. "I have my work cut out for me."

"Okay, but the offer still stands." He said goodbye to Chaz, then headed toward the door, but two women stopped him to chat on his way out. At least the coach had been friendly to Tawny-Lynn and hadn't treated her like a piranha like other people did.

If he remembered correctly, she'd been the star of the team and had won the game for them that last day.

His sister had adored the coach, too, just like all the girls had. And Coach Wake had cried like a baby at the funerals of the girls who hadn't survived the crash. He'd also been a leader in organizing search parties for Ruth and Peyton in the days following their disappearance.

"Are you okay?" Chaz asked.

A weary sigh escaped Tawny-Lynn. "Yes. But seeing him reminds me of…"

"Peyton and that day."

She nodded, her eyes glittering with tears as she looked up at him. His heart ached for her. Had anyone comforted her after the crash?

Did she have a boyfriend back in Austin?

He motioned to Hilda to bring the bill. It didn't matter to him if she did have a boyfriend. She didn't want to be here in town, and he had a job to do.

He wouldn't let himself even think about a relation-

ship with anyone until this case was solved and he gave
his parents closure about Ruth.

TAWNY-LYNN NEEDED some air. The conversation with Coach
Wake had stirred memories she tried hard to keep at bay.

Heck, everything about the town roused memories.

The diner was starting to clear as everyone paid their
checks and left for work. A young man with blond hair,
wearing jeans and a flannel shirt strode up to the table just
as Chaz reached for the bill. Her fingers touched it at the
same time and that annoying frisson of awareness sent a
tingle through her.

"Chaz?"

"I've got it," he said with a look that warned her not to
argue.

"Hey, Sheriff," the blond man said. "I got your message."

Chaz shook the guy's hand. "Yeah, Jimmy, this is Tawny-
Lynn—the woman I told you about. She owns White Forks
and needs new locks."

His eyes flashed a smile at her as he tipped his cowboy
hat. He was handsome in a rugged, good-old-boy kind of
way. "Hey, ma'am. I'm Jimmy James, I own the locksmith
shop."

Tawny-Lynn shook his hand, annoyed that his hand
didn't make her tingle.

No, only Chaz Camden's touch made her body quiver.
The one man in town she could never be close to.

"I can get to those locks right away if you want."

"Thanks. I'm going to pick up some groceries, then head
back out to the ranch."

He handed her his business card. "Give me a call when
you get home, and I'll run out."

Home? White Forks was not her home anymore. But
she didn't argue. She accepted his card, then sat stiffly as

Chaz paid the bill. They walked outside to her father's truck together. Chaz leaned against it as she dug out her keys.

"I don't know if you should use Keith Plumbing to do those repairs." His mouth twitched into a frown. "There's something about the man that rubs me the wrong way."

"What?"

Chaz shrugged. "I don't know. But he was questioned after Ruth and Peyton went missing."

Tawny-Lynn jerked her head up. "You mean he was a suspect?"

"He was a person of interest," Chaz said. "He did some odd jobs for my parents, and he'd worked in Sunset Mesa around the same time the two girls went missing from that area."

Tawny-Lynn gritted her teeth. She didn't remember the man.

"How about the ranch? Did he do repairs there?"

Chaz shook his head. "Not according to your father."

"Was anyone else questioned as a suspect?"

"Barry Dothan," Chaz said. "Do you remember him? He was my age, but is mentally handicapped."

"I do remember seeing him around town. He was odd, used to hang out by the field and watch us practice," Tawny-Lynn said.

Chaz shrugged. "The sheriff found pictures of all the girls on the softball team and swim team plastered on his walls. But his mother claimed he was home the day of the crash."

"You think she'd lie to protect him?"

"That's hard to say. He has problems. She feels protective."

"I don't think he'd hurt anyone."

"Maybe not intentionally. But he could have gotten confused. Maybe he showed up and Peyton and Ruth were hurt and scared of him. He got mad. There were rocks out there. He could have used one on Ruth or Peyton."

And if her sister and Ruth had been injured, they might have been too weak to fight back.

"If he did hurt them, then why didn't you find their bodies? Surely, he wasn't smart enough to hide them somewhere."

"That's the reason the sheriff didn't think he did it," Chaz said. "And the reason he was never arrested." Chaz reached for the truck door to open it for her. "I'm telling you so you'll watch out for him and Plumbing. If one of them had something to do with Ruth's and Peyton's disappearance, he might be worried about your memory returning."

Tawny-Lynn nodded. But she didn't intend to run like the person who'd written those bloody messages wanted.

If Plumbing or Barry Dothan knew something, she'd find out. She needed to know the truth in order to move on.

Chapter Seven

Tawny-Lynn left the diner, then walked across the street to the general store. She should have thought to buy groceries the night before, but she'd been overwhelmed by the dust and mess, and her only thought had been about cleaning.

She grabbed a cart as she entered, reminding herself that although she enjoyed cooking, she didn't have time for fancy meals and wouldn't be entertaining anyone. Most of her time would be spent cleaning out the house and working in the yard. She didn't plan to be at White Forks long. Maybe a week, no more.

Once she put the ranch on the market, she'd go back to Austin, and let the real-estate agent handle the rest.

She gathered coffee and sweetener, eggs, milk, cereal, bread, cheese, sandwich meat, added a few canned goods and soups, then decided to pick up ingredients to fix her favorite chili and nacho pie. Both would make enough to last her a couple of nights and were simple to prepare.

Relying on her favorite go-to recipes, she dropped in corn, black beans, tomatoes, tortillas and seasonings, then sour cream, avocados and limes to make guacamole.

The store was fairly empty, but as she rounded the corner to the produce section, she almost bumped into a middle-aged woman with an overflowing cart. A gray-haired man she assumed to be the woman's husband plucked a bag of oranges from a display table.

He scratched at his forehead when he spotted her. "Tawny-Lynn, is that you?"

Her hands tightened around the cart. "Sheriff Simmons?"

He chuckled and shook his head. "I'm not the sheriff anymore. Retired a couple of years ago. Chaz Camden took over."

"Yes, I know. I saw Chaz earlier."

Mrs. Simmons eyed her over her wire-rimmed glasses. "Sorry about your daddy, dear."

"Thanks." People probably judged her for not honoring him with a memorial service. Yet another reason for people to disapprove of her.

"What have you been doing with yourself?" Mr. Simmons asked.

"I started a landscaping business in Austin. I just came back to take care of the ranch."

He squeezed her arm. "I'm sorry we never found out what happened to Peyton and Ruth. That case will always haunt me."

Her throat thickened with emotions. "I know you did your best."

"Did your memory of that day ever return?" Mrs. Simmons asked, a hopeful note in her voice.

Tawny-Lynn shook her head. "No. I guess the doctor was wrong when he said the amnesia was temporary."

Guilt crawled through her, making her itch to run again. She gripped the cart and started away. "Well, it was nice to see you. I have to get back to the ranch."

"Nice to see you, too," the Simmonses said at once.

At least they'd been cordial to her, Tawny-Lynn thought, as she grabbed some fruit and headed to the checkout counter. The last time she'd talked to the sheriff he'd come out to the ranch when she'd been released from the hospital.

Everyone in town was hounding him to find Ruth and

Peyton and get answers for the dead girls, and he'd interrogated her as if she'd caused the accident herself.

She paid for the groceries, then carried them outside and loaded them in her car. But as she pulled away, an eerie sense crept over her.

Was someone watching her?

She looked around, searching, but didn't see anyone suspicious. A mother and her baby strolling in the park, a family climbing into their SUV, an elderly man walking into the hardware store leaning on a horsehead cane.

She was just being paranoid.

Still, she stayed alert as she drove through town, then found herself driving the opposite direction from home, out on Dirt Dauber Road, a road named after the mud daubers that had built nests in the cylinder of a small plane, causing it to crash. Oddly, that crash had occurred only a mile from where the school bus had collided into the boulder below the ridge.

Perspiration beaded on her neck as she parked, but she took a deep breath to calm herself. She had visited this site twice during the year after the accident, each time hoping it would trigger her memory.

Both times she'd had such panic attacks that she'd collapsed.

She was not going to do that today. She had to hold it together.

Determined, she walked over to the edge of the ridge. The guardrail had not only been repaired, but a sturdier metal one that was at least four inches higher had replaced it. Still the distance to the bottom of the ravine was daunting.

The wind stirred the leaves in the trees, their rustling sound mingling with the rumble of the brewing storm. The skies had darkened again, blotting out the sun.

She stared at the boulder below, an image of the bus

teetering over the edge flashing into her mind. Was that a memory or simply a figment of her imagination due to the pictures and descriptions she'd seen?

A scream echoed in her head and she closed her eyes for a moment, launching back in time.

The ball game, the victory, they were going to get pizza, Ruth and Peyton whispering about some guy...then the jolt.

Had she looked back to see what had hit them?

No...no time. The bus lurched forward, was losing control. Screams, blood, glass shattering, metal scraping... then a loud crunch. She was falling, falling, struggling to grab hold of something to keep from going through the glass...

Then pain and she couldn't move, and...darkness. Then hands touching her, a low voice whispering she would be all right. Fresh air hit her, and she gulped, her chest aching as she drew in a breath. But when she opened her eyes the face was dark. Blank. As if wearing a mask.

No, not a mask. As if there was no face...

SHE OPENED HER eyes, her breathing coming in erratic pants. Why couldn't she see the face?

Frustrated, she kicked at a rock and watched it tumble down the dirt into the ravine.

Suddenly that eerie feeling swept over her again, and she felt someone behind her. Watching her.

She must be paranoid, she reminded herself.

But when she glanced over her shoulder, a shadow moved. Trees rustled. Leaves crunched.

It wasn't her imagination this time. A man was standing in the shadows, half hidden by the thick trees.

Not just any man—Barry Dothan.

And he was taking pictures of her from his hiding spot in the woods.

CHAZ DROVE TO Sunset Mesa and parked at the sheriff's office. He'd phoned ahead and Amanda Blair, the new sheriff of Sunset Mesa, had agreed to meet him.

He smelled coffee brewing as he entered and found a young woman in her twenties with amber hair pulled back into a ponytail pouring a mug at the scarred counter across from the front desk. She was petite but athletic looking, and as she turned, he noticed a steely glint in her eyes.

She might be compact, but her attitude screamed that she was tough and could handle the job.

He tipped his hat. "I'm here to meet the sheriff."

She offered him a smile. "I'm the sheriff, Amanda Blair." She extended her hand, and he shook it. "And don't even start with how young I look. My father was a Texas Ranger. I started solving crimes when I was in diapers."

He chuckled. "Sheriff Chaz Camden. Thanks for agreeing to meet me. And I wasn't going to comment on your age."

Her wry look indicated she knew he was lying. "Right." She gestured toward the coffee, and he nodded, then waited while she poured him a mug. Then she led him to a desk in an adjoining office.

"What can I do for you, Chaz?"

He liked her directness and dropped into a wooden chair across from her desk. "I don't know if your former sheriff shared information about our cold case with you."

She drummed her nails on the desk. "He didn't, but then again, Lager was having memory problems." She sighed. "The mayor gave him a lot of leeway, but finally they had to ask him to step down."

"I'm sorry." He laid the file he'd brought with him on the desk. "A few years ago, two girls went missing from Sunset Mesa. That same year, a bus carrying the local softball team crashed in Camden Crossing and took three girls' lives. One survived, but two others—Peyton Boulder and my sister, Ruth—disappeared. We still don't know what happened to them."

"I read about the cases," Sheriff Blair said. "I made it a point to familiarize myself with all the old files when I took office. Besides, I grew up around here and remembered the town's devastation when the girls went missing." She pulled a file from the drawer in the desk, opened it and placed it so he could read the contents.

"This is what I have so far on the missing girls from our area."

"Avery Portland was fifteen, popular, a cheerleader. Parents dropped her off for a school dance. According to her boyfriend, she was acting funny all night, picked a fight and she went outside. He went after her, but she was gone."

"Boyfriend's story check out?"

Sheriff Blair shrugged. "He appeared to be devastated. His buddies all gave him an alibi, too."

"How about girl two?"

"Melanie Hoit, sixteen. On the dance team at school. Disappeared from the mall in Amarillo where she was supposed to meet her girlfriends on a Saturday night. Security cameras turned up nothing. According to parents, everyone loved her."

"Were either of the girls ever in trouble?"

She shook her head. "According to the families, no. Neither had any kind of arrest record. Both excelled in school. No problems with authority, although Avery's father had abandoned the family eight months before, and her friends said she was angry and had been to see the counselor about the divorce."

"Were she and Melanie friends?"

She nodded. "Since fifth grade."

Like Ruth and Peyton, except they'd disappeared without a trace.

"No ransom calls. No phone calls from the girls." Sheriff Blair rubbed her hand over her forehead. "No leads."

Chaz spread the notes from the Camden case on the desk. "Sounds similar to our missing girls."

"Except for the bus crash," Sheriff Blair pointed out. "Avery and Melanie disappeared at different times."

Chaz chewed the inside of his cheek. "True. One theory is that the kidnapper was obsessed with one of them. But when the crash occurred, he had to take both."

Sheriff Blair narrowed her eyes. "But he left that other girl, Peyton's sister."

"Yes, Tawny-Lynn Boulder," Chaz said, his chest clenching. "That's true, but she had a broken leg and was unconscious."

"So how did he make two girls go with him? Were there signs of a struggle?"

Chaz grimaced. "It was hard to sort out what happened." He slid a photo of the crash site and tapped it. "There were skid marks from the bus and another vehicle, although the sheriff and crime team never tracked down the vehicle."

"What about blood from a fight? If the girls struggled with the abductor, there might have been evidence."

"The scene was a mess," Chaz said. "Blood and glass were on the rocks, but the fire destroyed most evidence. And it rained that day so the rain washed away the rest."

"I suppose if the kidnapper had a gun he could have forced the girls to go with him. But if Tawny-Lynn was injured, how did her sister and yours escape the bus unharmed?"

Chaz's chest tightened. "They could have been hurt, which would have made it harder for them to fight back," he said. "No one knows."

"What about the girl who survived? It says in the file that she might have witnessed the abduction."

Chaz nodded. "She sustained a head injury, had amnesia and can't remember details of that day."

Still, someone wanted her dead. Which confirmed in his mind that she had seen foul play.

Chaz removed three other photos and showed them to her. "These three young women have also gone missing during the past five years from various counties in Texas."

"You think they're connected?"

"I'm not sure, but maybe. The M.O. is the same. The victims are around the same age. All went missing in the spring, and vanished without a trace."

"Spring?" Sheriff Blair scowled. "The time of year might be significant."

Chaz nodded. What worried him most was that they had no leads. "If the same perpetrator kidnapped all these girls, that means another girl might go missing any day now."

TAWNY-LYNN FROZE, her nerves sizzling with tension.

Barry Dothan had seemed harmless when she'd known him years ago. He was almost childlike in his speech patterns, and walked and behaved like an oversize kid. He'd gained weight and had a pudgy look about him now, his jowls were sagging, his dirty blond hair wiry and choppy as if he'd cut it himself.

But he was hiding and taking pictures of her. And the police had found pictures of Peyton and Ruth as well as other teenagers on the bulletin board in his room.

She shivered.

Was he going to add hers to that wall?

She slowly moved toward the woods, determined to talk to him. But panic flashed in his eyes when he saw her, and he started to run.

"Wait," Tawny-Lynn called.

He planted one hand on a tree, his eyes darting in all

directions. She glanced around for a car, then noticed a bicycle tucked against a copse of trees.

"Barry?"

"I...didn't do anything wrong."

Tawny-Lynn forced her expression to remain calm. "I just want to talk to you."

"I didn't do anything," he mumbled again. "I just like to take pictures."

"It's all right," she said. "But why are you here?"

He shook his head from side to side, back and forth in a frantic motion, his eyes widening in a crazed expression. "I didn't do anything!"

Then he jumped on his bike and raced back through the woods, weaving and swaying as if she'd frightened him.

Her heart raced as she jumped in the truck and fired up the engine. Barry might have been obsessed with her sister or Ruth, but would he have hurt them?

Maybe he'd tried to help them that day, but one of them had fought him and things had gone ugly....

But Chaz was right. He didn't have the intellect or enough emotional control to have hidden a body or kept quiet all these years.

Still, the way he protested so vehemently made her wonder if he knew something that he hadn't told. Maybe he'd been here that day and seen something?

The truck chugged around the winding road, her mind trying to picture the blank face in her memory. Could it have been Barry who'd pulled her from the fire?

She turned down the drive to White Forks, angry that her mind refused to give her the answers she needed.

The answer everyone in town needed, especially the Camdens and the parents of the deceased girls.

She threw the truck into Park, retrieved two of the grocery bags and started toward the porch steps. But she froze at the bottom, her breath catching.

A dead animal, maybe a deer, had been slaughtered and left on the porch. A bloody trail was smeared on the steps.

And another message had been written in blood on the door.

Leave, or this will be you next.

Chapter Eight

Chaz had just left Sunset Mesa when his phone rang. His stomach knotted when he saw Tawny-Lynn's number on the screen.

"Hello."

"Chaz, I hate to bother you—"

"What's wrong?"

"Someone left a slaughtered deer on my front porch with another message."

Chaz silently released a string of expletives. "Don't touch anything and don't go inside."

"I haven't. I'm sitting in the truck."

"Good. I'll be there as soon as I can." He jogged outside, jumped in his squad car, flipped on the siren and sped away from Sunset Mesa, his phone glued to his ear. "Did you see anyone when you pulled up?"

"No," Tawny-Lynn said.

"Has Jimmy been there to redo the locks?"

"Not yet. I'm expecting him any minute."

"Okay, just keep your eyes peeled. If you see anyone, get out of there. Don't try to confront them on your own."

"Don't worry. I don't have a death wish," she said.

But someone else had one for her. He turned onto the main highway leading back to Camden Crossing. "I just came from talking to the sheriff in Sunset Mesa about the two girls that went missing from there the year before Ruth and Peyton did."

"Didn't Sheriff Simmons already cover that?"

"Yeah, but it turns out the sheriff in Sunset Mesa was suffering from dementia. I thought fresh eyes might see something they missed back then."

"Any luck?"

"No. But I'm not giving up." A thick silence fell between them. "Tawny-Lynn, are you okay?"

"Yes," she said, although she didn't sound okay.

How could she be with threats being made against her? "Did something else happen?"

A weary sigh echoed back. "I stopped by the site of the bus crash."

A heartbeat passed. He didn't know what to say. Everyone had pushed her to remember, yet that day had been traumatic and painful for her. "And?"

"I remember someone slamming into the bus and us careening over the side of the ridge," she said. "But I didn't see who hit us. And…then I remember being unconscious and waking up and someone was pulling me from the wreckage. Smoke was billowing around me, and the heat… it was so hot and I was scared."

Chaz's heart was pounding, but he didn't push. He simply waited to see if she would elaborate.

"But that's it," she whispered. "The face is…blank."

He slowed as he rounded a curve, then passed the high school.

"Maybe you didn't actually see the face," he suggested.

"I…don't know." Her voice cracked. "I feel like I did, but there's something in my way, blocking out the image."

"You were injured," Chaz said softly. It was about time someone cut her some slack.

Another tense minute passed, while he veered down the driveway to the ranch.

She cleared her throat. "There's something else."

He scrubbed a hand through his hair as the farmhouse slipped into view. "What?"

"Today when I was at the site. I felt like someone was watching me, and when I looked over my shoulder, Barry Dothan was there, hiding in the woods, taking pictures of me."

Fear slammed into Chaz. "Did he hurt you?"

"No," Tawny-Lynn said. "But it was spooky. I tried to talk to him, but he kept shouting that he hadn't done anything wrong."

"Did he say what he meant by that?"

"No. But why would he go back there if he wasn't there when the accident happened?"

"Good question. I'll have a talk with him and his mother. Maybe he did something to the girls accidentally. If not, maybe he knows something."

Chaz raced up beside the truck and parked, then jumped out, his gun drawn. Tawny-Lynn opened the truck door and climbed down, her face pale.

He took one look at the bloody deer carcass and message on her porch and fury railed inside him.

"I have to do something to stop this," she whispered.

"It's not your fault," Chaz said between gritted teeth.

Then he did what he'd wanted to do when he saw the very first message. He pulled her up against him and wrapped his arms around her.

TAWNY-LYNN LEANED into Chaz, her body trembling. Ever since that awful accident, she'd felt alone.

Persecuted, confused, terrified and guilt-ridden.

She'd learned to deal with it and to stand on her own, but for just a moment, she allowed herself the comfort of Chaz's arms.

He stroked her back, rubbing slow circles between her

shoulder blades. "You don't deserve this, Tawny-Lynn, and I'm going to make sure whoever did this doesn't hurt you."

Tension slowly seeped from her tightly wound muscles. She felt the warmth of his arms encircling her, the soft rise and fall of his chest against her cheek, the whisper of his breath against her ear.

Finally she raised her gaze to his. "I'm sorry, Chaz. I guess that dead animal shook me up more than I thought."

His eyes darkened with concern and other emotions that made her want to reach up and touch his cheek.

Kiss his lips.

Foolish.

A muscle ticked in his jaw. "I promise you I'll put a stop to this cruelty."

She pulled away and struggled for bravado. "Whoever did it probably just wants to scare me off."

"Maybe so. But I won't tolerate this kind of crap while I'm in office. When I find the bastard who did it, he'll pay."

She folded her arms, missing his contact already. The sound of an engine rumbled, and a black pickup rolled up.

"There's Jimmy now." Chaz flicked a hand up to greet the locksmith as he emerged from his truck. "We have a problem here," he said, indicating the carcass on the front porch. "Let me check the house out first, then you can get to work."

Chaz gestured to Tawny-Lynn. "Stay here with her until I return." Then he raced up the steps to the house.

Tawny-Lynn hissed a breath, praying the person who'd threatened her wasn't inside.

Jimmy shuffled back and forth. "Sorry you're having trouble, ma'am."

Tawny-Lynn forced a polite smile. Jimmy was probably in his thirties and wore jeans and a khaki shirt with the name *James's Locks* embroidered on the pocket. His smile was flirty like it had been at the diner although a devilish gleam lit his eyes.

But Chaz must trust him or he wouldn't have called him.

"You didn't grow up in Camden Crossing, did you?" she asked.

"No, ma'am," Jimmy said. "I came from Sunset Mesa. But I moved here a couple years ago."

Chaz returned to the doorway and waved that the house was safe. "I'll clean up this mess, Jimmy, and you can start with the locks."

Jimmy nodded, grabbed a kit from his car and headed up to the porch. "You want a security system?"

Tawny-Lynn frowned and shook her head. "I don't think installing a security system is worth the investment."

Chaz didn't look convinced. "Put dead bolts on all the doors and check the window locks. Then install a hidden camera and aim it at this porch. If this guy shows up again, we'll nail him."

Tawny-Lynn waited until Chaz hauled the bloody deer carcass off the porch. He carried it into the woods, and she retrieved the groceries, sidestepping the blood on the porch floor as she carried them inside.

She quickly sorted and stored the items, glad she'd cleaned the pantry of the outdated canned and boxed goods. Chaz came in for more bleach and a bucket of water and sponge.

Jimmy started in the kitchen with the back door, giving Chaz time to clean the front porch. She brewed a pot of coffee and left it for the men, then started to clean the den.

But the memory of Barry Dothan at the crash site made her rethink her plan. Instead of starting downstairs, she'd start in Peyton's room.

She and Ruth had been whispering about boys those last few weeks, sharing secrets and giggling and talking in hushed voices. Every time she'd tried to join the conversation, her sister had shut her out.

What if her boyfriend knew something?

Maybe there was some clue in Peyton's room as to the secret they'd been sharing.

CHAZ HAD PHOTOGRAPHED the deer and bloody message before he hauled the carcass into the woods. Then he searched for fingerprints on the door, but other than the blood, the door had been wiped clean. There were also no footprints in the blood so the perpetrator had sidestepped the bloody trail he'd left on the steps.

Someone knew what he was doing and was covering his tracks.

But who?

There were a dozen or so people who didn't want Tawny-Lynn here.

Because they didn't want her to remember what happened that day? To remember the face she said was blank?

Because he or she had done something to Ruth and Peyton?

That thought made his gut churn, and he punched the number for the crime lab and asked to speak to Lieutenant Willis Ludlow, the CSI chief he'd met at a police seminar.

"What can I do for you?" Lieutenant Ludlow asked.

Chaz quickly explained the circumstances. "My deputy couriered over some blood samples I took at the crime scene."

"Yeah, hang on a minute, and I'll pull the results."

Paper rustled, then a tapping sound followed, and he realized Ludlow was on his computer. Seconds later, he returned. "Okay, the blood sample on the mirror came from an animal. It was dried and had been there a couple of days."

Two days—the same day Tawny-Lynn's father had died. "Deer blood?"

"No, a rabbit."

"And the blood on the wall?"

"That one was from a deer. Maybe your guy is a hunter."

"Possibly." Or anyone with enough imagination to kill a deer and use its blood to frighten Tawny-Lynn.

His mind ticked away possibilities. It had to be someone fairly strong to have dragged the deer up onto the porch. Someone who didn't have a weak stomach.

Most likely a man.

"How about the prints?"

"The only ones we found were Boulder's and his daughter's."

Chaz was frustrated but not surprised.

"Sorry, I know that's not much help."

"This perp is covering his tracks," Chaz said. "But I'll catch him sooner or later." He just hoped it was before the creep tried to make good on his threats and hurt Tawny-Lynn.

His conversation with his father echoed in his head, and he went to tell Tawny-Lynn that he was leaving.

He needed to have a talk with his old man.

But there was no reason his father wouldn't want Tawny-Lynn to remember. In fact, he'd driven the theory that she'd been hiding something and demanded she stop faking the amnesia.

But his father didn't want her here, and he had a hunting rifle. Deer hunting was his sport.

Then he'd talk to Barry Dothan about those pictures and see if he was stalking Tawny-Lynn.

TAWNY-LYNN SHIVERED as she stepped into her sister's old room. It was as if she'd walked back in time.

Peyton had always been his favorite because she was more of a girly-girl, and her room reflected her personality.

Though she and her father had argued those last few

months. Mostly about the length of Peyton's skirts, her makeup and boyfriends. Peyton had been hormonal, determined to date when their father told her no, and had snuck out several times late at night.

Her father had also found her slipping alcohol from the house.

Twice, she'd come in so drunk she could barely walk, and Tawny-Lynn had covered for her. She and her sister had argued the next day, and Tawny-Lynn had begged her sister to stop acting out.

Peyton had yelled that she was almost eighteen, that she was in love, and that she'd do whatever she pleased.

A couple of weeks later, she'd run in crying one night, and when Tawny-Lynn asked what was wrong, Peyton refused to talk.

She'd figured it was boyfriend trouble, but then she'd heard Peyton and Ruth arguing over the phone later, and thought the two of them had had a falling out. But Peyton had never shared what had upset her or what happened between her and Ruth.

She slid into the desk chair in the corner and searched the drawers, finding assorted junk—spiral notebooks with old algebra problems, a science notebook, movie ticket stubs, old hair bows, ribbons and report cards. Peyton had been an average student, but popular because of her good looks.

She checked the other drawers and found a few photographs of her sister and Ruth. The two of them at pep rallies, Peyton playing midfield, Peyton in her homecoming dress, Ruth in hers on the homecoming court.

Her finger brushed the edge of something, and she discovered another photo jammed between two school albums.

Her heart squeezed as she stared at the picture. It was Peyton, her and their mother. Peyton had probably been two and she was an infant. Her mother was smiling as she cradled her in her arms.

Tawny-Lynn wiped at a tear and placed the photo in her pocket to keep. If her mother had lived, how would their lives been different? Would her father have stayed away from the bottle?

Satisfied the desk held no clues, she checked the nightstand by the bed. Her sister had kept a diary, but Tawny-Lynn searched for it after Peyton disappeared and never found it. It could have been in her gym bag in the bus and burned in the fire.

Another lead lost.

In the drawer beneath an old compact and brush, she found a box of condoms. She opened the box of twelve and noted they were half gone. Peyton had always had boyfriends, but she hadn't known her sister was sexually active.

Who had she been sleeping with?

Hoping to find some clue about the mysterious boyfriend or the missing diary, she rummaged through the closet, searching the shoeboxes on the floor but found nothing but sneakers, sandals, flip-flops and a pair of black dress shoes.

Deciding it was time to throw out her sister's clothes—she could donate them to the church along with her father's belongings—she gathered several garbage bags and began pulling sweaters, shirts and jeans off the shelves and rack and dumping them inside.

She spotted Peyton's letter jacket and pulled it off the hanger, but a folded scrap of paper fell from the pocket. She opened the note and read it.

Dear Peyton,
Please don't leave me. I love you, and you said you
loved me. Call me tonight.
Love & Kisses,
J.J.

Tawny-Lynn struggled to remember J.J.'s last name. The class yearbooks were in the desk drawer, so she grabbed the latest one and searched the names and photos from the senior class.

J.J. McMullen.

Yes, Peyton had been dating him around Christmastime. Did he still live around town?

She used her smart phone to look up his number and found a James McMullen living right outside town. She punched his number but a woman answered. "Hello?"

Tawny-Lynn wiped dust from her jeans. "I'm looking for James McMullen."

"He's at work. Who is this?"

A baby's cry echoed somewhere in the background.

"Where does he work?"

"At the meat market in town. Now who is this?"

Tawny-Lynn didn't reply. She hung up, trying to picture the dark-haired boy who Peyton had once dated butchering meat all day, but the image didn't fit.

But his father had owned the place so he must have gone to work with him.

She finished cleaning out the closet, then stripped the dusty bedcovers and stuffed them in another bag. The notebooks and papers went into the trash. When she finished, she dragged the bags downstairs.

"I'm finished down here," Jimmy said. "I'll check the windows upstairs."

"Thanks."

She hauled the bags of clothes outside, tossed them into the pickup truck and headed to the church. She dropped the bags with the secretary, thinking the woman looked familiar, but she didn't take the time to introduce herself.

Ten minutes later, she parked in front of the meat market and went inside. Glass cases held dozens of cuts of beef, pork and chicken while shelves to the side were filled with homegrown vegetables, sauces and spices.

An older man with a receding hairline stood behind the counter, his apron stained.

"Mr. McMullen?" Tawny-Lynn asked.

His reading glasses wobbled as he peered over the counter at her. "What can I do for you, young lady?"

"I'd like to talk to your son, J.J."

The man frowned, but yelled his son's name. A second later, J.J. appeared, looking more like his father than she remembered. Maybe it was the receding hairline or the nose that was slightly crooked. The bloody apron didn't help.

"Tawny-Lynn?" J.J. said, his eyes widening in recognition.

She nodded, then removed the note and gestured for him to take it. He rounded the counter and leaned against the potato bin as he read it.

"You were the last guy I remember dating Peyton before she disappeared."

His sharp gaze jerked toward her. "You think I had something to do with that?"

"No," Tawny-Lynn said, although the anger in his tone made her wonder. Had he been questioned seven years ago?

"In the note, you were asking her not to leave you. What happened?"

He cut his eyes toward his father, then shoved the note back in her hands. "She dumped me, that's what happened. She found someone else."

"Did she say who it was?"

He shook his head, his anger palpable. "No, but I got the impression it was an older man. She kept saying that it was complicated, but that he was sophisticated and he'd take care of her. That one day they'd get married." His gaze met hers. "Hell, when she went missing, I thought maybe she ran off with him."

Tawny-Lynn had heard that rumor. But the sheriff had found no evidence to substantiate the theory.

It was complicated.

What if her sister had been seeing an older man, maybe a *married* man? If she told J.J. her intentions of marrying, maybe Peyton had pressured him to leave his wife.

Would he have hurt her sister to keep their affair quiet?

Chapter Nine

Chaz should have been relieved that the messages had been written in animal blood instead of human blood, but the fact that someone had threatened an innocent woman in his town infuriated him.

He parked in front of the bank and strode in, then headed straight to his father's office, but the secretary stopped him on the way.

"He's not here. He went home to have lunch with your mother."

That was a surprise. But it probably meant that he'd found some discrepancy in their finances and wanted to interrogate his mother. Gerome Camden was a control freak who had made a fortune because he obsessed over every penny, kept his wife on a tight budget and didn't allow frivolities.

Except where Ruth had been concerned. He'd doted on her and spoiled her rotten.

Chaz drove to his parents' house, tossing a quick wave to the gardener trimming the shrubs, then buzzed the doorbell. He didn't wait for the maid to answer, but had only buzzed to alert them he was on his way.

His boots clicked on the polished-marble floor in the entryway as he crossed to the dining room. His mother looked up with a smile, her china teacup halfway to her mouth. "Chaz, this is a surprise." She started to rise. "I'll get Harriet to bring you a plate."

"No thanks, Mom, I'm not here to eat." He crossed the room and gave her a quick kiss on the cheek.

"Of course you'll eat with us," his father said in a tone that brooked no argument.

Chaz rounded on him. He hated to broach this subject in front of his mother, but if anyone could calm his father—and keep him from doing something stupid to Tawny-Lynn—she could. Where Gerome Camden ruled the finances, Beverly Camden ruled the house and had impeccable manners and morals.

"What's going on?" his mother asked.

Chaz set the file he'd brought with him on the table in front of his father. "When Dad heard Tawny-Lynn Boulder was coming back to town, he paid me a visit and ordered me to run her out of town."

"What?" His mother fanned her face. "Gerome, you didn't."

Guilt streaked his father's face. "We suffered enough seven years ago because of that girl. I didn't want her stirring up old hurts."

"You act as if she caused the bus accident," his mother chided. "She lost her sister, too, and she spent a week in the hospital."

"That's right." Chaz opened the folder and spread out the photos of the bloody messages. "When she arrived, she found this on the mirror in her room. That night someone ran her off the road into a ditch." He tapped the photo of the bathroom wall. "Then someone left this."

"Is that blood?" his mother asked.

Chaz nodded. "Rabbit blood on the mirror. Deer blood on the wall." He showed them the picture of the bloody deer carcass. "When she got home from the grocery store today, this was waiting for her."

His mother made a choked sound and grabbed her water, but his father simply glared at him. "I told you no one wanted her here."

"Did you do this, Dad? Or did you hire someone to?"

His father slammed both hands on the table, jarring the silverware. "How dare you accuse me of such a thing. Just look how you've upset your mother."

Chaz planted his fists on his hips. "I'm not going anywhere until you answer my question."

"Chaz, you can't really believe—"

"Mother, please, let him answer." Chaz turned to his father. "I know that you want Tawny-Lynn gone. Did you set this up to scare her off?"

"Of course not." His father shoved the pictures back into Chaz's hands. "Now take these offensive things and get them out of here."

Chaz gripped the folder. "I hope you're being honest, Dad. Because if I find out you had anything to do with this, I'll be back."

He mumbled an apology to his mother, then strode toward the door. Behind him, he heard ice clinking in a glass as his father fixed himself a scotch.

TAWNY-LYNN TRIED to remember the names of Peyton's other friends.

The softball team had been Tawny-Lynn's core group, and she'd been devastated at the deaths of her fellow teammates.

But Peyton had run in several groups. She'd chaired the prom committee her junior year, had worked on the class yearbook and joined the dance team during football season.

Cindy Miller, the cheerleading captain, had invited Peyton to a sleepover a few weeks before the accident. Desperate, Tawny-Lynn looked up the girls' name online and found her home address, so she called the number.

"Mrs. Miller speaking."

"Can I speak to Cindy please?"

"Cindy's not here. She's at her house. Who is this?"

Tawny-Lynn hesitated over revealing her name. "I'm calling from the high school reunion committee. We had a worm in the system that trashed our files, and we lost married names and current contact information."

"Oh, well, Cindy wouldn't miss a high school reunion for anything. She married Donny Parker from the class two years ahead of her. They live outside Camden Crossing in one of the homes on the lake. Donny developed the property himself."

So they were probably rolling in money. "That's wonderful. Can I have her phone number and address? And oh, if she works, I'd like that number, too."

She scribbled down the numbers as Cindy's mother read them off.

"Cindy doesn't work. She stays home with the twins."

Tawny-Lynn rolled her eyes. She probably had a nanny and spent her days at the tennis courts.

"Thanks. I'll give her a call." She disconnected, then wheeled the truck toward the lake. The storm clouds brewing all day looked darker as she passed farmland that would soon be rich with crops. White Forks once had a nice garden but her father had let it dry up along ago.

A few wildflowers had sprouted along the entrance to the lake community, the sign swaying in the wind. She followed the road through the wooded lots, noting that it was new and most of them weren't developed yet. No doubt expensive homes would be popping up, drawing newcomers to Camden Crossing.

Those lots would need landscaping. Designs rose to her mind, but she squashed the thought. No one in Camden Crossing would likely hire her to design their properties. No use in even going there.

She passed an estate lot where the house sat back in the woods and realized it was the address she was looking for. A personalized sign with the name Parker on it dangled from the mailbox, and as she veered down the driveway tall trees surrounded her, offering privacy and shade from the relentless Texas sun.

The stucco-and-stone house looked like a lodge nestled in the woods, and a BMW was parked in the garage. Beside the house, a boat ramp held a customized pontoon. Tawny-Lynn walked up the cobblestone steps leading to the front door and rang the doorbell. Seconds later, a commotion sounded inside with the sound of children squealing.

When the door opened, a pair of redheaded little boys stared up at her, their faces streaked in something that looked suspiciously like mud but smelled like chocolate pudding. She guessed them to be about four years old.

"Boys, I told you not to open the door!"

Tawny-Lynn swallowed her surprise when Cindy appeared. Maybe it was baby weight, but she'd gained at least thirty pounds.

"Tawny-Lynn?" Cindy said in a croaked whisper.

"Hi, Cindy. I wasn't sure you'd remember me."

"How could I forget?" The annoyance at the boys morphed into a wary look. Cindy did not look happy to see her.

"Mind if I come in and talk to you for a minute?"

"I can't imagine what about," Cindy said warily.

Bored, the boys took off running up the winding staircase behind them, screaming as they went.

"Please," she said. "I'm only back for a few days to get my father's ranch ready to sell."

Cindy bit her lower lip, shifting from one foot to the other as if struggling with her thoughts. Finally she motioned for her to come in.

"You have a gorgeous place," Tawny-Lynn said. "Your

mother said you married Donny Parker, that he built these houses."

Nerves flashed in Cindy's eyes. "You talked to my mother?"

"I was just trying to remember some of Peyton's old friends."

Cindy's brown eyes widened. "Why? Have you heard from your sister?"

Tawny-Lynn fought the temptation to fidget as she took a seat on a leather sofa in the giant-size den. The view of the lake was magnificent, reminiscent of a postcard.

Cindy seemed to have everything in life. So why did she seem so anxious?

"No. Have you?"

Cindy raked kids' toys off the couch. "No, of course not. I just thought…maybe you found out what happened to her and Ruth."

"That's why I'm asking questions," Tawny-Lynn said. "I talked to J.J. McMullen earlier and he said that Peyton broke up with him for an older guy. He hinted that he thought the man might have been married. Did she ever mention anything to you about a man she was seeing?"

The sound of the children tearing down the stairs echoed in the cavernous house, and Cindy jumped up. "No, I don't remember that. Now I really need to take care of the boys. It's time for their karate lesson."

Tawny-Lynn stood, wondering if the boys really had a lesson, or if Cindy just wanted to get rid of her.

Because Cindy ushered her out the door and practically slammed it in her face.

Irritated, Tawny-Lynn drove down the long drive, then parked off to the side in a vacant lot and watched as seconds later, Cindy flew past.

What in the world was she in such a hurry for? The boys'

lesson, or had her questions upset Cindy? Did she know whom Peyton had been seeing?

And if so, why hadn't she told her or the police?

CHAZ WAS STILL stewing with anger as he left his father's. Maybe he'd jumped the gun in his accusations.

His father was a businessman, a well-respected member of the town, a man who used his money and connections to run the show.

But he'd never been violent or used physical force to get what he wanted. He'd never had to.

And smearing blood on a wall was not his style.

He drove to Barry Dothan's house, contemplating his approach. He'd found pictures of teenagers in the sheriff's file from the original investigation.

But Barry's mother had given him an alibi.

Still, he didn't like the fact that he'd been watching Tawny-Lynn.

He pulled over at the trailer park, noting the weed-choked yards dividing the mobile homes. Children's toys were scattered around, a mutt was tied to the porch that had been added on to the second trailer, then he spotted Barry's bike.

Chaz walked up to the trailer and knocked, remembering the stories he'd heard about the family. When she was younger, Mrs. Dothan had been a stripper and that's where she'd met Barry's father. He was now serving time in prison for selling cocaine.

Complications during childbirth had caused Barry's brain damage.

He knocked again and heard shuffling inside. The door screeched open and Mrs. Dothan stood looking at him with blurry eyes as if she'd been drinking. She wore a ratty housecoat that she tugged around her, then lit a cigarette, inhaled and blew out smoke.

"What do you want, Sheriff?"

"To talk to you and Barry." Chaz didn't wait on an invitation. He shouldered his way past her into the tiny den, which was riddled with dirty laundry and reeked of smoke and alcohol.

She dropped into a recliner that had seen better days, focusing on her cigarette.

"Is Barry here?"

"What you want him for? He do something?"

"I don't know," Chaz said. "Did he?"

She shrugged. "He's a good boy. Not bright, but he ain't bad."

Chaz walked toward the bedrooms. "Barry?"

"He ain't here," she said in a smoker's voice. "Now tell me what you want with him."

"I heard he was out at the site of the bus crash." He didn't have to elaborate. Everyone in town knew the place, the date, the time. It had been embedded in their memories forever. Some even used it as a reference point—before the bus crash, after the bus crash.

She shrugged. "He likes to ride his bike all over."

"He likes to take pictures, too. I saw the ones the sheriff confiscated seven years ago."

Her right eye twitched. "They were pictures of the girls at school, after softball practice, at the swim meet," she said. "Not like they were naked pictures."

Chaz arched a brow. "Does he have pictures of naked girls?"

She took another drag of her cigarette. "He may not be bright, but he's a guy," she said.

"Are they of real girls or are you talking magazines?"

"Those magazines. I don't know where he gets 'em but he keeps them under his bed. He doesn't know I found 'em."

Chaz shifted, curious. "Do you mind if I take a look in your son's room?"

She flicked ashes into a misshapen ashtray that Barry had obviously made out of clay. "Not if you're trying to pin something on him. I told the sheriff years ago Barry was with me the day of that crash. He didn't have nothing to do with it."

"I didn't say he did, but earlier he was taking photographs of Tawny-Lynn Boulder. It spooked her."

"Barry's not dangerous. Why's she acting like that?"

"Because someone left bloody threats on her doorstep and in her house."

Her eye twitched again, and she reached for a half-empty vodka bottle on the table. "He didn't leave any threats."

Chaz gestured to the bedroom with the posters of the high school swim and soccer teams. "If he's innocent, then it won't hurt for me to take a look." This time he didn't wait for her response.

He ducked inside and studied the room. There was a single bed covered with a navy comforter with baseballs on it, a dinosaur-shaped lamp and a collection of Hot Wheels cars that filled a shelf next to the bed.

He glanced at a desk and saw a stack of yearbooks and realized Barry collected them, even though he'd never graduated himself.

In the desk drawer, he found childlike drawings of a house with the sun shining above it, and stick figures portraying a family. Was Barry dreaming of finding a girl and marriage?

Chaz studied the photographs on the wall. He'd added a plastic rose above the girls' team from the crash, a tribute to the lost lives.

Frowning, Chaz dropped to his knees, checked under the bed and found the stash of girly magazines Mrs. Dothan had mentioned. He also discovered another box and pulled it out, then lifted the lid.

His gut clenched at what he found inside. Pictures of

teenage girls outside the school. A photograph of Ruth and Peyton from years ago when they'd worn harem costumes for a halftime show. Pictures of them dunking water over each other after a softball win.

A picture of the two of them at the swimming hole in their bikinis.

Then one of Tawny-Lynn in her bathing suit standing by the dock ready to dive into the lake.

Barry might not be dangerous, but the pictures were disturbing, and this spying had to stop.

He carried the pictures out to show Mrs. Dothan. She barely reacted when he laid them on the table. She simply lit another cigarette.

"Boys will be boys."

He opened his mouth to make a point, but the door bust open and Barry stumbled in.

Chaz frowned at the blood on Barry's shirt and hands.

Chapter Ten

When Barry saw Chaz, he turned and bolted. Chaz jumped up and caught him by the arm of his denim jacket. "Wait a minute, Barry."

"I didn't do anything wrong!" Barry shouted. "I didn't."

He gripped Barry by the arms. "How did you get that blood on your shirt and hands?"

"My nose. I crashed my bike into a tree."

"So it's your blood?"

Barry nodded but he was shaking, his eyes darting around for an escape. "Yeah, I didn't hurt nobody."

Mrs. Dothan stumbled over from her chair. "Barry, don't say anything."

Chaz reached for the strap of the camera slung over Barry's shoulder. "What were you doing in the woods? Were you taking pictures?"

"There's nothing wrong in taking pictures," Mrs. Dothan cut in.

Chaz flipped the camera over and hit the replay button to view the pictures Barry had shot. An uneasy feeling traveled up his spine.

Various shots of Tawny-Lynn at the crash site. She looked so sad, so vulnerable, so tormented that his heart gave a painful tug.

"You took pictures of Tawny-Lynn this afternoon," he

said. "I know how you obsess over girls," Chaz said. "Did you get mad when she told you to leave her alone?"

Barry started babbling about how he hit his nose on the tree again. "Didn't do anything wrong. Tawny-Lynn... wouldn't hurt her."

"You took pictures of my sister and Peyton Boulder years ago, Barry. I found them in your secret box."

"Pretty girls," Barry said. "I just like pretty girls."

"What do you like to do with them?" Chaz asked through gritted teeth.

"My boy doesn't do anything to the girls." Mrs. Dothan pulled Barry toward her. "He just likes to look."

Chaz reminded himself to be calm. He had no evidence that Barry had committed a crime. He removed his phone from his belt and retrieved the photos from Tawny-Lynn's porch. "See that threatening message, Barry. Are you sure you didn't get blood on you from the deer when you killed it and wrote on Tawny-Lynn's porch."

Barry's eyes widened in panic and a second later, he crumbled to the floor, wrapped his hands over his head and broke into incoherent sobs. "Don't kill deer, don't like blood. Stop it, stop it...."

"Sheriff, you need to leave," Mrs. Dothan said.

Chaz glared at Barry's mother. "If he hurt someone in the past, Mrs. Dothan, you're not helping him by protecting him."

"My son isn't dangerous," she cried as she stabbed her cigarette into the ashtray and knelt by her son. "Now get out!"

Chaz's heart hammered as Barry continued to wail. Was he innocent, or was he more dangerous than his mother and everyone thought?

Now that Tawny-Lynn was back and asking questions, she didn't want to stop. Seven years ago she'd been too traumatized and grief-stricken to think clearly. She barely remembered the sheriff talking to her or any of the leads he might have pursued in the investigation.

But she was sure someone—a male—had dragged her from the wreckage. Only no man had ever come forward to claim his hero status.

Which made everyone wonder if he had done something to Peyton and Ruth.

Seeing Cindy triggered memories of the other girls on the softball team. Not just the three who'd died, but the other players on the team who hadn't taken the bus that day. Two had been sick with a flu that had swept through the school, another girl had been out of town due to a death in the family, Judy Samsung had been benched due to a broken arm and Rudy Henway and Paula Pennington had gone home with their parents because they'd planned to take the SATs the next morning.

Tawny-Lynn drove into town and stopped by the drugstore to pick up a refill of her migraine medication, then found a local phone book on the counter at the pharmacy. She grabbed it, slipped into a chair in the corner and thumbed through it, searching for each of the girls' names to see if any of them still lived in town.

Paula showed up under her maiden name, but not Rudy. But there was an ad for the Sports Barn, owned by Rudy Farnsworth. It had to be the same Rudy.

She punched Paula's number but the phone had been disconnected. She dialed the Sports Barn next and a woman answered.

"Hello, this is Rudy at the Sports Barn. What can I do for you?"

Tawny-Lynn panicked and hung up. She berated herself as she took a deep breath, then hurried out to the truck and drove to the shop on the edge of town. The ancient building had been renovated since she'd moved away, but as she entered, she realized the inside hadn't changed. Jerseys, shirts, trophies, bumper stickers and every other sports parapher- nalia related to the local teams, both elementary, middle, high school and club teams were represented.

When she was small, she'd coveted the gleaming tro- phies in the glass cabinet.

"Be right with you." A young woman with striking red hair in a ponytail stood behind the counter writing up what she assumed was an order.

Tawny-Lynn remembered the tough-girl attitude Rudy had always emanated. She'd always wondered about the girl's home life.

A second later, the woman looked up, her amber eyes flashing with surprise. "Tawny-Lynn, you really are back?"

Tawny-Lynn shifted, her hands jittery although she didn't know why. "Not for long. Just to settle my daddy's ranch."

Rudy's expression softened. "Well, good luck with that."

"Thanks." Tawny-Lynn gestured at the jerseys and tro- phies. "So you own this place now?"

Rudy grinned. "Yes. I guess the tomboy in me never died." At the word *died,* she winced. "Sorry. I didn't mean it—"

"Don't apologize," Tawny-Lynn said. "I always loved this store. It's nice to know it's in the hands of someone else who appreciated it."

Rudy walked around the counter, and Tawny-Lynn no- ticed she was pregnant. "Oh, when's the baby due?"

"A couple of months," Rudy said. "I married a guy I met at A&M, Jo Farnsworth. He played football for the Aggies."

"Congratulations." A silence fell, and she fidgeted with one of the sweatbands on the shelf. At least Rudy had moved on and seemed happy.

Something she'd been unable to do. Even miles away

in Austin, it was as if she were permanently stuck here in the past.

"I'm so sorry they never found Ruth or Peyton," Rudy finally said.

Tawny-Lynn gave a slight shrug. "I wish I could have helped more. Remembered…"

"It wasn't your fault," Rudy said. "Everyone was way too hard on you."

"Thanks." Unexpected tears burned Tawny-Lynn's eyes. "Can I ask you a question, Rudy?"

Rudy rubbed a hand over her belly, but a wary look pulled at her face. "What?"

"Did you ever hear my sister talking about a boyfriend after she broke up with J.J.?"

Rudy started refolding a stack of jerseys that were perfectly folded. "It was a long time ago, Tawny-Lynn, and you know Peyton and I weren't close friends. She was the pretty popular girl and I was…a dork."

Tawny-Lynn laughed for the first time in a long time as if she might have found a friend. "I always felt that way around her, too."

Rudy gave her a sympathetic look. "I always liked you. And I'll never forget that last game. You were awesome."

Tawny-Lynn blinked back more tears. For so long, she'd associated everything about Camden Crossing with that horrible day. But there had been some good memories and people here.

"Thanks, I thought you were cool, too."

They both laughed.

"Good luck with the baby." A seed of envy sprouted inside Tawny-Lynn. She'd closed herself off from relationships for so long that she hadn't bothered to fantasize about marriage and a family of her own. She'd been too busy grieving the one she'd lost.

She turned to go, but Rudy rushed up behind her.

"Tawny-Lynn, I…didn't want to say anything because…I don't want to speak bad about Peyton, but…"

"But what?" Tawny-Lynn clenched Rudy's hand. "Tell me. J.J. said he thought Peyton might have been involved with a married man."

Rudy's eyes flickered with regret. "I think she was, too."

"What makes you say that?"

"A couple of days before the accident, I left my bag in the locker room and went back to get it. I heard Peyton and Ruth talking."

"What were they saying?"

Rudy rubbed her swollen belly again. "Peyton was crying and said that she thought he'd leave his wife for her, but he wasn't going to. She sounded really upset."

"Did she say who the man was?"

Rudy shook her head. "No. Apparently he told her she'd better not tell anyone about the two of them, that he'd ruin her life if she did."

Tawny-Lynn's heart hammered. She had to find out who Peyton had been sleeping with. The man who'd made that threat could have killed her.

And if Ruth had known about him, he might have killed her to keep her quiet.

"Mrs. Dothan," Chaz said as he paused at the doorway. "If I find out you're lying to protect Barry, I'll come back and arrest you."

"I said get out!" Mrs. Dothan shouted over Barry's wails.

"I'm leaving, but watch your son. Taking pictures may seem innocent to you, but it also can be construed as stalking." He hesitated. "And, Barry, stay away from Tawny-Lynn Boulder."

He closed the door behind him, hoping they would heed his warning.

Tawny-Lynn's face flashed in his mind, and he itched to go see her. An itch he knew he should avoid scratching.

Because holding her felt too damn good. So good he wanted to hold her again.

Not going to happen.

His phone buzzed as he climbed into his car and drove back toward town. "Sheriff Camden."

"Sheriff, this is Sergeant Justin Thorpe with the Texas Rangers."

"What can I do for you, Sergeant Thorpe?"

"In the past month, two young women have gone missing in the counties next to Camden Crossing. Due to the cold cases in your town and Sunset Mesa, a special task force has been created to investigate the connection, if there is one."

"Tell me about the disappearances," Chaz said.

"A month ago, Carly Edgewater disappeared from a pep rally at the school where she teaches. So far, no one saw or heard anything."

"How about her family?"

"Prominent parents. They were at a charity fund-raiser the night she went missing, so we've cleared them."

"Boyfriend or girlfriend trouble?"

"Not that we've uncovered, but I'm just starting the investigation."

"What about the second woman?"

"Name's Tina Grimes. Disappeared last week. Supposedly had a dentist appointment one morning, but never made it. When we checked, there was never a dentist appointment."

"So she lied? Why?"

"We don't know that yet. She supposedly had a boyfriend, but they broke up six months ago. Mom died last year of cancer, single father adores his daughter. He appears to be pretty distraught. Said the last few months had been difficult with his daughter. She was moody and depressed but refused therapy."

"So it's possible she ran off or hurt herself?"

"It's possible. But the sheriff never found a body and there was no suicide note."

Chaz pulled up to his office, parked and strode inside. "You've spoken with Sheriff Blair over in Sunset Mesa?"

"She's next on my list."

"So you think we're talking about one kidnapper?"

"Maybe. That's the reason for the task force, to coordinate efforts and see if we find a connection."

"If this perpetrator has been doing this for years and gotten away with it, he has to be pretty damn smart." Which would rule out Barry.

"He definitely knows how to stay under the radar."

His deputy must be making rounds as the office was empty. Chaz claimed his desk chair and turned to the computer. "Send me all the info you have on the cases. I'll compare it to our cold case. How old are these women?"

"Mid-twenties."

Hmm, maybe the cases weren't related. The first two victims had disappeared from Sunset Mesa when they were in their teens. These young women were in their twenties.

"Thanks. The more eyes we have on this, the better."

Chaz hung up and made himself some coffee while he waited on the information. When it came in, he printed out copies of the files to take home to study.

He jotted down some quick notes on the dates of the disappearances, and frowned. Just as Sheriff Blair mentioned, all the girls and these two women had gone missing in the spring.

Was the time of year significant for a reason? And if so, what the hell did it mean?

TAWNY-LYNN TACKLED her father's room when she got home, but as she dumped liquor bottles and beer cans into the trash, her conversations with Cindy and Rudy replayed through her head.

Who was the older man Peyton had been in love with?

Cigarette smoke permeated the air, so she gathered the bedding and towels in the bathroom and piled them in the trash. She tackled her father's closet next, a well of emotion bubbling inside her as she folded his pants and shirts to donate to the church. Some were too stained, tattered and smoke-riddled to save, but she found two hats he'd bought but never worn and Sunday ties that hadn't been seen in a decade and added them to the church bag.

She flipped on the radio while she sorted and cleaned, tuning in as the weatherman forecasted rain by the weekend. Tomorrow she'd tackle the outside of the ranch. She could finish cleaning and do minor repairs on the rainy days.

Her shoulders ached with fatigue as she hauled the bags out to the truck, then she scrubbed the walls and bathroom, determined to cleanse the smoky scent. But two hours later when her hands were practically raw, the scent still lingered.

Deciding she needed to clear the braided rug out, she rolled it up, dragged it outside and tossed it into the back of the truck to dispose of.

A noise sounded from the corner of the house, and her breath caught. Slowly she inched around the side to see what it was, and found a stray cat pawing at the ground by the old flowerbeds.

Relieved, she hurried back inside and locked the door. She finished in her father's room by taking down the ancient curtains that had turned from white to a yellowed brown, then tossed them into a trash bag.

She found another stack of mail on the desk and sorted through it. A crinkled envelope caught her eye, and she opened it, surprised to find an offer to buy the ranch from Chaz's father. Her eyes widened at the amount he'd offered. The letterhead held the bank's logo, and had been dated three weeks before.

Why would Mr. Camden want to buy the ranch?

Because he owned almost everything else in town.

Maybe he'd tried to run her father off like he'd done her because he reminded him of Ruth.

Did Chaz know about the offer?

She carried the envelope to the kitchen and dropped it into the basket with the unpaid bills, then returned to finish the bedroom. She found a shoebox of photos and put them in the den to sort through later.

Next she attacked the fireplace. It was full of old ashes and soot, so she swept it out and cleaned the hearth, then wiped down the fireplace tools. Then she swept and mopped the wood floor in her father's room.

Muscles aching, she stood back and admired her work. The house was old, but cleaning it made a huge difference. Exhausted, she climbed the steps, showered, then collapsed into bed.

Her landscape work was physical, but this heavy lifting had strained muscles she didn't even know she had.

She closed her eyes, praying the nightmares would leave her alone, and fell into a deep sleep. But sometime later, a noise startled her awake.

Cool air floated around her, giving her a chill. The house was old and drafty, but she remembered leaving the windows open in her father's room to air out the smoke, so she grabbed her robe, tugged it on and tiptoed down the stairs. She reached for the light to flip it on, but suddenly someone grabbed her from behind.

Tawny-Lynn screamed and threw her elbow back in defense, but her attacker threw her facedown and straddled her. She kicked and bucked, but he was heavier than her, and he pinned her to the floor.

Then he wrapped his hands around her throat, his fingers digging into her windpipe.

Chapter Eleven

Tawny-Lynn struggled to breathe, but her attacker tightened his grip and she gagged for air. Furious at herself for leaving the window open, she channeled that anger into adrenaline, shoved her hands beneath her chest and pushed herself up, bucking to throw her attacker off her.

The tactic worked, and he loosened his hold for a brief second, just long enough for her to crawl toward the fireplace. The poker was only inches away. If she could just reach it…

But he was fast. He gripped her ankle and tried to drag her away from it. She used her other foot to kick at him, then clawed her way toward the fire poker. A blow to her back made her cry out in pain, and tears burned her eyes.

But she blinked them back. She didn't intend to let this creep kill her.

She kicked backward again and heard his grunt as she connected with his nose. Panting for air, she scrambled to her knees and grabbed the poker.

Then she flipped around just as he charged toward her. It was dark, but she squinted to see his face.

Impossible. He was wearing a ski mask, two dark eyes glaring at her as he heaved for a breath.

She clenched the fire poker in a white-knuckled grip and swung it just as she used to do the bat. He ducked to the side and she missed his head by a fraction of an inch.

But the poker connected with his shoulder. He roared in anger and lunged to wrestle it from her, but she swung it toward his knees. She hit one and he crumpled with a curse.

Taking the fire poker with her, Tawny-Lynn jumped up and ran past him, stomach churning as she raced upstairs to get her phone. She stumbled once, but caught herself, then raced into her bedroom, grabbed her phone and locked herself in the bathroom.

Her hands trembled as she punched Chaz's number. God help her, she wished she'd grabbed her father's rifle from the closet. From now on, she'd sleep with it by the bed.

Downstairs, footsteps pounded, and she prayed he wasn't coming up the steps for her. The phone rang twice, then Chaz finally answered.

"Chaz, it's Tawny-Lynn. Someone's in the house. He tried to choke me."

"I'm on my way. Where are you?"

"Locked in my bathroom. Hurry…" She pressed her ear to the door to listen. "Oh, God, he's coming up the steps."

CHAZ GRABBED HIS GUN and raced to his car, fear for Tawny-Lynn spiking his adrenaline. He pressed the accelerator to the floor, tires squealing as he sped down the road toward White Forks.

Night cast shadows across the road, and he watched for cars in case Tawny-Lynn's intruder was escaping.

He hoped to hell the bastard had run and that Tawny-Lynn was safe.

He rounded the curve on two wheels, grateful he lived so close to the ranch and that hardly anyone was out on the road this late at night. His father had had a saying, that nothing good happened after midnight. One sentiment they agreed on.

A dark SUV flew past him, and he glanced back, wondering if it might be the intruder, but it had a Montana tag. Probably a tourist traveling through.

He swung the squad car down the drive to White Forks, then cut the siren, his headlights paving a path on the dark dirt drive. It was a moonless night, the stars hidden behind the ominous clouds that so far had held back their wrath.

He bounced over the ruts, his heart racing as he scanned the property. Except for Boulder's old pickup, there were no vehicles in sight.

Had the intruder parked down the road and hiked in through the woods?

He slammed his car to a stop, flipped off his lights and climbed out, easing his car door shut. He held his gun at the ready as he approached, checking in all directions for an ambush.

The sound of an animal scrounging through the woods echoed in the distance—or maybe it was Tawny-Lynn's attacker escaping.

He had to check the house first. Instincts on alert, he eased his way up the porch steps, mentally seeing that damned bloody deer carcass.

Apparently the threats had been real.

The front door was locked, so he jiggled it but the new dead bolt was in place. Damn. How had the intruder gotten in?

He rushed down the steps and walked around the side of the house until he found an open window in old man Boulder's room. Cursing beneath his breath, he climbed through the window, then tiptoed across the room, bracing his gun.

The room was clear. *Clean* and clear, he thought, shocked at how much work Tawny-Lynn had done in such a short time.

Holding his breath, he inched into the hall to the living room and kitchen and scanned the rooms. Though it was dark as hell, he didn't see or hear anything.

Tawny-Lynn said she was locked in her bathroom. He checked the laundry room off the kitchen and the back door. Still locked. The intruder had to have either left through the window or he was still upstairs.

Silence fell around him, tense and almost debilitating it was so thick with his own fear. He imagined finding Tawny-Lynn dead and his knees nearly caved beneath him.

He gripped the stair rail as he climbed the steps, then glanced in Peyton's room. Tawny-Lynn had obviously cleaned out the room, as well. The old posters, bedding and memorabilia had been packed up, the shelves empty. The room even smelled of Pine-Sol and furniture polish.

But no one was inside.

He inched toward Tawny-Lynn's room next, pausing to listen at the door. His mind traveled down a dangerous road, envisioning Tawny-Lynn's brutalized body, but he blinked to purge the disturbing images and turned the doorknob.

The door squeaked open, and he cut his eyes across the room. More shadows and darkness. He crept through the door, then checked the closet, relieved when no one jumped him, then rapped on the bathroom door.

"Tawny-Lynn, it's me, Chaz."

He waited a second, his breath tight, then rapped again. "Tawny-Lynn, it's me. The house is clear."

Suddenly the door swung open and Tawny-Lynn stood in front of him, a fire poker clenched in her hands, her face stark-white with fear.

TAWNY-LYNN WAS shaking so hard she could barely stand. She'd imagined her attacker breaking into the bathroom and finishing her off.

Then she'd never see Chaz again. Or find out what happened to her sister.

"He's gone. Are you all right?" Chaz asked in a gruff voice.

She nodded, but her throat was too thick to speak.

Then she didn't have to talk because Chaz stowed his gun in his holster, pulled her up against him and wrapped his arms around her. "Shh, it's okay now," he murmured against her hair.

"He tried to choke me," Tawny-Lynn whispered.

Chaz's breath brushed her cheek as he lifted her chin. "Did you see who it was?"

She shook her head, shivering as she remembered the man's hands gripping her throat. And his face…it was as blank as the man who'd dragged her from the fire.

Was it the same person?

"It was dark, and he wore a ski mask," she said. "All I saw were his eyes. I think they were brown."

Chaz examined her neck, his jaw tensing. "Did he say anything?"

"No…he just jumped me and threw me down."

He touched the handle of the fire poker. "You used this on him?"

She nodded, and he took it and dropped it to the floor. Then a slow smile spread across his face. "Good for you."

In spite of the tears pressing at the back of her eyelids, she smiled. "I hit him in the shoulder and his knee."

"Then I'll look around in town for someone hobbling."

Tawny-Lynn laughed softly, and Chaz stroked her back with slow circles. "I'm sorry this happened, Tawny-Lynn." He pushed a strand of hair away from her cheek. "Sorry I wasn't here to protect you."

Tawny-Lynn laid her hand on his chest. His heart was racing, but he felt so strong beneath her that she felt his warmth seep into her, comforting.

"Thanks for coming."

Chaz squared his shoulders. "It's my job to protect the town."

So she was just a job to him? A way to find out what happened to Ruth…

She had to remember that.

She started to pull away, but he held her tight. "Wait, Tawny-Lynn, I didn't mean it like that."

Her gaze met his, tension rippling between them. "I understand, Chaz. I know I let everyone down."

"No, your father and everyone in the town let *you* down." He traced a finger along her jaw. "I let you down back then."

Tawny-Lynn's chest squeezed. "Chaz…"

"I promise I won't let you down now, though."

Tawny-Lynn couldn't remember when she'd had anyone to lean on. Anyone who cared about her.

But she couldn't lean on him. Could she?

Then he cupped her face between his hands, lowered his head and closed his mouth over hers. And she forgot about reservations and gave in to the moment.

CHAZ PRESSED HIS lips to Tawny-Lynn's mouth, his body hardening with arousal as she clung to him. He hadn't realized how much he wanted to protect her until he'd heard her terrified voice on the phone.

Or how much he wanted to be with her until he'd looked into those sea-green eyes.

Her soft whispered sigh urged him to deepen the kiss, and he flicked his tongue against her lips, coaxing them to open. He drove his tongue inside, tasting her, teasing her, aching for more.

He pulled her tighter against him, one hand going to her back to massage the tension from her shoulders. She raked a hand across his chest, sending fiery sensations through him that intensified his need.

Hunger and desire heated his blood, and he eased her back into the bedroom. But they nearly stumbled over the fire poker, reminding him of the reason he'd raced to her house like a madman.

Silently chiding himself, he looped his arms around her waist and ended the kiss. But he missed her already as she pulled back and looked up at him.

"Chaz?"

"I'm sorry, I shouldn't have done that."

"Why not?" Tawny-Lynn whispered. "Because of who I am?"

He shook his head. "No, because of who *I* am." Self-disgust underscored his tone. "I'm supposed to protect you, not take advantage of you."

"You didn't take advantage of me," she said softly.

He fisted his hands by his sides, desperately wanting to draw her back into his embrace. To kiss her and give her pleasure and alleviate the tormented look in her eyes,

But the only way to do the latter was to find out who'd tried to kill her.

And getting to the bottom of the cold case that had haunted Camden Crossing for seven years was the key to it.

"I should look for forensic evidence," he said. "Fingerprints."

"He wore gloves," she said, her finger automatically rubbing the bruise forming on her slender throat.

"Okay, but maybe he left fibers from his clothing, a hair, something that will help nail him when we catch him." He gestured around the room. "Was he in here?"

"No, he attacked me downstairs."

"He climbed in through a window in your father's room?"

She released a weary sigh. "I opened it earlier to air out the room when I was cleaning. I was so exhausted I forgot to close it when I went to bed."

"Don't beat yourself up over it," Chaz said. "If he wanted to get in, he would have found another way."

She nodded in acceptance, then tightened the belt around her robe.

"Let me get my kit and camera. I want to take pictures of your neck and the crime scene, then I'll do a search."

"I'll meet you downstairs."

He hated to leave her for a second but duty called. So he jogged down the steps and retrieved his crime kit and camera.

Anger mounted as he tilted Tawny-Lynn's head backward and photographed the bruises on her neck. The imprint of a man's fingerprints discolored her skin. Only Tawny-Lynn said he'd worn gloves.

Still, they might be able to compare the sizes of the prints, so he took some close-up shots. Tawny-Lynn watched silently as he searched the room for forensics.

"You cleaned earlier?" Chaz asked.

She nodded.

He plucked a tiny black thread off the floor. "Then this must be from the intruder. I'll have the lab analyze it."

"It probably came off his ski cap."

"Maybe we can trace what kind of cap it is, where he bought it." It was a long shot, but he had to try it.

"I paid Barry Dothan a visit this afternoon," Chaz said.

Tawny-Lynn narrowed her eyes. "And?"

"He admitted to taking pictures of you and the other girls at school. But his mother claims he's innocent. She alibied him years ago."

"The sheriff really thought he could have hurt Ruth and Peyton?"

"He was a person of interest. But he became really upset when I accused him of stalking you. I don't know if he's dangerous, but I warned him to stay away from you."

"Thanks."

A frown puckered between his eyebrows. "Honestly though, judging from what I saw, I don't think he kidnapped our sisters. Over the years, he would probably have broken down and told someone."

"That's probably true," she said.

He shone a flashlight along the floor, looking for blood, an eyelash, anything that might help. "A Texas Ranger named Justin Thorpe called this afternoon. Two young women went missing from neighboring counties in the last two months. If the cases are connected, Dothan can't have done it. He only travels by bike."

"So he couldn't have gotten rid of Ruth's and Peyton's bodies if he'd killed them," Tawny-Lynn said.

"Right."

A heartbeat passed. "Chaz, this afternoon I talked to J.J. McMullen, Peyton's old boyfriend."

Chaz glanced up at her. "What did he have to say?"

"That Peyton dropped him for an older man. He thought the guy might have been married."

That was news to him. "Did he give you a name?"

She fidgeted with the belt of her robe. "No, he said he didn't know who it was. But it started me thinking about Peyton's other friends and that they might have known something about who she was seeing, so I went and talked to Cindy Miller, I mean Cindy Parker, and Rudy Farnsworth at the Sports Barn."

"Did they know who Peyton was seeing?"

"Not exactly. But Cindy got really nervous when I asked her. And Rudy said she'd heard Peyton crying, and telling Ruth that she thought her lover was going to leave his wife for her. But when Peyton pressed him, he threatened to ruin her life if she told anyone about them."

Chaz ran a hand through his hair. "There wasn't anything in the sheriff's report about a married lover."

"She obviously was with someone because I found condoms in her nightstand." Tawny-Lynn paused. "And if what

Rudy said was true, this man might have panicked at the idea of Peyton exposing their affair."

"So he killed her to keep her quiet?"

"It's possible."

Chaz grimaced. Her theory made more sense than anything they'd considered so far. "Yeah, and if Ruth knew who he was, then that would have given him motive to kill her, too."

DAMN TAWNY-LYNN. She'd nearly broken his knee with that fire poker. She was tough—a fighter—that was for sure.

Just like she'd been on the softball field.

Not as soft and sweet as her sister. Or Ruth.

Ruth… Oh, beautiful Ruth.

He'd hated losing her. Had never meant for things to turn out the way they had…

The wind stirred the trees below, and now the curtains had been stripped in the old man's room, he could see every move the sheriff and Tawny-Lynn made.

Dammit. Camden was getting way too chummy with her. Didn't he have any allegiance to the town?

He'd watched the sheriff through his binoculars from his perch at the top of the hill and seen him making out with her.

That would be a complication. If the two of them got too close, he'd have to do something fast.

Killing Tawny-Lynn would be easy.

But killing the sheriff would be risky.

Still he'd do whatever he had to in order to protect his secret.

Chapter Twelve

Tawny-Lynn rubbed her aching back as she saw the wheels turning in Chaz's head. For the first time in years, she sensed he wasn't sure he wanted the answers.

Because they might find that Ruth and Peyton were both dead.

She'd long ago accepted that possibility. After all, if they had survived, why wouldn't one of them have contacted their families?

"I'm finished here if you want to go back to bed," Chaz said.

Tawny-Lynn shrugged. "I don't think I can sleep."

He gently touched her arm. "I'll stay downstairs and keep watch. Go get some rest."

"You don't have to stay, Chaz."

Worry knitted his brow. "Yes, I do, I'm the sheriff."

That's right. He was just doing his job. Maybe she had totally misread that kiss. But she could have sworn she'd felt his passion.

"I can't send this stuff to the lab until morning," he said. "Then I'm going to talk to Sheriff Simmons and see if he remembers any rumors about Peyton having an affair with a married man."

Good heavens. She'd known her sister was boy crazy and out of control those last few months, but how could she have slept with a man who already had a wife? Did he have children, too?

Did he still live in Camden Crossing?

If so, maybe he was worried that Tawny-Lynn knew his identity. Or that she'd find something in the house that would trigger her memory.

"Was there anything left from the fire?" she asked.

Chaz narrowed his eyes. "What do you mean?"

"Like Peyton's backpack. She liked to scribble J.J.'s name in her notebook. Maybe she scribbled this man's name in it, and the notebook was in her bag."

"I'll ask the sheriff," Chaz said. "You didn't find anything in her room?"

She hadn't searched every notebook. "Just the condoms. But I'll keep looking."

Chaz rubbed a hand down her arm. "This has been a helluva night for you. Go back to bed, Tawny-Lynn."

She was exhausted. But the thought of the nightmares returning—and a new one with the strangler in it—made her breath hitch.

She wanted to ask Chaz to go with her to bed. To hold her and comfort her through the night.

His gaze locked with hers for a moment, heat sizzling between them along with unanswered questions…and desire.

Desire was dangerous, though. It led to emotional entanglements like love, and she wasn't ready for that in her life.

Working with Chaz to find answers would have to be enough.

So she climbed the steps to her room and crawled into bed alone.

But she tossed and turned and sleep eluded her. Every time she closed her eyes she saw that masked man diving toward her. Felt his hands twisting her neck and squeezing the life out of her.

He hadn't succeeded tonight.

Which meant he would be back.

Would he kill her next time?

WATCHING TAWNY-LYNN retreat to her bedroom alone was one of the hardest things Chaz had done in a long time.

Ever since the day Ruth went missing, he'd blamed himself and turned his focus on finding out what happened to her. That was all tied to Tawny-Lynn, and her reappearance in Camden Crossing had given him hope.

But, hell. He was lying to himself if he didn't admit that there was more. He was attracted to her. That kiss had only whetted his appetite for more.

Even worse, he liked her.

She was strong and gutsy, a fighter, a survivor in spite of all she'd endured. She didn't even seem to hate his family or the town, which she had every right to do.

And she wanted the truth as much as he did.

Only being this close to her, touching her, holding her, made him want something else just as much.

He wanted to keep her safe. Wanted to kiss her again and make love to her and...

He couldn't go there.

Instead, as he stood watch over Tawny-Lynn's house, he stewed over the information Tawny-Lynn had shared, mentally tossing around names of men in town who might have had an affair with Peyton.

He immediately dismissed the old-timers who hung out in front of the general store to play checkers. There were friends of his father's, but they were so much older he couldn't imagine Peyton being attracted to any of them.

Thanks to the new development on the lake and the mayor who'd spearheaded the project to renovate the exterior storefronts to give the town a cohesive Western look, the town had doubled in population in the last seven years.

New families and businesses meant progress for the town.

But whoever had taken Peyton and Ruth had lived in or near Camden Crossing seven years ago.

Keith Plumbing had been a suspect because he'd done odd jobs in Camden Crossing and Sunset Mesa, but he'd gone to Austin for a job that day. Only the job fell through. Plumbing claimed he was upset, bought a bottle of bourbon and spent the night in his truck.

But he had no one to corroborate his story. Still they'd had no evidence against him.

He tried to remember Plumbing's age and guessed he was early thirties now so he would have been young enough to attract a teen, yet old enough to be considered an older man by Peyton or Ruth.

Wind rattled the windowpanes in the house, and he combed through the downstairs rooms, making sure the locks were secure. His eyelids felt heavy so he brewed a pot of coffee and wandered outside to sit on the front porch.

Boulder had let the ranch go downhill. Not that it was a big working spread, but the place had potential. Two barns, a stable and riding pen. And enough pasture for a small herd of cattle.

An investor would probably sweep up the place, then Tawny-Lynn would be gone from his life forever.

An odd feeling pinched his gut at the thought.

She could have died earlier.

Hell. Someone still wanted her dead.

He sipped his coffee and watched as dawn streaked the sky. Pinks and reds and oranges smothered the gray clouds from the night before, making the ranch look peaceful. Yet an eerie feeling washed over him, as if death had already taken hold of this land.

But he wouldn't let it claim Tawny-Lynn. She'd suffered enough. He'd protect her with his life.

Tawny-Lynn waited until the sun had lifted into the sky, then finally slipped from bed. She was exhausted from staring at the ceiling and thinking about her attacker.

And the kiss she'd shared with Chaz.

She wanted to kiss him again.

But that would be risky to her heart. As soon as the ranch was ready to be put on the market, she'd return to her life. A life that didn't include Chaz.

Only could she leave with unanswered questions? And what if the man who'd attacked her last night had followed her?

She washed her face, brushed through her tangled hair and secured it into a ponytail. With rain on the horizon tomorrow, she dressed for yard work today.

The scent of coffee wafted up the stairs as she descended, and morning light washed over the den and kitchen. The place looked different now without the clutter and dust. Almost…homey.

With a little paint and some new furniture, someone *would* make it a home again. She could almost see a baby in a bassinet in the corner, a little boy with dark hair, running across the room with a football in his hand, a dog curled on a braided rug in front of the fireplace.

Good grief. The little boy she'd pictured had looked just like Chaz.

You are crazy, Tawny-Lynn. Crazy. Even if you and Chaz ever got romantic, his parents would never accept you.

She filled herself a coffee mug, then retrieved her father's rifle from the gun cabinet and set it by the stairs.

Then she found Chaz on the front porch in the swing with his own mug. Sunlight streaked his chiseled face, adding to his masculinity.

But when he glanced at her, shadows darkened his eyes.

"Did you sleep at all?" she asked.

The swing creaked as he pushed it back and forth with his feet. "No. Did you?"

"Not really." She sank into the swing beside him.

For a long moment, they sat in silence, just sipping their coffee and looking out over the ranch. The grass was dry, weeds choked the flowerbeds, and the barn and stables needed repairs.

So much to do.

Yet in the quiet of the morning, there was also something almost peaceful about the scenery. And something intimate about sharing it with Chaz.

Chaz slid his hand over hers, and Tawny-Lynn's breath caught. Unable to help herself she curled her fingers into his. His touch felt warm, sensual, titillating.

"I'm headed out to see Sheriff Simmons today."

Anxiety wound Tawny-Lynn's stomach into a knot, any sense of peace evaporating.

"After what happened last night, I don't want to leave you alone, though. You can come with me."

Tawny-Lynn considered his suggestion, but being with him was playing havoc on her senses. "No, go ahead. I need to stay here and work outside today."

The sooner she fixed up the place, the sooner she could leave.

He slanted her a worried look. "It's not safe for you to be alone."

"No one is going to attack me in broad daylight. Besides, I found Daddy's rifle. I'll keep it with me outside just in case."

He arched his brows. "You know how to shoot?"

She smiled, grief twisting her heart. "That's the one thing my father and I did together. He taught me. I used to clean off the cans he set on the fence in ten seconds flat."

"There's a helluva difference between shooting cans and shooting a person."

She squeezed Chaz's hand, her gaze glued to his mouth. Her body ached to be held, her lips yearned to touch his again. But the memory of that man's hands around her throat as he tried to strangle the life out of her, taunted her.

"I can do it if I have to."

He put his coffee mug on the porch floor, then took hers and did the same. Then he lifted a finger and traced it along her jaw. "You're strong, Tawny-Lynn. I admire that about you."

She shook her head. "I'm not strong, Chaz. If I was, I'd be able to remember, to see that man's face."

A silence fell between them, fraught with old pain and anguish.

Chaz leaned forward and kissed her again. This kiss was tender, sweet, full of passion and promise. Tawny-Lynn leaned into him, savoring his taste and wishing it could last forever.

He probed her lips apart with his tongue and deepened the kiss, their tongues dancing in tandem. Raw need flooded Tawny-Lynn.

She wanted more, to take him upstairs and get naked with him.

But he ended the kiss, then pulled away and stroked her cheek again. "Are you sure you can handle the rifle?"

She smiled. "I won the skeet shoot at the county fair when I was twelve."

"I wish I'd seen that."

Maybe if she stuck around she'd show him.

She froze. Where had that thought come from? She would never stay in Camden Crossing.

He squeezed her hand again then stood. "Call me if you need me. I'll check in after I talk to Simmons."

She lifted their joined hands, then kissed his palm. "Thanks for coming last night, Chaz. And for staying."

He paused, his eyes flickering with emotions she couldn't define. Worry? Hunger? Desire?

"I promise you I'll find the man who hurt you."

She licked her bottom lip, hating the reminder as he walked to his car. But for once in her life, she didn't feel alone. Chaz would keep his promise.

Still, she grabbed the rifle for protection as she headed outside to work in the yard.

As much as Chaz hated to leave Tawny-Lynn, he wanted to talk to Simmons and question Keith Plumbing, and thought it might be best if she wasn't with him for the latter in case Plumbing admitted to an affair and disparaged Peyton.

But tension coiled inside him. Although her attacker most likely wouldn't come back during the day, Chaz didn't like the fact that someone wanted to hurt her.

He drove home and showered, then went straight to Sheriff Simmons's place, a rustic log cabin he'd built for retirement on the creek. Gravel crunched beneath his boots as he made his way to the front door. The sound of water gurgling over rocks echoed from behind the cabin.

He knocked again but no one answered, so he walked to the side of the cabin and spotted Simmons sitting on a rock, holding a fishing pole. Simmons glanced up at him, squinting at the bright morning sun.

"Hey," Chaz said. "Are they biting?"

Simmons chuckled. "No, but I'm not giving up."

Chaz gestured at the bait bucket on the ground. "Looks like you're enjoying retirement."

Simmons shrugged. "Gets lonely sometimes. This was mine and Dorothy's dream. Not so much fun alone."

A pang stabbed at Chaz's heart. Simmons and his wife had been married thirty years, but the very year Simmons retired, he lost his wife to cancer.

"But you didn't drive out here to listen to me complain," Simmons said. "What's up, Camden?"

Chaz explained about Tawny-Lynn being back in town and the trouble. "Someone attacked Tawny-Lynn last night."

Simmons whistled. "That poor girl. She's been through hell." He wiped his forehead with the back of his hand. "Her daddy treated her like Peyton's disappearance was her fault. I wasn't surprised when she didn't want a memorial service."

Sympathy for Tawny-Lynn swelled inside Chaz, mingling with his growing admiration for her.

Chaz sat down on another rock and watched the birds dipping toward the water.

Simmons pulled in his pole, checked the bait then cast it again. "So what can I do for you?"

"Tawny-Lynn talked to a couple of former classmates and thinks that Peyton might have been having an affair with a married man. Did anyone mention that when you investigated?"

Simmons scowled. "No. I talked to a few of the kids at the memorial services, but everyone said Peyton was dating J.J. McMullen. Your folks said Ruth wasn't involved with anyone."

Chaz picked up a rock and skipped it across the water. "What if J.J. was pissed off about the breakup? Maybe he followed the bus and ran it off the road, then abducted Peyton and Ruth?" After all, he'd been strong even at eighteen. He could have subdued the girls one at a time.

"That's possible, although I remember talking to J.J. and he was pretty broken up. He had an alibi, too. One of the cheerleaders said he was with her during the time of the crash."

"He could have convinced the girl to lie for him," Chaz suggested.

Simmons shrugged. "I suppose that's true."

"Did any of the teenagers mention that someone had a grudge against Peyton or Ruth?"

"Not that I recall. At the time, we assumed the case was connected to the missing girls from Sunset Mesa."

"We have to consider all the possibilities," Chaz said. "Did anyone go missing about that time? A man, I mean?"

"No. I checked in case one of the girls ran off with someone but no names came up."

He'd have a chat with J.J. McMullen. If he had done something to the girls, maybe guilt had set in and he'd be ready to confess.

If not, he'd look at Plumbing again.

Hell. He understood the reason the case had gone cold. One question only led to another, and different theories where they'd chased lead after lead ended up yielding no results.

Tawny-Lynn seemed to be the only one who might have seen something.

But that secret was locked in her head.

The very reason someone wanted her dead.

TAWNY-LYNN STACKED the dishes in the dishwasher, retrieved the few gardening tools she could find in her father's shed, stuffed an old high-school ball cap on her head and walked outside. She surveyed the front property and realized the most she could do short-term was to clean out the weed-infested flowerbeds and plant some roses.

That would require a run to the lawn-and-garden supply store for compost and a good sprayer. But first she needed to weed the beds in front and the one on the side of the house.

She yanked on gardening gloves, knowing she had to take advantage of the early-morning temperatures before the hot Texas sun climbed the sky.

She yanked and pulled and tore the weeds from the two beds flanking the porch steps, then checked the pH level of the soil. Yes, it definitely needed the nutrients provided by bonemeal so she mentally added that to her list.

Perspiration beaded on her forehead, and she swiped at it with the back of her sleeve, dumped the weeds into the wheelbarrow, then hauled it around to the right side to work on the last flowerbed. She'd probably need a new trellis here and would put climbing roses, maybe a mixture of red, yellow and pink to add color against the faded white house.

The entire structure needed painting, but she didn't have the money for that. The new owners could fix it up the way they wanted.

A momentary pang of sadness assaulted her as she actually imagined the for-sale sign in the front yard.

Good grief. She couldn't get sentimental now. This place would be an albatross around her neck if she kept it.

And too much of a reminder of the family she'd lost.

Something sparkled in the sunlight and she squatted down and realized it was a bracelet nearly buried in the dirt.

With gloved hands, she brushed away dirt until the bracelet was uncovered fully, then picked it up. Her heart slammed against her rib cage as she turned it around and studied the charms.

Both Peyton and Ruth had worn charm bracelets. Her sister's favorite charm had been a heart she'd said her secret boyfriend had given her. At the time, she'd thought Peyton was joking about the boyfriend.

But this bracelet didn't have a heart charm. Instead, there was a tulip, a cougar for Camden Creek Cats, a telephone, pair of red high heels and a small key, which said Key to My Heart.

This bracelet had belonged to Ruth.

Her heart pounded. Why was it here in the old flowerbed? Had Ruth lost it one day when she was on the ranch?

Although Ruth and Peyton never worked in the garden. That had been her job.

Only, she'd lost interest for a while after the accident.

She held the bracelet up to the light, her eyes widening as she spotted a dark stain on the band of the bracelet. It looked like…blood.

Her imagination went wild. But reality interceded, and she realized Ruth could have lost it months before the accident. An animal or even the wind could have tossed it in the dirt. In fact, she'd seen the cat pawing in this flowerbed the night before.

She tucked it in her pocket. She'd save it and give it to Chaz. He'd probably want to keep it.

Curious still as to how it had come to be in the flowerbed, she raked her hand through the weeds.

The ground was uneven. Slightly curved at the top almost like a…grave.

Pulse clamoring, she grabbed the shovel and began to dig. One shovel of dirt, another, a third…and the shovel tip hit something.

She knelt to examine it and gasped.

Dear God, no…

The shovel had hit bone.

Chapter Thirteen

After leaving Simmons, Chaz stopped by the butcher shop. J.J. stood behind the counter, his apron bloody from cutting meat for the morning shopping crowd.

He'd always thought it odd that J.J., who'd been a popular football player, had come back to help run his father's store. He'd called his deputy on the way over and asked him to run a check on McMullen and had learned some interesting stuff.

The former football star had a record.

J.J. looked up at him, a wary look creasing his beefy face. He handed the woman her order, then she went to the register to pay J.J.'s father.

Chaz crossed his arms. "We need to talk."

J.J. shot his father a wary look, but his father motioned for him to take a break.

J.J. led him through the back work area, and Chaz grimaced at the bloody meat on the stainless-steel tables. The meat-cooling locker stood to the right.

A good place to hide a body.

"What do you want?" J.J. asked.

Chaz decided to use the direct approach. "Someone tried to kill Tawny-Lynn Boulder last night. Where were you?"

The man's mouth fell open, then he shut it, his eyes livid. "You think I tried to hurt her? Why the hell would I do that?"

"Just asking." Chaz lifted his brows, waiting.

J.J. ran a hand over his apron and heaved a breath. "Listen, it wasn't me."

"You know who it was then?"

"No. I just mean I wouldn't hurt Tawny-Lynn."

"You left college because you were arrested for assaulting a girl."

Shock streaked J.J.'s face. "That was bull. Someone at a party gave this girl some coke. She went crazy and accused me of coming on to her. But I never touched her."

"Then why did you leave school?"

"Because her father was rich and, at that point, I'd blown out my knee and couldn't play ball." He gestured at the butcher shop. "As you can see, my family doesn't have money like yours. I couldn't afford a fancy lawyer, so the court-appointed attorney, some kid barely out of diapers, talked me into a plea."

Chaz gritted his teeth. "What about Peyton Boulder? She left you for another guy, an older man. That make you mad?"

J.J. glared at him. "Yeah, it made me mad. But not enough to kill her. For God's sake, I loved her."

"All the more reason for you to try to win her back. Maybe you chased down the bus, accidentally hit them, then pulled her out. When she wouldn't go with you, you lost your temper."

"That's not true. I wasn't even in Camden Crossing that day," J.J. growled. "I was…never mind."

"Where were you?" Chaz asked.

J.J. looked down at his apron, then his bloodstained hands. For God's sake, he could have cut the girls up to pieces and stored them in his father's meat locker until all the commotion died down.

"Where were you?"

"I don't have to tell you anything," J.J. said.

"Sheriff Simmons said one of the cheerleaders gave you an alibi. If I talk to her, is she going to change her story?"

A frisson of fear streaked J.J.'s face. "If you're going to arrest me, I want a lawyer."

A bold move since he'd just claimed that his first one had failed him.

Chaz jerked him by the collar. "If you're innocent and have nothing to hide, you'll tell me. Then I can eliminate you as a suspect."

J.J.'s nostrils flared. "Coach caught me smoking weed and threatened to cut me from the team unless I went for treatment. I was in a drug rehab class that day. *All* day."

That would be easy to check.

Chaz had one more question. "Did Peyton tell you the name of the man she was seeing?"

J.J. hissed between his teeth. "No. But she said she was going to marry him, and he'd give her everything she ever wanted. Things I couldn't."

J.J.'s angry gaze flattened, grief replacing the anger. "I didn't hurt Peyton," he said. "Besides, if I knew the jerk she was seeing, I would have gone after him, not her."

Chaz's phone buzzed, and he quickly checked the number. Tawny-Lynn.

"Don't leave town," he told J.J. as he walked away to answer the call.

"Chaz," Tawny-Lynn cried. "You have to come quick."

He jumped in his car and flipped the engine. "What's wrong? Did the guy come back?"

"No," Tawny-Lynn said, her voice cracking. "I found a body on the ranch."

Dread balled in his belly. If it was on White Forks, odds were that it was Peyton. And if Peyton was buried there, would Ruth be there, too?

TAWNY-LYNN'S HAND trembled as she jammed her phone into her pocket. She couldn't take her eyes off the grave.

For a moment, she'd hoped, prayed, that the bones belonged to their old dog who'd died when she was a freshman in high school. But she'd raked enough dirt away to see one of the blankets they used to keep in the barn in the hole.

Someone had used the blanket to wrap the body in.

And judging from the length of the grave, a human body lay inside.

A noise from the woods startled her, and she grabbed the rifle and swung it toward the direction of the sound. Seconds later, a baby doe scampered away, and she blew out a breath of relief.

Damn. Her hands were shaking so badly that if that had been her attacker from the night before, she would have missed him by a mile. That is, if she managed to fire a shot before he jumped her.

Struggling to calm herself, she walked back to the porch and sat down on the steps. But she kept her eyes peeled for trouble, the rifle in her hands.

Her phone buzzed again, and she saw it was the auto-shop number, so she snapped it up with one hand.

"Tawny-Lynn, about your car…"

God, she'd forgotten to call him. "Yes?"

"I had to realign it and we pounded out the dent. I figure we'll check out the brakes while it's here. You can pick it up tomorrow."

"Okay, great. Thanks."

An engine roared down the driveway and she looked up, grateful to see Chaz zooming up to the house. He screeched to a stop, jumped out and ran toward her, then eased the rifle from her hands and laid it on the porch. He gripped her arms. "Where's the body?"

Tawny-Lynn swallowed hard and pointed toward the

flowerbed. "I was digging up weeds to plant some roses when the shovel hit something."

Chaz squeezed her hands. "Stay here. I'll take a look."

"Chaz?"

"Yeah?"

"At first I thought it might be the dog we used to have, but…the body's wrapped in a blanket from the horse barn. And the grave…it's too big."

His eyes flickered with myriad emotions, then he walked around the side of the house. Tawny-Lynn dropped her head in her hands, her mind spinning.

Her father and sister had argued the night before Peyton went missing. But he hadn't hurt her….

She'd been in that bus accident. So how would Peyton's body have ended up here?

DREAD BALLOONED IN Chaz's chest as he rounded the house and stooped by the flowerbed. Tawny-Lynn was right.

The hole was a grave, although she'd barely uncovered enough for him to see the size. Odds were, though, that her sister was buried here and that a domestic dispute between father and daughter had occurred.

Hadn't Tawny-Lynn been through enough without finding Peyton's body on her homestead?

Still, the grave triggered more questions.

How had the body gotten here? He tried to piece together a possible scenario in his mind. Her father had discovered Peyton was having an affair with a married man, then found Peyton at the crash site and brought her to the ranch and…what? Killed her? That didn't make sense. Especially when police were crawling over the crash site and Tawny-Lynn had been injured.

He'd have to check and see what time Boulder had shown up at the hospital.

He phoned the crime team from the county, knowing he

needed help. With a body this decomposed, they needed a forensic specialist and an M.E., all with skills he didn't possess.

While he waited on them to arrive, he strode to his car, retrieved his camera and snapped some pictures of the scene, capturing the grave, blanket and bone poking through the soil. When he finished, he found Tawny-Lynn still sitting on the steps, her forehead creased with anxiety.

"The M.E. and crime lab techs will be here soon. They'll transport the body to the morgue for an autopsy."

She nodded, but she looked numb. He took her hands in his and realized they were icy cold, so he rubbed them between his own to warm them.

"I'm so sorry, Tawny-Lynn."

"I'm going to make some coffee," she said as if rallying. "I have a feeling it's going to be a long afternoon."

He wished he could make this nightmare easier for her, but he couldn't. And if Peyton was in the ground, where was Ruth? They'd assumed all these years that the same man had abducted the two of them.

Now he didn't know what to think.

THE CRIME UNIT AND M.E. arrived, and Tawny-Lynn stepped back outside for introductions. "Lieutenant Levi Gibbons," a big, dark-haired man said. "I'm with the crime lab and M.E.'s office." He gestured toward two younger men, a blond with a buzz cut and a brown-haired guy with a goatee. "This is Seth Arnaught and Corey Benson."

Chaz introduced himself, and Tawny-Lynn shook their hands. "There's coffee and sandwiches inside whenever you want them."

The lieutenant removed his sunglasses and leveled Tawny-Lynn with a concerned look. "You found the body, ma'am?"

Tawny-Lynn nodded and lifted her chin. Some of the

color had returned to her face, but her eyes still looked list-less. In shock.

But she was trying her damnedest not to show any weakness.

"I came back to the ranch to fix it up to sell it. I was digging through the flowerbeds when the shovel hit bone."

Another man, mid-fifties with silver hair, emerged with his own team. "I'm the chief medical examiner, Stony Sagebrush."

Another round of introductions were made, then Chaz asked, "Are you men familiar with the case of the two girls who disappeared from Camden Crossing seven years ago?"

They indicated that they were.

"You think this is one of the girls?" Lieutenant Gibbons asked.

Tawny-Lynn cleared her throat. "Yes. Maybe my sister, Peyton."

"What would make you say that?" Lieutenant Gibbons asked. "Didn't your father and sister get along?"

Tawny-Lynn gave Chaz a pleading look.

"Her father liked to drink," Chaz said. "But Peyton went missing from the bus accident, so there are a lot of missing pieces to the puzzle."

"All right, let's get to work," Gibbons said. "No use speculating until we verify whose body it is."

They all agreed, and Chaz led the crime team and M.E. around the side of the house to the grave. They snapped photographs of the house, surrounding property and gravesite before the team exhumed the body.

Tawny-Lynn remained on the porch with a cup of coffee, a faraway look in her eyes.

"You said there were two missing girls?" Lieutenant Gibbons glanced across the property. "Do you think the other girl is buried here somewhere?"

Chaz swallowed the lump in his throat. "I don't know. If

Peyton's father took her from the accident and killed her, it was probably in a fit of rage. I still can't figure out how he'd have gotten her to leave the accident scene anyway. Tawny-Lynn was hurt and rushed to the hospital, and there were rescue workers and law enforcement officers everywhere."

"Maybe the two girls escaped but were disoriented and wandered away from the scene. Then Boulder showed up and found them?"

"I suppose it's possible, although there are still too many holes in the theory."

"If I were you, I'd organize a search party to comb this ranch just in case," Lieutenant Gibbons suggested.

Chaz considered the idea. "I'll get right on it."

He walked back to the porch to ask Tawny-Lynn's permission before he phoned his deputy to organize the search.

She wiped at a tear that had escaped as he climbed the steps. When he explained the lieutenant's suggestion, she readily agreed. "We said we wanted answers, didn't we?" She sipped her coffee, her eyes blank. "We may not like what we find, Chaz."

He couldn't argue with that. But still they had to follow through. So he went inside, poured himself a mug of coffee and phoned his deputy.

Within an hour, ten men showed up to ride the property. While they did, Chaz went to search the barn and stables.

If someone had been in a hurry to dispose of a body, that would have been a likely hiding spot.

TAWNY-LYNN REMEMBERED the bracelet she'd found and fingered it as Chaz headed out to the barn. The deputy and the search party rode out, half on horses they'd brought in trailers, the other half in Jeeps and SUVs.

She needed to give the bracelet to Chaz. But seeing it would upset him and raise questions as to how it had come to be in the flowerbed.

Because Ruth was buried in the ground there instead of Peyton?

That made absolutely no sense. Her father would never have hurt Ruth. And if Peyton had survived, she would have never left her best friend.

Besides, showing Chaz the bracelet now would only make him feel the unbearable sense of anguish and panic that had seized her chest at the thought of the body belonging to Peyton.

She cared too much about him to put him through that torture until they knew for sure.

She stuffed it back into her pocket. She would give it to him after they received the M.E.'s report.

Decision made, she went inside, grabbed more trash bags and retreated to her room. She'd cleaned out her father's and Peyton's rooms, now it was time to do the same to hers. The sooner she did, the sooner she could leave this godforsaken ranch and town.

She plowed through the closet, yanking out clothes she hadn't seen or worn in years. T-shirts, jeans, skirts, shoes… everything went into the bags. When the closet was empty, she attacked the desk in the corner, embarrassed when she found an old notebook where she'd scribbled Chaz's name a dozen times like a love-struck teenager.

He hadn't given her the time of day back then, but she thought he'd hung the moon.

She still did, dammit. He'd only grown more handsome and stronger in her eyes.

Suddenly a board squeaked and a man's voice boomed from the doorway. "What are you doing, Ms. Boulder?"

Tawny-Lynn swung her head toward the lieutenant. "Just cleaning out my old room."

"Stop." He strode forward and snatched the notebook from her, raising his eyebrows in question at her silly teenage scrawls. She didn't realize Chaz was with him until she heard his quick hiss of breath.

Embarrassment heated her cheeks. "That was a long time ago, in high school."

"This house, the property, it may have been the scene of a crime. Are you trying to get rid of evidence?"

Shock slammed into Tawny-Lynn. "No, of course not. I told you, I'm getting the property ready to sell."

"We'll need to search your room, your father's and sister's," the lieutenant said.

Tawny-Lynn froze. "I…already cleaned out their rooms."

"Really. First you throw things out, then you report a body." Lieutenant Gibbons's eyes flared with suspicion. "It sounds like you're trying to get rid of evidence."

Panic fluttered in her belly. "That's not true." She stood, bracing her hands on her hips. "I didn't know that body was out there, Lieutenant. I only came home because my father died and I wanted to sell this place."

The lieutenant indicated the notebook. "Were you jealous of your sister, Ms. Boulder? Did something happen between the two of you and things got out of hand?"

"That's enough," Chaz cut in. "My sister and hers were alive when they boarded the bus after the softball game that day. Tawny-Lynn was seriously injured and transported to the hospital from the scene. There's no way she could have—or would have—hurt either Peyton or Ruth."

Tawny-Lynn gave Chaz a grateful look, but she sensed the lieutenant wasn't satisfied. "Maybe not, but she could have covered for her father all these years."

Anger railed inside her. She'd heard those accusations before.

"I suggest you wait on the porch until my men search the house." He gave her a warning look. "And tell me where your father's and sister's things are. My men will need to search those, as well."

Tawny-Lynn glared at him. "I took the trash to the dump, the clothes to the church."

He spoke into the mike at his lapel and ordered one of his guys to go to the church.

"Come on, Tawny-Lynn." Chaz took her by the arm and escorted her down the steps and onto the front porch, while the men went to work in her house.

She fell into the porch swing and stared at the sky while the crime team searched her house and toolshed and went to confiscate the items at the church. The hours dragged by while the men from town combed her property.

Emotions pummeled Tawny-Lynn, and by the time the team had finished and left, dusk had long set and night had fallen. She felt defeated, numb, helpless.

And furious that once again her life was being turned upside down, her innocence questioned.

"It'll be morning before we receive the M.E.'s report, if then," Chaz said as the last of the search party left. Thankfully they hadn't found another grave or body.

He handed her a drink, a shot of scotch from the only bottle she'd saved because it hadn't been opened. She willingly took it and downed it, needing the warmth of the alcohol to stir her blood.

He brought her another and kept one for himself, then sank onto the porch swing beside her. The creak of the swing rocked the night as they finished their drinks in silence.

"I'm going to shower," she said, suddenly feeling dirty and as if a bath could wash away the shame of what had happened today.

He nodded. "I'll keep watch."

"You don't have to stay, Chaz."

"I'm not leaving you tonight," Chaz said gruffly.

She didn't have the energy to argue. Worse, she didn't want to be alone.

So she headed up the steps, dropped her clothes on the floor by the bed, then grabbed her robe. But as soon as she climbed into the shower, the floodgates unleashed. She cried for Peyton and her father and herself.

And for Chaz and what she wanted between them that could never be.

CHAZ HEARD TAWNY-LYNN crying after he'd locked up and walked upstairs. Finding the body had shaken them both up, but having Gibbons accuse her of protecting her father had obviously resurrected bad memories of the past and driven her over the edge.

He removed his holster and placed his weapon on the nightstand, the rational side of his brain ordering him to go back downstairs. Tawny-Lynn needed rest, sleep, to be alone.

But he needed to be with her. To hold her and assuage her pain.

The sound of the shower water faded, then seconds later, the door squeaked open. Steam oozed from inside, then Tawny-Lynn appeared in the doorway, her damp hair hanging in ringlets around her pale face, her eyes haunted.

She looked so beautiful, though, that his gut clenched.

She glanced at the bed, then into his eyes. "What are you doing?"

He stood and walked over to her. "I told you I wasn't leaving you tonight."

Her lower lip trembled, then hunger flared in her eyes. That moment of raw emotion was all he needed.

He pulled her into his arms and closed his mouth over hers. She clawed at his shirt, popping buttons in her haste, then raked her hands over his chest as he plunged his tongue into her mouth.

Chapter Fourteen

Chaz cradled Tawny-Lynn's face between his hands, deepening the kiss as he backed her toward the bed. Her damp hair brushed his cheek as he lowered his head to nibble at the sensitive shell of her ear, then he dipped lower, trailing kisses down her neck.

The bruising from her attacker angered him, and he traced a finger gently over the imprint of the man's fingers.

No one would ever hurt her again. Not as long as he was around.

She threaded her fingers into his hair, need igniting between them, and he raked a finger across her nipple through her robe. She whispered a pleasured sigh, then pushed his shirt to the floor.

Breathing in her feminine scent was intoxicating and stirred his hunger to a burning fever. He parted the top of her robe and kissed her delicate neckline, dipping lower to tug one bare nipple between his teeth.

She groaned and arched her back, then reached for his belt. Her fingers made quick work of unfastening it, then she unsnapped his jeans. His length hardened, bulging against his fly.

He couldn't remember the last time he'd been with a woman. But even then, he hadn't wanted her the way he wanted Tawny-Lynn. He laved one breast, moving slowly to the next and suckling her nipple until she cried out and shoved his jeans down his hips.

He pulled away long enough to step out of them, one hand working the belt of her robe. He slipped the knot free, his breath catching as he stripped it and feasted on her naked body.

"You're lovely," he whispered.

Tawny-Lynn blushed. "Chaz—"

"Shh. I've been thinking about this for a long time."

"Me, too."

Her whispered confession sparked a fiery heat in his belly, and he eased her down on the bed and climbed on top of her. Her skin felt silky soft and tasted like berries as he kissed her again, tracing his tongue from her neck down her breasts to her center. She pulled at his arms, but he parted her legs and dove his tongue into her core.

Tawny-Lynn's fingers dug into his hair and she moaned, her body shuddering as she succumbed to the pleasure. Her sweet release dampened his tongue, making him even more desperate to be inside her.

She shivered, twisting at the sheets as he shed his boxers and grabbed a condom from his pocket. Desire flared in her eyes as she helped him roll it on, then she curled her fingers around his thick length and stroked him.

He grabbed her hand, determined to prolong their pleasure, then pushed her legs apart with his thigh and settled between her.

"Chaz," she murmured in a hoarse whisper.

"I want you, baby." His fingers toyed with her sensitive nub for a moment, then he deftly replaced his fingers with his sex and guided himself to her damp center. She arched her back, lifting her hips to accommodate him as he thrust inside her.

She was warm, soft, sensational.

Fire rose inside him, creating a burning ache that only

she could quench, and he pulled out and thrust into her again, filling her over and over until she cried out his name again, and he lost himself inside her.

TAWNY-LYNN'S BODY quivered. She'd had sex a couple of times, both meaningless encounters, but none that had aroused her emotions and stirred her body to the heights Chaz had.

Because she was falling in love with him.

Panic tightened her chest. She couldn't be in love with Chaz. She had to leave Camden Crossing soon, and he… would stay here with his family.

But he rolled them to the side, wrapped his arms around her and she nestled into him and closed her eyes.

Tomorrow she'd face reality. Tonight she wanted to lie in his arms, hold him and pretend that they had a future together.

But in the back of her mind, the truth gnawed at her. The M.E. would determine the identity of the body found on White Forks. They still had questions. Answers to find.

A killer to track down.

But Chaz kissed her again, and she forgot about the body and murder and all the reasons she and Chaz shouldn't be together. She wanted him tonight and he wanted her.

That was all that mattered.

So she gently stroked the side of his jaw and teased him with kisses along his neck and chest. Moments later, the passion ignited between them again, and they made love a second time—this time long and slow, exploring each other's bodies.

And when she finally fell asleep, she dreamed about a happy time, where she and Chaz were riding on horseback across the ranch with the wind blowing, flowers blooming and their future bright and happy—a future they would spend together.

THE SOUND OF his phone buzzing woke Chaz long before he wanted to get up or leave the bed. He reached across Tawny-Lynn and retrieved it from the nightstand, his stomach knotting at the sight of the M.E.'s number.

Dragging on his jeans, he walked to the window and looked out as the call connected. "Sheriff Camden speaking."

"This is Dr. Sagebrush. I have some news about the body."

Chaz glanced back at Tawny-Lynn and watched her roll over and stretch. Her long hair was splayed across the pillow, her beautiful breasts exposed as the sheet slipped down to reveal nipples, tight and begging for attention.

He wanted to hang up the damn phone and go back to bed with her. To make love and bury themselves in each other until they forgot about the past.

But he couldn't do that.

"Yeah?"

"Maybe we should meet, Sheriff. I hate to give bad news over the phone."

"Look, Tawny-Lynn and I have both been in the dark for years. Just tell me—did the body belong to her sister?"

Tawny-Lynn must have heard him because she sat up, rubbing her eyes with a frown.

"No, I checked dental records, Sheriff. The body is not Peyton Boulder." He paused and Chaz's heart hammered.

"Then who was it?"

"It was your sister, Sheriff."

The room seemed to spin out of control. Hot air swirled around Chaz, nearly suffocating him.

He blinked, swallowed hard, leaned his head against the windowpane. Outside the sun was shining, but he couldn't see anything but those bones.

Then his sister's face when she was ten and had bounced into the room to beg him to take her fishing. Pain, deep and raw, immobilized him as more images of Ruth flashed through his head.

Ruth at six with her gap-toothed smile, holding her doll and standing in front of the Christmas tree. Ruth at twelve when she'd taken up in-line skating and broken her arm. Ruth at her first school dance where he'd watched over her like a hawk to make sure the boy she was with didn't make a play to get her behind the bleachers.

All these years he'd hoped…what? That Ruth would be alive and living somewhere doing what? He'd known this was probably the outcome.

Except, why the hell had her body been found on White Forks?

"Sheriff?"

He scrubbed a hand down his chin, struggling for composure. "Yeah, I'm here. You're sure about this?"

"Yes. I have both dental and medical records. She had an old injury, a broken arm?"

"Yes."

"I'm sorry, Sheriff."

His detective skills finally breached through his shock. "Do you know how long she's been buried there?"

"About seven years."

So she had never really escaped or left Camden Crossing. "What was the cause of death?"

"Judging from contusions on the skull, she died of a blow to the head. It looks like from a sharp object."

"A sharp object?"

"Yes, but I can't say whether it was accidental or intentional."

"But the force was hard enough to kill her?"

"In my opinion, yes."

Chaz choked back grief. He'd considered telling his parents about the body but hadn't wanted to panic them because they'd all assumed Peyton and Ruth were together.

"Thank you, Dr. Sagebrush. I'll talk to my parents and we'll be in touch."

Then they could finally lay Ruth to rest the way she deserved.

Still, as he ended the call, the questions pummeled him again.

He didn't realize Tawny-Lynn had gotten out of bed until she touched his arm. "What's wrong, Chaz?"

His gaze raked over her. She'd pulled on her robe again, but she looked rested, and her lips looked swollen from his kisses. His first instinct was to drag her back to bed and lose himself inside her, to chase away the darkness eating at his soul.

But something shiny sparkled in the sunlight, catching his eye. Something on the floor by the bed…

Realization suddenly hit him and he pushed past Tawny-Lynn, knelt and picked it up. A charm bracelet.

Ruth's charm bracelet.

"Where did you get this?" he asked, his throat so dry he nearly choked on the words.

"Chaz—"

Anger seared him as his gaze met hers. "Where did you get it?"

"Yesterday, outside," she said, her voice cracking.

"By the grave?"

She nodded, her hands digging into her robe. "Chaz, was that the M.E.? Was it Peyton's body?"

"You know what he said." Chaz's voice turned cold. "You found this, you knew it was Ruth in that grave instead of Peyton, didn't you?"

"No…that's not true." Tawny-Lynn shook her head, her face paling.

"Yes, you did." He dangled the bracelet in front of her. "You knew yesterday and you let me believe it was

Peyton." His fingers dug into her arms. "Or did you know before that?"

"What? No, of course not."

"Is that what you forgot seven years ago? That Ruth was buried on your ranch?" A muscle tightened in his jaw. "Did you know she was here all along, Tawny-Lynn? Is that why you left town, because you knew and you were lying to everyone?"

"No," she said, although her voice sounded weak, defeated.

"You *did* know. What happened? Did Ruth and Peyton drag you from the crash, then leave?"

"No— I don't know," Tawny-Lynn whispered. "I told you I don't remember. I didn't see the person's face."

"Then why was Ruth buried here? How did she get from the crash to your ranch?"

Tears blurred Tawny-Lynn's eyes. "I have no idea," she murmured.

Chaz struggled to piece together the facts, for some scenario that made sense. "You said Peyton was involved with a married man. Maybe she saw the accident as a way to escape. Or—" his mind took a dangerous leap "—maybe he caused the crash, then Peyton was going to run off with him. Ruth could have tried to stop her and the man...or Peyton...hit Ruth, then buried her here so we wouldn't find her."

"But," Tawny-Lynn said, her eyes filled with denial, "Peyton loved your sister. Peyton would never have hurt Ruth or have left her."

He released her so abruptly she stumbled backward. "Then tell me what happened, dammit!"

"I told you, I don't know. Maybe whoever killed Ruth forced Peyton to go with him."

"Or—" he said between clenched teeth. "Hell, your father was a drunk. Maybe Ruth came to tell your father

that Peyton was running off, and they argued—and he
killed her."

"Chaz, you're jumping to conclusions."

Chaz dropped his hands from her, wishing he'd never
touched her. "Or Peyton ran away with her lover and left
my sister here in the ground."

"How could you believe Peyton would do that?"

"Where is she?" he barked. "Where's she been all these
years?"

"I don't know!" Tawny-Lynn cried. "If I did, don't you
think I would have told you?"

His stomach was churning, his eyes blurry. He didn't
know what to believe anymore. What to think.

Whether he could trust Tawny-Lynn or not.

So he finished dressing, grabbed his gun and holster
and headed to the door.

He had to bury his sister and give her the rightful memorial she deserved.

But first he had to tell his parents. And that would be
the hardest thing he'd ever done in his life.

TAWNY-LYNN BRUSHED away tears as Chaz stormed out the
door. Her heart was breaking.

How could Chaz believe that her sister had killed Ruth?
Or that her father had?

He had no reason to hurt Ruth.

But she had no answer for how Ruth's body had come
to be buried at White Forks.

Still, she hadn't lied to Chaz....

But he thought she'd covered up for Peyton. If he believed that after the intimacy they'd shared the night before, then everyone else would.

If only she knew who Peyton had been involved with.

She paced the room, racking her brain, then remembered
that Chaz had mentioned that Keith Plumbing had been a

suspect years ago. He would have been in his early twenties and was nice looking.

What if he and Peyton had been in love?

Maybe her sister had pushed him to leave his wife, and he'd flown into a fit of rage and killed Peyton? Maybe Ruth witnessed the murder, or she'd known about him, and he killed her to keep her quiet, then buried her on White Forks to throw suspicion off himself and onto her father.

They hadn't found Peyton's body on the ranch.

That didn't mean it wasn't there.

Determined to uncover the truth, she quickly showered and dressed, then looked up Keith Plumbing's address. She could confront him at work, but she'd probably get more information if she faced him in person at home.

And his wife… If he'd cheated on her with Peyton, odds were that he'd cheated another time. Maybe more.

Twenty minutes later, she parked at Plumbing's house, an older, brick ranch in a moderate subdivision near town. The community was run-down and needed some landscaping, but most of the houses looked decent with his repair and renovation business. Plumbing probably did odd jobs in his own neighborhood.

She parked in the drive, noting the tricycles in the yard. Apparently the Plumbings had young children.

A MORNING BREEZE stirred, lifting her hair as Tawny-Lynn walked up the steps to the front door. She rang the bell, anxiety plucking at her at the sound of children screeching inside. If she accused Plumbing of an affair and his wife didn't know, she might be tearing apart a marriage.

The door opened, and a woman in her late twenties with bleached-blond hair answered, a baby on one hip, two toddlers holding on to her legs.

"If you're selling something, I'm not interested," the woman said.

Tawny-Lynn caught the door edge before the woman could close it. "I'm not selling anything, Mrs. Plumbing. My name is Tawny-Lynn Boulder. I need to talk to you."

A nervous tick tugged at the corner of the woman's mouth. She patted the towheaded little boy beside her. "Herman, you and Jerry go watch cartoons." The boys raced off, sliding on the floor as if they were skating. Mrs. Plumbing patted the baby's back. "What's this about?"

Tawny-Lynn explained that she'd come back to sell the ranch. "Mrs. Plumbing, I know the police questioned your husband seven years ago when my sister and Ruth Camden first went missing."

"They harassed him, you mean." She hugged the baby tighter to her. "Keith is a good man. A good father."

Tawny-Lynn inhaled. "Since I returned, I learned that my sister was having an affair with a married man before she disappeared. I'm not proud of that, but if it's true, I need to know who it was."

Mrs. Plumbing narrowed her eyes. "You think she was seeing Keith?"

"I don't know," Tawny-Lynn said. "But yesterday we found Ruth Camden's body on my father's ranch. If Peyton had pushed this man to leave his wife, then—"

"You bitch," Mrs. Plumbing snarled. "How dare you come to my house and suggest that my husband slept with your sister. And now you're trying to make out like he killed her and Ruth Camden."

"I'm sorry. I'm just looking for the truth—"

"Well, the truth is that Keith never slept with your sister, and he sure as hell didn't kill anyone." She grabbed the door. "Now get off my property before I make you leave myself."

Tawny-Lynn knotted her hands. "All right. But if I find out you're lying, I'll be back. And next time I'll bring the sheriff with me."

The woman slammed the door in her face. Tawny-Lynn gritted her teeth and rushed back to the car. She'd certainly made another enemy now.

But Mrs. Plumbing had been defensive and nervous when she'd first realized who she was. Was she lying to cover for her husband?

Chapter Fifteen

Chaz forced his emotions at bay as he delivered the bad news to his parents. His mother was hunched in her favorite armchair, crying quietly, while his father had poured himself a drink, downed it and paced the living room.

"You found her on the White Forks Ranch?"

"Yes," Chaz said. "Actually Tawny-Lynn discovered the grave when she was weeding the flowerbeds."

His father whirled on him, eyes enraged, a vein throbbing in his forehead. "I told you that girl was lying years ago. She probably knew our baby was there all along."

"I can't believe her body was this close all these years." His mother dried her face with a handkerchief. "I always held out hope that somehow she'd survived."

So had he. But she'd been dead all along. Dead while they'd organized search parties, posted fliers, made television appearances to plead for her return.

"Boulder was nothing but a lousy drunk," his father growled. "And Tawny-Lynn covered for him."

Chaz's head ached from trying to sort through the situation. He'd accused Tawny-Lynn of the same thing. But as rational thoughts returned, he couldn't imagine her having hidden such a secret for so long.

Not when the police and town had persecuted her.

She would have broken if she'd known something.

Unless her father had killed Ruth instead of Peyton's lover, and Tawny-Lynn had been afraid of her old man.

But the hurt in her eyes had been too real for her to have lied. Besides, if she'd known the body was there all along, why report it now?

Chaz knelt in front of his mother and cradled her hands between his. "Mom, I promise you, I will get to the bottom of this."

She leaned forward and hugged him, her body trembling with grief. "I don't want to lose you, too, Chaz."

"You won't," he said softly. He glanced at his father who was still pacing, his agitation mounting with every second. Obviously Gerome Camden wasn't calm enough to comfort his wife. The day Ruth had gone missing, something inside his father had died, and he'd never been the same.

The confirmation of her death would probably change him even more, make him retreat deeper into his shell. "Is there anyone I can call to come and stay with you, Mom? How about your friend LuAnn?"

She nodded and released him, but squeezed his arm. "Yes, honey, LuAnn would be nice."

"All right. Then I'm going to issue a statement to the press. Maybe airing the story again will trigger someone's memory, or prompt a witness to come forward."

Like Peyton's married lover. What did the man know about Ruth's death?

His father paused, the lines around his mouth sagging. "Do you think talking to the press is a good idea?"

"Tawny-Lynn learned that her sister was seeing a married man. If we find him, he might fill in the blanks."

"You think he killed Ruth?" his father asked.

"It's possible. And if he did, he'll pay for it."

"I suppose we'll have to make arrangements," his mother said, another round of tears flooding her eyes.

"I'll let you know when the M.E. releases her," Chaz said.

"When you do that press conference, tell the public we're offering a reward of $50,000 for any information leading to an arrest," his father said. "This time maybe it'll do some good."

Chaz agreed, kissed his mother then called her friend LuAnn as he walked back to his car. LuAnn expressed her regrets and promised to rush over to be with her.

He phoned the mayor, the head of the local paper and the nearest television station along with the FBI agent Justin Thorpe who was spearheading the task force to look into the case of the other missing women. By noon, Chaz stood in front of a podium to address them.

He began by reiterating the details of the original case. "With deep sadness, I'm here today to announce that we have located the body of my sister, Ruth Camden. Her body was found on White Forks Ranch, but at this time we have not located Peyton Boulder. We've recently learned that Peyton may have been having an affair with a married man before the accident and that affair may have played a part in her disappearance. At this point, we do not know the man's identity. If anyone knows the name of this man, or has any information regarding his whereabouts or the death of Ruth Camden, please contact the police. Ruth's parents, Mr. and Mrs. Gerome Camden, are offering a reward of $50,000 for information that leads to an arrest in this case. Thank you for your time."

Several hands flew up and the questions began.

Chaz answered them as best he could, silently praying that unlike years before, this time someone would come forward.

TAWNY-LYNN STARED at the television screen, her heart in her throat. Relaying the news about Ruth's death had to have been difficult for Chaz.

The Camdens probably blamed her, too.

But she no longer cared what they thought. She'd lived with the pain of knowing they'd hated her for years.

But she did care about Chaz.

And she wanted justice for Ruth.

Fresh tears threatened, and she stood, deciding to purge her anxiety, but she couldn't stomach working in the flowerbeds or outdoors.

Not after her earlier discovery.

Although if Peyton were buried on the ranch, surely the search party would have found her grave.

Desperate to block the images from her mind, she resorted to more cleaning, her stomach clenching at the sight of the drawers and cabinets the crime team had rooted through. She washed and dusted and polished walls and floors and furniture until the afternoon bled into evening.

Exhausted, she showered, then poured herself a glass of wine as she fixed a salad, but before she had a chance to drink it, the house phone rang.

She jumped, startled. She'd forgotten to have it disconnected. It was probably a solicitor, but on the off chance it was Chaz or someone calling about Ruth's body, maybe with a tip, she grabbed the handset.

"Hello."

Silence echoed over the line, then she heard the sound of someone breathing.

Anxiety ripped through her. "Who is this?" The person who'd left those bloody messages? The one who'd tried to kill her?

Another heavy breath, and fury shot through Tawny-Lynn. "Listen to me, if you're the person who tried to kill me, I'm not going anywhere until I find out the truth."

Her fingers felt clammy as she tightened her grip on the phone. "Okay, you coward, I'm hanging up—"

"No, don't."

Tawny-Lynn froze, her chest heaving for air. The voice

belonged to a woman. But it was muffled. Still it sounded… almost familiar.

"Who is this?" she asked again.

"I…know who your sister was sleeping with."

Was this Keith Plumbing's wife? Maybe she'd changed her mind and decided to come forward.

"Tell me his name."

"Not over the phone," the woman whispered. "Meet me at the park at the creek and I'll tell you everything."

"What do you mean 'everything'?"

The line went dead before the caller replied.

Tawny-Lynn sat for a moment, contemplating what to do as the wind rattled the windowpanes of the old house. If the caller had been Plumbing's wife, then why didn't she identify herself?

Maybe her husband had been in the house.

But why the clandestine meeting?

Could it be a setup? Someone working with the man who'd tried to kill her?

Or…what if the person who'd killed Ruth was a woman? Maybe the wife of the man Peyton had been sleeping with? She could have killed Peyton and then Ruth.

And now she wanted her dead.

She picked up the phone to call Chaz, but hesitated, her heart aching as she remembered the accusations he'd hurled at her.

No, she'd go alone.

But she grabbed the rifle to carry with her just in case she was walking into a trap.

CHAZ MET WITH the Texas Ranger and Sheriff Blair from Sunset Mesa after the press conference, then spent the afternoon fending off calls, hoping to get some valid tips.

But as dusk fell, nothing had come through.

The front door of the sheriff's office burst open, and

Keith Plumbing stalked in, his face blazing with anger. He yanked off his work hat, then propped his hands on Chaz's desk.

"How dare you send Tawny-Lynn Boulder over to question my wife, and make accusations against me?"

"What?" Chaz forced his voice to remain calm. "I didn't send Tawny-Lynn to do anything."

Plumbing lifted his hands from the desk and folded his arms. "Then why the hell did she go to my house and ask my wife if I was running around with her sister?"

Chaz blew out an exasperated breath. "I guess because she wants answers." He stood, towering over Plumbing by at least a foot. "Did you have an affair with Peyton?"

"You've got to be kidding me!" Plumbing cursed. "I can't believe this crap. I didn't deserve the law coming down on me seven years ago, and I sure as hell don't now."

"You didn't answer the question," Chaz said calmly. "Did you sleep with Peyton Boulder?"

"No," Plumbing shouted. "For God's sake, she was a teenager back then. I'm not stupid."

Chaz simply stared him down. "Then why did the sheriff question you?"

"Because I was in the wrong place at the wrong time," Plumbing said. "My wife and I'd only been married a couple of years and were having money trouble. Then she gets pregnant on top of that, and I blew one out at a bar one night. Wound up in a bar brawl and got arrested. Once you get in the system, you're an easy patsy."

"Maybe," Chaz said, wondering if Plumbing simply had a chip on his shoulder or if he was lying to cover his butt. "But maybe you deserved to get looked at."

The man shot him a seething look. "Listen, Sheriff, I learned my lesson. I've been clean for seven years, go home to my wife every night. I didn't sleep with Peyton, and I sure as hell didn't kill your sister. So tell Tawny-Lynn that if she keeps harassing me, I'm going to get a lawyer and sue her six ways till Sunday."

Plumbing rattled the chair with his hands as he turned and stalked out the door. Maybe the man had control of his drinking, but he wasn't sure about his temper.

Chaz had to put aside his feelings toward Tawny-Lynn, jumbled as they were, and make sure she was safe. He'd also better pass on Plumbing's warning and tell her to let him do the police work.

He grabbed his Stetson and keys and headed out to his squad car. Plumbing's truck was already disappearing out of sight, headed in the same direction as White Forks.

Chaz turned from the parking lot and followed, riding Plumbing until the man made the turn toward his own sub-division. Relieved Plumbing hadn't planned to pay Tawny-Lynn a visit in the mood he was in, Chaz sped toward the ranch. But just as he neared the mile-long drive, Tawny-Lynn barreled from the ranch, cut a right and drove away from town.

Curious, Chaz followed behind her, maintaining enough distance not to spook her, but staying close enough that if someone else was following her, he'd be able to detect it.

Two miles down the flat country road, she veered onto the graveled road leading to the creek park. The place used to be a popular teen make-out spot, but he thought they'd found a new location for their rendezvous. Although it was dark and deserted, he'd discovered dopers out here twice. Last month he'd even broken up a deal going down.

He made a mental note to have the city fix the street-lights as half of them were burned out. The playground needed reworking, as well. No wonder the residents didn't use the park much anymore.

He spotted Tawny-Lynn driving to the section where the picnic tables were located and he flipped off his lights, not wanting to alert her he was following.

She veered into a spot in the parking lot, then sat for a few minutes, and he did the same, making sure he was hidden by a cluster of trees. Finally another car rolled up, a small sedan that slowed as it neared Tawny-Lynn's car.

She must be meeting someone. But why the hell would she agree to meet someone out here in the dark where it was deserted?

He thought she had more sense than that.

Protective instincts rushed to life, and he checked his gun, then watched as a woman clad in all black clothing with a hoodie climbed from the sedan.

Tawny-Lynn's truck door opened, and she stepped out. A breath of relief escaped him when he saw her swing the shotgun up beside her.

He opened his door, careful to close it without making a sound, then slowly eased his way along the creek edge until he was hidden behind a tree near the park bench. The woman in the hoodie gestured toward the bench, then Tawny-Lynn dropped the rifle to her side and followed.

He tilted his head, waiting on the woman to step into the moonlight so he could see her face.

When she finally did, his heart stopped. It couldn't be…

Chapter Sixteen

Tawny-Lynn stared at the woman in front of her in shock. It wasn't possible…was it?

"Hello, sis," the woman said.

Tawny-Lynn shook her head in denial. She'd expected Mrs. Plumbing, but never Peyton.

But it *was* her.

Her hair had darkened, streaked with red now, unnatural as if she'd dyed it. But she lowered the hood and those same blue eyes looked back at her. Blue eyes she'd looked into so many times.

She had to swallow twice to make her voice work. "You're alive. What? How?"

"I'm sorry, Tawny-Lynn," Peyton whispered. "Sorry I left you to deal with everything, but I was scared."

Relief mingled with stunned surprise, but anger followed, nearly choking her. "You let me think you were missing, kidnapped, maybe raped or murdered…." Fresh tears made her voice turn to gravel. "How could you do that to me?"

"I can explain," Peyton said. "But please put away Dad's rifle."

Tawny-Lynn had forgotten about the gun. "I thought you might be the person whose been trying to kill me."

"What?" Peyton gasped. "Oh, my God, I— Why would someone try to kill you?"

Tawny-Lynn laid the rifle on the table with a huff. "Because they think I know something about the accident. Everyone in town thinks I've covered up for whoever took you and Ruth." Her voice rose an octave. "But you've been alive all this time and Ruth was dead and buried on our ranch."

"I...didn't know about Ruth," Peyton cried. "I...thought she'd run off, too."

Tawny-Lynn massaged her temples where a headache pulsed. She had missed her sister so much, had wanted to see her again, had prayed she was alive so many times.

And now here she was, and she didn't how to react.

Tawny-Lynn sank down at the picnic table, numb. Peyton followed her, then sat down next to her, and pulled her sister in close.

"I'm so sorry, honey, really, I...wanted to call you. To come back. To explain."

"But you didn't," Tawny-Lynn said in a pained whisper. Still, she didn't fight her when Peyton wrapped her arms around her.

"I was a coward," Peyton said against her ear. "And a terrible sister. But...I had my reasons."

A noise sounded nearby, gravel and twigs snapped, then a harsh male voice echoed in the wind.

"So you did lie, Tawny-Lynn. No wonder you went away. Have you been living with Peyton all this time?"

Tawny-Lynn pulled away from Peyton and glanced up, her heart racing. Chaz glared at the two of them with rage in his eyes.

"No...that's not true," she said in a hoarse whisper.

"Then what is the truth?" Chaz said coldly. "Because I sure as hell don't know anymore."

Tawny-Lynn's head was swimming. "I don't know," she said, "but I didn't lie to you."

"Yet here you are with your long-lost sister."

Memories of the night in Chaz's arms seemed so distant that she ached to turn back the clock. But too much had happened.

Whatever closeness they'd shared had dissipated in the light of day. And if Chaz believed that she'd lied and covered up his sister's murder, then he didn't know her at all.

And he certainly could never love her.

CHAZ REACHED FOR his handcuffs. He wanted to haul both Tawny-Lynn and her sister in for lying, for leading the police on a wild-goose chase for Peyton when for all he knew she'd killed Ruth and left her at White Forks.

"None of this is Tawny-Lynn's fault." Peyton shot up from the bench like a protective big sister. Only where had she been when the town and their father had persecuted Tawny-Lynn?

She couldn't have known where Peyton was back then. She'd been too traumatized and had that head injury. And her reaction when his family and the town had turned on her had been too real.

"Did you kill my sister, Peyton?" he asked.

Peyton's eyes widened. "No! Heavens no, Chaz. I loved Ruth." She crossed her arms and shifted onto the balls of her feet, the ground crunching beneath her shoes. "In fact, I didn't know Ruth was dead until I saw your press conference earlier. That's when I called Tawny-Lynn to meet me."

His gaze shot to Tawny-Lynn's, but she was watching her sister with a mixture of awe and hurt. "Where have you been?" Tawny-Lynn whispered.

Peyton cleared her throat. "In Tennessee," she said softly. "I...had to leave town. I didn't know what else to do."

"You could have come home," Tawny-Lynn said. "The entire town was looking for you. I was looking for you. And Dad..."

"Dad and I weren't getting along back then," Peyton said. "That's one reason I left."

"You were having an affair with a married man," Chaz said sharply.

Peyton's eyes widened. "How do you know about that?"

"I talked to J.J. and Cindy and Rudy," Tawny-Lynn said.

Peyton's face paled in the dim moonlight. "What else did they tell you?"

"Nothing," Tawny-Lynn said. "So who was he? Did you run off with him?"

"No." A shudder ripped up Peyton's body making her look scared and vulnerable. "But he is the reason I left."

"And what about Ruth?" Chaz asked. "Did you two fight about him, then you killed her to keep her quiet?"

Peyton shook her head fiercely. "I told you, Chaz, I would never have hurt Ruth."

"But you did argue about him," Tawny-Lynn said. "You were arguing and whispering on the bus."

"You heard us?" Peyton asked.

"I didn't understand what you were saying, but I knew you were upset. Then someone ran into the bus and the driver lost control, and we crashed into the ravine."

Peyton tucked a strand of Tawny-Lynn's hair behind her ear. "Yes, and when I came to, I smelled smoke. You were hurt, sis, and I pulled you out before the bus exploded."

"What about Ruth?" Chaz asked.

"She was gone," Peyton said. "I...looked around and couldn't find her."

"What do you mean, you couldn't find her?"

"She wasn't in the bus," Peyton cried. "You have to believe me, Chaz. If she had been, I would have saved her, too."

"How could she have been gone?" Tawny-Lynn asked.

Peyton shrugged, her expression tormented. "I don't know. At first I thought that maybe he... That she left with him. I was scared so I ran and hitched a ride with a trucker. That's how I wound up in Tennessee."

Chaz gritted his teeth. "Who did you think she ran off with?"

"You have to understand, we were young. I was petrified," Peyton said.

"You didn't answer my question," Chaz barked.

Peyton gave Tawny-Lynn a pleading look. "Tell us what happened, Peyton. Ever since I came back, someone's been threatening me. A man even broke into the ranch and tried to strangle me."

"I'm so sorry. I thought when I left it would be over."

"It's not over until we lock him up," Tawny-Lynn said.

Peyton sank back on the park bench, twisting her hands together. "I can't believe he actually killed Ruth. He was married, and when he broke it off with me, I was devastated. I was stupid and thought I was in love with him."

"You wanted to marry him?" Tawny-Lynn asked gently.

"Yes, then he started hitting on Ruth, pressuring her to have sex with him."

Chaz's pulse pounded.

"I realized then that he'd used me. That I wasn't the only one, so I told Ruth to stay away from him. That if he harassed her, she should tell her folks." She looked up at Chaz. "That's what we argued about. She didn't want to tell them. But he threatened us and…that's why I ran."

Tawny-Lynn took her sister's hands in hers. "Who was it, Peyton? You have to tell us his name so we can make this right."

Peyton nodded, although her voice quivered when she spoke. "It was Coach Wake."

ANOTHER SHOCK WAVE rolled through Tawny-Lynn at Peyton's words. Coach Wake had seduced Peyton? Had hit on the other girls?

"Our softball coach?" Tawny-Lynn asked. "He slept with you?"

Peyton dropped her head as if ashamed. "He seduced me, and I fell for him like a fool. But then he went after Ruth, and I heard other girls talking about how he'd done the same to them. That he'd come on to them in the locker room. I had to stop him from bothering Ruth. So after the game that day, I told him we were going to go to your parents."

"That's when he threatened you?" Chaz asked.

Peyton nodded. "He said he'd ruin both our lives if we told anyone." She gave Chaz a pleading look. "Ruth was terrified of your parents finding out. She didn't want to embarrass your father and begged me to keep quiet."

"Then you dragged Peyton out. Where was Ruth?" Chaz asked.

"I don't know."

"You should have stuck around and told someone. Then my sister might still be alive."

"I know, but I was terrified. The coach was so mad when I talked to him after the game that he followed the bus. He's the one who caused us to crash."

Tawny-Lynn recognized guilt in her sister's eyes and knew that she blamed herself.

"I should arrest you for not coming forward," Chaz said. "For covering up for a murderer."

Tawny-Lynn's protective instincts surged to life. "Listen, Chaz, Peyton told you the truth. She didn't hurt Ruth, she tried to save her. And she ran because she was scared, not to cover for the coach."

"Your sister was the best friend I ever had," Peyton said earnestly. "If you arrest the coach, I'll testify about the sexual harassment and that he hit the bus."

"Sexual harassment?" Chaz muttered. "That's only the beginning of the charges I'm going to bring against the monster. On top of sexual assault, I'm charging him with five counts of murder."

Tawny-Lynn realized he was right. If Coach Wake had caused the crash, he'd killed three of her teammates, and the bus driver.

And now it appeared that he'd killed Ruth.

Had he tried to kill her because he thought she knew about his affair with Peyton? Or was he afraid she'd remember that he caused those four deaths?

CHAZ STUDIED PEYTON for a moment before he left. "Can I trust you not to leave town?"

"Yes." Peyton curved her arm around Tawny-Lynn. "I was seventeen and scared back then, Chaz. I'm not a kid anymore. I want to make up for the past. And I'm not going to allow Ruth's killer to get away."

"We'll go back to the ranch together," Tawny-Lynn said.

Peyton rose and took Chaz's hand. "I promise you that I won't run again. It's time Coach Wake got what he deserves." Regret lined her face. "Besides, I feel terrible that I didn't come forward seven years ago. No matter how many young girls he's pressured into having sex with him since then."

Rage heated Chaz's blood at the thought. She was right.

"You two go back to the ranch. I'll let you know when he's in custody."

Tawny-Lynn nodded, and he waited until they got in their cars and left for White Forks, then he strode back to his squad car. He replayed images of Coach Wake in his head. He was always friendly, outgoing, a real charmer with the moms.

Because he was taking advantage of their daughters behind their backs. Pressuring them into sex, then threatening them so they wouldn't reveal his dirty little secret.

A secret he'd killed for to keep quiet.

Chaz started the engine and peeled from the park. He checked his watch for the time and realized the coach should be home from school by now. That is, unless they had a game.

His body teemed with anger as he drove straight to Wake's house, a nice two-story in a new development close to town. The yard was well kept, the flowerbeds filled with flowers, the house freshly painted.

Everything that shouted that Coach Wake was a nice, family man.

Now Chaz knew differently.

He checked to make sure his weapon was secure, his handcuffs intact, then walked up to the front door and rang the bell. A few moments later, the man's wife, Susan, answered the door. She was pretty with brown hair and green eyes. And she was very pregnant.

"Sheriff, what can I do for you?"

"Is your husband home?"

She propped her hip against the door frame. "No, they had a game."

"Away or home?"

"Home."

Sympathy for the woman in front of him clawed at him. But then again, what if she'd known about the sex with the young girls?

Either way, if he told her his plans to arrest her husband, she might warn him and he'd probably run.

He didn't intend for the creep to get away.

"All right, I'll catch up with him later."

She cleared her throat. "Can I tell him the reason you stopped by?"

"No, thanks," he said. "I just need to talk to him, that's all."

He walked away as if the conversation could wait, but the town had already waited seven years for justice, and he refused to hold off another day.

He climbed back in the squad car and drove to the high

school, parked and headed to the bleachers. The stands on both sides were filled with parents, teens and kids. The game was in the last inning, the score tied.

Memories of watching Ruth, Peyton and Tawny-Lynn play haunted him. If he'd known back then what Coach Wake was up to, he would have stood up for the girls, especially his sister.

Why hadn't she come to him?

Maybe she'd planned to. But the coach had killed her first.

One of the girls hit a ground ball and the other team's player missed it, allowing the Camden Cats to score the winning run.

Cheers erupted taking him back to that fatal day when Tawny-Lynn had won the game for the team.

And everything else had been lost.

The team raced onto the field, cheering and shouting and hugging each other. The coach was beaming, high-fiving the girls, as he joined the players to celebrate.

The handcuffs jangled at Chaz's hip as he strode onto the field. The other team was heading to their bus, but family members and friends of the Cats stood shouting and clapping in the stands.

Coach Wake's face went ashen when Chaz reached for the cuffs, as if he knew the past had finally caught up with him.

"You're under arrest, Coach Wake." Chaz jerked the man's arms behind him. The girls on the team paused in their celebrations, shocked. The stands grew quiet, curious whispers rumbling through the crowd.

"You don't have to do this in front of everyone," Coach Wake growled.

Chaz snapped the handcuffs into place.

"Yes, I do. You should be grateful I don't shout the

charges over the intercom." He knew arresting Wake in front of the team and town might be considered cold.

But he didn't give a damn.

It was only fitting that the residents see the man who'd torn their town apart handcuffed and hauled to jail.

Chapter Seventeen

"Where exactly did you find Ruth's body?" Peyton asked as they parked at the ranch.

Tawny-Lynn led her sister to the side of the house. "There. I was weeding the flowerbeds and found her bracelet. Then…the body."

Peyton studied it with a solemn face. "I don't understand how she ended up here. This is miles from the site of the crash."

"I don't understand, either," Tawny-Lynn said. "Unless the coach took her from the site, killed her then decided to hide her body here in case someone discovered her."

Peyton nodded, although she looked unconvinced. Shadows plagued her eyes as she turned toward Tawny-Lynn. "I'm so sorry I left you to deal with everything. I—that's the one thing I regret most."

"I was so scared," Tawny-Lynn admitted. "Every time I thought about what might be happening to you—"

Peyton drew her into a hug. "I'm so sorry I put you through that. I never meant to hurt you or Dad. I just didn't know what to do."

Tawny-Lynn wanted to forgive her sister with no questions asked, but she had suffered for years and she needed answers.

"Come on inside. I want to hear where you went, what happened after you left."

They hooked arms together and walked around to the front porch. Tawny-Lynn remembered the bloody deer and threats and made herself glance around the house and yard in case her attacker had returned.

But hopefully Coach Wake was locked up so they were safe.

She unlocked the door but Peyton hesitated in the doorway. "I don't feel like I belong here," she said in a haunted whisper.

Tawny-Lynn squeezed her hand. "Neither do I. You should have seen the place when I came back. Dad's drinking was really bad the past few years, and he'd turned into a hoarder. There wasn't an inch of clean, empty space anywhere."

Peyton walked into the den and stood by the fireplace. "I…should have let him know I was alive before he died."

Tawny-Lynn simply looked at her sister, unable to let her off the hook. Peyton's disappearance had sent her father over the edge and drastically changed all their lives.

Knowing they both needed something to dispel the tension, she went to the kitchen, opened a bottle of wine and brought them both a glass.

Peyton cradled it in her trembling hands. "Thanks."

Tawny-Lynn sipped hers, needing liquid courage. "Dad took your disappearance hard. He…blamed me."

"You?" Peyton sank down onto the hearth. "Why? You were injured."

"Didn't you read the papers or watch the news?" she asked, a trace of bitterness in her voice.

Peyton shook her head. "Not at first. I was…confused. Terrified and alone, trying to figure out where to go and what to do."

Tawny-Lynn swallowed hard. "I had a concussion from the accident, and my memories were all scrambled. I knew someone rescued me from the bus, but I couldn't see a face.

The parents of the other girls, Chaz's parents, even Dad blamed me. They thought if I could remember, they'd be able to find you and Ruth."

"Oh, Tawny-Lynn." Peyton stared into her red wine. "I never thought about that. I…guess I didn't think at all. I felt so stupid to have slept with the coach, especially when I realized he hit on other girls."

"You and Dad argued a lot those last three months. Did he know about Coach?"

Peyton shook her head. "He caught me sneaking back in one night, and accused me of being a slut. We got into a terrible fight…. But he was right."

Tawny-Lynn softened. "You weren't a slut, Peyton, just a vulnerable girl. Coach Wake took advantage of that."

Regret flickered in Peyton's eyes. "But I should have come forward and spoken up. No telling how many girls he's done the same thing to since."

She was right. Seven years—seven *teams* of girls…

"Well, you're here now, and Chaz has gone to arrest Coach Wake so he can't hurt anyone else."

Peyton swirled her wine in her glass. "But it won't bring back Ruth."

She sat down beside her sister, soaking in the fact that she was alive. "No, it won't. But she'll finally get the justice she deserves. Then all of us can move on."

CHAZ PHONED HIS parents on the way to the jail and asked them to meet him at his office. He didn't want them to learn the news about the coach's arrest from the gossip mill. They deserved to hear it from him, and to face the man who'd killed Ruth.

Coach Wake sat with his head down, his jaw set as Chaz parked. He walked around the car, opened the door and hauled him out, keeping a firm grip on the man's arm as he escorted him inside.

His deputy's eyebrows shot up, but he watched silently as Chaz fingerprinted Wake and booked him.

"I don't know what the hell you think you're doing, Sheriff, but you've made a huge mistake," Coach Wake snapped.

"You've harassed your last girl," Chaz said through clenched teeth.

"Where did you dig up these phony charges? None of the girls on my team would say anything bad about me."

Chaz shoved his face into the coach's. "And why is that? Because you threaten to destroy their lives if they talk." It wasn't a question, but a statement.

The coach stiffened. "I would never threaten one of those kids."

"I have a witness who says differently."

A seed of panic flared in Wake's eyes. "Who are you talking about?"

"All in due time." He grabbed the man by his arm and hauled him through the double doors to the back.

"You're going to be sorry for this," Coach Wake said angrily as Chaz threw him into a cell.

Chaz slammed the cell door shut and jangled the keys. "I don't think so. You're finally going to pay for what you've done."

"I want a lawyer!" Wake shouted. "Give me my phone call now."

"You'll get it," Chaz said as he headed back to the front. He needed time to compose himself before he interrogated the man, needed to have evidence compiled and to build his case. He would need a formal statement by Peyton, as well.

In the front office, he paused to explain the situation to his deputy. "Send those prints over to the lab," Chaz said. "Tell them to compare them to the prints found at the Boulder place and any they might have found on my sister's bracelet."

Seconds later, his parents stormed in the door, looking haggard. "What's going on, Chaz?" his mother cried.

His father's expression bordered on irate. "You arrested Ruth's killer?"

Chaz nodded. "I did make an arrest, but I need to explain some things to both of you before word gets out."

His mother clenched his arm. "What things?"

"Did you or did you not arrest Ruth's killer?" his father bellowed.

"Just come in my office and sit down." He led them to his private office and offered them coffee, but they both declined.

"Just tell us what's going on," his father demanded.

Chaz crossed his arms and began by explaining that Peyton Boulder was alive.

His mother gasped. "What? Where's she been all this time?"

His father gave him a scathing look. "Did she kill Ruth?"

Chaz shook his head. "No, I believe Coach Wake did, but I need time to build a case. I have motive, though."

His mother paled. "What motive?"

Chaz pulled up a chair and faced her, noting that his father was still standing, his body ramrod straight as if bracing himself for more bad news.

"Peyton claims that Coach Wake seduced her, that she had an affair with him, then he hit on Ruth."

His mother's eyes widened in shock. "No...."

Chaz nodded. "When Ruth told Peyton, Peyton realized that the coach was sexually harassing other girls. After the game that day, Ruth threatened to come to you two and tell you about it, but the coach warned her that she'd be sorry if she did."

"He threatened her?" his mother asked.

"That son of a bitch," his father muttered. "Where is he? I'm going to kill him."

Chaz blocked his father from exiting his office. "No, Dad, you aren't going to do anything. You're going to let me handle this. He's in custody now."

"What did he do to our little girl?" his mother whispered.

Chaz stood his ground against his father when he tried to push past him. "Peyton said he chased the bus down and hit them. Coach Wake is the one who caused the accident that killed those other three girls and the bus driver."

His mother dropped her head into her hands. "Oh, my God...."

"Then he dragged Ruth away and killed her," his father said. "He deserves to die for what he did."

Yes, he did. But first Chaz had to make a solid case. "Now, I want you two to go home. Don't talk to anyone about this. I need Peyton to make a formal statement, then I have to gather as much evidence as possible to make sure Coach Wake doesn't walk."

"If he walks, he won't live long," his father muttered.

"Dad, I understand how you feel, but don't go around saying that to anyone else."

Although his father was right. If Wake walked, the town would probably form a lynch mob and hang him themselves.

TAWNY-LYNN FINALLY put together her famous enchiladas for dinner.

"This is delicious, sis," Peyton said. "You've turned into a good cook."

Tawny-Lynn shrugged, wondering if Chaz would think so. "Cooking is like gardening, it's relaxing to me."

"I can't believe how rundown the ranch looks," Peyton said.

"There's still a lot to do. The weatherman predicted rain the next couple of days. That's why I was working outside, weeding the flowerbeds. Spiffing up the landscaping should help attract a buyer. Although the house needs repairs and my finances are low."

Peyton poured them both more wine. "Did you ever consider moving in and staying here yourself?"

Chaz's face flashed in her mind, and her heart tugged. But any love between them had been one-sided. "No. There's nothing for me in Camden Crossing except bitter memories of how much the town hated me after the accident."

Remorse darkened Peyton's eyes. "That's my fault. And I'll make sure everyone knows it."

Tawny-Lynn sighed. "I'm not sure how everyone will react, Peyton. They may be angry that you didn't come forward sooner."

Peyton's expression turned determined. "I know, but it's time the truth came out. The lies ate at me over the years. And I missed you." Peyton blinked back tears. "When I heard that Ruth's body was found, I realized I couldn't live with myself if I didn't come forward."

They ate in silence for a few moments before Peyton spoke. "Where did you go when you left the ranch?"

Tawny-Lynn bit into her enchilada. "I got a partial scholarship at Texas A&M. The money wasn't enough though, so I took a part-time job at a local lawn-and-garden shop. I guess I'd felt so depressed, dead for so long, that I discovered I liked growing things, watching them come to life. So I majored in landscape architecture."

"You're amazing," Peyton said.

Tawny-Lynn chuckled. "Not really. I started my own business last year, but it's been tough going. When Dad died, I figured I could sell the ranch and put the money into my business."

"You can still do that," Peyton said.

Tawny-Lynn set down her fork. "The ranch belongs to both of us."

Peyton shook her head. "I don't deserve it, not after I let you and Dad down."

"You were a victim," Tawny-Lynn said. "Now let's clean up the dishes, and I want you to tell me where you've been, what you've been doing all this time."

They lapsed back into silence as they cleaned the kitchen, then they retreated to the den in front of the fireplace.

"Now tell me about you," Tawny-Lynn said. "Where have you been living? Did you finish school?"

Peyton curled on the sofa. "I hitched a ride across the country, then wound up staying on the streets for a few weeks."

The images that flashed in Tawny-Lynn's mind terrified her.

"I was scared," Peyton admitted. "Then I met this girl who took me to a group home for teens. She showed me how to make a fake ID and how to get by. I got a job washing dishes at a little diner, then one of the waitresses took a liking to me and invited me to live with her while I earned my GED."

"What did you tell her about your family?"

Heat flooded Peyton's cheeks. "That my mother was dead and that my father was a mean drunk—that I had to run away."

She'd told the partial truth. "What happened then?"

"I lived with her almost five years, then she passed away. But during the time she was alive, she encouraged me to attend a technical school. I became a paralegal and have a decent job."

"It sounds like you did okay."

"I managed, but I was lonely," Peyton admitted softly. "I never stopped missing you and Ruth and wanting to see you." A small smile tugged at her lips. "But I did meet a man through work, and last year we moved in together."

Tawny-Lynn thought about Chaz again and her heart ached. "Maybe I could meet him sometime."

"I'd like that," Peyton said softly.

Tawny-Lynn's cell phone buzzed, and she snatched it up. "Hello."

"I arrested Coach Wake," Chaz said. "Is Peyton still with you?"

"Yes, she's right here."

"Tell her that I need her to come in and sign a formal statement in the morning." His voice sounded terse.

"Okay, we'll be there first thing."

"Thanks." He hung up without another word, and Tawny-Lynn felt bereft. But she pasted on a brave face for her sister. "That was Chaz. He arrested Coach Wake and wants us to come to his office in the morning to sign a statement."

Peyton's hand trembled as she set down her glass. "Tomorrow the town is going to go into shock."

For the second time in seven years. "At least this time, they'll have answers."

Peyton yawned. "I'm going to call Ben in a minute to tell him what's going on."

"Does he know about me? About what happened?" She paused. "About Coach Wake?"

Peyton nodded. "I told him the night before I left to come here. When I heard about Ruth, I broke down. He... was amazing, so supportive."

"I'm glad," Tawny-Lynn said. Maybe there was a happily ever after for one of them in the cards.

HE WATCHED THE ranch from a distance, his nerves on edge. Coach Wake had been arrested. He'd caused the crash that had killed three girls and the bus driver.

And he had killed Ruth.

Soon everyone would know that. Or at least they would *believe* it.

Then *he* would be in the clear.

Unless…Tawny-Lynn remembered his face. That he'd been there that day.

Damn her and her sister, Peyton. All these years he'd wondered where in the hell she was. Why she hadn't come forward.

It was all her fault. She'd seduced that coach and made him want the other young girls on the team. How many had he taken advantage of?

The man deserved to die. But if he went to jail for four counts of murder, at least he'd rot in jail without parole.

But Tawny-Lynn… She was a problem. She had seen his face today.

One day she still might remember….

It was time he got rid of her for good.

Chapter Eighteen

After his parents left, Chaz decided to question Coach Wake. He wanted his gut reaction before the lawyer showed up and stalled the case with legalities.

Chaz strode back to the cell and found the coach sitting on the bare cot with his head in his hands.

"Talk to me, Coach."

Coach Wake shot him an angry look. "You made a mistake. I never hurt any of those girls."

"Really?" Chaz folded his arms. "Because I have a witness who claims that you pressured her to have sex. That she wasn't the only teenager or girl on the team that you slept with."

"I love my wife," Coach Wake said. "And I love coaching. I can't help it if some impressionable student has a crush on me. It happens to coaches all the time. Doesn't mean I did anything about it."

"This girl has no reason to lie," Chaz said.

"If that's true, then tell me who she is."

Chaz shook his head. "Not yet. But I wanted to give you the opportunity to do the right thing and confess before things get dirty."

"They will get dirty because I intend to sue you for false arrest and defamation of character."

Chaz grunted, his hands tightening around the bars of the cell. He wanted to choke the truth out of the bastard.

"When I finish with you, you'll be begging me for a deal. You killed my sister and you're going to pay for it."

"I didn't kill Ruth," he shouted. "She got out of that bus alive."

"Then you *were* following the bus and caused it to crash."

"That's not what I said."

"I know for a fact that you tried to pressure her into having sex, and that when she threatened to tell my parents, you chased down that bus, ran into it and forced it over the ravine."

Panic streaked the coach's face. "That damn Tawny-Lynn. That's what she told you? Did she finally remember something?"

The quiver in his voice confirmed his guilt in Chaz's mind. "So you admit to being there. But you didn't do anything to save those girls, did you? You left them there to die."

The coach scrubbed a hand over his face, stood and paced the cell. "I'm not admitting anything."

"And when Tawny-Lynn came back, you got worried so you tried to kill her."

Wake clammed up. "I want my lawyer."

Chaz simply glared at him. "Fine. But you are going to jail, Coach. And tomorrow everyone in town is going to know what you did to their children."

"I'm innocent," Coach Wake protested.

Chaz simply turned and left the man to stew in the cell. It would be the first of many nights he'd sleep alone on a cold cot. Maybe one day he'd even feel remorse for what he'd done. Although he didn't appear to feel anything now except the need to protect himself.

But for the first time in years, especially the last two weeks since Tawny-Lynn had returned to Camden Crossing, Chaz allowed himself to relax when he got home.

Even though they'd found out Ruth was dead, they had closure in the arrest of Coach Wake. They knew what had happened to Peyton.

And Tawny-Lynn was safe.

Maybe she'd even decide to stay at White Forks.

He paused as he set the take-out meal he'd picked up at the diner on his table, wondering where that thought had come from. He'd known all along that Tawny-Lynn was here to put White Forks on the market, and that there was no love lost between her and the town.

Hell, some of the townsfolk would probably be furious at Peyton for staying away and leaving them in the dark for so long.

He opened up the foam box and inhaled the savory scent of homemade meat loaf and mashed potatoes and gravy. His mouth watered. He tried to recall what he'd had for lunch, then remembered he hadn't eaten.

No wonder he was ravenous.

He'd deal with the fallout from the arrest and Peyton's arrival in town tomorrow. His deputy was staying at the jail, watching over their prisoner.

Tonight he was going to steal some much-needed sleep.

He wolfed down the food and chased it with a cold beer, then walked to his office nook and studied the photographs on the wall.

Wake would probably have a lawyer and bail in the next twenty-four hours. Unless Chaz could convince the judge to remand him until his trial.

He phoned his contact at the paper and TV station and requested another press conference. As soon as he had Peyton's official statement in the morning, he'd announce the news of Wake's arrest.

The parents of the dead teens would be riled at the coach, and it would no doubt be an emotional day, but at least now they would have justice.

When his parents finally buried Ruth in the graveyard at their church, her killer would be rotting in jail. And if Wake had pressured other girls to sleep with him, maybe once Peyton went public, the others would, too.

Then he'd make sure Coach Wake never hurt anyone else.

THE BUS WAS ON FIRE. Flames burst through the air, eating at the ceiling and seats. Smoke clogged Tawny-Lynn's lungs as she opened her eyes.

Someone had dragged her from the bus. Her sister. Peyton was alive.

She struggled to sit up, but pain throbbed through every cell in her body. Her leg hurt the most. Then she looked down and saw that it was twisted at an odd angle.

Broken.

"Peyton!" She tried to scream over the noise of the exploding glass as the bus blew, but her voice came out a hoarse whisper.

Where was Peyton?

She blinked, but smoke clogged her vision. Then she saw him...a man...dragging Ruth away.

Panic bubbled inside her. She tried to see the man's face, but he was too far away. Then he turned and looked at her, and she cried out....

His face was blank. An empty black hole....

Tawny-Lynn startled awake and sat up in bed, her pulse clamoring as she looked around the room. It was empty. No one inside.

Only the man from her nightmares. She felt his evil permeating her. Felt his eyes boring into her.

She clenched the sheets, desperately forcing the image back into her head.

A man dragging Ruth away. He wore a dark coat....

something gold glinted in the darkness. A ring of some kind?

Or had she imagined it? Maybe it had been embers sparking from the flames.

Was the man Coach Wake? Had she blocked out his face because she'd been too shocked to see him hauling Ruth away?

CHAZ'S CELL PHONE trilled, jarring him from sleep at 6:00 a.m. He reached for it as he climbed from bed and walked to the kitchen to make coffee.

"Sheriff, you'd better get down here now."

Chaz blinked. "What's going on?"

"The parents of the three girls who died in the crash are here along with your father. I swear, we've got a lynch mob on our hands."

Chaz cursed. He should have foreseen that his father would call the other parents.

"I'm on my way." He ended the call, rushed to the bathroom and splashed water on his face, then hurriedly dressed. He picked up coffee on the way, knowing he needed a clear head, and to calm down, because he felt like throwing his father in jail for stirring up trouble.

By the time he arrived, Coach Wake's wife and Alvin Lambert, Wake's attorney, had joined the scene. His deputy stood by the door leading to the back of the jail with his hand at his gun. Lambert had strategically pushed Mrs. Wake to the opposite side and was guarding her as if he expected the parents to physically assault her.

"No one sees Wake until the sheriff says so," his deputy said as Chaz entered.

Chaz's father stood to the right of the other parents, calmer today, although his eyes were livid, revenge flaring in their depths.

Chaz shot him a scathing look. He'd deal with him later.

"Is it true?" Mrs. Pullman asked, her face tormented.

"Coach Wake forced girls to have sex then killed our children!" Mr. Marx shouted.

"Did he?" Mrs. Truman cried.

Chaz held up a hand to calm them. "Listen to me, and listen good. I did make an arrest, but I need time to gather evidence and interrogate Coach Wake."

"If he killed our daughters, you can't let him go free," Mr. Truman said sharply.

"Please, Sheriff," Mrs. Pullman whispered. "We've waited all this time for the truth."

"Trust me, I know how you feel. We all want justice." Chaz cleared his throat to stop another onslaught of questions. "But you have to leave now and let me do my job."

"Sheriff," Lambert cut in. "I need to speak to my client."

"Why are you doing this to my husband?" Mrs. Wake cried. "He's a good man. He would never hurt one of his students."

The door opened and Peyton and Tawny-Lynn walked in. Shadows rimmed Tawny-Lynn's big eyes, but Peyton looked much calmer than he expected. Still, when they spotted the group in the office, they both halted warily.

Shouts and chaos erupted.

"Oh, my God!"

"Peyton Boulder?"

"You've been hiding your sister!"

Chaz stepped in front of the two women, a protective stance. "If everyone will calm down, I'll explain."

"You knew she was alive?" Mr. Marx asked.

"Why did you leave our girls to die?" Mrs. Pullman demanded.

Chaz motioned for them to be quiet with his hand. "I've called a press conference in an hour to announce this arrest. Now everyone listen."

A strained hush fell over the room. Chaz stepped aside

and ushered Tawny-Lynn and Peyton inside, then separated them from the ill-tempered group by indicating they stand behind the desk.

His father was shooting daggers through both the Boulder girls, his mother wringing her hands together, the others in the room studying them in muted shock.

"Now," Chaz began. "Peyton Boulder survived the crash seven years ago, but she ran and left town out of fear."

"What were you afraid of?" His father asked. "That everyone would find out you were a tramp?"

Chaz spun toward his father. "Dad, if you say one more word, I'm going to throw you in a cell. Now shut up and listen."

Mrs. Wake leaned into her husband's lawyer as if her legs were about to buckle. If she hadn't known about her husband's affairs, he felt sorry for her.

Then again, everyone was innocent until proven guilty. But he believed Peyton's story.

He gestured toward Peyton. "I'm sorry that I ran," Peyton said. "But I was scared."

"Scared of what?" Mrs. Pullman asked gently.

Peyton sank into the chair behind the desk. Tawny-Lynn stood behind her with her hand on Peyton's shoulder for support. Then she spilled her story, the same one she'd told Chaz.

Gasps of outrage and sorrow rumbled through the room. "Did he pressure our daughters into sex?" Mr. Marx asked.

Pain radiated in Peyton's eyes. "I don't know. Honestly. We…never talked about it. In fact, I didn't tell anyone except Ruth. She knew I had a crush on him and, when he approached her, she wanted me to know. I realized then that he was a user and told her to go to her parents. The coach met up with her after the game, and she told him she was going to tell her parents. He exploded and threatened us."

She rubbed her temple, her voice strained. "I saw his car

come up behind the bus, then he hit us and the bus spun out of control. I guess I hit my head when we went over the embankment, because when I came to, blood was everywhere. My sister was on the floor, trapped, and I dragged her out. But I didn't see Ruth anywhere. I was running back to try to save the other girls, but…the bus suddenly burst into flames." Tears trickled down her face, her voice cracking on a sob. "I—I'm so sorry, I wanted to help them, but fire was shooting out on all sides. And I couldn't get back in."

A deafening silence fell across the room, everyone lost in bitter memories and grief and the horrific images Peyton had painted in their heads. Images that obviously tortured Peyton every day.

"What happened then?" Mrs. Pullman asked as she dried her own eyes.

"I saw Coach Wake at the top of the ravine where the bus went over. He was watching the bus burn."

Gasps of outrage filled the room. "That son of a bitch," Mr. Marx muttered.

"I can't believe he just stood there," Mrs. Pullman whispered.

Peyton nodded, the shock of the memory haunting her eyes. "Then I realized that if Coach could just stand there and watch, that he would make good on his threats. That he'd kill me to keep me from going to the sheriff, so I ran."

Mrs. Wake had stood by and listened, but her cheeks blazed with anger. "My husband… He wouldn't have left those girls like that. He was their mentor. He cared about them."

Peyton's gaze rose to meet the woman's. "He did leave them, Mrs. Wake. I'm sorry, and I don't mean to hurt you. I was a stupid teenager back then, but he slept with me, and then he tried to sleep with Ruth. And he caused the others to die that day."

Mrs. Wake planted her hands on her hips. "No, you seduced him and now you've come back to ruin his reputation."

"That's not true," Peyton said. "I came back to do the right thing because Ruth is dead."

Mrs. Wake moved toward Peyton, but the lawyer caught her. "Come on, this is not helping. We'll talk to your husband and get to the bottom of this."

Chaz faced the group. "Folks, I know you're angry and feel like exacting your own revenge, but you will go home and let me handle this situation the legal way."

Mr. Marx started to protest, but Chaz ushered the parents out the door with a stiff reminder that he'd lock them up if they interfered with the case.

Mrs. Wake had dropped into a chair and was massaging her belly. As soon as the parents left, Lambert and the coach's wife demanded to see Wake. Chaz's parents hovered, as well.

His mother knelt by Peyton and squeezed her hands. "I know you loved Ruth."

"I did," Peyton said in a low voice. "I'm so sorry. I thought— I'd hoped that she'd escaped that day. I didn't know he'd killed her."

His father wasn't as forgiving. "If you'd stuck around and come to us, maybe we would have found her in time and she'd still be alive."

"That's not fair." Tawny-Lynn stepped in front of Peyton and jutted her chin up at his father. "First you blamed me, now Peyton. My sister tried to warn Ruth about the coach. He's the one you should be mad at, not her."

"Dad," Chaz warned, breaking up the staring contest between Tawny-Lynn and his father. "Take Mother home. I have a press conference in a few minutes."

"You'll let everyone know you caught Ruth's killer?" his father said.

Chaz nodded. "I can't divulge details, but I will announce his arrest and the charges we're filing. But you and Mom remain low key, and don't stir up any more trouble. The last thing I want is for the town to crucify Wake, or for some kind of vigilante to make things worse."

If that happened, he'd have to protect Wake.

And that was the last thing Chaz wanted to do.

He needed to keep him behind bars before his anger got the best of him and he beat the man to a bloody pulp himself.

A SHUDDER COURSED up Tawny-Lynn's spine. She'd known for years that Chaz's father hated her, but his animosity toward Peyton made her furious.

Couldn't he see that Peyton had suffered? She'd left her home out of fear, run because a mentor and man she'd trusted had used her and threatened her. And she'd lost Ruth.

She saw the guilt in her sister's eyes, but she didn't know how to alleviate it. Maybe in time Peyton would be able to forgive herself.

She gave Mr. Camden a cool look, then took Peyton's arm. "Come on, sis, let's go home. A little more work, and we can hang that for-sale sign and both of us can leave this horrible town behind us."

But the memories would haunt them forever.

So would Chaz's handsome face. Why had she gone and fallen in love with him?

His troubled gaze met hers. "You should be safe now, but let me know if there's any more trouble." He angled his head toward Peyton. "Will you write out everything you've told us and sign it? Then I'll let you know when the trial date is set so you can come back and testify?"

So that was it? Chaz was resorting back to business as if nothing personal had happened between them.

"Of course," Peyton said.

Tawny-Lynn's heart was breaking as they left the building. She finally had her sister back and the answers she'd yearned for.

But she would never have the man she loved.

Chapter Nineteen

Chaz finished the press conference with a knot in his gut. He wanted to see Tawny-Lynn again, but she probably hated him now. After all, he'd been rough on her when they'd found Ruth.

He would deal with his feelings for her later. Today he had a job to do, and that meant tying up this case so Coach Wake would never see the light of day again.

With the story airing at noon, word would spread quickly in the small town. He'd left his deputy with Wake's lawyer and wife, and was grateful they'd left by the time he made it back to his office.

He had a message to call the M.E. and another from the lab. He phoned the M.E. first. "What did you find?"

"Unfortunately we didn't find any DNA from Coach Wake," the M.E. said. "There were some broken ribs, which probably happened in the accident. We think that she fell backward on a sharp object and hit her head. Could have been a rock. That's what killed her."

Chaz mentally pieced together the facts. Ruth must have crawled out of the bus, and Wake saw her. He chased her, maybe caught up with her and they argued. Then he pushed her and she fell and hit her head.

"Is that all you found?"

"I'm afraid so. Any DNA that might have been under

her nails was long ago washed away by the elements and decomp."

"Thanks." He hung up and phoned the crime lab, hoping they had more. "This is Sheriff Camden. Tell me you have good news."

"Nothing condemning yet, but we're trying to recover some DNA from one of the stones left at the gravesite."

"You think it's the one that killed her?"

"No, but the way it was stuck in the ground indicates it might have been used as a grave marker."

Chaz contemplated what he'd said. Had Wake marked the grave so he could come back and visit Ruth? Or maybe he'd planned to move her at some point?

"How about the bracelet?"

"There's a partial print we're working on. I'll let you know if we find a match."

A knock sounded on his door, and the deputy poked his head in. "Sheriff, there's a couple of people here to see you."

Chaz frowned. So the circus was starting.

He thanked the crime tech, then strode into the front area and was surprised to see Cindy Miller Parker and Rudy Farnsworth standing together.

"We need to talk to you," Cindy said.

Rudy bit down on her lip. "It's important. It's about the coach."

Chaz's stomach knotted. Surely to God they weren't here to say Peyton was lying.

"All right. Can I get you ladies something to drink? Coffee? Water?"

They both shook their heads, half-clinging to each other as he led them into his office. "Okay, what can I do for you?"

Cindy cleared her throat. "We heard about Coach Wake's arrest, and that Peyton Boulder said Coach seduced her."

Chaz nodded, steepling his hands on his desk and waiting.

"What she said is true," Rudy said, her voice quivering.

"How do you know?" Chaz asked.

They spoke at the same time, both looking straight at him with conviction. "Because he did the same thing to us."

"I KNOW THAT was difficult for you," Tawny-Lynn told her sister after they'd eaten lunch.

Peyton shrugged. "It felt good to finally come clean." She gave a sad smile. "I'm so sorry I left you to deal with the fallout after the bus crash."

"I'm sorry you felt like you couldn't come to Dad or me," Tawny-Lynn said.

Peyton shrugged. "Maybe one day we'll stop saying I'm sorry."

Tawny-Lynn lifted her glass of tea in a toast. "Let it be today. It's time to move forward from the past."

Peyton picked up her plate and carried it to the dishwasher. "Right. Now what can I do around here to help you get this place ready to sell?"

"The rain hasn't set in yet, so let's work outside," Tawny-Lynn suggested.

"We should probably hire someone to paint the house," Peyton said.

"Probably," Tawny-Lynn agreed. "But I can't afford that right now."

"I'll pay for it," Peyton said. "I have some money saved."

"All right. But you can take the expenses out of the ranch when we sell it."

"Who knows," Peyton said. "When you fix this place up, you might not want to leave."

Tawny-Lynn's heart squeezed. "I have to. I can't stay here."

"Why not?" Peyton said. "Is there someone special waiting in Austin?"

"No," Tawny-Lynn said. "Just my business."

"Maybe Camden Crossing needs a good landscaper. I saw several new developments going up on my way into town."

Tawny-Lynn shrugged. "It's just too difficult to be here, Peyton."

"Because of what happened, or because of Chaz?"

She narrowed her eyes. "Why would you ask about him?"

"I saw the way you two looked at each other," Peyton said. "You're in love with him, aren't you?"

Tawny-Lynn hadn't been close to anyone in so long that it felt strange to have her sister back, watching her, reading her so well. "He doesn't feel the same way," she said instead of denying the truth.

"Are you sure about that?" Peyton asked. "Because it looked to me like he was crazy about you."

"His family hates me," she said. "Mr. Camden crucified me after the crash, accused me of intentionally holding back information about you and Ruth."

"I'm sure he didn't mean it."

"Oh, he meant it all right. You know Chaz's father is rich and owns the town. He turned others against me. I would never be good enough for his son."

Peyton caught her arm. "If Chaz loves you, it doesn't matter what his father thinks."

"That's just it," she said, her voice cracking. "He doesn't love me." She headed to the kitchen sink. "Now, enough about the Camdens. I thought we'd plant some rosebushes today."

Peyton teared up again. "Let's plant yellow roses in the place where Ruth was buried."

Tawny-Lynn stacked her own plate in the dishwasher. Yellow roses for friendship seemed appropriate.

Tawny-Lynn's cell phone buzzed. She glanced at the

caller ID and saw it was Chaz, so she snatched it up.
"Hello."

"I wanted to let you and Peyton know that Cindy Miller
Parker and Rudy Farnsworth came in my office after the
press conference."

She frowned. "Really? Were they shocked about the
coach?"

Chaz made a low sound of disgust. "No. In fact, they
both made statements that Coach Wake pressured them
into having sex when they were in school, too."

Tawny-Lynn paused. No wonder they'd been standoff-
ish when she'd approached them. "So they'll testify and
back up Peyton's story?"

"Yes, so tell Peyton she's not alone in this."

Thank God.

"I have to go. I'm going to push Wake for a confession
now, so we can speed this process along."

Tawny-Lynn ended the call, then turned and told Peyton.

"I'm sorry he did the same thing to them," Peyton said.

"Me, too," Tawny-Lynn murmured. "But with their tes-
timonies, the charges should stick."

Peyton nodded, that haunted look back. "Let's go plant
those roses for Ruth."

FOR HOURS, CHAZ FENDED off calls from local citizens asking about Coach Wake's arrest. Parents were freaking out,
wanting to know details—if he'd only targeted girls or if
he'd sexually abused boys. When? How many?

The questions went on and on.

He finally let the machine pick up, deciding he'd listen
to the messages. If anyone had pertinent information, he'd
return the call.

A knock sounded on his office door, and his deputy
poked his head in. "Sheriff, there's a couple of people here
who insist on seeing you."

Chaz stood. "All right. Check the messages and let me know if we need to follow up on any of them."

When he stepped into the front, two sets of parents were waiting, along with two teenage girls.

"I'm Sheriff Camden," Chaz said. "What can I do for you?"

One of the fathers spoke up. "My name is Joe Lansing. We want to press charges against Coach Wake."

Chaz glanced back and forth between them. "Go on."

The mother of the first girl wrapped her arm around her daughter, a petite blonde they introduced as Joan. "After we saw the news, Joan came to me. She told me the coach forced her to have sex with him this past year."

Chaz narrowed his eyes at the girl. "Is that true?"

Joan lowered her head and nodded. "I was afraid to tell anyone. He said he'd cut me from the team."

"He said he loved me," the other girl said. "That if I wanted to play first string, I'd show him I loved him, too."

Chaz hesitated. He'd read about cases where teenagers made up stories to get attention. But the more he talked to the girls, the more he was convinced they were telling the truth.

"I'll need your statements written down," he said. "And will you testify in court?"

They both agreed, and so did the parents. Then he watched as the girls wrote out details that sickened him and made him want to go after Coach Wake all over again.

By the time they'd left, his deputy joined him with three more complaints from girls whose parents had called in. He phoned them all back and explained they would need to make formal statements.

Apparently, after word leaked about the coach's arrest, the team had met and the parents had encouraged their daughters to break the code of silence, that confessing what the coach had done didn't reflect badly upon them.

He admired them for their courage.

He strode back to the jail cell with the other two complaints in his hand.

Coach Wake stood, his anger palpable. "When is my arraignment? I want out of this hellhole."

Chaz folded his arms. "I don't think that's going to happen, Coach. I have two more written statements here from girls you've coached confirming that you forced them to have sex with you. And I'm getting calls about more."

"They're lying," Coach Wake said, although fear laced his voice.

"Really? You mean Peyton Boulder came all the way back here after seven years of silence to lie. So did Cindy Miller and Rudy Farnsworth. And those girls on your current team are lying, too."

"They wanted to have sex," he shouted bitterly. "They asked for it!"

"My sister didn't ask for it," Chaz said between clenched teeth. "In fact, she was going to tell my parents."

"She just wanted to play hard to get," Coach Wake muttered.

Chaz fisted his hands. He wanted to wrap them around the sicko's neck. "No, Ruth wasn't like that. You used your power and influence to rope the girls into your bed. And Peyton had the courage to stand up to you. Others have found it, too."

Chaz swallowed back bile. "In fact, Ruth stood up against you. That's why you killed her."

"I didn't kill her." Coach Wake's voice cracked. "I admit I had sex with Peyton and the other girls, and I was mad and chased after the bus, but I didn't mean to run into it. My car hit a wet patch and I skidded. It was an accident."

"An accident, but you stood and watched the bus explode and didn't even try to help those girls inside."

"It happened too fast. There was nothing I could do."

Chaz wasn't buying it—Wake was a lowdown coward. "You were angry and afraid your dirty secret would come out, so you found Ruth and killed her, then buried her out at White Forks to make the police think Peyton's father killed her."

Coach Wake gripped the bars. "I didn't kill Ruth. I saw Peyton pull Tawny-Lynn from the bus, then she went back, and I figured she'd get Ruth out. Then I heard a car coming."

"So instead of going down to try and rescue the other girls, you ran off and left them there in that burning bus."

Resignation and sorrow, the man's first hint at true emotions, lined the coach's face as he sank onto the cot again. "I panicked—I just panicked—and then I was scared to come forward. I didn't want to go to jail."

"So you let those girls die, then stood by while the town crucified Tawny-Lynn. Then you went back to your same old ways, sexually assaulting the students who trusted you."

"You don't understand, the girls, they're so young and flirty—"

"They are minors, teenagers, students who trusted you, and you took advantage of them."

Coach Wake scraped a hand over his chin. "So I had sex with some of them, but I didn't kill Ruth," Coach Wake said firmly. "I swear I didn't."

Chaz studied the man with a sick feeling in his belly. Wake had just admitted to sexual assault and causing the accident. So if he'd killed Ruth, why not confess to that, too?

Unless he hadn't murdered her…

But if he hadn't, who had?

Wake's wife's face flashed in his mind. She'd defended her husband. What if she'd known he was cheating with those younger girls?

She could have followed the bus or even been following her husband, then killed Ruth.

TAWNY-LYNN COLLAPSED into bed exhausted from the day's ordeal and the manual work she and Peyton had done outside. Not only had they planted flowers, but they'd cleaned out the barn, bought pine straw and spread wood chips around several trees in the yard nearest the house.

Knowing Coach Wake was in jail and Peyton was sleeping in the next room, she fell into a deep sleep. Surely the nightmares would leave her in peace now.

But some time later, a cold chill stirred her from sleep. The room was dark, the scent of a man's cologne suffusing her. She gasped, the dark blank face that had haunted her for years was back.

She blinked, hoping she was dreaming, but when she opened her eyes, he was there. Coming toward her.

She tried to scream, but a hand clamped over her mouth, then she felt the cold barrel of a gun against her temple.

Chapter Twenty

Chaz stewed over his conversation with the coach long into the night when he should have been sleeping.

Wake would go down for multiple counts of manslaughter for the bus driver and three teens. Coupled with the sexual assault charges, he would spend years in prison.

So why not confess to Ruth's murder?

His phone trilled, making the nerves in his neck tighten. Yesterday he'd thought he'd solved the cold case and maybe the town could heal. But now he wasn't so sure.

Another peal of the phone and he saw the number for White Forks on the caller ID screen. He gripped the phone, knowing it could be Peyton or Tawny-Lynn. "Sheriff Camden."

"Chaz, it's Peyton. Someone took Tawny-Lynn."

"What?" Cold sweat burst on his brow.

"I heard a scream and ran to her room, but she wasn't inside," Peyton cried. "Then I ran down the steps and saw someone in dark clothes dragging her outside."

"Who was it?"

"I don't know, I couldn't see. I'm scared, Chaz." A sob from Peyton echoed over the line. "You have to find her."

His mind raced. Tawny-Lynn had been in danger since she'd pulled into town. After making the arrest, he assumed

Coach Wake had been trying to scare her into leaving and keeping quiet.

But now?

"Chaz, I can't lose her," Peyton said. "Not when I just got her back."

He couldn't lose her, either. Not that she'd ever been his. But they had made love. And he'd thought she cared about him.

Then he'd blown it by hurling accusations at her.

"Tell me what else you saw. Was it a man or a woman?"

"I don't know," Peyton said. "It was so dark outside and whoever it was had on black clothes and a hood."

"Did her abductor say anything?"

"No, but I thought I saw something shiny glint in the darkness. I…think it was a gun."

His stomach knotted. "Lock the doors, Peyton. I'm going to send my deputy out there while I look for your sister."

Peyton agreed in a shaky voice, and he ended the call, then phoned his deputy and explained. "I don't want Peyton left alone for a minute. She may be in danger."

"I'm on my way," Deputy Lemone said.

Chaz hung up, grabbed his gun and holster and strapped it on. Several people in town, especially the parents of the girls in the crash, along with his own parents, had despised Tawny-Lynn for years. But after the arrest, there was no reason to go after her.

The only person he could think of with motive was the coach's wife. She was pregnant and obviously distraught over the accusations against her husband. She wouldn't want the father of her baby in prison when her child was born.

And maybe she thought that Tawny-Lynn had seen him—or her—at the crash site that day with Ruth.

He raced to his car and sped toward the Wake's house, praying that she hadn't hurt Tawny-Lynn.

TAWNY-LYNN STIRRED from unconsciousness. As soon as her abductor had gotten her to the car, he'd knocked her over the back of her head with the butt of his gun.

She blinked through the darkness, trying to see him and figure out where they were.

"Good, you're awake. Now it's time to write your suicide note."

Fear seized her at the sound of the voice. A very familiar voice.

She blinked again, struggling to sit up, then realized her legs and wrists were bound. He gripped her arm and hauled her to a sitting position.

Moonlight illuminated the dark face. The one that had been blank all these years.

Now it slid into focus.

Chaz's father.

Suddenly the past rushed back to her. She had roused from unconsciousness that day. And she'd seen him dragging Ruth away. Ruth was crying and shouting for him to let her go, but then Mr. Camden had struck her. Ruth fell against a rock, then the world had gone dark for her again.

"Why are you doing this?" she asked, her heart hammering. "Chaz arrested the coach. And I didn't remember anything."

"But you would have," he growled. "It was only a matter of time. I saw the way you looked at me yesterday." He shoved a notepad and pen into her hands. "You seduced my son, too. I can't take the chance—"

"On Chaz learning that you killed Ruth," Tawny-Lynn spat out. "You were at the crash site that day. You grabbed her and were arguing—"

Pain wrenched his face. "It was an accident," he said, his voice warbling. "She told me about Coach Wake and wanted me to go public."

"But you didn't want her to, did you?" Tawny-Lynn

started struggling with her hands, but he pressed the gun to her chest and she froze.

"Of course not," he snapped. "Everyone would have talked about it, talked about her, thought she was a slut. I couldn't let that happen."

"You could have stood up for her and stopped the coach," Tawny-Lynn said. "Instead you cared more about your pride and appearances, and your daughter died for it."

He gripped her arms and shook her. "Shut up. I told you it was an accident."

"Then why did you hide it? And how could you put her in the ground instead of giving her a proper burial?"

Tears streamed down his face. "I wanted to bury her right," he said. "But my wife wouldn't have understood. And Chaz… He would have hated me."

"So you turned the town against me?"

"Because if your sister hadn't started the affair with Coach Wake, he never would have come after Ruth."

"You're delusional," Tawny-Lynn said. "Chaz called me last night and said two other girls from our class came forward and made the same accusations. Who knows how many more girls will speak up now?"

"It doesn't matter," Camden said. "My wife and Chaz can't find out what happened that day, they can't." He tapped the notepad. "Now take that pen and write what I tell you to."

"Please, you don't have to do this," Tawny-Lynn whispered.

He jammed the pen between her fingers.

"No one will ever believe I killed myself," Tawny-Lynn said.

"Oh, yes, they will," Camden said in a sinister voice. "You're going to confess that you were jealous of Ruth and your sister, jealous of Ruth and the coach, and that you pushed Ruth down and made her fall."

CHAZ WAS SURPRISED to see a light on in Mrs. Wake's house. He glanced through the front living room window, searching for movement.

Footsteps sounded inside, and he held his gun at the ready in case Mrs. Wake was armed. How else would she have been able to force Tawny-Lynn from the ranch house?

He didn't see anything through the front window so he moved to the side and peered in. The window gave him a view of the kitchen where he saw Mrs. Wake pacing with her hand over her belly. She doubled over and cried out, and Chaz froze.

Was she in labor?

He eased around the side of the house, looking in other windows, but it was dark and he couldn't see anything. He craned his head to listen for sounds indicating Tawny-Lynn was inside, but nothing.

Finally he moved back to the kitchen window and saw Mrs. Wake collapse into a chair, one hand reaching for her phone. She knocked it off the table and leaned her head on her hands, heaving as she breathed through the contraction.

Dammit. Did she have Tawny-Lynn?

He circled back to the front door and pounded on it. Afraid the woman was in trouble, he jiggled the door but it was locked. "Mrs. Wake, it's Sheriff Camden. Open up please."

Seconds bled into minutes, then he heard her feet shuffling. When she opened the door, her face was contorted in pain, and she was clutching her belly.

"You're in labor?"

"How did you know?" she asked through a deep breath.

"I didn't. I'm looking for Tawny-Lynn Boulder."

Her cheeks reddened with exertion as she gripped the door. "Why would I know where she is?"

"Because someone kidnapped her from her house tonight."

Her eyes widened in shock, but another contraction seized her, and her legs buckled. He caught her before she hit the floor and put his arm around her waist.

"Come on, I'll drive you to the hospital."

"I need my husband," she whispered.

That wasn't going to happen. "Is Tawny-Lynn here?" he asked.

She shook her head. "Of course not." She made panting sounds as he helped her to the car. She fell into the seat, her face ashen.

He had to get her to the E.R. But he had to search the house first just in case she was lying.

"I'll be right back."

"Where are you going?" she cried.

He didn't answer. He ran back in the house, racing through each room and flipping on lights. He searched closets, the pantry, the attic, but the house was empty.

He noticed a suitcase on the floor and assumed it was Mrs. Wake's so he grabbed it and jogged down the steps. She was clutching the seat, heaving through another contraction, when he jumped inside.

"I got your bag."

"Get me to the hospital," she said. "Or I'm going to deliver this baby in your car."

He flipped on the siren and peeled from the drive. Thankfully traffic was nonexistent and the hospital was close by. Five minutes later, he roared into the emergency room driveway and threw the car into Park. He jumped out, yelling for help.

"This woman is about to deliver," he said as two E.R. workers raced out to meet him.

"Please, Sheriff, my husband should be here."

"I'm sorry." He couldn't make that happen right now, not with Tawny-Lynn missing and in danger. And his deputy was guarding Peyton. "Is there anyone else I can call?"

She shook her head. "My mother." She recited the number, and he called as he jumped back in his car. Five rings later, a woman answered, her voice laced with sleep.

"This is Sheriff Camden. Your daughter asked me to call you. She's in labor. I just dropped her at the hospital."

"Oh, thank you, Sheriff. I'll get there as soon as I can."

His phone was buzzing with another call as he pulled away. He checked the number and saw it was his mother. Why would she be calling him at 4:00 a.m.?

"Mom?"

"Chaz, I need you," she said in a shaky voice.

"What's wrong?"

"Your father…"

Had his father gone after the coach? "What happened?"

"He's gone."

"Gone where?"

"I don't know, but you have to come over here. We need to talk."

Fear rolled through Chaz. First Tawny-Lynn was kidnapped. Now his father was missing?

What the hell was going on?

He sped away from the hospital, siren blaring as he raced toward his parents' house. Worry clawed at him as he tried to make sense out of the situation. If Wake hadn't killed Ruth, then Tawny-Lynn had seen the killer that day after the crash, and the killer was afraid she'd still remember his or her face.

But why do something to his father?

He rounded the curve on two wheels, tires squealing as he swerved up the drive to his parents' estate. Sweat beaded on his head as he threw the car into Park and ran inside.

His mother met him at the door, her complexion pasty, her eyes red-rimmed. She'd been crying. "Oh, Chaz, I'm so afraid."

He hugged her and ushered her into the den to sit down. "What happened, Mom?"

She burst into tears. "I...don't know. He was so upset last night when we got home, and he started drinking. Then he pulled out all the old pictures of Ruth, and then I saw him looking at pictures of the crash and all the articles that ran afterward. The pleas we made for information on Ruth and Peyton, the story about Tawny-Lynn and the story about the coach's arrest."

He handed her a handkerchief and waited while she dried her eyes.

"I tried to talk to him, but he was so upset. Shouting and saying crazy things about blame and guilt and Tawny-Lynn seeing something."

A bad feeling gnawed at his gut. "Then what?"

"He grabbed his gun from his desk and said he had to finish things, to finally put everything to rest."

"What did he mean by that?"

"I don't know," his mother said in a shaky voice. "He just said he had to do it for our family. Then he took the gun and left."

"Was he going after Coach Wake?"

"No, I don't think so."

Chaz inhaled sharply. "Mom, Coach Wake admitted that he had sex with the girls and caused the bus crash, but he denied killing Ruth. If you know something, anything... please tell me."

Another storm of tears rained down her face, and she hugged her arms around her middle as if she might fall apart if she let go. "I don't know...not anything really."

Emotions threatened to overwhelm him. "But you suspect something?"

She nodded miserably. "That night...of the accident..." She heaved a sob. "That night I found Ruth's softball bag...I saw him hiding it."

"Dad had her bag?" The bag that was never recovered from the accident. They'd assumed it had burned in the fire.

"Yes. When I asked him, he went crazy and refused to talk about it. I...forgot about it for a while, but tonight when I saw him with the pictures, he had that bag again."

Chaz's blood ran cold. If his father had Ruth's gym bag, that meant he had been at the crash site.

He could have seen Ruth, talked to her...and if she'd told him about the coach...

No...it was impossible.

His father had a temper, had been overprotective of Ruth, had worried about appearances...

Cop instincts kicked in, and his mind took another dangerous leap. His father had been the one to lead the animosity against Tawny-Lynn. He'd barged into her room at the hospital.

Dear God. Had his father killed Ruth?

"You won't get away with this," Tawny-Lynn said as she finished the suicide note. "Chaz will figure out the truth."

Mr. Camden laughed harshly. "No, he won't. If he really does care about you, he'll be devastated to learn that you're the one who killed his sister, and that you used him all this time."

"He's smarter than you think," she said. "He doesn't let emotions interfere with his job." Sadly, she knew that firsthand.

He waved the gun in her face. "Shut up and get out."

"Chaz will never believe I killed myself."

"I'll take care of that." He dragged her toward the ravine. He'd parked at almost exactly the same spot where the bus had gone over the edge seven years ago. It fit with his plan.

Everyone would think that she was overcome with guilt and decided to end her life where she'd taken Ruth's.

"Even if Chaz believes you, my sister won't. Besides,

you've forgotten that I had a broken leg. There's no way I could have killed Ruth." She struggled against him. "How did you get her on White Forks without my father seeing you?"

Mr. Camden's voice trembled. "I buried her while he was at the hospital with you. Now it's time to end this."

He squeezed her arm. "You grabbed Ruth's leg and pushed her down," he said with a shrug of his shoulders. "She hit her head on a rock."

Tawny-Lynn shook her head. "Killing her was an accident. If you explained that Ruth fell, everyone would understand," she said, "but killing me is premeditated murder."

He shoved her toward the edge. "With you gone and your heartfelt confession, no one will ever know about either."

She stumbled forward, the ravine below resurrecting memories of the crash that day. She could hear the screams of the other girls as the bus went over.

Remembered the cries of the parents as they'd arrived. Her terror in searching for Peyton.

She'd finally found Peyton again. She couldn't die like this.

And she couldn't leave this world with Chaz thinking that she'd killed his sister.

Chapter Twenty-One

Panic crowded Chaz's chest. "Mother, someone broke in and abducted Tawny-Lynn tonight. Do you think Dad would hurt her?"

"I don't know, Chaz," she cried. "I've never seen him like this. He was…out of his head."

"I have to find him before he does something to her," he said. "Do you have any idea where he might take her?"

She shook her head as more tears filled her eyes and spilled over. "He just kept saying that the day of the crash ruined our lives. That Tawny-Lynn did."

If he was thinking about the crash, then he might go there, take Tawny-Lynn back to the place where everything had fallen apart.

He squeezed his mother's hands. "I have to go. If you hear from him, call me."

She nodded, terror streaking her face. "Please find him, stop him," she whispered. "If he hurt Ruth, he didn't mean to. But if he hurts Tawny-Lynn—"

"I know," he said. "I know."

He pushed to his feet and jogged back outside. His tires screamed as he accelerated, sped down the drive and veered onto the highway.

He phoned his deputy, relieved when he answered. "How's Peyton?"

"Worried." He paused. "Did you find Tawny-Lynn?"

"Not yet. But I have a lead. Stay with Peyton. I'll call you back."

He hung up, then swung onto the road leading to the bus crash site, his heart throbbing. Dawn was on the horizon, red and orange swirls painting the sky, promising a clear day instead of the rain the weatherman had predicted.

As he rounded the curve, he spotted his father's car on the side of the road, parked sideways, nose heading toward the ravine. He slowed, his breath stalling.

His father stood behind Tawny-Lynn, a gun pressed to her back.

He rolled the car to a stop several hundred feet back, then eased his door open. In spite of the fact that he was careful, gravel crunched beneath his boots as he slowly walked toward them.

His father swung his head toward him. His mother was right. He'd never seen his father looking so crazed. He tightened his hold on Tawny-Lynn's arm. "Don't come any closer, Chaz."

"Dad, you have to stop this right now," Chaz said. "You don't want to hurt Tawny-Lynn."

"She has to die—don't you see that?" his father snarled. "She saw me that day. She'll ruin everything for our family."

"It's not her fault." Chaz's gaze met Tawny-Lynn's. She looked scared, but gave him such a look of sorrow and trust that he nearly choked on his love for her.

Love?

Yes, he did love her, he realized. But he'd been such a fool that he'd never told her.

Instead he'd run from his feelings for her by turning on her like everyone in the town had.

TAWNY-LYNN HATED the anguish in Chaz's eyes. She'd never once suspected his father of killing Ruth. And neither had Chaz.

He had to be in shock.

"Just walk away, Chaz, and let me handle this. You'll see. She wrote out a confession." He waved the barrel of the gun at her temple. "She was jealous of Ruth and Peyton, jealous of the coach because he wanted Ruth, not her. Isn't that right, Tawny-Lynn?"

She cut him a scathing look. "You know that's not what happened, Mr. Camden."

"I can't lose my family," Camden said, anger radiating from his every pore. "I won't."

"You will if you kill Tawny-Lynn, Dad," Chaz said in a gruff voice. "Right now, Mom and I know that what happened with Ruth was an accident. But doing this, intentionally hurting Tawny-Lynn is not the same thing."

"I didn't mean to do it," he said. "Ruth was arguing with me. She said she was going to tell everyone about Coach Wake. I just tried to stop her and I grabbed her arm, but she fell. Her head hit a rock." Tears clogged his voice. "I loved Ruth…."

"I know that, and so does Mom." Chaz slowly inched toward his father.

"We can forgive that, Dad. It was an accident. But we can't forgive you if you hurt Tawny-Lynn."

His father's hand trembled, the gun shaking as he waved it back and forth between himself and Tawny-Lynn.

"Dad, please put down the gun." Chaz held out his hand. "Just set it on the ground and we'll talk."

"No, then everyone will know…" He swung the gun up and aimed it at his own head, and fear seized Tawny-Lynn. If Chaz's father killed himself, Chaz would never get over the guilt.

Camden clenched his hand tighter on the gun, but Tawny-Lynn threw a sharp jab to his side with her elbow and knocked his gun hand up into the air. The gun fired, a bullet flying upward, but in his panic, Camden shoved her aside.

Chaz lunged toward his father, wrestling for the gun. The gun fired again, but Chaz managed to wrangle it from his father's hands and tossed it a few yards away, then threw his father onto the ground.

She stumbled, lost her footing and slid. Gravel rained down the ravine as she slipped over the side.

She screamed, grappling for something to hold on to so she wouldn't plunge into the ravine below.

CHAZ FRANTICALLY SEIZED his father's hands and yanked them behind his back, then snapped handcuffs around his wrists. He didn't want to arrest him, but he had to take him in.

Tawny-Lynn's scream brought him out of his shock, and he jerked his head up and saw her going over the edge. She'd saved his father's life by throwing that punch.

He couldn't let her die.

"Stay put, Dad," Chaz said in a low growl in his father's ear. He ran to the edge of the embankment, then knelt. Tawny-Lynn had managed to grab a rock jutting out, but dirt and gravel were spewing down the embankment in her face, and her fingers were slipping.

"Hang on," he shouted. "I've got you."

He wrapped his fingers around one wrist, then reached for the other hand but she lost hold. Her hand missed, and she dangled over the ravine. His arm muscles strained as he braced himself in the dirt and stretched to reach for her.

"Chaz!" she cried. "I can't hold on."

"Yes, you can! You have to," he said. "Trust me."

She was trembling, her body flailing to grab hold. He fell to his belly and stretched, finally latching on to her other arm. Her fingers dug into his wrist, and he grunted and slowly hauled her up over the edge, crawling backward and pulling her with him until they were safely away from the overhang.

His father lifted his head and looked up, his expression defeated as Chaz folded Tawny-Lynn into his arms.

"I'm sorry," he whispered into her hair.

"I…didn't remember, not until tonight."

No wonder she'd blocked it out. "I know, I know." He cupped her face between his hands and checked her for injuries. "Are you all right?"

She nodded, although tears trickled down her face. "I'm sorry, Chaz…. Sorry about Ruth."

"Shh," he murmured. Then he wrapped her in his embrace. "I love you, Tawny-Lynn. I was so afraid I was going to lose you before I could tell you."

She looked into his eyes, the sweet passionate, courageous woman he'd come to know staring back. "I love you, too, Chaz."

His heart swelled with emotions, with the need to hold her, possess her, to keep her near.

They had to talk about the future, deal with his father, with his mother…

But not yet.

For now, he bent his head and kissed her, savoring the fact that she was alive and in his arms.

Epilogue

Tawny-Lynn couldn't believe how happy she was. Today was her wedding day.

Peyton peeked in, then straightened her veil. "You look beautiful, sis."

"Thanks." Tawny-Lynn hugged her sister, thanking God every day that Peyton had survived. "I like Ben."

Peyton smiled. "He's a good guy. He's been patient with me. And—" she wiggled her finger, a diamond glittering on her left hand "—he asked me to marry him."

"That's wonderful." They hugged through their tears, then Peyton pulled away, grabbed them tissues and laughed. "Now, stop crying or you'll mess up your makeup."

Tawny-Lynn dried her eyes, and Peyton hurried to the door. "Come on, they're about to play the wedding march!"

A sliver of sadness dampened her mood as she opened the door and saw Chaz's mother sitting alone in the front row in one of the chairs they'd set up for the ceremony. Arresting Chaz's father had torn Chaz apart, but he didn't blame Tawny-Lynn. He'd had to do it for Ruth.

His father had pleaded guilty to kidnapping and threatening her, and was spending time in a psychiatric facility to receive counseling. Mrs. Camden, though heartbroken about her husband, had actually apologized to Tawny-Lynn for the brutal way they'd treated her years ago. Occasionally things were tense, but they were working hard at a relationship because they both loved Chaz.

She and Peyton had decided to keep the ranch. Chaz was moving in with her and planned to help her repair the house. Cindy Miller had introduced Tawny-Lynn to her husband who'd hired her to do all the landscaping at the new developments around town.

For a girl who'd felt shunned by the town, she finally felt a part of it.

Peyton had worked with one of their old classmates, Andrea Radcliff, who had opened a bridal shop, to set up the wedding on the lawn of the ranch. With the garden she'd planted, a gazebo draped in lace and fresh flowers and a white tent complete with champagne and wedding cake, the place looked gorgeous and more romantic than she could have imagined.

Peyton, dressed in a summery pale blue sundress, carried a bouquet of lilies. Tawny-Lynn smiled as she followed her sister down the center aisle between the rows of white chairs.

When she saw Chaz standing at the foot of the gazebo in his long, dark duster and cowboy hat, her heart leaped with joy.

CHAZ'S GAZE MET his bride-to-be's beautiful eyes, and he couldn't believe this day had finally arrived.

The day he was going to make Tawny-Lynn his wife.

His deputy surprised him by admitting that he played guitar, and now was strumming the wedding march as Tawny-Lynn walked down the aisle.

She was so beautiful that it made his heart hurt every time he thought about the fact that he'd almost lost her. That wild wheat-colored hair of hers fluttered in the wind as she approached, the red roses she carried stark against the soft, white, strapless dress hugging her curves.

He couldn't wait to take it off her.

She paused in front of him, and he took her hand and led her up the steps of the gazebo. The reverend commenced the short ceremony, and minutes later, announced them man and wife.

Chaz turned to Tawny-Lynn and framed her face between his hands. "I love you, Mrs. Camden."

"I love you, too," she whispered.

Then he claimed her mouth with his lips, pouring his heart and love into their first kiss as husband and wife.

* * * * *

Look for the sequel to
COLD CASE AT CAMDEN CROSSING,
COLD CASE AT CARLTON'S CANYON,
featuring Texas Ranger Justin Thorpe and
Sheriff Amanda Blair as they tackle
the case of the missing girls from Sunset Mesa!

Coming January 2014, only from Intrigue!

"Best thing you ever tasted. Right?"

With a run of his tongue across his lips, he stared at her. "Yeah, and the cookie's not half-bad, either."

"I want to—" Before her brain stopped her, she pressed her lips to his mouth, and her body leaned into him.

Daniel didn't resist. His arm snaked around her waist and tightened his hold, drawing her to him. He took over, parting her lips, exploring her mouth, holding her captive with his caress.

Lord, he could kiss.

Forget chocolate. She had a whole new favorite taste. Raven wrapped her arms around his neck and held him closer, taking the kiss even deeper.

With a groan he eased back. "This is a bad idea," he said softly.

"I don't care," she whispered against his mouth. And she didn't. She just wanted to feel.

THE CRADLE CONSPIRACY

BY
ROBIN PERINI

MILLS & BOON

First published in Great Britain 2013
by Mills & Boon, an imprint of Harlequin (UK) Limited,
Eton House, 18-24 Paradise Road, Richmond, Surrey TW9 1SR

© Robin L. Perini 2013

ISBN: 978 0 263 90384 3

46-1213

Harlequin (UK) policy is to use papers that are natural, renewable and recyclable products and made from wood grown in sustainable forests. The logging and manufacturing processes conform to the legal environmental regulations of the country of origin.

Printed and bound in Spain
by Blackprint CPI, Barcelona

Award-winning author **Robin Perini**'s love of heart-stopping suspense and poignant romance, coupled with her adoration of high-tech weaponry and covert ops, encouraged her secret inner commando to take on the challenge of writing romantic suspense novels. Her mission's motto: "When danger and romance collide, no heart is safe."

Devoted to giving her readers fast-paced, high-stakes adventures with a love story sure to melt their hearts, Robin won a prestigious Romance Writers of America Golden Heart Award in 2011. By day she works for an advanced technology corporation, and in her spare time you might find her giving one of her many nationally acclaimed writing workshops or training in competitive small-bore-rifle silhouette shooting. Robin loves to interact with readers. You can catch her on her website, www.robinperini.com, and on several major social-networking sites, or write to her at PO Box 50472, Albuquerque, NM 87181-0472, USA.

Dedicated to the warriors from all walks of life who battle post-traumatic stress disorder, and the families who fight beside them every minute of every hour of every day. May your journey find light, hope, love and peace.

Chapter One

She came to slowly, her head throbbing, crippling pain skewering her temple like an ice pick digging deep. Without opening her eyes, she tried to lift her hand to touch the side of her head, but her arm wouldn't move, almost as if it were pinned against her body. Confusion swept over her, and she forced her eyes open to sheer, cloying darkness. The air around her was fetid and stale, stinking of dirt, wet wool and…

And blood.

Oh, God. Where was she? Desperation clutched at her throat.

She struggled to move, but her arms were numb. Something held her as if she were encased in a straitjacket. Frantic, she lifted her head, and her face bumped up against what felt like cheap shag carpet. She clawed her fingers beneath her and identified the distinctive weave. This couldn't be happening.

Instinctively she gasped for air, the darkness pressing down like a vise clamped on her chest.

Was she buried alive?

Her stomach rolled, and bile rose in her throat. She couldn't get sick. She had to escape.

She twisted and turned, struggling against the suffocating prison, scratching at the rough fabric. It was above her, below her, around her. She fought to free herself, panic mounting from deep within.

She rocked back and forth. Dirt and dust shook free. She sucked in a breath, and her lungs seized on the foul air. She had to get out.

"Help," she tried to scream, then fell to coughing as if she'd used up the meager air supply.

Worse, the rug had muffled the sound of her voice. Wherever she was buried, would anyone hear her cries? "Oh, God. Someone help me. Please," she croaked in a voice she didn't recognize.

Her breathing turned shallow. The air had thinned.

She sucked in one more desperate breath and froze, aware of a new scent, far more subtle than the rest. It penetrated her mind. Sweet, familiar, and so very, very wrong. Baby lotion.

Nausea suddenly churned, and her dread escalated. Strange visions stirred through her. A pink blanket. A tiny crib. But along with the images came stabbing pain in her head that nearly shattered her.

Her thoughts grew fuzzy, and she fought to hold on to reality. Somehow she knew, if she closed her eyes, she would never wake up. She couldn't pass out. She had to find...

A name flitted at the dark edges of her memory, then slipped away, leaving despair and terror. She turned toward the sweet scent again and breathed deeper. More flashes. Pain. Fear.

A stranger's voice screaming, "No!"

Lights exploded behind her eyelids and darkness engulfed her, closing around one wisp of memory.

The last sound she heard was a baby's terrified cry.

THE AFTERNOON SUN beat down on Daniel Adams from a bright West Texas sky. He adjusted his dusty brown Stetson to block the back of his neck and stood at a fork in the road, not a cloud in sight, not a car to be seen, nothing to tempt him to travel one way more than the other. He could choose a twisting blacktop leading into the Guadalupe Mountains or the county road veering east.

The dirt road headed in the general direction of Carder, Texas. He had friends there who'd made it clear he had a place waiting at Covert Technology Confidential. Staffed with former Special Forces, CIA and FBI operatives, CTC helped people in big trouble with nowhere to turn. The only rule they followed: justice.

Daniel wanted to be there, but he couldn't put himself back into the battle.

Not yet.

He was still too screwed up from his imprisonment and torture in the small European country of Bellevaux. Right now all he wanted was to find his way back to normal from the PTSD and not eat a bullet like his old man had done to deal with the same thing.

Daniel looked around again, frustrated he couldn't even decide which way to go next.

He *normally* made split-second, life-or-death decisions, but that was before. Before he'd been thrown in a dungeon, before the bastards had taken a whip to every inch of his body, an iron bar to his legs, and so flayed his mind with lies and threats that he'd almost broken.

For what seemed like an eternity, he'd fought every damn day with every ounce of strength to stay alive, to not give the interrogator the information he'd wanted.

In the end, Daniel had prayed for death.

Like his old man.

But Daniel was still alive. He'd been found, then stuck full of tubes and even now had more metal holding him together than Wolverine. Against the odds the doctors had given him, he'd healed, then stood and, after six months of recovery in the States, had walked again.

Daniel was broken. He knew it; the CTC operatives knew it. Only his family and his therapist held out hope. *Talk about delusional.* Daniel knew better.

What other reason would a man sleep outside and walk the highways and dirt roads from Langley, Virginia, ending up in Texas months later? A bit Forrest Gump, but Daniel couldn't face his team till he knew his PTSD didn't endanger anyone, until the memories and flashbacks no longer turned him into a terrified beast, striking out at everyone. So here he was, facing miles of desert plateaus, prickly pears and the occasional rattler.

Alone. Mostly.

Trouble followed him. Literally.

Trouble was the name he'd given the foolish dog he'd rescued, who'd warily taken up residence about ten feet from Daniel's side. He glanced at the mixed breed—some odd combination of Newfoundland and Irish setter that made him look like Chewbacca. *Dog must be dying in this heat with all that fur.*

Daniel knelt down and slid the duffel from his shoulder. He tugged a metal bowl from one pocket and set it on the ground. He didn't dwell on why he'd taken to carrying it with him; he just filled the dish half full from his canteen. He rose and stared at the water, then the dog. "What are you waiting for?"

Trouble tilted his head and sat on his haunches, his expression all but saying, *Move back, stupid. You know how this works.*

Daniel sighed and retreated. "Fine. But one of these days, you're going to have to come closer than ten feet."

As soon as Daniel reached the required distance, the

mutt bounded to the water, burying his face in the cool liquid.

Daniel had found the fuzz face lying on the side of the road with his leg and hip scraped up after losing a one-sided battle with a car. Since Trouble wouldn't let Daniel touch him, Daniel had been forced to rig a makeshift travois and drag the miserable canine five miles to a vet's office. The doc tranquilized the dog and patched up his injuries, but the moment the vet had given him the opportunity, Trouble had hightailed it out the front door and down a back alley.

A couple miles later, the animal had taken up residence parallel to Daniel, walking along the highway, never again getting close enough for even a scratch behind the ears. They'd passed a road sign, listing Trouble, Texas, three hundred miles away, and the dog instantly had a name.

That was a couple of weeks ago. The dog limped less now, Daniel a bit more.

Yesterday they'd made it to the small Texas town bearing the dog's name. Daniel had stood in the cramped, dark foyer of a B and B, testing his body's reaction to it, but knew he still couldn't sleep inside. Nothing to do but move on.

The waitress at the diner had told him there was nothing but lost dreams for miles around. She hadn't been lying. The beat-up sign he now leaned against—Cottonwood Creek Copper Mine—could've come from the 1950s.

He really had traveled west of hell to end up a few miles east of nowhere.

Trouble finished his water, nosed the empty bowl toward Daniel, then moved away.

"We're a pair, aren't we, boy?" Daniel said softly. "Too damaged to do anyone any good."

As Daniel repacked the dish, the dog's ears perked up, and he growled low in his throat.

"What's the matter with you?" Daniel turned to see what had upset Trouble and noticed a black vulture circling nearby. "Relax. It's probably eyeing the carcass of a cow that wandered away from the herd."

The dog's hackles rose as he focused his attention on a hill jutting up from the desert. Without a backward glance, Trouble bolted toward the mound. And that vulture.

What the hell? The dog hadn't left Daniel's sight since they'd become traveling companions. "Trouble!" The hairs on the back of Daniel's neck rose, and a warning chill ran through him. He started after the dog that had disappeared from view.

Within a minute the mutt bounded toward Daniel, skidding to a halt a few feet away. Trouble barked urgently several times, ran back a short distance, then turned and barked again.

"What's going on, boy? Show me."

Trouble whined and yipped, then ran. Daniel, his gait uneven, took off after the dog.

The vulture still circled but lower now.

He followed Trouble over the small rise, past a dead rabbit, then came to an abrupt halt.

Trouble circled in front of the dilapidated opening to an old mine, the mouth leading into the dark interior of the mountain. When he saw Daniel, the dog barked again and raced into the tunnel.

A mine shaft. Complete with a condemned sign and evidence of a partial cave-in. Rock walls, claustrophobic darkness. He couldn't go in there. Daniel sucked in a panicked breath, trying to quell his racing heart and the terror that bubbled up from his gut.

The dog didn't come out of the mine.

While Daniel watched, more loose stones fell from the mine's ceiling. "Trouble!"

The dog appeared several feet inside the opening and barked furiously.

Perspiration slid down Daniel's temple. He couldn't do it. Not now. Not ever. The dog growled, racing back and forth, entreating Daniel to follow.

Bracing himself, Daniel stepped barely into the opening, kicking something metal that clanged off the rocks, like the slamming of iron prison bars. A medieval dungeon. Memories assaulted him. The darkness echoing with screams. No, he was in a mine shaft. Still, he heard the footsteps of his captor. The crack of the bastard's whip.

Daniel fell to his knees, fighting to stay present, to escape the horrific memories, until Trouble dropped something in front of Daniel and bit his sleeve. Daniel broke free, panting, and his hand landed on a woman's shoe. Daniel's gut clenched. High heels weren't exactly appropriate for trudging around the Texas desert.

Hell. Was there a woman in here?

Trouble grabbed his shirt again and tugged hard. Daniel snagged a small but powerful flashlight clipped to his belt and shone the beam into the tunnel. The crumbling shaft veered left, debris and broken supports everywhere. Trouble bolted ahead and waited at the bend.

Grasping at his primary PTSD tool, Daniel focused on the grounding techniques he'd learned in therapy and forced himself forward into the shadows. An all-too-familiar panic squeezed his lungs. The walls pressed in until the cave morphed into a stone cell.

Pain level, eight.

Fighting to stay in the present, Daniel clutched the flashlight in a white-knuckled grip. He stared at the illuminated circle, narrowing his gaze. Sounds still reverberated. Trouble's barks morphed into sadistic laughter. The dirt seemed to hold the scent of torture and blood.

He fought against every survival instinct that raged within, that urged him to run. Struggling for control, Daniel moved forward. He wasn't in Bellevaux, he was in Texas. Broken, but free.

"Anyone here?" he shouted.

His words echoed in the darkness, but only silence answered him.

A sprinkling of dirt fell on his head, and the timbers creaked. He froze. The flashlight's beam hit a large heap of rocks, filling half the tunnel.

"Trouble?" Where the hell had the dog gone?

Suddenly he heard an odd moan coming from around the tunnel bend. Was that Trouble...or a human?

"Hello? Is someone there?"

Trouble barked, then reappeared to tug on Daniel's pant leg, frantic now.

Daniel followed the dog into the blackness, concentrating on the small beam of light that helped him keep the nightmares at bay.

The dog rounded the debris and led Daniel to a six-foot-long pile of rocks and dirt, hidden behind the mound from a cave-in. The dog scrabbled among the rocks, desperately trying to dig through them.

Daniel knelt down just as several stones fell away, revealing a bloodstained patch of multicolored carpet and silvery-gray tape.

Duct tape.

Another high-heeled shoe lay a few feet from the mound, and a quiet wail sounded again from beneath the rocks.

Trouble whined and pawed at the carpet.

A steely calm came over Daniel, not complete, but

closer than he'd felt in almost a year. Someone was alive and needed him.

His damn freak-out would have to wait until later. He needed to keep it together now.

After propping the flashlight so he could see, he shoved several rocks to the side. The smell of blood hit him, nearly slamming him into a flashback, but he fought for control.

Daniel swept aside the small rocks that covered the carpet, then threw the larger ones to the side.

"Help me…" The voice faded to silence.

He grabbed the Bowie from his leg sheath and slashed through the two taped areas with the knife, then rolled the carpet open. A woman, beaten and bloody, lay half-comatose on the filthy carpet.

Daniel pressed his fingers against her throat and felt the thread of a pulse.

She was chilled and in rough shape, but alive.

Relief loosened some of Daniel's tenuous hold on his emotions, so he quickly ran his hands over her arms and legs, knowing he needed to get them both out of this death trap fast. His examination didn't reveal any broken bones or severe lacerations on her body, but blood caked one side of her face and hair. The rest of her long hair spread across the carpet like a raven's wings.

He'd seen enough of the birds growing up in Texas, and he'd befriended one in Bellevaux while on surveillance. Sitting in the tree above his hideout, for the price of a few breadcrumbs the damn bird had kept Daniel from going insane while he'd been stuck in one location for weeks. After being forced into that godforsaken dungeon, Daniel had imagined the raven's life. Outside his cell. Outside the prison. Free. Daniel would imagine being free someday like the raven, and used the memory as a lifeline when the world had seemed hopeless.

Maybe this was a sign?

Or maybe he had totally lost his mind, and it was just dawning on him now.

The ground trembled slightly.

Daniel cursed, then scooped her into his arms and stood. "Let's go, Trouble."

The woman's eyes opened, gorgeous, fear-filled eyes, the color of cinnamon. "Who are you? Did I come here with you?"

"I'm not the one who put you here," he said. A rumble sounded from somewhere overhead. He let out a curse. "We're in an unstable mine, and we have to get out. Now."

Her eyes widened. He clutched her close against his chest and took off toward the bend.

The mountain shook again, then a spray of dirt and debris showered over both of them before one of the ceiling supports gave way with a loud crack.

"Cave-in!" Daniel curled her beneath him and covered her with his body, hoping she wasn't bleeding internally. And hoping to hell the roaring panic slamming through his mind didn't make him explode. They were being buried alive, and he was losing it fast.

DIRT AND ROCKS pelted the ground around her, but they didn't hit or hurt her. The man lying on top of her let out a soft grunt, his broad shoulders protecting her from the onslaught.

The dog she'd seen momentarily, before all hell broke loose in the cave, now sidled up against her and whined, burying his cold nose against her hand. She grabbed its fur, then slowly released her grip enough to pet it, trying to calm the animal's fears as well as her own.

The man groaned and shifted against her; the contours of his hips and thighs settled over her, pinning her down.

She took a panicked breath. Who was he? She couldn't remember him, and yet he'd protected her.

And why had he said he wasn't the one who put her here?

She couldn't be sure of anything with the incessant pounding in her head. Her mind spun with confusion. A bevy of rocks cascaded down the wall, thudding on the ground. At any moment the cave could bury them both.

She knew they had to escape but couldn't focus on anything except the feel of strong arms holding her and the hard body shielding her from the cave-in. She couldn't let reality in because something was horribly, horribly wrong. She was supposed to be somewhere. Doing…something. Something important but she couldn't remember what.

Her heart seized, and she struggled to regain control.

"Hey, you okay?" the man on top of her whispered. "I'm going to try to move and see what shape we're in."

As he spoke, his warm breath caressed her ear, helping her relax a bit. She didn't know why, but she felt safe with him. Which was stupid, considering where they were.

The mountain around them rumbled again, and she trembled, gripping his shirt. He wrapped her closer, pressing her cheek against his chest. Despite his calm demeanor, his heart raced. Did he think they would die here? Her head throbbed like the devil pummeling his way into heaven, but she didn't want to move. She didn't want to know they were trapped.

When the tremors stopped, he raised his head. She blinked and stared at his face. The beam from the flashlight had gone dim in the dust, but she could make out his features. Barely. His dirt-filled hair fell over his forehead and nearly reached his chin. The scar down one side of his cheek made him look like a pirate, and the hard pulsing line of his jaw seemed to confirm her worst fears. "Are we going to die?"

The shadow that swept through his hazel eyes was there and gone so fast she thought she'd imagined it.

"No."

"Thank you, if you're lying." She reached up to his face and touched his cheek, his jaw still clenched, contradicting his assurances.

He met her gaze, and his eyes flashed with gold. "Are you hurt?"

She tried to sit up, but rocks surrounded them. Oh, dear God, how would they get out of here? She couldn't breathe. Her head throbbed worse whenever she moved, and her heart thudded against her chest like she had run a sprint. The feeling that she had to do something struck again. What was she supposed to be doing? Every time she tried to focus, pain stabbed through her brain, triggering flashes of light and odd sounds...and terror.

"My head feels like it's going to explode, and I'm seeing double. I can't think."

She struggled to rise, and the world grayed. She clutched at his shirt, twisting the fabric hard. She panted and stared at him, unblinking, willing the world to come into focus.

The first thing she noticed was the bloodstained carpet, and she gasped. "Was I inside that?"

The man backed away, preparing to stand aside, but she clung to his cotton shirt. She didn't want him to leave. She needed him close. He was the only thing real in this craziness. "Someone tried to kill me, didn't they?" she asked, pressing her hand to her bloodied forehead.

She should know the answer, but her entire mind was blank.

"I don't know what happened," he whispered, his voice deepening. He stroked the back of her hand, his touch gentle but steady. "But you're fine. Just breathe in. I need you calm for us to escape."

His gaze held her captive. He took in a deep but shaky breath.

She did the same. The dog pushed against her leg, and she curled her fingers in its fur again. Daniel exhaled, and she mimicked him, breath for breath. Unable to look away, she pinned her focus on him, inhaling through her nose, letting her lungs expand and fill.

Her grip eased a bit on his shirt, but not enough that she couldn't feel the rapid heartbeat beneath her hand. "Are *you* okay?"

Something dark and haunted crossed his face again. A second later it was gone.

"I'm fine, but you've got a hell of a knot on your head."

She raised her hand and felt the swelling and the sticky residue. A small whine escaped her. "It hurts."

"I bet it does." He pressed his fingers gently against her scalp. "Why don't you sit back down and drink while I dig us out." He tugged a canteen from his belt, tilting it against her lips.

Gratefully she let the water sluice down her throat. "Thank you." Her voice cleared somewhat.

She took another sip. "How did you find me?"

"Trouble must have heard you." The man turned and started pulling stones to the side to clear the passageway.

"Trouble?"

"The dog. I'm Daniel, by the way." He threw a large rock farther away. "And your name?"

She opened her mouth, and nothing came out. Why couldn't she think of it? Everyone knew their own name. In an instant the crushing pain was back. The flashes of light. Muffled cries and hazy images. Trying desperately to stop her head from spinning, she clutched the heart-

shaped locket around her neck like a good-luck talisman.
"Oh, my God…"

Daniel turned around at the panic in her voice.

"I don't know my name." Her hands clutched at his.
"Daniel, how can I not know my own name?"

Chapter Two

The dust from the mine filtered the beam from the flashlight, but it was more than enough to let Daniel know they were screwed. Sweat that had nothing to do with exertion slid down his back. He was fighting off a PTSD meltdown and now this. How could he comfort her when he felt borderline psychotic?

He had to get outside. Fast.

"What's my name?" the woman repeated, her voice shaking.

Daniel's grip tightened on the rock he held. He hated the fear and bewilderment in her words, and he'd be damned if he let her see his alarm for both of them.

The blood on her temple oozed again, droplets landing on her dusty silk shirt. Someone had wanted her dead. That person might still succeed if Daniel didn't dig them out quickly. He had no answers for this terrified woman, and couldn't give her much in the way of comfort except to wrap her in his arms and hope she mistook his trembling as her own.

Daniel stroked her dark hair. "You're going to be okay," he reassured, knowing his words may not be true. "Once that bump goes down, you'll remember everything."

"What if I don't?" She shivered.

He pressed her closer. "You will. It's common with head injuries to be a little fuzzy."

She shook her head, then winced, pressing her hand to her temple. "This isn't fuzzy. *I. Can't. Remember. My. Name.*" She paused, her eyes widening, then she whispered, "I can't remember...anything."

Swearing internally, Daniel gently stroked her black hair and forced what he hoped was a confident smile to his face. "Maybe we should call you Trouble. You deserve the moniker more than the mutt over there."

At the sound of his name, Trouble's head cocked.

"Or we could go the princess route. Sleeping Beauty might be appropriate." Daniel kept his tone light, trying to divert her focus...and his. "Except she had blond hair. You could be Snow White. Her hair was black."

A small smile tilted the corners of the woman's mouth. "You're an idiot, but thanks." She bit her lip. "Seriously I can't just pick a name out of thin air."

"Then I'll do it for you." He studied her amazing brown eyes and once more touched the long, silky strands of hair. Black as night. Or *like a raven's wing*... "How about I call you Raven for now? After your hair color. Just until you remember."

"Raven, huh?" she said, her voice small and vulnerable.

"Raven suits you," Daniel admitted. "It's striking and unforgettable. Like you." He pulled back his hand. "Now I have to get back to work."

Methodically he picked up one rock after another, telling himself he'd break through soon. But he could feel the churning in his mind and gut. He took a cleansing breath, praying for control.

His hands grew slippery with sweat. He would not give in to the panic.

The shrinks had diagnosed him with post-traumatic stress disorder soon after his rescue from Bellevaux.

Like Daniel hadn't recognized the symptoms already.

His combat-vet father had suffered from PTSD nightmares and flashbacks as long as Daniel could remember—until his dad had ended it with a bullet to his brain. Daniel had found him, and the sight haunted him still.

At the memory Daniel's heart raced, pounding against his ribs as if it would burst through any second. He closed his eyes to stall another attack.

A furry nose nuzzled its way beneath his hand. What the hell? Now the dog decided to make friends? Daniel's fingers curled through Trouble's coat. If Trouble could work through his issues, Daniel wasn't about to succumb to his. He had no time to wallow in imaginary fears. Even if they felt completely real.

"We'll be fine," he announced, perhaps as much to hear the words aloud as to calm Raven. But he'd noticed it getting harder to breathe with all the dust. He came upon a few large stones, and he lugged them away, one at a time.

Each time he rose to his feet, steadying himself on the leg his captors had broken in three places, it became harder. If his leg gave out, they'd be in a world of hurt. He dragged a wooden beam toward the back and bumped into something. He turned, noticing a big painted box with a large letter *C* carved into the top. One corner of the lid was bloody, with a few pieces of black hair stuck to the surface. It didn't take Sherlock Holmes to recognize the match to Raven's head wound. Besides, kids' toy boxes didn't wind up in deserted mines by accident.

Using the edge of his shirt, Daniel opened the lid. Empty. "Raven? Do you recognize this box?"

Before she could respond, Trouble snapped to attention. He whined and let out a loud bark, pacing back and forth in the confined space. Another rumble sounded from somewhere inside the mountain.

"We're out of time. I think if I pull out a few more rocks, you can get through."

She tried to walk, but her legs buckled beneath her.

He grabbed her, and she held her body stiff. "Forget me. Dig." She pushed on his chest. "Go!"

Another rumble resonated through the earth surrounding them. The mine was collapsing. They had to get out.

Daniel yanked a rock out, then another, speed counting more than finesse now. Within minutes a small hole had appeared.

He shone the light through the opening. The entire cavern beyond was intact. For now.

Raven's small hand clutched his arm as she crawled up beside him. "I can help."

"Raven…"

With two hands she grabbed a rock and tossed it into the pile he'd started. "Shut up and dig."

"Stubborn woman," he grumbled, but he admired her grit.

They worked side by side, and before long, they'd created an opening large enough for her and Trouble to escape. He peered through the hole. "Can you slide through?"

She studied the gap. "I think so. What about you?"

"I'll be fine. Trouble," Daniel ordered, "go on."

The dog looked at Daniel; then the stupid mutt seemed to roll his eyes. He lifted his paws to the hole and climbed through.

Daniel grasped her waist. "Go on. I'll be right behind you."

"Your shoulders won't fit through that opening."

"I'll move a few more rocks, then follow you."

She hesitated. "Promise?"

"Believe me, honey, I want out of here worse than you do."

Finally she nodded and reached her arms into the hole. Trouble whined from the other side. Her body slithered through. The rocks groaned in protest and shuddered around her.

Raven stilled.

Dust and gravel landed on her back.

"Don't stop! Move!" Daniel batted a falling rock away.

Daniel shoved her hips forward, and she tumbled to the ground with a moan, clutching her head. Trouble nudged her cheek, giving her a quick lick.

"Hey! Are you all right?" Daniel asked, as loud as he dared given the avalanche just waiting to happen.

"Yes."

She rose unsteadily and faced him, too wobbly for his liking. He peered at her through the frame of rocks. "Get outside. Stay at least twenty feet from the mine's entrance."

The obstinate woman just shook her head and came toward him. "I won't leave you. I can dig from this side."

Another warning grumbled around them.

"Look, lady. This place is coming down soon. A few more rocks, and I'm running like hell out of here. I don't need to be concerned about you, too."

She hesitated.

Daniel tossed a stone aside. "Don't worry. It takes more than a cave-in to do me in. This little challenge doesn't even break my top five. Now get the hell outside."

With one last look, she stumbled around the bend toward the mine opening.

"Go," Daniel said to Trouble. "Guard her."

A soft whine escaped the dog, but he followed her.

Daniel widened the hole, his adrenaline ratcheting higher with every second. The stubborn woman didn't weigh more than a hundred twenty pounds, and she'd nearly brought the unstable wall down on them. At over two hundred, he might get one shot to reach the other side, but these stones were like the last blocks in Jenga. Very precarious…and dangerous.

If he was going to die, he wanted it to be out in the open, under the sky, not like a rat trapped in a hole. At least the fight to stay alive was beating back the past—just barely.

He tried to squeeze through, but his hulking six-foot-four frame scraped the edges of the passageway. Damn football shoulders.

Two more rocks should do it.

He moved one, and a spray of dirt sifted over him.

One more to go.

Daniel took a deep breath then tugged out the rock and heard the cracking start.

He shoved through the hole, ignoring the rocks hitting his body. He dragged his bad leg through just as the roar grew louder.

Then the whole damn mountain started coming down on top of him.

"DANIEL!" THE GROUND around Raven shook, tossing her to her knees as debris scattered over her.

She'd made it to within three feet of leaving the tunnel, and despite several attempts, she couldn't stagger to her feet. Her aching head spun in the dimming light from outside.

Oh, God, she couldn't leave Daniel alone. He'd rescued her. She had to get up and help him somehow.

Suddenly he burst around the corner, plowed into her and knocked her flat.

"You're supposed to be outside!" He scooped her into

his arms as if she weighed nothing and hauled her outside through a cloud of dust.

Daniel stumbled, and they went down hard, just a few feet outside the cave's opening. Dirt and dust spewed from the mine, raining down on them, but Raven didn't care. They'd made it.

Trouble bounded next to them, barking until Daniel finally rolled onto his back, his face screwed up in agony. He sucked in several gulps of air, then glared at Raven. "What were you thinking? I told you to get out."

"I wanted to help—"

"Are you always this obstinate?" he growled, shifting his leg, his jaw tightening.

"I don't know," she whispered. "I really don't." The blankness in her mind scared her, terrified her. She rubbed her temple. Why did everything seem like a foggy void, one she couldn't see past?

His lips thinned into a grimace, then he sighed. "It's a miracle we made it out in one piece." He scanned up and down her body. "You look like hell. I don't suppose I look much better."

She gazed at his dirt-covered figure. He looked great, actually. His dusty clothes didn't take away from the fact that he appeared every inch the hero. From the stubble on his chin to the mussed light brown hair kissed with sunlight, to the V-shaped body, there wasn't anything to complain about. When he walked over and grabbed a brown Stetson from the ground, dusted it off and settled it on his head, the look was complete.

She didn't know what kind of guy had attracted her before, but this one was doing it for her now. She struggled to a seated position. Actually she was seeing two of him now, which couldn't be a good sign.

"Let me help you up." Daniel held out his hand to her.

"We're in the middle of nowhere, my canteen is behind a wall of rock, and you need a doctor. We have to get moving."

She placed her small hand in his and stood beside him. "I can make it."

He glanced over at her. "I have no doubt of that, honey. We just have to walk to my phone and call the sheriff who patrols these parts. I'd like to try to get you into the shade."

She took a step and swayed into him, then bent over, resting her hands on her knees. Her stomach roiled, and she swallowed down the nausea.

He snuck his arm around her waist. "We'll go slow," he said softly. "It's been a tough day."

She leaned against him but tried to mostly stand on her own two feet. Daniel hadn't said anything, but the hitch in his step told her that he'd been injured. Maybe it was because he'd come to her rescue, but the closer she looked at the scar on his face, she could tell his skin was still healing from recent wounds. He looked like he'd had a rough year, not just a rough day. War veteran, maybe?

The bright sun in the clear blue sky blinded her after the dark mine, so she stared at her feet and concentrated on putting one foot in front of the other. That's all she had to do.

One step.

The world spun a little.

Another step…gray clouded her vision. The darkness enveloped her, blocking out the sun.

From far, far away she heard a loud curse and watched the ground tilt toward her.

Then all went silent.

THE BLAZING SUN hung low in the sky. Daniel's leg protested with every step, his body apparently not thrilled with carrying Raven's extra weight, no matter how slight. Shards of pain dug through the spots where the plate and screws held his bones together. All he could do was keep walking.

He'd tried dialing 9-1-1 for help, but signals in the middle of nowhere were hard to come by. Once he thought someone answered, but he never could connect. Hell, he couldn't even reach Information to get the local sheriff's department number.

Trouble had taken up his customary position out of reach, though instead of ten feet away, the mutt had moved closer. More like six feet, eyeing the woman in Daniel's arms the whole time.

"If you were a horse this would be a lot easier," Daniel groused to his traveling companion.

The dog just quirked his ear and kept walking.

With a quick shift of his arms, Daniel adjusted his burden. Raven had scared him when she'd keeled over. She hadn't responded when he'd attempted to revive her. Head injuries were nothing to mess with, and for a moment, he'd feared the worst.

When her chest had risen and fallen, his heart had restarted. At least she was breathing, even if her face had taken on the color of buttermilk.

He'd debated whether to turn back to Trouble, Texas, or go forward to Nickel Creek, just south of the Texas–New Mexico border. But he knew Trouble had a medical clinic, so for the first time since leaving Langley, Daniel retraced his steps. He still had a good ten miles to go. Even one more seemed impossible right now.

His foot snagged a rock, and he stumbled forward. Daniel's arms held Raven snug against his body, but a sharp pang pierced his knee. Something had stabbed or bitten him. He hadn't heard a rattler. He backed up and righted himself, a long, slow breath escaping him at the sight of

the devilishly sharp plant at his feet. The lechuguilla re-
sembled the base of a yucca, but its three-inch-long black
spikes at the ends of the flat leaves could spear through
leather or skin with ease. Thank God, he'd been moving
slow. Those suckers could do some real damage.

He was lucky he hadn't dropped Raven.

The jostling hadn't caused a gasp or the slightest movement from her, and he didn't like it. She'd been out too
long. He glanced behind him. As dusk approached, the
merciless sunlight dimmed somewhat. Even when he'd
been in top shape, it would've taken him until full dark
to reach Trouble. His leg wouldn't hold out much longer.

A siren sliced the silence. Daniel tamped down the ir-
rational urge to run in the opposite direction. He had to
remind himself he wasn't in a country where the national
police could stuff you into a dungeon, and people forgot
about you like you were never born.

He waited as the sheriff's vehicle pulled a few feet from
him.

A cop stepped out and rounded the car. Not your average small-town sheriff. This guy walked with precision
and a determined quiet. He had the look of some of CTC's
operatives, and his narrowed expression took in the three
of them. "You the one who tried calling 9-1-1? We caught
the tower location, and this is one of the only paved roads
around. You need some help? Your lady's not looking too
good."

"She needs a hospital," Daniel said, shifting her in his
arms so the sheriff could see her head wound. "And I need
to talk to you."

The man took one look at the blood on her head and
ran to his car. He opened the back door and helped Daniel slide inside the idling vehicle with Raven still cradled
against him. The dog hesitated by the side door.

"Come on, boy." Daniel tapped the backseat.

The dog hunkered back, then scampered into the desert.

"Trouble!" Daniel called.

The mutt didn't stop, just disappeared behind a shrub bush.

Daniel sighed and gazed at Raven. The cop shut the door on them. "You want me to go after him?"

With a pang, Daniel scanned the empty landscape. Yeah, Daniel wanted the sheriff to go after the dog. Trouble had no water, no food, and it would be dark soon, but Raven was still unconscious. "She needs an emergency room. The dog lands on his feet." At least Daniel prayed Trouble would.

"He yours? Will he go home?"

"I'm not sure either of us currently has a home," Daniel said. "We met on the road."

"I see." The cop pulled onto the road and studied Daniel through the rearview mirror. "You wouldn't be that drifter Milly mentioned who came through town yesterday?"

Daniel stiffened. He didn't like the fact that someone had noticed him. He prided himself on being invisible to most, but the waitress had been way too friendly in that small-town-nosy kind of way.

"She didn't mention you had a traveling companion. You gonna tell me what happened, and why you're carrying an unconscious woman down a county road? Or did you find her along the way, too?"

At the suspicious tone in the sheriff's voice, the hairs on the back of Daniel's neck straightened. He didn't need any more problems, so he told the man what he knew.

The sheriff cursed. "Those mines have been abandoned for years. I occasionally find some kids out there playing stupid games of truth or dare. One kid died because he couldn't find his way out. The state should seal them up."

"You need to get the carpet and the toy box out of there first. Maybe you'll find some fingerprints."

The sheriff plucked his radio speaker. "I don't have a lot of help, but I can call in some assistance from Midland. If it's not too dangerous to enter the mine, they'll retrieve the evidence." He waited a beat. "You say this woman doesn't know her name? Do you believe her?"

Daniel met the sheriff's gaze. He understood what the man was asking. "Wrapped in carpet held together with duct tape? She didn't do that to herself. Yeah, I believe her."

The sheriff zipped across the desert and soon reached the Trouble, Texas, Medical Clinic. Daniel carried Raven inside.

A grizzled doctor took one look at her wounds, grabbed a gurney, then wheeled her into a closed area. Daniel followed.

"You with her?" the nurse asked, obviously ready to evict him.

Daniel nodded. He wasn't about to let Raven out of his sight. Not while she was so vulnerable.

The doctor immobilized her neck first, then bent down. "Can you hear me, miss?" he asked loudly.

She didn't respond at first, until a child in a different examining room cried.

Raven's eyes blinked open, and she stared up at the doctor in panic.

"Where am I? Where's my baby?"

PAMELA WINTER EASED the rocking chair back and forth, back and forth, her aging muscles aching as she held the child closer.

Squeak. Squeak. Squeak. "Mommy's going to take care of you."

The baby cooed in her sleep, pursing those sweet little

lips as if she were nursing. Pamela wished she could do it, but it was impossible at her age.

"You'll be fine, my precious girl."

Pamela let her wrinkled hand stroke down the soft cheeks of the healthy eighteen-month-old baby. So healthy when…

No. Pamela wouldn't think that way. Everything would be fine. She'd done what she had to do.

The television filtered through the room. Another game show, one she'd watched nightly for twenty-five years. The recliner near the fireplace mocked her with its emptiness.

This wasn't the home it was supposed to be. She wasn't supposed to be alone. She was supposed to be here with her husband, with their new daughter. A perfect, happy family. A second chance. A do-over after the horrific way their first attempt at parenthood had turned out. She'd believed her husband had changed. He'd certainly been quieter toward the end. He hadn't used his fists or his threats as much after Christopher left.

Until earlier that day before her husband died.

Pamela hummed a lullaby and touched the rosy cheek of the beautiful baby in her arms. A perfect daughter. Unlike Christopher, the child from hell. A child with no conscience who, even when he grew up, never felt the need for one.

Thank God his father had finally found an alternative. After yet another stupid stunt, he'd told Christopher to choose the army or jail. Christopher had picked the army, so now he was trained to kill, with no conscience to stop him. Pamela shivered, even though the temperature hadn't turned cold. Every day she prayed she'd get a telegram, or a knock at the door, along with a military chaplain saying her son was dead, and the world was a safer place for it.

What a blessing that would be.

A key sounded in the lock. She tensed. Her husband was dead. Her son was gone.

No one should have a key.

"I'm home."

Oh, my God. Christopher.

Pamela vaulted out of her chair, clutching the infant in her arms. What was *he* doing here? Her son wasn't due for leave from deployment for another six months.

She couldn't deal with his horrible temper, his manic and depressive rages. Not now. What was she going to do? He'd kill her if he found out the truth about what she'd done. She settled the baby in the nearby cradle and rose from the rocker.

He could *never* find out.

Heavy steps clunked across the hardwood floor. She bit her lip.

The tall, strapping man, as handsome and dangerous as his father, strode across the room, the once long, shaggy hair now cut military short. He dropped his duffel in the marble-covered foyer.

"No hug for your baby boy?"

He gave her a smile. A smile she hadn't seen since he'd become a teenager.

She allowed herself a smidgen of hope. Was the good Christopher back? She embraced him carefully like one would a cobra. He could be that lethal.

Her son stared at her. "Is the baby sleeping?"

She nodded, her throat closed off in fear. Would he be able to tell?

With a grin, he crossed to the cradle and stared at the infant. "She's even more beautiful than her pictures. Chubby, rosy cheeks. You've been plumping her up. I'm glad. She was so pale in the last set of photos." He kissed the top of the baby's head. "I'm home now, kiddo. Anyone messes with you, and they're dead."

Pamela turned so he wouldn't see the tears trailing down her cheeks, tears that were an all-too-common occurrence these days. Her arms felt empty again. She picked up the baby and then faced her son. Forcing a false smile into place, she reached a trembling hand to Christopher. "I'm glad you're home," she lied. "Safe with us. Safe and sound."

"I opted out early. I'm back for good."

She tried to swallow down the terror that clutched at her heart. This wouldn't work. She couldn't keep the truth from him forever. Someone would tell him, or he would guess.

Why was this happening?

Pamela hadn't thought he could leave the service before his five-year enlistment was up. Nothing had worked out like she'd planned.

Everything was so hard now. So wrong.

The baby squirmed in Pamela's arms and opened her striking green eyes.

"Hello, beautiful," he said, scooping up the baby from his mother's arms.

He walked across the room, past the darkened hearth, then sat in his father's chair, an obvious act of defiance to the man he'd hated.

Christopher examined the infant in his arms. "She reminds me of someone. Who do you think?"

Pamela swallowed, unwilling to answer. She had to get him out of here, away from the baby. She would have to come up with some way to hide the truth.

The television volume rose as a news banner flashed across the screen.

Breaking news. Trouble, Texas.

The picture of a battered and bloody woman took up the entire screen.

Pamela almost cried out in shock at the sight. With a trembling hand, she grabbed the remote and pressed the volume control so she could hear.

"The sheriff's office revealed the woman was found in an abandoned mine west of Trouble. Referred to as Jane Doe, she cannot identify herself due to a head injury. They're asking anyone who knows or has seen this woman to contact them immediately."

Pamela dropped the remote. She glanced at her son, then swayed. "This can't be happening. That woman is supposed to be dead. She tried to steal my baby."

Chapter Three

"Open your eyes, darlin'. Please."

Daniel's soft, deep voice soothed Raven's senses. She wanted to do what he asked, but she couldn't seem to function. She hurt too much. The rhythmic pulses slammed in her temples like a bass drum reverberating through her mind. She wanted to let sleep overtake her again, except for some urgent feeling that drove her to wake up and move. She needed help for some reason. *His help.* For something very important…

Dazed, she struggled to lift her lids. Through her lashes, unfamiliar images coalesced. The room was dark, save a low light glowing from above the headboard. An IV and monitor were hooked up by her bed. Panic started, then she heard someone speak again.

"That's it. Wake up now. Just a little more."

It *was* Daniel. What a relief. She knew his voice. Trusted his voice.

A callused finger traced her forehead, and she peered blearily over at the fuzzy double image of the man sitting beside her.

"There you go. Keep those beautiful eyes open."

"Daniel." His face, handsome and troubled, held her enthralled. He was familiar. The only thing that was. She reached up and touched his cheek, the one with the scar.

He clasped her hand in his and drew it away. "Don't exert yourself. Are you really awake this time?" he asked. "Awake enough to answer some questions?"

"I think so," she croaked.

Daniel gave her a small smile, and she could see the relief in his eyes.

"But I don't know where I am."

"We're in Trouble, Texas, at their medical clinic. You had me worried, passing out like you did."

She licked her lips. Her mouth was so dry. "My head hurts. I can't think straight."

"I'll tell the nurse. Want some water?" he asked.

"Please."

He cupped her head and held a straw next to her lips. With one sip, the cold fluid coated her throat. She smiled at him. He knew just what she needed.

Even that small movement made the throbbing restart. She lifted her hand to her temple and encountered a bandage. "What's this? What happened?"

"Before or after the cave-in?" he asked.

"Cave-in?" Hazy images of darkness and falling rocks assailed her. The scent of panic and fear, from a…a dog and Daniel. Dust. Blood. There were some memories there, but none were very clear. She touched the bandage once more. "How did I do this? Did the rocks hit me? What was I doing in a stupid cave anyway?"

"I don't know the answers to all your questions, but falling rocks only did some of the damage." He leaned forward, glancing at the curtain. "Look, I don't have much time before someone comes in, but I do want to help you. Can you try to think about being in the mine shaft before it caved in? Do you remember who hurt you?"

"Someone hurt me?" She furrowed her brow, trying to

reconstruct the strange images in her mind. "Why would anyone do that?"

"Think. What do you remember?" he asked.

"My name is Raven."

"Raven's not your name." The man's expression held nothing but pity. "We made it up because you were panicked about not remembering yours."

"That's crazy." She dug her fingernails into his palm. "That's the only name I know. And I know you. You were holding me and telling me everything would be all right. We were in the cave together. You held me. I remember you."

He squeezed her hand. "I was only holding you to calm you down. I'm sorry. We never met before today."

"It doesn't seem possible. You're...you're Daniel. I know you." She grasped at the small straw of sanity remaining. "I was in your arms. How can you deny we know each other? Why are you lying?"

The curtain surrounding them was yanked back, the sound of the metal rings scraping like nails on a chalkboard.

A man in uniform entered the room. "Yeah, Adams, that's something I'd like to know. You sure looked involved with her when I saw you."

"I was trying to save her life. What was I supposed to do? Dump her and run?"

"No, but you informed the charge nurse you were together when you arrived. You were in the exam room the whole time. Didn't look like a total stranger situation to me. So what gives?"

A deep-seated fear took hold in Raven's chest when anger rose to Daniel's face.

He slowly stood and faced the lawman. "My dog found her, and I tried to get her help. End of story."

"I also warned you not to come back here alone with the Jane Doe. You make a habit of going against the law? You got a prison record somewhere I should check out?"

Daniel blanched, darkness in his eyes once more. "You go ahead and check."

"I intend to," the sheriff shot back. "Now, why don't you wait outside, while I have a talk with this lady you claim not to know."

Raven gripped Daniel's hand. He was her only touchstone. "Please, don't make him leave."

"I'm Sheriff Galloway, ma'am." His gaze sliced across Daniel. "It appears you've been the victim of a crime. I need to ascertain the threat. I said, step away from her, Mr. Adams."

Daniel glanced at their intertwined fingers. "Why don't you let the lady decide, Sheriff? She doesn't look all that eager to be alone with you."

"I said move away." Galloway grabbed Daniel by the arm. "Don't press me. You're two seconds from a cell."

Daniel yanked his arm from Galloway's grasp and pushed aside the curtain.

"Don't leave, Adams. I'm talking to you next."

Not attempting to cloak his obvious fury, Daniel settled against the wall just outside the partition.

Raven couldn't believe what was happening. None of this made sense.

"That man claims he doesn't know you, ma'am," the sheriff said, pulling a small notebook from his uniform pocket. "Yet you say you *do* know him. Which is it?"

Her gaze went back and forth between the two men. "I…I don't know."

"Did Adams hurt you?"

Did he? She was already injured when she came to in the mine. She pressed her hand against her head. That damned throbbing was getting worse, scrambling her thoughts. "I...I don't think so." She blinked hard against the blur Daniel's face had become. "I think he just helped me. I can't really remember what happened before the cave-in."

"So he could have put you there?"

"No. He specifically told me he didn't do that."

"What?" Galloway strode out to Daniel. "Okay, Adams, that's it. You're coming with me until I sort this out." The sheriff slapped a cuff on Daniel's wrist.

Daniel stilled, his face stiff as he stared at the silver bracelet. "Great, just great. Good Samaritan bites the dust one more time. When will I learn?"

Raven stared at him in handcuffs, horrified. Her mind whirled in confusion. She didn't think he had hurt her, but could she be wrong? Nothing made sense.

His gaze went flat, the light behind his eyes dimming. Expressionless, lifeless, soulless. Instinctively Raven reached out to him, needing something, anything to hold on to, but Daniel turned away from her. "I guess I know where I'm headed. Thanks, sweetheart."

The sheriff snagged his prisoner's free arm and snapped the second cuff closed, pinning his arms behind him. The loud click echoed in the room, and Daniel's jaw throbbed, his neck muscles bunched together. He didn't look back at her.

She wanted to call out to Daniel, but she didn't know what to say. She just couldn't remember. She had to be Raven. Didn't she?

Then why had he lied about not knowing her?

"I...don't...remember." The words stuttered from her. Desperation clawed at her insides.

The sheriff gave her a sympathetic grimace. "If Adams

is telling the truth, he'll be out soon. If not...you have nothing to be sorry about. You're safe now."

Sheriff Galloway escorted Daniel out.

The nurse whipped the curtain closed, shutting her in. Alone. Abandoned. The cream-covered cloth fluttered still, a barrier to the world. She wrapped her arms around her body, trying to stop the aching loneliness. Her hands and heart felt empty.

She turned to her side in the bed, staring at the curtained wall. She didn't blink. Her vision grew blurry. Why couldn't she remember? Try as she might, just a few glimmers sifted through her. A fuzzy dog's face, a toy box, *and Daniel.*

She sighed. Daniel. What had she done? Why hadn't she defended him? Why hadn't she fought to make the sheriff understand that she felt safe with Daniel? She reached out her hand, wishing his strong fingers were there for her to grasp.

Her belly clenched. She had the unsettling feeling she'd just made a terrible mistake in letting Daniel go. She curled into a ball. Her fingernails bit into her palm.

Oh, God, what had she done?

THE NIGHTMARE WOULDN'T end. Raven knew she was asleep, but she couldn't escape. Wrapped in a carpet. The dust, the dirt, the blood.

She fought against the memory suffocating her, struggling to break free from the prison. Her hands clenched at her side. Not carpet. Sheets.

The clinic. And a presence watching over her. She could feel its malevolence.

She squeezed her eyes tighter, unable to battle the unexpected terror seizing her body and her mind. She swallowed and forced herself to open her eyes.

"Daniel?" she mumbled, praying he was there, despite her letting him down.

Her blurry vision focused. A man stood above her, his face half-hidden by a surgical mask. Not Daniel though and not the doctor who'd treated her before.

"Who—"

Before she could ask, he pressed his fingers around her throat, then clamped his other hand over her mouth and nose. He tightened his grip, cutting off all air.

Please, God. She couldn't breathe. She twisted against him, each movement sending shafts of pain and light through her brain. He pressed harder, then braced himself and used his knee to hold her to the bed. He was crushing her windpipe.

Panicked, she grappled for the call button, but he yanked it from her hand. White spots filled her graying vision. She couldn't die this way. She wouldn't.

Frantic, relying on pure instinct, Raven used all of her remaining strength to drive the flat of her palm into the man's nose as hard as she could. She heard the crunch of breaking bone.

Her attacker yelled and stumbled back, blood spewing over his mask.

A string of expletives exploded, and he slammed his fist into her head. Pain like a thousand pieces of shrapnel penetrating her skull shattered her control, but she had one chance to live.

Screaming for help, she clutched her head and curled up to protect herself.

Shouting and approaching footsteps sounded from beyond the curtain.

"Damn it!" Her assailant, wearing a white doctor's coat over jeans, shoved through the curtain, covered with his own blood. He slammed a metal cart to the side and barreled over the doctor.

Raven struggled to take in air through her damaged throat. She heard frantic cries to call the sheriff, and the thud and crash of more bodies and equipment hitting the floor.

The doctor staggered to her side, blood streaming down the side of his face. "Are you all right? What happened?"

"That man tried to kill me," Raven croaked. "I need Daniel. Someone please get me Daniel."

The doctor yelled out some orders then bent over her. "Stay with me, Raven. Don't give up."

She blinked through the agonizing pain. All she wanted to do was sleep. She couldn't keep her eyes open. She sucked in a shallow breath. She should have trusted her gut. She should have trusted Daniel.

She *had* made a horrible mistake. She just prayed Daniel wouldn't hold it against her.

THE JAIL CELL was too small.

Daniel lay rigid on the bunk and stared at the tiles on the ceiling, counting the dotted patterns within them. He refused to look at the gray cinder-block walls, and he sure as hell wouldn't look at the bars holding him in this prison.

Cringing and screaming on the floor, fighting off phantoms only he could see, would go a long way to convincing Galloway he had a psycho on his hands. If Daniel didn't get out soon, he wouldn't be able to hold it together. That time was coming closer every second.

His gut filled with panic until one mind-blowing thought intruded. Raven was vulnerable, and he couldn't help her from in here—or from the psycho ward.

He'd tried not to let her get to him.

Who was he kidding? She already had.

Daniel gritted his teeth, sat up and stared through the bars, clenching and reclenching his fists, his knuckles turning white. His hands were clammy, and he fought the urge to rock in place. He rubbed his wrists. At least the sheriff had finally removed the cuffs. Just in time. Daniel had been ready to throttle Galloway to get the keys.

He hadn't done it. He'd maintained control.

Barely.

When the bars had clanked closed, the crisscross of scars on Daniel's back had started to burn. He'd promised himself he'd never be in this situation again. Never be incarcerated. Never be captive and powerless again.

He wiped the sweat from his eyes, restless, edgy, like he was jumping out of his skin. He should have left Raven at the clinic and moved on. He didn't even know her. She was none of his business.

An image of her pain-filled eyes haunted him, though, hitting him harder than the echoes of remembered screams in his mind. Stronger than the memory of his torturer's laughter. The snap of the whip. The sound of bones breaking. Those were all trumped by Raven's small whimper of pain and the way she'd looked at him with such trust.

Good God, lady, don't depend on me.

Unable to sit still any longer, Daniel rose and grabbed the cold steel bars and shook them, testing the lock. Nothing gave at all. He was trapped. Trapped again. He crumpled to his knees, unable to fight his demons anymore. His fingers ached from gripping the bars, and an animal sound of terror rose within him.

His shoulders shook, and he struggled not to break. Not that it mattered anymore.

The other cells were empty.

"Help me, Lord," Daniel prayed. "Don't let me crack. *Don't let me become like my father.*"

The doorknob separating the sheriff's office from the jail twisted.

Daniel stood swiftly, bracing himself to bear his full weight, despite his legs shaking. He froze his emotions inside, hoping his face had gone blank.

The sheriff stepped inside and stared at Daniel.

Galloway leaned his shoulder on the jamb, his relaxed stance feigned. Daniel recognized the tension in the guy's body. Militarylike awareness. Maybe Special Forces.

"Well, Adams, Milly at the diner verified your identity as someone she served yesterday—solo. Said you were a *lone* handyman looking for work. She didn't have anything for you, so she sent you down the north county road to ask at one of the ranches on the outskirts of town."

Daniel shifted his feet, the urge to shake the bars nearly overwhelming, so he just nodded.

Galloway rested his hand on his gun. "I also had a very interesting conversation with Blake Redmond, the sheriff in Carder, Texas, who said he knows all about you."

"Fantastic." Even a good friend like Blake couldn't have vouched for him with all the rumors flowing during Daniel's disappearance. He'd been called traitor until he'd been rescued from his captivity, and now he'd just gone for a walk—across the country. Blake could very well have told Galloway to throw away the key.

"Actually, in your situation, it is. The man vouched for you. Said you're a lot more than a regular handyman. Said you possess some serious skills in a lot of areas. Not that I'm surprised. Your whole vibe says ex-military or mercenary. Doesn't necessarily say sane."

Daniel gritted his teeth.

The sheriff crossed one boot over the other. "I know men like you, Adams. I know about the nightmares. The panicked look when you're trapped in a cell." He strode over to the door and yanked out an impressive set of keys. "I'm letting you go—"

Daniel's heart slammed in his chest.

"—but there's a condition."

Daniel stared down the sheriff. "Name it."

"There are no missing person reports filed on Raven, or Jane Doe, or whoever the hell she is. Milly swears you couldn't have had supper at the diner and made it to the mine fast enough to hurt the woman. Now me? I'm harder to convince, but my gut says it's not you."

Galloway stood with the key in his hand, just inches from the lock. Daniel's breath caught. *Open the damn door.*

The sheriff turned the key in the barred door. "But, Adams, I think you should keep drifting through. Just because my town's name is Trouble doesn't mean I ask for it. And something about you smells like trouble."

Daniel walked through the cell door, not letting Galloway see his enormous relief or his shaking hands. He grabbed his duffel bag off the floor from where Galloway had tossed it earlier. Daniel slung it over his shoulder, then turned to the sheriff.

"Whether you believe me or not, Raven is in serious danger. Somebody left her to die. She couldn't have escaped on her own." If it hadn't been for Trouble, she might never have been found. She wouldn't have survived. The thought made him shudder. "I hope you're better than good at your job, because when the killer discovers she's alive, he'll track her down."

Galloway nodded. "She'll be taken care of."

"Because if something happens to her, I'll—"

Galloway stilled, his stance poised and coiled like a dangerous animal. "You'll do what, Adams?"

"I'll be back to find out why," Daniel warned.

Just then a skinny young man slammed into the room,

his cheeks red, huffing and puffing. His new uniform, creased pants and bit of peach fuzz on his chin screamed *rookie*.

"Sheriff." The nervous deputy skidded to a halt in front of Galloway. "Sheriff, that Jane Doe from the hospital… someone just tried to strangle her."

LIGHTS FLASHED THROUGH the night sky, and the siren rang out. The few people on the streets of Trouble turned their heads to stare as the sheriff's car raced by. This time Daniel rode in the front seat.

"You said she was safe," Daniel accused, his biting words cold as he attempted to tamp down the fury building in his gut.

"I didn't expect someone to attack her in the middle of the emergency room," Galloway snapped.

"You're paid to expect the worst. She should never have been left alone."

Galloway yanked the steering wheel hard to the right, and the car squealed into the parking lot.

Daniel leaped out and ran toward the building, despite the pain in his leg. He raced inside the clinic, to the desk. "Where is she?" he demanded. "Where's Jane Doe?"

The shaking nurse pointed to the same examining room Raven had been in before. Daniel flung aside the wall of fabric, the squeal of the curtain rings barely registering this time. "Raven!"

She lay on the bed, her eyes closed. Bruises encircled her neck.

At the sight, rage erupted in his gut.

He sat down next to her and gently touched her hand. "Oh, darlin'. I never should have let the sheriff take me."

Raven's eyelids fluttered open, then her eyes widened. "Daniel."

He scarcely recognized the raw, hoarse voice she used.

"Daniel, you're here." She clasped hold of his hand. "Don't leave me, please. He almost killed me."

"I won't," he promised. "Not until you're safe." Whoever had attacked her had come too close to cracking her voice box. "I'll be right by your side."

He glared at Sheriff Galloway, daring him to challenge Daniel's vow.

The man gave a slight nod and stepped behind the curtain.

"Thank you. I'm sorry about before." She closed her eyes. "I'm so glad you're here…" Her voice trailed off in sleep.

Daniel positioned himself as best he could to watch over her until the shuddering left her and her breathing steadied into the rhythm of sleep. He eased the still-tight grip of her hand, then stalked to just beyond the curtain to where the sheriff stood checking his notes.

Daniel crossed his arms, struggling to stay civil. "Well?"

"No one saw him come in. From what Raven relayed to the staff, someone dressed as a doctor tried to choke her. He appeared to be acting alone. She fought back and must have hit him just right. She probably broke his nose, and he ran out. Nearly took out the doc and the crash cart."

"You get samples of his blood?" Daniel asked.

"Yes, and I can send them to Midland for forensics, but unless the guy is in one of the government databases, we're not going to be able to identify him. As it is, it's gonna take a while for the results."

Daniel gave the sheriff a sidelong glance. "What if I told you I had contacts with serious forensic resources? Would you give me a blood specimen?"

"These 'contacts' of yours could fast-track it?" Galloway's brow arched.

Daniel nodded. "They can hit all the federal databases a hell of a lot faster than your lab. And they're certified. You can use the results for the court case."

The sheriff paused for a moment, his gaze settling on Raven's bruised throat and head wound. "I'll get you a second sample. We keep this between us."

Daniel agreed, then studied the small emergency department. Double doors leading to hospital rooms, a few cabinets and a second triage area. Only two or three staff members that he could see. "How'd the perp know Raven was here?"

The sheriff grimaced. "Local news picked up the story after I called into the clinic to say we were on our way. We don't get that many emergency calls around here. A few illegals who chose a bad stretch of border to cross, some domestic disturbances and the occasional drunk driver. Can't sneeze in this town without someone knowing about it."

"Great." Daniel swore again silently. "If this story has hit the news, you'll need a guard on her 24/7. Right now whoever attacked her has all the advantages."

"I know you're right, but no can do," Galloway said. "I'm down one man already, with half the damn county to cover. That's nearly two thousand square miles. Even if I could spare the deputy I have left, he can't watch her nonstop."

"I wouldn't let you put that prepubescent kid on her, anyway. He couldn't protect her from a puppy, much less a killer."

Galloway crossed his arms. "I can stick her in jail for her own protection."

Daniel's entire body tensed at the idea of Raven surrounded by bars. "She didn't do anything wrong."

"At least she'd be safe."

"How do you know?" Daniel challenged. "If you can't guard her in the clinic, how can you guard her in the jail? Someone wants her dead. All he'd have to do is create a diversion pulling you two away from the station, and you'd be leaving her vulnerable."

Galloway tilted his head. "So we're at an impasse. I don't have the manpower. I don't have the money. Unless..." He stared at Daniel for a long moment.

"Unless what?"

"Unless you really are some whizbang hotshot military type. Sheriff Redmond said you're handy with tools a lot more lethal than a hammer and nails. And you're one of the best trackers and investigators money can buy."

"Blake Redmond should learn to keep his mouth shut."

"He was trying to save your butt from an attempted murder charge. Kissing his feet is the least you could do." Galloway paused. "Seriously, as you so delicately pointed out, I could use the help on this one. The doctor said Raven has traumatic amnesia. Her memory may or may not return. Until we know better, we have nothing else to go on except whatever clues come out of that mine."

"And the blood sample from her attacker," Daniel pointed out.

"That, too," the sheriff agreed. "But, like you said, she needs someone protecting her 24/7. How about it? I could deputize you."

"That's a switch. An hour ago, you were running me out of town."

"Yeah, well, things change. I just need your signature on a form, and you have to take a quick oath."

Daniel looked back at the curtain behind which Raven slept. He'd promised he wouldn't leave her until she was safe. He couldn't let her fight this alone. Someone had tried to kill her twice. Daniel didn't have a choice, and Galloway knew it. "I have your resources available to me?"

"Whatever you need, though you may have more than I do."

"Your name makes the request more…official. And just so we're clear, this isn't a permanent assignment, Sheriff. You understand that? Once I find out who's after Raven, I'm back on the road."

"You won't hear me complaining. I want my quiet town back."

"If I need more help—more manpower from my contacts—can I make a few calls?"

"Exactly what are you saying?"

"I won't get any flack for bringing outsiders into your county?"

The sheriff shot him a speculative glance. "Does Sheriff Redmond also know these mysterious *resources?*"

"Most definitely. Feel free to call him to check them out."

"Just what are these 'outsiders' going to do?"

"I know people who can look in a lot of gray areas with finesse and speed," Daniel replied easily. "Their only goal is justice."

The men's gazes met. They understood each other.

"I won't look the other way, Adams, if you go beyond the law…that is, if I know about it," Galloway said.

Daniel rolled the sheriff's comments around in his mind. So Galloway believed in justice more than rules. Daniel's kind of law enforcement. "Understood."

Galloway signaled his deputy, who had brought Daniel's duffel into the clinic. "I left your Glock in there. I imagine you know how to use it. You require anything else?"

Daniel shook his head at the dig. "I have what I need."

"Then I'll set up the paperwork for you to sign."

Daniel gave Galloway a nod, then eased aside the curtain and walked over to Raven's bed. After setting down his pack, he unzipped the duffel, pulled his Glock from its case and checked the magazine. Everything seemed set. With calm precision, he tucked the weapon in the back of his jeans, then yanked his knife and ankle sheath from the duffel's side pocket. After one quick buckle of the sheath's strap around his leg, Daniel was able to slip in his knife. Relieved at having his two primary weapons within easy reach, he settled down to wait.

It was odd that being in the tight enclosure in the examining room didn't seem as bad now. Almost as if the fact that he was officially guarding someone nullified some of the usual discomforts of small places. Of course, it helped that the walls were made of cotton, not stone.

The next two hours sitting on a hard wooden chair didn't help Daniel's leg. He adjusted his position, but he couldn't get comfortable. At least the twinges kept him awake.

Not that he hadn't been mesmerized by the rise and fall of Raven's chest or the temptation of her full lips as they parted with each breath, but the shadows under her eyes reminded him of the danger stalking her and exactly why he was here.

The curtain at the end of her bed shifted slightly. Daniel tensed. He palmed the Glock and held it at his side.

The fabric parted. A woman in pink scrubs stepped through. Daniel hid the weapon from her sight as the nurse checked Raven's vital signs.

"How is she doing?" Daniel whispered.

"Everything seems normal."

"What about her memory?"

The woman's sympathetic look evoked an ache deep in Daniel's chest. He didn't want his concern for Raven to be so obvious. He was just worried about her safety.

None of this was personal.

It couldn't be.

His recent stint in the jail cell had shown him just how messed up he truly was. He wouldn't saddle anyone with that crap to deal with for life. Been there. Done that. Had his father's spent bullet casing from his suicide to show for it. Daniel wouldn't put anyone through that.

The nurse checked the IV needle before turning back to Daniel. "The doctor said her memory could come back anytime—or not at all," she said. "She has a concussion, and he wants to keep her for observation."

"Isn't there a quieter location we could stay? A private room maybe? Away from everyone else?" *Especially murdering psychos.*

"I'm sorry. The clinic only has a dozen beds. They're all taken," she said. "This will have to do until something comes available."

Not good enough. Daniel wanted security, minimal entrances and exits. And distance. As it was, three-quarters of this room could be moved with a harsh breath to the fabric curtain. Besides, the perp knew her location. Nowhere in this clinic was safe.

"Does she have to stay in the hospital tonight? I've had enough concussions to know the drill. I'll check her status every hour, and I can bring her back if there are changes, but I need to take her somewhere more secure."

The nurse frowned. "I'll contact her physician. After what happened earlier, I understand your concern."

"Is there a hotel nearby?"

"There's a *motel,* the Copper Mine, just at the edge of town. Run by a bit of a character, but Hondo keeps a clean place."

Daniel chewed on his lip, not liking the idea of sleeping indoors, but at least in a motel room he had a chance to protect Raven. One entrance and solid walls. "Thanks for the tip."

The nurse left, and he pulled out his cell phone, powering the thing on for the first time since leaving the mine. He still had battery life—and twenty-four messages, since he hadn't bothered to listen to them in the past month.

He ignored the voice mails and stared once more at Raven lying on the bed. Who was she really? What was her name? Who wanted her dead?

He put in a call to Galloway's office requesting a list of missing persons reported in Texas and New Mexico. Galloway, apparently a man of his word, sent Daniel the information quickly to his phone. After a quick review of the small number of cases and watching the room's TV for any updates, he let out a sigh.

Nothing. The local television story on Raven hadn't hit the national news or even the big affiliates. At this point Daniel wished it had. Since the person who had buried Raven in that mine knew she was still alive, they were playing against time. More extensive news coverage might give them her name.

His gaze swept Raven's still body. How could no one be missing her? Then again, maybe she was a loner. Some people didn't reach out, didn't create spheres of friends. Some people were totally on their own. Might be nice on occasion. Daniel had tried to disappear, and no one would let him.

A glint of gold around Raven's neck flickered under the fluorescent light. Daniel leaned forward in his chair and tugged on the chain, pulling the heart-shaped locket free of her hospital johnny.

He shifted closer in his seat and palmed the locket, the necklace she had clutched with such desperation. Maybe there were clues inside. His fingernail pressed the latch and opened the heart.

"What are you doing?" she asked groggily, her voice still raspy.

Her cinnamon-colored eyes opened, and he nearly drowned in them.

He gave her a small smile, relieved she'd regained consciousness. "Checking out your necklace." He ran a gentle finger down the smooth skin at her temple. "Trying to find out who you are," Daniel said softly.

She glanced at the small heart locket he'd opened. "Is that a picture inside?"

"Yes, of a raven-haired baby, and a lock of hair tied with a pink ribbon," Daniel said. "Recognize her?"

Raven sat up, her hand trembling as she studied the picture.

"Do you think it's me as a baby? It's my hair. Or could my dream be real?" she whispered. "What if that pink blanket and that poor baby's cry are memories?"

She rubbed her upper arms with her hands as if warding off a chill; then she stared at him, dread lacing her gaze. "Could the person who tried to kill me have taken my baby girl?"

NIGHT IN TROUBLE, Texas, hid a man and his bloody nose well. A few streetlights, a few houselights, but Christopher could disappear in this small town. He was good at disappearing and not being seen as he went about his business.

His footsteps pounded the pavement, the rhythm a little slower now. He sucked in a few breaths. He could do this. The run wasn't nearly as tough as in boot camp. In fact, he'd feel great if it weren't for his broken nose.

God, he wanted that woman dead. He couldn't believe she'd done this to him. She barely weighed as much as his duffel bag from Afghanistan, but she packed a helluva punch. He hadn't expected that, and now he was on the run, covered with blood, wearing stolen clothes and stealing down dark streets to get back to his car.

All because of that bitch.

He heard the sound of not-so-distant laughter and took off again. Alley after alley, corner after corner on foot.

He rounded another dark turn, leaned back against a cinder-block wall and tilted his head to hold his nose at the bridge, knowing it was a bad bone break, and he'd have to be careful until it healed.

If the woman had known a little bit more about what she was doing, he'd be dead. Apparently she'd taken enough self-defense training to do damage. A little harder, a slightly different angle and shards of bone would have sliced up into his brain. He'd have dropped on the spot. The fact that he was in a medical clinic at the time wouldn't have saved him.

Two sets of sirens blasted into the night. Christopher shrank into the blackness. They wouldn't find him.

This whole situation pissed him off. This was *not* how he'd planned his welcome home.

His mom had panicked when that news report had come on. His emotions had taken over. He knew better. He never should have let his mother influence his plans.

Yeah, he liked killing, but he hadn't taken the time to study the layout. He'd be lucky if that fiasco at the clinic didn't put his butt in a sling. They probably had security cameras. He'd screwed up and given too much away about himself. He rubbed his thumb along the barrel of his HK, almost wishing he'd used the gun instead of trying to strangle her.

He wouldn't make the same mistake again.

But they'd be watching her now, closely. He needed the

element of surprise and a bit of help. Someone who understood the stakes and the joys of a good kill.

Christopher untucked his cell phone from his pocket and dialed his buddy's number. "Pick up, you loser."

Ring after ring. Just as he was about to give up, Tad answered.

"This better be good, or you're in a serious world of hurt," the voice at the other end muttered, sleep clogging the words.

"Wake up, you lazy slug. Wanna go hunting?"

Christopher could almost see his ex-platoon-mate's face perk up in interest. "I'm listening and assuming you're not talking about quail."

"I have a woman who needs to disappear. For good. Get my drift?"

"Chelsea?"

"No, I haven't even seen her yet. It's someone you don't know."

"No rules?"

"Just help me make her go away."

"What's the lucky lady's name?"

"That's the best part. She hasn't got one, and I'd kinda like to keep it that way."

Chapter Four

Daniel didn't know how long he had waited for Raven's breathing to even out in deep sleep. He eased the curtain closed and walked across the room. Sheriff Galloway stood whispering with the doctor.

"You checking up on me, Sheriff?"

"Always."

"You know I can handle this. Or are you here to kick me out of town again for some reason?"

"I have an investigation to follow up." Galloway gave Daniel an irritated glance. "You have *your* job. How's she doing?"

"She finally fell asleep. Raven can't remember anything, but she thinks she might have a baby out there."

Galloway stilled. "What the hell… We have a missing baby on top of everything else?"

"I don't know." Daniel described the locket. "The truth is, I have no idea if she's remembering something or not. She doesn't know, either. All I can tell you is that her only memories are of a pink blanket and hearing a baby cry."

The sheriff thrust his hand through his hair. "Nothing's hit my radar. Damn it." Galloway looked at the doctor. "Has she had a baby? Can we tell?"

The doctor shifted uncomfortably under the sheriff's gaze.

"Could Raven have a baby out there?" Daniel glared. "The attacker may have her."

The man cleared his throat and shifted his feet, then finally let out a long breath. "Since Raven doesn't have a memory, and there might be a child at risk…I can reveal that she has given birth. I can't tell you when. Only that it wasn't recent."

Galloway grabbed his phone and made a call. "I want a search statewide on missing children over the past two weeks. See if anyone reported a mother *and* child missing. And check on the status of Jane Doe's prints. I need to know who she is." His expression turned deadly as he listened. "No, it can't wait until morning." He snapped the phone closed and faced the doctor. "What else can we do?"

"Not much, until she remembers."

"How long will that be?" Daniel asked.

"I wish I could tell you. We know a lot about the human body, but the brain is one organ that I'm sorry to say is, in many ways, a mystery. She has a traumatic brain injury even though the MRI doesn't show any swelling. Honestly there doesn't appear to be any physical reason she shouldn't remember."

Daniel paced back and forth. "That's not good enough. She needs to remember—for her own safety as well as the baby's—so how can we speed up the process?"

"Look, *Deputy,* you can't force a brain that's been injured to work on a timetable. And we have no idea what happened to her out there. Her body is protecting her right now. We have to let her heal."

Daniel lifted his gaze to the ceiling. "This is crazy. Every hour we delay is more time for her attacker to try again."

"And the harder you push, the more she may bury the memories until they never come back." The doctor narrowed his gaze at Daniel. "I know you're impatient. I'm concerned about the baby, too, but I'm more concerned about the patient who I know exists. You have to go slowly."

"You're giving me nothing, doc."

"Maybe if you retrace her steps, the familiar *might* bring something back. *If* this isn't all in her imagination. Scent is also a strong trigger. Get some baby lotion or shampoo and introduce it naturally, with no expectations. She'll remember more. Other than that, she needs rest and no stress."

Daniel glanced back at the closed curtain. "That I can do. I can keep her safe and calm," he said quietly. "She will remember." Daniel pinned the sheriff with his gaze. "My gut tells me there is a child. Raven's reaction was visceral. It was the first thing she said when she woke up. Can you use your network to find out if the baby exists?"

Galloway nodded. "I'm on it."

"I'll protect Raven. The perp obviously knows she's here. She can't stay."

The sheriff's phone rang. "Galloway."

As the person on the other end spoke, the sheriff's jawline went tense. "Keep digging. She didn't come out of nowhere."

He ended the call.

"No leads?" Daniel asked.

"Her prints didn't get a hit. Nothing on the missing persons reports that matches her or a dark-haired child of any age. We've got squat."

"How does a woman—and perhaps a child—vanish without anyone reporting it? Something's not right." Daniel thrust his hand into his pocket and worried the bullet casing.

Galloway nodded. "Her husband—"

"She's not wearing a ring," Daniel said harshly. He

pounced on the statement. He didn't want anyone to be in Raven's life. No one but him.

His fingers flicked against the brass's metal edge. That was wrong. He knew better than to let himself get involved. He could hurt her. She was simply a woman who needed help, but somehow, over the past few hours, she'd become important to him. More important than she should.

"Husband or not, every baby has a father. Most of the time child abduction is a family member, typically a parent. We have to consider the father the prime suspect."

"Except we don't know her identity. Or his. Or even if there *is* an abduction. Until we know who Raven is, we have no leads."

"Catch twenty-two," Galloway muttered.

"Doesn't matter. She's still in danger. I'm taking her out of here," Daniel said. "When can she leave?" he asked the doctor.

Daniel wanted to grab her and get her away from this place. Even as he looked around the waiting room, all he saw were opportunities for an attack. Numerous entrances and easy access.

"Tomorrow." The doctor stroked his jaw. "I can't do anything else for her, but she has a concussion. I want her here for the remainder of the night just in case of complications. I'll check her again first thing in the morning. If she doesn't have further symptoms, you can take her, but you'll need to watch her closely. If she gets nauseous or dizzy or starts seeing double again, bring her back in."

Daniel's body tensed in resistance. She was open and vulnerable here. This was a bad idea. He could feel it. He opened his mouth to argue—

"I'm not backing down," the doctor said. "If she takes a turn for the worse, she'll need immediate medical intervention."

"In the meantime, I want all staff to deny Raven's presence here. Got it?" Daniel told the doc.

He received a nod in return from the physician.

A loud ruckus outside the hospital interrupted the discussion. Daniel whirled around, hand on his weapon. A television news crew pushed their way into the emergency room lobby. Daniel glared at the sheriff and whirled behind the curtain hiding Raven, letting him and the doc deal with the intrusion.

After several minutes of heated argument, the sheriff got rid of the news crew. Galloway stuck his head through the curtain and nodded. "Doc's distracting them in the parking lot."

With a last check on the woman who hadn't regained consciousness even in the turmoil, Daniel stalked back into the emergency room's lobby. "We leave in the morning. Until then, I'll take watch." He turned to the sheriff and, after a quick look around verifying no one was eavesdropping, lowered his voice. "I hear there's a decent motel at the edge of town. Any reason for us not to stay there?"

"I'll call Hondo," Galloway offered, his voice lowered, as well. "The guy's discreet and knows his way around a weapon or two. If Raven feels safe enough, like the doc said, maybe she'll remember."

"A motel is better than fabric walls. But I still want to see the place before she goes anywhere near the joint."

Galloway took out his phone. "I'll make the arrangements."

"Keep it quiet, Sheriff. I don't like how much this guy knows."

With a quick nod and agreement to return at dawn to watch Raven while Daniel checked out the motel, Galloway left.

Daniel stepped back through the curtain protecting

Raven. Shadows marred her pale complexion. He couldn't stop staring at the porcelain of her skin or the vulnerability of her expression. Her full lips had parted slightly, but they turned down at the corners, her troubles painted on her face. He could understand that. His hand hovered centimeters from the skin he knew would be softer than a breath of fresh air.

He closed his fist and pulled away. She deserved better than he would ever be. That bullet in his pocket was his reminder that not everyone made it back from hell.

With a sigh, he settled into the chair next to Raven's bed. Anyone looking in would think he was relaxed. Not a chance. Her fear-filled eyes haunted his memory.

But no one would get near Raven again.

Not on his watch.

CHRISTOPHER GINGERLY PRESSED against his swollen nose. He swore and scanned the eerily quiet surroundings in the alley behind the sheriff's office before catching sight of the phone line coming down the side of the building.

Thank God this decrepit town hadn't updated the system in decades.

"This is stupid," Tad hissed. "Are you trying to get us caught?"

"You a coward?" Christopher egged on his friend. He knew what buttons to push with Tad. He hadn't wanted an accomplice, but this was clearly a two-man job. Christopher had to stay out of sight until his nose healed. He needed backup.

No one better than the guy he'd grown up with. They'd gotten thrown in jail together, had joined the army together and had found a way to get kicked out of the military together.

Christopher could count on Tad. "Look, the nurse didn't

know anything 'cept Jane Doe left the hospital. If anyone knows where that woman is, it's Sheriff Galloway, and we can't just ask. We need intel."

"I saw the sheriff. Former Special Forces, I bet. He's dangerous. Just like the lieutenant," Tad said.

"We took care of him just fine."

"Yeah, but not quick enough. Still got booted out," Tad grumbled. "No pension, no nothing. Can't even get a frickin' job now. All that time wasted."

"I wouldn't say it was a total waste. I learned a few things and made some pretty good connections." Christopher pulled a small electronic device from his pocket. He clipped it on the phone line that had been tacked to the side of the building and tucked a small earpiece inside in his ear. "Now we'll know exactly what the good sheriff is talking about no matter where we go. When he hears where that woman is, she's dead."

"And what about the sheriff? What if he interferes?"

"If he gets in our way, well, bullets kill Special Forces, too."

THE CLOP OF worn boots sounded on the linoleum floor of the hospital. The owner paused, just visible beneath the curtain. "Come on in, Sheriff," Daniel said, his voice barely above a whisper.

Galloway pressed back the fabric. "You said dawn, so here I am. Any change?"

"The nurse woke Raven about a half hour ago. She seems better."

"Did she remember anything?"

Daniel shook his head and rose.

"I'll watch over her," Galloway said, his hand on his Beretta.

"I won't be long." Daniel paused for a moment and sent

the sheriff a sideways glance. "What are you doing in this Podunk town, Galloway? Something about you doesn't quite fit."

Galloway's lips twisted. "Pot. Kettle."

"Touché," Daniel muttered with one last long glance at the sleeping woman in the bed. He'd teased her about being a sleeping princess, but damned if she didn't fit the part. Just looking at her made his heart ache. "I'll be back, Raven. Count on it."

He shoved aside the unwanted desires. He had to remember the past, the reason he couldn't let himself care. He strode through the small clinic and out the exit. He had a job to do, and nothing, especially not his own weakness, would stop him from protecting her.

The sight greeting him outside the clinic made him shake his head. Trouble. The fuzz face had dust and grime on his coat, but he sat there with a rag in his mouth and expectations on his face.

"What the hell did you get into, boy?" Daniel asked, stepping forward cautiously so as not to run the skittish dog away.

Trouble cocked his head, then dropped his trophy before taking a few steps back to his now customary six feet.

Daniel knelt down, noticing a triangle of material looking like torn jeans. Several red splotches decorated the worn blue fabric. Blood, maybe? "Seems like you had a battle with someone."

His senses pinged with awareness. Raven's attacker had worn jeans. Could he be that lucky? He raced into the hospital and returned wearing a glove on one hand and carrying a bowl of water in the other. Daniel set the liquid down. Trouble didn't hesitate. While the mutt lapped up the drink, Daniel picked up the fabric by the corner, studied it for a moment and dumped it into a paper lunch sack. "Who'd you go after, Trouble?"

He kept his hands by his side, kneeling down, meeting Trouble's gaze at eye level. "You hurt, boy? Will you let me check you over?"

Daniel focused on making his voice calm and smooth. Normally he would've let the dog be, but there was blood on the animal's side.

"I'll be quick." His movements slow and steady, Daniel made more effort than he had in weeks to get close to the dog. As if he understood, Trouble sat quiet but alert. Daniel ran his hands over the mutt's fur.

When he reached the dog's side, Trouble yelped.

"Someone hurt you?" Daniel's gaze hardened, and he palpated the animal's ribs. They didn't seem broken, and there were no cuts, but whoever the canine had attacked had fought back.

"Not too bad. You'll live, boy." Daniel tried to scratch behind the floppy ears, but Trouble's patience had ended. He scooted away.

Daniel stood. "You are one strange dog. I'll drop off your little trophy and see if you tangled with Raven's attacker."

He hurried in and out of the hospital. Trouble hadn't moved. "I'm going for a ride. I don't suppose you want to come?"

Trouble let out a bark. Out of his pocket Daniel pulled the keys to the truck the sheriff had loaned him. The casing from his dad's gun fell to the ground. Daniel scooped it up. He couldn't lose the reminder. That mutt, and now Raven, had somehow embedded themselves behind the protective wall Daniel had constructed around his heart. All he had to do was look at the cylinder of brass to remind him of what he'd come home to that horrible afternoon.

Blood and brains splattered on the wall of his father's bedroom. His sisters' screams when they'd followed him into that death room.

He shook his head to dispel the memories. No time for the past.

With a quick tug he opened the door of the truck. "Well?"

He half expected Trouble to skedaddle, but the dog surprised him yet again. He jumped into the vehicle and sat on the passenger seat.

"So you hate cop cars and uniforms, do you, but not trucks? I can't say that I blame you. Just takes one psycho in uniform to sour the taste."

Daniel put the truck into gear and exited the hospital parking lot. Trouble stuck his head out the window, letting the wind blow through his reddish hair, with that crazy dog smile on his face. The trip didn't last long, though. Within a few minutes, Daniel had traveled from one end of the small town to the other.

He pulled inside the parking lot of the Copper Mine Motel. The place should have been a dump, but a fresh coat of paint brightened it up, and two iron kettles of pansies lined each side of the screen door entrance, giving it a vintage and welcoming vibe.

Daniel pressed the buzzer.

A curtain pushed aside. A tiny woman with scraggly gray hair and piercing blue eyes peeped through the gap. "You Daniel Adams?"

"Don't be asking him his name, Lucy. How many times have I told you, you give away too much? What if it's a bad guy?"

She pouted, then shrugged. "How many visitors we get at the crack of dawn? Besides, I can spot a bad guy a mile away. Quit babying me, big brother. You're not my keeper."

A large barrel-chested man opened the door. His brown hair was wild, but his beard well kempt. Tattoos covered his arms. A steel loop pierced his lip.

Incongruously, oven mitts encased his hands, and he held a fresh-baked pan of chocolate chip cookies. "Sorry for the delay. Had to get these out of the oven."

So not a picture Daniel had expected. The cookies should belong to his sister. This guy should be greased up, taking a wrench to a Harley. "You're Hondo?"

"You got it. This is my place."

His sister cleared her throat and glared at him.

"Yeah, well, Lucy here got it in a settlement from her lyin', cheatin' ex-husband." He glanced at his sister. "But I'm the one who keeps the place from falling down around your feet. Isn't that right, little sister?"

"Just don't you forget who's in charge," she huffed. "I'm going to watch wrestling."

"Keep the volume down," he commented with a smile in his eyes. He turned back to Daniel. "She's far too trusting. I hear you need a room."

"For a while."

"I also hear you prefer no record that you're staying here," he said with a scowl. "I don't want no problems. I see any funny business goin' on, I won't hesitate to call the sheriff. I'm only lettin' you stay 'cause he vouched for you."

"Agreed." Daniel pulled out his wallet.

Hondo raised his hand. "Sheriff took care of one week's rent. We'll talk after that if we're both still interested."

Daniel studied the man in front of him. He didn't see deception behind Hondo's eyes. "That's fair." He shoved his billfold back into his pocket. "One week."

"Good." Hondo smiled and held out the baking sheet. "Cookie?"

RAVEN PEERED THROUGH the pickup's window at a succession of mom-and-pop shops down Trouble's main drag and clutched the hospital blanket tighter around her. The big stores hadn't invaded yet. A few doorways had been blockaded, but for the most part, this little Texas town looked to be doing all right. Better than she was, certainly.

She shivered, then huddled against the truck's worn seats. Despite the temperatures in the seventies outside, she couldn't stop the chills from skittering down her arms. She clutched at Trouble's fur. His big brown eyes peered up at her from his spot on the floorboard. The dog could very well be the only reason her legs had stayed warm. He didn't want to move away from her. She appreciated the loyalty.

"I can't believe he's letting you pet him like that," Daniel muttered.

Raven scratched Trouble's floppy ears. "I like dogs. And he's well trained. A service dog, do you think?"

"Maybe," Daniel said. "He didn't have any tags, and he doesn't act like a K-9, but I gotta wonder if he might be search and rescue after watching him find you in that mine. He wouldn't stop until I dug you out."

She lifted Trouble's chin. "So, boy, you're a smart one, aren't you? You saved my life." The animal tilted his head into her touch, and she fondled his soft ears and bent down. "Thank you," she whispered.

Daniel pulled the truck into the parking lot of a motel and turned off the keys. "This place should be safer than the hospital."

She peered at the newly polished sign. *Copper Mine Motel.* Her fingers explored the bruises on her throat that the attacker had made. "I'm not sure if I should be relieved or worried."

After Daniel turned off the engine, he twisted in his seat, his gaze intense, his expression unrelenting. "Even if your attacker finds us, there's only one entrance. He'll have to go through me and Trouble to get at you. We won't let that happen." He touched her arm lightly. "I promise you that."

His words made her want to believe, to put herself into his hands. She couldn't do this alone. If she'd been totally alone throughout this whole ordeal, she would be dead right now. Of that she had no doubt. She nodded at Daniel, regretting the action the moment her chin bobbed down. She could almost feel her brain banging against her skull. Even though the pain meds had taken the edge off, she could still sense every small movement from her neck up.

She winced, and he must have caught it.

"You're hurting again," Daniel said. He opened the door and stepped outside. "Stay here. I'll be right back."

He walked a few feet across the porch and knocked on the side jamb. A huge, scary-looking man stood in the doorway. Raven tensed, her gut winding in a knot. Trouble whimpered and laid his head in her lap. She gripped his fur and reached toward the door. She didn't have a plan, but she couldn't let Daniel fight the big man alone. If nothing else, she could be a distraction.

Then the mountain smiled, tilted back his head and chuckled. He slapped Daniel across the back and disappeared inside.

Daniel looked toward her and offered her a reassuring nod. He scanned the surroundings, and she knew he kept watch for her. Raven sagged in the seat and leaned her head against the soft back, uncertain why she'd been expecting an attack. The bright blue of the morning sky didn't appear real. Nothing did. Gingerly she ran her finger along the bandage still covering the cut on her head. She pressed gently against the injury. A sharp stab of pain needled her temple.

At least the pain proved this wasn't some crazy dream.

She was real. The locket was real. She snapped opened the catch. Was the baby real, too?

Searching for something to ground her, she let her gaze wander, looking for anything familiar. She could identify the steering wheel; she recognized the windmill looming above the motel. Her gaze swept the motel sign again. Copper.

The symbol for the element was *Cu*.

Her heart fluttered. She looked around. Where had *that* come from?

The wrought iron windmill. Iron, *Fe*.

She clutched her locket. Gold, *Au*.

Her head ached, but an almost desperate excitement rose within her. She *knew* this information. The knowledge was second nature. She could identify the elements clearly, easily. Was she a chemistry teacher? A scientist?

She glanced at the cantina across the road. Drinking alcohol, ethyl alcohol or ethyl hydroxide. *EtOH*. Flash point: pure EtOH caught fire at just under seventeen degrees centigrade.

She grabbed Trouble's fur. "I remember something from before."

Daniel opened her door. "We're in room number six," he said.

She barely heard him, digging her fingers into his arm. "I know the periodic table of the elements. I know chemicals. Benzene. C6H6. An organic chemical compound. A natural constituent of crude oil. It has a sweet smell." Her body shook. "It's like breathing air. I know it the same way I know Trouble is a dog, and you're a man, and that knob turns on the radio."

She smiled up at him. "My head hurts like the devil, but I know my chemistry."

"Chemistry," Daniel muttered. "It's a good start." He slid his hands under her and swept her into his arms, then glanced around. "You can tell me all about it once we're inside."

"I'm too heavy," she protested.

"I carried you a couple miles down that highway," he said, tightening his grip. "I'm getting used to the feel of you in my arms."

Daniel balanced her against his chest, and she couldn't help feeling small against his broad shoulders. He was a bit lean for his build, as if he hadn't eaten right, but every sinew of muscle oozed strength.

With a quick turn of an old key, he pushed into the motel room. Trouble bounded in ahead of them, checking out the place, his nose against the carpet.

Daniel's arms tightened around her as if he didn't want to let her go. His gaze dropped to her mouth, and suddenly the sheer joy of knowledge transformed into something else. His eyes grew dark, a flicker of green sparking in the hazel depths. Her breath caught. She was hurt, dusty and so not-sexy, but she couldn't help but lean into him. In the uncertainty of her current existence, he had become a constant.

Her hands flattened on his strong shoulders. His fingers moved along her back, and a flash of awareness tingled through her. Her lungs tightened, and her mouth went dry. She wet her lower lip, and his chest rumbled against hers.

Sparks she recognized ignited between them, and she squirmed.

In two steps Daniel laid her on the regular-sized bed taking over the room. His movements gentle, he placed a pillow behind her back.

She looked to the other side of the mattress, clutching the simple quilt with her fingertips. Not much room.

If he wanted to sleep in the bed with her, they couldn't help touching each other. Her gaze lifted to his, and she bit her lip.

The heat in Daniel's gaze dimmed, and he took in a shuddering breath, as if fighting for control. He doused the fire burning between them and took a step back. "Sorry. They didn't have a room with two beds available." Daniel placed his hand on her arm, his touch reigniting that shiver of awareness she couldn't deny. She may not know her name, but she knew the electricity sparking between them didn't happen often.

He snatched his hand back from her arm. "We need to lay down some ground rules. You don't answer the phone or the door. You don't stand by the windows. You let me enter first wherever we go. Got it?"

"But—"

"It's not negotiable, darlin'. You sleep here, as far away from the door as possible while I'm keeping watch by the window. You don't have to be afraid." His face took on a somber expression, and he trailed his finger down her cheek. "Not of anything or anyone."

Including me. He left the unspoken words in the air around them. She shouldn't be afraid of him, and she wasn't, but she couldn't help but be terrified of what she already felt building between them. "I can't let you sleep on the rug."

"It's near the window. I like the open air," he said, his voice soft but certain. "So does Trouble."

Immediately the mutt bounded up on the bed, circled twice and settled on top of Raven's feet. His ears flattened, and he stared at Daniel with a *Who me?* expression on his face.

She bit back a small chuckle.

"Traitor." Daniel glared at the dog with a shake of his

head. "I obviously spoke too soon. He's been hanging with me for weeks, and he wouldn't so much as come near. To you, he's pretty much pledged his undying devotion."

Raven scratched Trouble's ears.

"Guard her, Trouble. I'll get our stuff from the truck." He disappeared out the motel room door.

She watched him leave and glanced down at the dog next to her. "Am I fooling myself, boy? Is he really the man he seems to be?"

She wished the animal could answer. Instead, she scanned the small room that would be her home until she remembered her own address. This place had to have been built in the fifties, but the pristine white tile of the bathroom looked new.

What little energy she'd saved had seeped out of her. Her eyelids wanted to close, but she couldn't stand lying down without a shower. She wanted nothing more than to wash the grime off her body, not to mention the blood out of her hair.

Determined to get clean, she swung her legs over the side of the bed and set her feet on the ground.

Daniel came in with his duffel and a grocery sack. "Whoa there. What do you think you're doing?"

"I need a shower." She stood, the back of her knees against the bed.

"Well, it's your lucky day, darlin'. The nurses gathered up a few things for you," he said, lifting the small plastic bag. "Tomorrow I'll try to get you some more clothes. The thing about small towns, there's not always 24/7 retail shopping."

"I don't have any money," she said slowly.

"Don't worry about that. You can pay me back when we find out—"

"You mean *if* we find out who I am," she finished.

"We'll figure it out."

"No one's come forward after the pictures on the news?" Her voice caught, and she wished it hadn't. She didn't like showing vulnerability.

"Not yet."

"How can I just disappear without anyone caring?" She couldn't bear to look at him so she opened the bag and shuffled through the items. Soap, a razor, lotion. Shampoo. She froze. Baby shampoo. She stared at the small bottle for a moment. Compelled, she twisted the cap and took a small sniff. Her head spun a bit, and she sat down quickly.

"Dizzy? Nauseous?" Daniel slipped his phone from his pocket. "I'm calling the doctor."

"It's not that. It's the baby shampoo." She held it up. "I smelled baby lotion in the mine and reacted the same way." Her eyes burned. "It's familiar, Daniel, and my heart feels *so* empty." She looked at the locket. "I know I have a child out there. Somewhere. Needing me."

"Then we'll find her." Daniel knelt at the edge of the bed. He took the small bottle from her and held it to her nose. "Breathe in. Close your eyes. Do you remember anything else?"

Raven let her lashes drop against her cheeks. She took slow, deep breaths, searching her brain for something, anything that would give her an answer.

Only a fog clouded her mind.

"Nothing." She frowned, the sharp words laced with frustration.

He entwined his fingers through hers and squeezed. "Not so fast. Close them again."

She let her eyelids fall. Blackness overtook her vision. Gray shapes swirled. "I see something." A pink blanket. She gripped his hand until her fingers had gone numb. "The blanket again."

"And unicorns," she whispered. "Rainbows and unicorns. It looks like a nursery."

"Okay, that's good. That's very good," Daniel said. "Where?"

The image faded away. She opened her eyes. "I don't know. It was there, but now it's gone."

"Was the light bright? Were you in the west? Here in Texas? Was it cloudy? Maybe Washington or Oregon?" he prompted.

"I don't know. I just don't know." She rubbed the bridge of her nose, then her eyes. Her head pounded with the futile effort.

Raven clutched the small bottle of shampoo and lifted her gaze to Daniel's. "I'm scared for her. I'm safe. I have you to protect me, but the baby's in danger. I can feel it."

A loud pounding at the door jerked Raven from the captivity of Daniel's gaze.

He slipped his Glock from beneath his jacket. "Get out of sight," he hissed. "Now!"

Raven rolled to the side and ducked behind the bed. She peered around the end. Trouble stood beside Daniel, his ears back, a low growl emitting from his throat as he stared intently at the doorknob.

Daniel stood to the side, gun at the ready. He flung open the door. "Don't move, or I'll shoot."

Chapter Five

Pamela gripped the steering wheel of the BMW and stared at the small ranch house situated on an isolated dirt road in the middle of nowhere. She studied the sheet of paper on the seat beside her, the map and phone number in her husband's writing. She'd never thought she'd have to sully her hands again with his less-than-honest *colleagues,* but she needed foolproof documents for her family to disappear out of the system.

She had no choice, not if she wanted to protect them. Her knuckles whitened with tension. A whimper sounded from the backseat. The baby clutched the blanket, her eyes tear-filled.

"You'll be mine soon, little one," she whispered softly. "Forever." She kept the air conditioner running, rolled down the windows and stared at the sweet little girl in the car seat. "You'll be fine in the shade of the tree. I won't be gone long."

She exited the car, clutching her handbag to her side. She set her jaw tight with determination, straightened her shoulders and strode across the dirt.

The door opened before she even reached the porch.

"Mrs. Winter?"

"Hector?"

The small gray-haired man with the wire-rimmed

glasses nodded once. He had to be four inches shorter than her own five-ten. Her confidence rose.

He waved her into the foyer, closing the door behind her. "I was sorry to hear about your husband. He was a *generous* patron."

Pamela reached into her back pocket and pulled out a thick white envelope. "I can be just as generous. You have the papers?"

"Of course." He held a large flat brown envelope. "The money first."

She laid the payment on the entryway table. Hector picked up the envelope and thumbed through the bills.

"You follow directions better than your husband," he said, handing her the documents.

Pamela's chest tightened as her fingertips closed over the envelope. She struggled to keep her hands from shaking and opened the top, sliding the papers out.

Certificate of Adoption.

She glanced at the signatures. "Perfect," she said, then briefly glancing at the other official-looking paperwork. "And the original birth certificates?"

"Inaccessible through a bit of misdirection." Hector shrugged. "Easier than providing citizenship paperwork for your husband, but more expensive." He walked to the door and opened it. "Just know, Mrs. Winter, that we now have a pact. I expect you to honor it. I look forward to working with you again in the future."

Pamela slipped the documents into her handbag and grasped the butt of her husband's revolver. "I won't be needing your help again, Hector."

She yanked out the gun and pulled the trigger.

A bright red stain bloomed on Hector's shirt. His mouth dropped open. He fell to his knees.

He keeled over, lying perfectly still. Pamela knelt down

to make certain he was dead, then rose and stepped over the body.

Wait. She couldn't leave. The money.

She rolled him over and grabbed the envelope of cash. "Thanks, Hector."

Without a glance back she locked the door and walked to the car. The baby blinked, her lower lip poking out. Pamela could see the tantrum coming.

"You be good, little girl, because you belong to me now. I'm your new mother. Well, I will be as soon as the procedure is completed."

Pamela tossed her purse into the seat, slid into the vehicle and shifted into Drive. Her lips tilted up in satisfaction, humming a lullaby.

Ashes, ashes, we all fall down.

DANIEL STOOD IN the doorway, his gun pointed at Hondo's sister. Lucy let out a high-pitched squeal, and her eyes rolled back into her head. Before Daniel could catch her, Hondo's sister had dropped a set of blankets and a pillow on the ground, and keeled over at Daniel's feet.

He let out a curse, lowered his weapon and knelt beside the unconscious woman.

An echoing curse roared from the motel's office three doors down. Hondo raced out and stared at Lucy.

"What the hell did you do to my sister?" He glared at Daniel.

"I guess I scared her." Daniel slid his weapon into the back of his jeans. "I didn't expect anyone."

Hondo scooped the slight woman into his arms. "Well, you want any extra blankets, you're coming to me. I sure as hell ain't knocking on this door again." He narrowed his gaze at Daniel. "That's one strike, Adams. You don't get three chances in my establishment. One more, you're out."

With Lucy in his arms, he turned his back to them.

"It's my fault," Raven said softly. "Daniel's worried about someone trying to hurt me."

Hondo looked over his shoulder, taking in Raven's pale face. His expression softened. "I'll take that into account, but y'all need to know something about my sister. Her husband damaged her bad. She used to be the sharpest kid in her class at school. Scholarship outta here and all. After what the bastard did to her, her mind is like a little girl's. She just don't understand this world no more. I won't be having her hurt again. By anyone."

He walked away, and Daniel closed the door, locking and chaining it. Guilt had him sucking in a long, deep breath. That and being inside. He didn't like the way the walls pressed in close around him. He flicked the window lock and shoved the glass up.

A slight breeze filtered from outside, and he slowed his breathing down, one count at a time. Yes, calmer. Much better. But he could use a minute.

He faced Raven. "You said you wanted a shower. Now might be the best time."

"Oh, if I could get clean right now, I'd love you for-ever—" Her eyes widened. "I mean...I'd really like that."

A blush crept up her cheeks, and a sudden tension rose between them. "Well," he said in an attempt to lighten the mood. "If that's what you offer when I say you can take a shower, I can't wait to see what happens when I ask you about dinner."

Her cheeks went crimson, and she looked away from him.

Her transparent emotion seduced him as much as her words. After years of wondering whether each person he spoke to was playing a game, he'd erected walls that she obviously hadn't. Honesty could be sexier than he imagined—and far more worrisome to his equilibrium.

He drew her to her feet, then tilted her chin up with his finger. "Don't be embarrassed. We're in a strange situation. Best find the humor in it when we can. How about we both agree that what happens in Trouble stays in Trouble? When you get your memory back, neither one of us leaves with any regrets."

She laid her hand against his scarred cheek. "You're a kind man, Daniel Adams," she whispered.

"You don't even know me, honey, if you're saying that."

"I know enough."

How could he respond? She didn't understand. What would happen if the PTSD hit while he was sleeping tonight? What if his phantoms reappeared, and he lost himself? What if he couldn't tell where he was, and he hit Raven like he'd hit that poor orderly during his recovery? Daniel had nearly killed the man who'd come up behind him and awakened him without warning. He'd been dreaming of Bellevaux, and the guy had almost paid the ultimate price.

She stood, a bit unsteadily. Shoving the fears aside, he guided her to the bathroom with a hand at her back. He paused at the door. "Do you need help?"

"Thanks, but…I can manage." She wouldn't meet his gaze.

"Sure. That's good." He scuffed his boot on the rug, anything to take away the awareness that Raven was going to be in that room, totally naked, water sluicing down that amazing body. He'd have to take a shower after her. A cold one. "Go easy on your wound."

She touched the injury. "The doc told me what to do."

Raven passed him and started to shut the door.

"Don't lock it," he said.

"I won't."

"Call me if you need me."

"I won't," she said. "Need you, I mean."

Daniel shook his head. "Go get wet."

The door closed a little harder than necessary, and he laughed. Then Daniel grabbed a chair and sat down at the window, staring outside into the now-darkened sky.

The stars weren't as bright as they'd been when he had bedded down in the middle of nowhere, but Trouble, Texas, didn't have many lights to drown out the flickering flames in the sky. He let out a slow, deep breath and closed his eyes, counting backward from one hundred.

Images swirled in his mind. Memories. His heart raced.

With a slight prayer, he opened his eyes.

The past dissolved. The ceiling remained the old popcorn texture. No centuries-old stone blocks in front of his eyes.

"So far so good, mutt," he grumbled at Trouble. He'd just keep looking out that window.

The sound of the shower's spray filtered through the bathroom door.

Oh, crap. Naked. She was naked in there by now.

The dog hopped off the bed and settled next to the thin walnut-colored barrier, as if guarding her in case Daniel succumbed to his lascivious thoughts. "You've fallen for her, haven't you, boy? So could I, if I'm not careful."

The phone in his pocket vibrated. He glanced at the screen. A familiar name flashed—*Noah Bradford*. He hadn't seen that name since he'd taken off from Langley.

"I thought you were out saving the world."

Noah Bradford, the operative whose moniker, The Falcon, sent fear and frustration through most terrorist organizations in the Middle East, chuckled. "I should be, but it looks like I've gotta save your sorry ass instead. Our friends in Carder put out the word that you were in jail, possibly facing some impressive charges. Figured I'd come laugh at you before I bailed you out."

"As you can tell, I'm already out."

"Yeah, heard that, too. Would have been nice if I had heard it from you. Don't you ever answer your damn phone?"

"I've been…busy."

"I bet you have, but you've been incommunicado for months. You okay?"

Noah had been in on Daniel's rescue. Noah, more than most people, knew exactly the damage that had been done to Daniel's body and mind.

"I was ready to track you down, Daniel, and you know once I get on a trail, I don't give up until I get my man."

Daniel had been dangerous as an operative, but Noah was downright deadly. "I'm doing better," Daniel said, staring through the glass. And he was doing better.

"Must be, if you're at that fleabag motel and not in jail. You inside or outside?" Noah asked, before Daniel could call him on how Noah knew his exact location.

Then again, the man collected high-tech classified gadgets like most men collected baseball cards or porn magazines.

"I'm inside."

"Yeah?" The surprise in Noah's voice was telling.

"Got the window open, and I'm half hanging out of it, but I'm inside four walls and not freaking," Daniel admitted.

"Good job. There's hope for you yet."

"So what's with all this concern for me all of a sudden?"

"First off," Noah said, sounding a lot more serious, "I didn't think you'd fare all that well in jail. Second, Sheriff Blake Redmond filled in CTC about your problem."

"Blake is one damn talkative guy lately. Not sure I'm liking that."

"Tough. Friends watch out for friends, especially the ones too stubborn to ask for help themselves when they're up to their ass in alligators."

Daniel exhaled a frustrated breath. "So what did my good ex-buddy Blake tell you?"

"That you've got yourself a woman who was buried alive and no leads. That, while your butt was in jail, someone tried to take her out again. Ransom takes his job as CTC head honcho seriously. He's pissed you never called him, seeing as this is what CTC handles. He told me to pull out all the stops to help you. He wants you on the team bad, my friend. Help is on the way."

"Where are you now?" Daniel asked.

"Approaching a certain copper mine outside of town," Noah said. "Blake wanted to make the trip, but Deputy Smithson just returned to duty after being in a coma. I'm here to make sure the new CTC forensics guy, Elijah, doesn't piss off the Midland crime-scene team with his off-the-chart brain and irritating tenacity. He's good, and he knows it, and he's not shy about expressing his opinion. He's probably forgotten more about the science of dead bodies than these yahoos ever learned."

"Have you seen the location where she was left?" Daniel asked.

Noah let out a low curse. "Just pictures some deputy took. I gotta hand it to you for going in there. That place is a claustrophobic death trap. I went stir-crazy viewing the stills, and I hadn't been held…" His voice trailed off.

Held captive in a dungeon for months.

Daniel heard the words in his mind as if Noah had uttered them.

"I had to go in the mine. The dog wouldn't let up, and

when I heard someone alive in there, I didn't have much choice," Daniel said.

"I'm impressed, but going in there had to have been tough."

"Knowing someone is out there now, trying to kill Raven, is worse."

"I see…"

Noah's tone of voice definitely changed, and Daniel cursed, hating that he'd revealed even that much about his feelings for Raven. "There's nothing to see."

"Right. Well, just know that we're doing our best. Some local engineers are bringing equipment and supplies to stabilize the mine, so we can get a camera into the pocket where you found her. With luck, we can shore up everything long enough to retrieve the evidence," Noah said. "I'll let you know when we get in."

"Thanks, Noah." Daniel paused. "I… It means a lot—"

"Don't you go all touchy-feely on me. I got a reputation to uphold."

Daniel let out a chuckle. "Sorry. It's all that psychobabble the shrinks fed me at Langley."

"I'm glad it's helping," Noah stated. "And I'm really glad you're doing better."

Noah ended the call, and Daniel stilled. *Am I doing better? Am I ready to face the past…and the future?*

He stared at his phone and clicked on the voice mail button. A long list of messages came up. One message from Noah. A couple from his loquacious buddy, Sheriff Blake Redmond. A half dozen from Ransom, the head of CTC. And fifteen from his mom that seemed to jump up and slap him upside the head with his rotten-son status. She must be furious with him by this time.

A sharp curse escaped. Man, he didn't want to call her. He'd pressed the first few buttons of her number when someone appeared about ten feet outside the window in the unkempt side yard.

"Hey, you in there," Hondo yelled. "Don't shoot me. Your phone is off the hook, and I wasn't about to knock on your door. I brought your friend some more cookies. They're still hot."

Daniel shook his head. Who was this guy? The Betty Crocker of Trouble, Texas, disguised as a Hell's Angel? "Okay, I'll unlock the door."

Hondo held up a bag to the window. "These are for your friend 'cause I made her feel bad." He scowled. "But none for you. It's your fault I had to give Lucy a sedative."

Daniel opened the door and took the bag. The smell of fresh-baked cookies filled the room. He groaned in appreciation and started to peer inside.

Hondo slapped Daniel's hand. "I said no cookies for you. Especially not my chocolate-chip-oatmeal specials. Won the county fair blue ribbon last year."

"I promise."

Hondo paused. "Maybe you can have one after your lady eats her fill—since you seem to be taking care of her all right. She looks like she needs a lot of help. Those are some bad bruises around her throat, and I confirmed with Galloway that you didn't put them there. He said you're protecting her."

Daniel glanced at the bathroom. "When she lets me."

"Women can be ornery like that sometimes." He looked around the hallway, then stepped closer. "If you need anything, I don't just bake cookies."

He lifted the pant leg of his jeans, and Daniel recognized the Bowie strapped to Hondo's ankle. A look of understanding passed between the two men.

"Hopefully it won't come to that, but it's good to know."

The big man slipped away, closing the door behind him,

and Daniel placed the white sack on the nightstand. He settled in the chair again, took a deep breath and dialed.

He braced himself for her anger, but if he was humble enough—

"Daniel Aaron Adams, why in tarnation didn't you call me back for the past three months?"

So much for a conciliatory greeting. He winced and held the phone away from his ear. "Hi, Mom. It's kind of a long story."

"I'm not going anywhere, so start talking. And remember, I can tell when you're lying."

THE MINE HADN'T changed except a few more piles of rocks had fallen from the ceiling. Not in the six years since Christopher's father had dragged him and Tad out of there during one very interesting spring break.

Tad's dad hadn't cared enough to punish them for messing around in the condemned caves, but Bill Winter had beaten Christopher enough for both fathers. The bruises had barely healed by the time school restarted. His mom had given him a note so he didn't have to undress during gym. No sense in inviting questions about the contusions decorating his back and legs.

Christopher twined the detonator wire on the dynamite and placed it near Christina's hand-carved box. He'd used his father's money to order online the best toy box ever for his adopted baby sister…and fill it with everything his dad had taken away from him over the years. What a waste, but it couldn't be helped.

He did a final check on his setup and handed the detonator cord to Tad. Back in the day they had used blasting caps they'd found in the old sheds near the mines. It's a wonder they hadn't blown themselves up. They were more sophisticated now.

"We're covering for your mom, dude?" Tad said, wrapping the explosives. He cut the cord, then wiped his hands on his jeans. "This is too twisted. I thought it was your old man who was one beer short of a six-pack." He rose from his charge and looked at the carpet. "She really did a number on that lady. With that much blood, I'm surprised she didn't die."

"Quit complaining. You wouldn't get to hunt if she were a corpse."

"Too true." Then Tad turned. "Shh." He stilled, listening intently. "Did you hear something?"

Christopher paused. "Sounds like a truck engine." He cursed, running around the bend to the mine's entrance. He peered into the light. The diesel engine of a huge flatbed loaded down with a small bulldozer rumbled down the road toward them. Smoke puffed in the air.

"Quick!" he shouted. "Hide the explosives."

Tad camouflaged his, and Christopher quickly concealed the dynamite behind the toy box and grabbed his hunting rifle. "Let's get out of here."

Tad at his heels with the detonator, Christopher raced toward daylight. The truck rumbled to a halt not too far from the mine's entrance. The driver jumped out. Dust spewed into the air as a sheriff's car pulled up beside the equipment.

Christopher shrank into the shadows. "Watch for an opening. We can't be seen."

An SUV pulled up, and the deputy turned his back on them.

"Now," Christopher hissed. He grabbed the detonator. Not looking around to see if Tad followed, Christopher sprinted to an outcropping of rocks and dove behind the cover.

Seconds later Tad slid behind him. "Leave me behind next time, why don't you?" he bit out.

"I knew you'd make it," Christopher lied. Belly first, he crawled between two mounds of rocks. A sharp stone scraped his belly, but he ignored the pain. They had to get far enough away to avoid the blast.

The desert offered more camouflage than he remembered. Christopher hunkered down behind a berm and peeked around a mesquite bush. A crime-scene van pulled up and two men filed into the cave, followed by a guy sporting a large case.

Then a deadly looking man exited an SUV. He pulled the deputy aside. Their conversation turned heated.

"I don't care what the forensics team wants. Sheriff Galloway gave us the leeway, so I'm ordering you *not* to remove any evidence from the crime scene. At least not until they get here."

Christopher couldn't make out the deputy's whine.

"Just do it," the man said. "If we're going to save Jane Doe's life, she needs to remember, and this cave is the only thing familiar to her. It needs to stay intact." He glanced at his watch. "They'll be here soon. If anything gets pulled out of that mine, you won't just have the sheriff to worry about."

Tad's eyes went wide. "Did I just hear what I think I heard?"

Christopher smiled. "I'm living right these days."

"The timing has to be perfect." Tad fingered the detonator. "But it was your dad's mine. They could tie it back to you."

"My father sold it years ago for a mountain of cash, most of it mine now," Christopher argued, setting the detonator to his side. A scorpion skittered across the sand.

Christopher slid his blade from its sheath and let the knife fly. He stabbed the creature in two without a breath.

"Must be nice to be rich," Tad said. "A dishonorable discharge doesn't do the bank account any good."

"Yeah, well, I'll pay you for the help. I deserve that money. At least a dollar a punch," Christopher said. "We just gotta wait until our target arrives. She'll go into that mine to figure out what happened to her, but it won't matter what she remembers. She won't be coming out."

DANIEL GRIPPED THE phone at his mom's stubborn words. She wouldn't let him hang up. He squeezed the guilt of not calling before now into submission. The motel room's air turned thin, and he sucked in a slow, deep breath. He leaned forward, huddling protectively over the phone as if his mom would be able to sense his desire to hug her. "I'm sorry I just disappeared like that."

A choked sob filtered through the phone. "God, I've been so worried. Are you okay?"

His throat closed off a bit. "Sure."

She didn't say a word. He closed his eyes for a moment and bit his lip.

"I told you not to lie to me, Daniel."

He shook his head. Damn the woman; she caught him every time. He'd never been able to deceive Jeanette Adams. Not as a kid. And obviously not as an adult. Even through the phone.

"How are you, son? Really?"

"Honestly?" He swallowed past the lump building in his throat. This was why he hadn't called her. He loved his family, and he knew they loved him, but his emotions had become like live grenades waiting for the pin to pull. One wrong touch could be deadly. He couldn't protect

himself, or her, from feelings that were too unpredictable.
"I don't know."

"The dreams still giving you trouble?" she asked, her
voice concerned, her sorrow seeping through.

Daniel closed his eyes, flashing on the nightmares,
when the darkness had shredded his soul. She'd witnessed
every horrifying moment of those first two weeks. She'd
seen him shut down, responding to nothing and no one.
She'd stroked his hair and whispered comforting words
like she had when he was ten, and he'd broken his arm
sliding into third base.

She'd seen him stare at the room and not see the hospital, but the dungeon walls of Bellevaux.

She'd held him when he'd cried out in pain during the
night, in a despair so raw he'd possessed no control. She'd
hurt for him when the orderlies restrained him to the bed
while he screamed and swore like a crazy man. She'd pit-
ied him, and he'd hated it, but that wasn't the worst of it.

The lowest moment he could remember was one horrible day. He'd thought he was better. The therapy session
had gone well. He'd come back to his room, and she'd
stood there, waiting for him, her hand adjusting the blinds
with the cord.

A lousy cord.

The twined string had morphed into a leather whip.
He'd lunged at her, death in his heart. She'd let out a small
cry, and he'd come back to reality, but he'd seen her eyes,
the second he'd recognized the fear on her face. Not *for*
him. Fear *of* him.

He'd seen that same expression when she'd looked at
his dad.

Something inside him had died in that moment.

The sound of the shower ceased. Daniel stiffened, but
Raven didn't come out. He wanted to hang up and knock

on the bathroom door to check on her, but she needed her time.

And he needed to make his mother understand.

"Mom," he said slowly, "I'm like Dad. I know it, and so do you." He couldn't live with destroying his family any more than his father had. He had to protect them, even if that meant hurting them—and himself.

Silence echoed through the receiver. He could barely make out a few shuddering breaths.

"The dungeon still comes back, Mom. I see it, where it's not. And the sounds. The screams. I live through that time every night. Even during the day. Just like Dad."

"But do you believe what you see is real?" she asked, her voice trembling with the question. "Do you think you're actually there?"

"It feels real," he said. "The stench. The pain." He rubbed his wrist. "I still wake up screaming, as if the whip is cutting into my back."

She bit back a small sob. "God, son, I want to kill the man who hurt you all over again, but that's a nightmare. You can't control it." She paused, and Daniel gripped the phone even tighter.

"Daniel, when you're awake—when an episode hits—do you believe you are in that dungeon in Bellevaux?"

He rubbed the scar on his cheek, then thrust his fingers through his hair. "Sometimes. Sometimes I have to fight really hard to remember, but mostly I have a double sense, and I can figure out where I am."

He heard a soft sigh. "I talked to your doctor," she said. "PTSD has a spectrum. You're not where your father was. Aaron couldn't tell the difference between the past and present. Ever. He was lost. You're not."

Daniel gripped the windowsill hard and breathed in the

cool evening air. He wanted to believe her. "Dad was okay sometimes," he whispered. "I remember."

"I know," she said. "Those days gave me hope, but they never lasted. Even years later, your father still couldn't find his way out of that mental hell. He couldn't bring himself back to reality. You can. That means you can regain your life."

"But—"

"You are *not* like your father. At all. You already have a control he never did." Her voice took on an edge he hadn't heard since one of his sisters hadn't come home by curfew one night. "Believe me. You are my son, and I will fight you for your survival."

Unable to keep still, Daniel rose, then paced back and forth, his mind whirling.

"Honey, come home. Try it. Your sister's getting married soon. It would mean the world to her for you to be there."

"I still don't trust myself." Daniel rubbed the base of his neck. "All those cars backfiring. Construction clanging like those damn metal bars closing. A crowd of people jammed into one room. Champagne corks popping. Nowhere to escape. I could snap just like he did. I won't ruin the wedding. Or their lives."

"They need you here. They trust you. So do I."

"You can't know I'll be okay," Daniel said. "You always said Dad would get better, but he never did. You told us he'd be fine, and he'd find peace, but he found it at the end of a gun."

The phone line went quiet. Too quiet. Daniel winced in regret. "I'm sorry. I didn't mean that."

"Yes, you did, and you're right. I let hope cloud my words and thoughts, seeing healing where there wasn't any. I wanted you and your sisters to still love him, to remember the man he used to be. I didn't understand just how deep his demons went."

"You don't know how deep mine go, either. I'm not the man I once was. Until I know for sure that I can keep it together, I'm not coming home. I love you and the girls. I don't want to let them down, but they've been through enough. I'd rather they hate me for what I didn't do than for what I did."

"I learned the hard way not to hide from this illness, Daniel. If I believed you were a danger to yourself or them, I'd snap you into the hospital faster than you could reach for your weapon." She paused. "Trust me."

"I do. It's trusting myself that's the problem. Bye." He ended the call and pressed the phone against his forehead.

I miss you.

Chapter Six

Raven stood frozen in place in the bathroom, holding on
to the door she'd just opened, staring at Daniel. Shock still
reverberated through her. Daniel had a home somewhere.
A woman and girls who wanted him back.

She wanted to be hurt…or angry…or something. She'd
come to think of him as hers. Her savior, her protector…
just hers. All of a sudden, the outside world had blown
apart the small bubble of safety she'd discovered in his
presence.

She'd been attacked, her memory lost, but that didn't
excuse not seeing his turmoil or his pain. How selfish
could she be? She didn't want to be that kind of person,
but she was scared. Her belly rolled at the thought of being
alone—without the one man she could trust. She needed
him. But not at this cost.

Her fingers bit into the wooden door so hard that they
cramped. She couldn't take her gaze off him. His entire
body sagged in despair.

Her feelings didn't matter. Seeing how broken Daniel
looked right now pushed her own needs aside. She wanted
to comfort him, but he straightened his shoulders. His face
went expressionless as stone as he shook off his emotions.

Doubting he would welcome her witnessing him so vulnerable, she cleared her throat and shoved the door so it

thudded against the wall, pretending she was just coming out of the bathroom.

His narrowed gaze snapped to hers. He hesitated for a moment, then rose and crossed the room, picking up a white paper bag on the way. "Hondo says hi."

She took the sack from him and studied his features, searching for some chink in his armor.

"What?" he demanded.

She didn't know if she'd been brave when she knew her own name, but his intensity didn't encourage questions. Would she normally have backed off? She had no idea, and she had to know.

"You're leaving, aren't you?" she said. "I don't blame you. I'm more trouble than you asked for. I understand."

He pocketed the phone and glared at her. "I told you. I'm not going anywhere. Not until you're safe. We may not know each other very well, but I keep my promises."

"Your wife—"

Understanding lit his eyes, and they crinkled at the corners when he gave her a slight grin. "I'm not married, Raven. That was my mom."

"Oh." The wave of relief that swept through Raven nearly buckled her knees. It wasn't right, though. She had no business feeling this way. She didn't even know him.

He sidled up to her. "How much did you hear?"

She couldn't meet his gaze, and his proximity sent a shiver up her spine. "I didn't mean to eavesdrop. And it was just the last few sentences. Something about not going home and loving the girls. I thought you might have kids."

"I was talking about my sisters."

"That's great. I mean, it must be nice to have siblings." She groaned, sinking onto the bed, burying her head in her hands. "Just hog-tie me and shut me up before I make an even bigger fool of myself."

He tilted her chin up. "I'm flattered," he said, his smile gentle. "Now, dig into the sack, and you'll find enough chocolate to distract you."

"Why would that help?"

"According to my sisters, it's a universal girl thing." He shrugged.

"I don't remember, but I'll take a chance." She opened the bag, and a sweet smell wafted from inside. She inhaled and her stomach grumbled. Chocolate chip. She lifted out one warm cookie, took a bite and closed her eyes, moaning in pleasure. "I think we have a winner. This is amazing." She pinched off a small bite, holding it to his lips. "Try it."

"Hondo has rules…"

"Then we won't tell him," she whispered. "But this cookie is orgasmic."

At the words, her shocked gaze captured his equally stunned one.

His eyes darkened, and Raven's breath stuttered. "I mean, it's really, really good."

"Then I'll definitely have some." His tone deepened, he leaned forward and snagged the morsel from her fingertips, licking off a small bit of chocolate that clung to her skin.

She cleared her throat. "Best thing you ever tasted. Right?"

With a run of his tongue across his lips, he stared at her. "Yeah, and the cookie's not half-bad, either."

She bit her lower lip. "I want to—" Before her brain stopped her, she pressed her lips to his mouth, and her body leaned into him.

Daniel didn't resist. His arm snaked around her waist and tightened his hold, drawing her to him. He took over, parting her lips, exploring her mouth, holding her captive with his caress.

Lord, he could kiss.

Forget chocolate. She had a whole new favorite taste. Raven wrapped her arms around his neck and held him closer, taking the kiss even deeper.

The room faded away until all she knew was his touch, his scent, his passion. She nipped at his lower lip, wanting even more, rocking against the hardness pressing into her belly.

With a growl he eased back. "This is a bad idea," he said softly.

"I don't care," she whispered against his mouth. And she didn't. She just wanted to feel. This crazy heat that was going through her was something she wanted to know more about. She couldn't believe she'd ever felt anything like what Daniel made her feel.

Surely I'd remember something like this.

Ignoring his intended retreat, she held his face in her hands and kissed him again, reveling in the lightning that sparked from her core, up through her breasts. She pushed them against his chest to ease the ache.

"Wow. Where has this feeling been all my life? I like it!" She couldn't stop the words and bit her lip. "The doctor said frontal lobe injuries often reduce inhibitions a bit. Is this what he meant?"

A small growl escaped from deep inside Daniel's chest. "I don't know."

"Well, I certainly hope so." She clutched at his shirt and tugged him closer.

Suddenly his phone vibrated on the table with an insistent hum. Daniel let out a long, slow breath. "I hate phones."

He clicked Talk and dragged it to his ear. "Adams." His voice came out husky.

Raven leaned in to listen.

"You two okay?" Sheriff Galloway asked. "You sound funny."

"We're fine." Daniel put his arm around Raven. "We're holed up in the motel. By the way, thanks for paying for a week in advance."

"I didn't figure you carried much cash, and Raven doesn't seem like she's going to be remembering her bank accounts anytime soon," Galloway said. "But on the good news front, preliminary blood tests on the denim material that your dog tore show it's a potential match for Raven's attacker. Type AB negative kind of narrows things down with this small-town population."

"Trouble knows whose it is. He'll recognize the guy if he comes across the scent again," Daniel said.

Trouble's ears perked up at the mention of his name, and he cocked his head. Raven petted the sweetie, and he leaned up against her leg. She caressed behind his ears and smiled as he pushed his head harder against her hand.

"What about samples from the mine? Can they retrieve them?" Daniel shook his head at Trouble, and Raven simply smiled.

"Your CTC colleagues indicated the engineering crew believes they can stabilize the mine long enough to process the crime scene. If nothing else goes wrong out there, they can be done by the end of the day."

"They haven't moved anything yet, have they?" Daniel asked.

"They're on hold until you get there," the sheriff said.

"We'll leave soon," Daniel said and ended the call.

Go back to the mine? Raven's stomach rolled at the thought. "I don't know—"

"The doctor said you should retrace your steps. See if anything out there triggers a memory now that your symptoms are improving."

Despite her fear, she nodded. "We're not going to find out the truth sitting in this motel room, are we?"

Daniel gave her an approving nod. "Exactly. And you'll be protected. I'll be there, and so will the deputy and two men from CTC." At her questioning glance, he shrugged. "I have a few friends with some skills that could come in handy."

Men like him. Raven didn't have to ask more. She clasped her heart-shaped locket. "I have a baby out there, and I need to find her. No matter what the danger."

He crossed the room and took out his gun. A click sounded, and the magazine fell into his hand. He checked it and then reloaded. "We're going to find out what happened to the baby. I promise you that."

Raven went still. Daniel hadn't said he would *find* the baby. Only that he'd discover what happened. Did he think her baby was dead?

For all her earlier bravery, Raven could not get up the courage to ask him.

THE ROAD TO the mine looked different from a truck. Daniel glanced at Raven. The afternoon sun hit the side of her face. Bruises had started rising near her temple—green, blue and yellow mottled in a painful-looking pattern. She'd been through so much.

She clutched the locket. "How much farther?"

He slowed the truck to a crawl, and Trouble let out a bark from the bed of the pickup. Daniel studied her expression, searching for any sign of recognition. "Anything look familiar?"

"I don't know. Dirt road, desert, shrubs, mountains in the distance." The intensity on her face didn't waver as she gazed out the front windshield at the curving road heading toward the mine where Daniel and Trouble had found her. But with each mile, he watched the light fade from her gaze. Her hand tightened on his, and his gut twisted. His shoulders tensed. Without Raven's memory, everyone they came into contact with was a suspect.

They came within a mile of the mine, and her chin fell to her chest. "This is useless. I don't recognize anything."

"This is the first try, darlin'. You still have healing to do. Cut yourself some slack."

She glanced over at him. "We both know this is the only lead. Don't patronize me. I may not have a memory, but I'm not a fool."

"Sorry," he said. "You're right. But wishing won't make it happen. There's forensic evidence in that cave, including blood. We have a lot of trails to follow."

Raven twisted in her seat. "DNA from the blood should help," she mused. "Comparing the thirteen core loci could get a match using CODIS."

Her eyes widened as he stared at her.

"Oh, wow, where did that come from?" She fell back into the seat.

"Well, Ms. Scientist. What else do you know about DNA profiling?"

He could almost see her mind whirl with effort.

"I know a lot. A whole lot." Excitement lit her face. "Did you know that if you have a CODIS profile or even a small sample of DNA, you can falsify the evidence? But you can also test for fake DNA."

She went on to describe in detail exactly what that entailed, but the explanation went way over Daniel's head.

"So you're a lab rat," he said. "That's pretty complex stuff to remember. You could give Elijah a run for his money."

"I don't know about that, but I think I was a scientist of some sort. That will help, right?"

"If you're from around here, we can narrow the search to biotech companies, universities and the like. Ask if they're missing a beautiful, brilliant brain," Daniel said.

She smiled at him, hope returning to her eyes. He'd wanted to see her smile again, to wipe away the hurt any way he could. More and more, he understood why his mother had kept the truth of his father's illness from them when they were kids. Hope meant everything.

The truck rounded the final curve leading to the mine. Several vehicles created a makeshift lot just east of the entrance to the mine.

Daniel pulled in near them, parked and turned in his seat. "Okay, let's take this slow. Focus on all your senses—sounds, smells, the feel of the earth beneath your feet. Memories are tied to those other senses even more than sight."

He knew that firsthand.

He exited the vehicle and scanned the cleared area in front of the mine for anything out of place. With a quick look toward the desert with its small hills and occasional shrub, he opened the door for her, as satisfied as he could be.

She slid out, and Trouble jumped from the back of the truck, standing guard beside her. Daniel motioned for her to stay put as he walked away, with her always in his sight.

Galloway's full-time deputy walked over and tipped his hat. "Deputy Adams, sir."

Daniel grimaced. Trouble's tail stiffened. His ears went flat, and a warning growl rumbled from him.

The deputy paused. "He bite?"

"Not usually, but he seems to hate uniforms. I wouldn't push it."

The kid backed off.

Noah Bradford walked up to Daniel and crooked a brow. "Did I hear him say 'deputy'?"

"It's temporary."

"CTC will be glad to hear that."

Daniel hadn't seen his friend for months. Noah now had a close-trimmed beard, which meant he was probably headed on a mission soon. Daniel liked to change up his appearance. Disguises had saved his life more than once.

Daniel held out his hand. "I'm glad you're here. What's going on?"

Noah swiped at the dust on his shirt. "The engineers shored up the entrance, but the place is a death trap. We were waiting for you."

"Thanks," Daniel said.

Noah glanced at the deputy. "Go keep an eye on Elijah, deputy. He might steal some of your evidence."

The deputy's face paled. "He wouldn't!" The kid took off back to the edge of the mine, where a tall man knelt next to several cases of equipment.

"That CTC's infamous new forensics lead?" Daniel asked, grinning at the deputy's nervousness. Elijah's ornery reputation had become legendary in a matter of months.

Noah smiled. "Yeah. Guy's a pit bull when it comes to evidence. Not much of a talker, though."

"And you are?"

"Compared to Elijah, yeah. I'm all about communication." Noah's sharp gaze took in Daniel's appearance. "You look better than you did on our last foray in Carder. Guess the two-thousand-mile trek did you some good."

"Maybe." Daniel looked over his shoulder at Raven, who stood off to the side staring intently at the mine. She closed her eyes for a moment, her brow furrowed.

"I read the report. You got her out of that cave, Daniel.

I'd have put up a few grand against those odds last time I saw you. Hell, your heart pounded like a rabbit's when you were sitting in a cockpit, and the damn thing had a window."

"She needed help." Daniel studied her black hair shining in the sunlight and the bruise on her temple. "She's got guts, Noah. She could have wrapped up in a ball and imploded, but she just doesn't quit."

"You like her."

Daniel rubbed the base of his neck. "Yeah. I shouldn't. What if—?"

Noah crossed his arms. "The man in front of me won't let her down." He paused. "I wasn't sure when I should give you this, but…I think now's the time." Noah turned to an SUV parked a few feet away. He opened the back door and revealed a small bag. Without words he reached in and pulled out a leather whip.

Daniel froze. Brown leather, braided, a brass seal around the handle. He recognized it well. The crest of the Duke of Sarbonne from Bellevaux. He couldn't take his eyes off the torture weapon. His palms went sweaty. A crack sounded in his memory. His gaze snapped to Noah's. "What the hell are you playing at?"

"Tough love, my brother." Noah shoved it at Daniel. "I brought it back from Bellevaux. I didn't know if I'd ever give it to you. The shrink said to use my own judgment." Noah glanced at Raven. "I think you're ready to break the hold the memories of this whip have over you."

Daniel shoved the whip at Noah. "Get rid of it. Bury it, burn it, trash it. Just get it the hell away from me."

"Conquer your demons." Noah gripped Daniel's arm and forced Daniel's hand around the whip.

With some sort of twisted need, Daniel let him and didn't throw him to the ground.

Noah clasped Daniel's shoulder. "The bastard who used this on you is dead, but he still lives in your head. Crack it until the sound doesn't haunt you any longer. Until you break its hold, Sarbonne wins. He stole so much from you, Daniel. Don't let him have your soul."

The leather felt stiff in Daniel's hand. His heart pounded; his gut bubbled with a fury unlike anything he'd ever known. His jaw throbbed until it ached. "Sometimes you can't win," he gritted. "My dad didn't."

"But you can. We've both seen the men who come home with more demons than they can live with. Some move on. Some don't. Go forward, Daniel. For yourself. And for her." Noah nodded over at Raven who'd turned to stare at them, her face concerned. She took a step toward them.

Daniel jerked the hand holding the whip behind his back. He wasn't ready for her questions. "Fine. I'll take it. But the first chance I get, I'm tossing it out the window. I want to forget."

"And that's worked so well for you, Forrest Gump."

Daniel bit out a four-letter word.

Noah's expression turned serious. "Look, do what you want with it, Daniel, however you can exorcise the demons. It's in your hands now." With that, Noah turned and headed toward Elijah.

Daniel crossed to the truck and tossed the whip into the back.

"Who was that?" Raven asked.

"Someone with a warped idea of friendship." Daniel frowned.

Raven touched his arm. "Are you okay?"

He turned to her. "I'll be fine," he lied, unwilling to reveal how much seeing that damn weapon nearly sent him to his knees. "How about you? Any more memories?"

"You," she said softly. "All I remember is you."

A rifle shot echoed through the air. Daniel shoved Raven into the ground next to the truck, then pushed her beneath the vehicle. In one swift movement he'd placed his body between her and the gunfire, and pulled out his weapon.

A bullet ricocheted off the metal just over their heads. "It's coming from behind that dirt ledge!" Noah shouted, pulling out his own weapon. "Everyone take cover in the mine."

Men ran from their positions, preparing to go into the cave. Several shots followed them in.

Almost simultaneously a thwack hit the ground near Daniel. "Two shooters!" Daniel shouted. No time for waiting. They were too vulnerable out here. "Cover us."

Elijah and Noah fired at the mound of dirt hiding the gunmen. Daniel grabbed Raven's hand. "Run!"

In seconds they dove into the cave. Elijah followed. He met Daniel's gaze with a hard look. "This the idiot who came after Raven before?"

Daniel had expected Elijah to be a science geek, but this man could hold his own in a battle. Huge, brilliant—and pissed.

Daniel nodded.

"Noah's positioned outside behind the rock outcropping, but he doesn't have an endless supply of bullets," Elijah said.

"What do you have for firearms?" Daniel asked. "No way we can stay in here."

Elijah nodded in agreement. "But it's almost like the shooter drove us in...or he's a horrible shot."

"I don't like this." Daniel grabbed the small flashlight still hooked to his belt.

"If he wants us in here," Elijah said, "there's got to be a good reason."

"Yeah. Or a damned bad one."

"Anyone with a flashlight, look around quickly for anything out of place."

Within minutes, a shout came out. "I found something."

Daniel raced around the bend.

Elijah pointed at the hint of red primer cord nearly concealed beneath a pile of rocks.

"It's rigged to blow," Daniel cursed. "Deputy, get everyone out. Cover them."

Elijah walked the area, then cursed. "There's another one." He pulled gloves from his pocket, snapped them on and pulled out a knife, taking it to the bloodstained carpet.

"No time for that," Daniel said. "Hurry."

He raced around the bend. "Everybody head east toward the rocks," Daniel shouted. "Don't stop until you reach safety. We'll try to cover you."

"Noah, we've got to come out!" Daniel yelled. "Lay down some cover."

A spray of bullets erupted from Noah's hiding place.

"Go! Now!"

The men hurled out of the opening just as Elijah skidded beside Daniel holding two evidence bags: one with a piece of carpet, the other with what looked to be wood shavings covered in blood.

Daniel glared at him.

"It's our one chance," Elijah said. "You know it as well as I do."

Daniel grabbed Raven's hand and bolted, his gun blazing. "Stay behind me."

Terror lined her face, but she ran. Bullets smacked the rocks above them. Daniel leaped behind a boulder and tugged Raven with him.

A fireball burst from the mouth of the mine, a conflagration shooting through the air. Heat seared the air around

Daniel and Raven, but the boulder blocked the worst of it. Nearby, two vehicles were engulfed in flames.

The second bomb exploded, and the ground beneath them shuddered. Daniel wrapped his arms around Raven's head and ducked down, shielding her. A rain of dirt pummeled them.

When the earth had settled, Daniel took a quick glance at the cave. The entire mouth of the mine was packed with dirt and rubble.

An engine revved. They both turned to see Noah and Elijah standing in the dirt firing at an escaping van. Where had that come from? The vehicle must have been hidden behind one of the large berms off to the side of the road leading up to the mine.

"Damn it, they got away," Daniel said.

She raised her gaze to his. "What's so important about me and my baby that they want me dead, and were willing to kill all these innocent people to make it happen?"

Daniel couldn't hold back the fury building in his gut. "I don't know, but we're going to find out."

RAVEN SAT IN Daniel's truck, gripping the armrest with a death hold, her fingers numb. The entire scene had been surreal. Noah and Elijah had declared the area clear. They'd discovered dozens of spent casings from what they'd called a semiautomatic varmint rifle, two sets of footprints and skidding tire marks, but the snipers had vanished.

Several trucks and a lot of equipment had been burned. The place looked like a war zone. For a few minutes most of the crime-scene investigators had been shell-shocked, then the anger had hit, and they started collecting evidence—what little there was. The mine was blocked off. Permanently this time. The whole infrastructure had collapsed.

Noah and Elijah had stayed to help, but Daniel had wanted her out of there.

Raven slid a sidelong glance at him. Once again he'd saved her life. The muscle in his jaw throbbed with fury. His knuckles had whitened with his tense grip on the steering wheel. He kept checking the rearview mirror and the side mirrors.

Even Trouble stayed at attention, as if on guard. The dog had nine lives. He'd been in the truck when the nearby vehicles had gone up in flames. The mutt had been shaken, but he'd come out of the attack none the worse for wear.

"Are we going back to the motel?" Raven asked.

"For the moment. I don't like it. Someone was waiting for us at that damn mine. I shouldn't have taken you there until they were caught. I should have at least had a chopper clear the area," Daniel said. "I'm off my game. I put you in danger." He swerved to the side of the road and shoved the vehicle into Park. "I've been thinking about this for a while, Raven. I might not be the best person to help you. Noah can protect you in ways I can't. I'd like for you to go with him."

"No. I don't know him." She grabbed his arm. "I know you. I trust you. You protected me."

"You don't understand." He let out a slow stream of air. "I was held captive in Bellevaux last November and December. I was tortured, beaten, whipped and starved. They shattered my leg in three places. My ribs and hands weren't much better. I'm put together with bolts and screws. They messed with my head. I've got claustrophobia and PTSD. I get flashbacks. If something happened to you because I didn't know where I was…I couldn't live with that, Raven."

He looked away, his face devoid of expression, and she knew under normal circumstances he would never have revealed the truth, but it explained so much. Their time in the cave, how he could calm her down. He understood the panic, the fear. She couldn't think of anyone better to help her.

She slid closer to him, and his entire body stiffened. "I see you fighting your demons," she said softly. "Help me battle mine. I *have* to remember, Daniel, and I'm not sure I can do this alone. I trust you to help me."

Daniel shoved his hand through his hair. "You're making a mistake."

She crossed her arms in front of her chest. "I don't think so."

He pulled back onto the deserted highway. No matter what Raven said, he'd contact Noah. He didn't trust himself. Just as they entered Trouble's city limits, Daniel's phone rang.

He punched Speaker. "Adams."

A crackling voice filled the cab. "Elijah's equipment is toast. He can't test the evidence he salvaged. I have to fly him back to Carder. Do you want another CTC crew?"

Daniel rubbed his face. "I'll let you know. Keep me posted on the results." He paused. "The data probably won't hold up in court due to the chain of evidence issues, but that doesn't matter. Run Raven's prints and DNA through every database we've got. Local, federal, international. We *have* to identify her. We have to find her child and the baby's father," Daniel ordered.

"We'll do everything we can," Noah promised. "If you decide to come back with us, call within the hour. Otherwise, I'll keep in touch. And, Daniel, think about working with what I gave you. What have you got to lose?"

Raven shuddered. She had seen Noah hand off the whip to Daniel, had watched his automatic response. She hoped Daniel threw the whip away. Horrible thing.

"Got it." Daniel ended the call and turned to her. "We

should go with them. The company headquarters in Carder is a fortress. CTC can protect you."

Raven squeezed the locket in her hand. "Whoever wants me dead probably has my daughter, don't they?"

"It's a safe bet."

He didn't offer any comfort. How could he? Raven closed her eyes, knowing what she had to do. "The men who attacked us are my only connection to my child. I won't hide away somewhere protected while she could be…" Her voice broke. "I have to stay close. I have to try everything I can to remember. Maybe, if I set myself up as bait, I could get close enough to see one of their faces—"

"No way."

"What choice do we have? We have no solid leads. I have this locket. There was a toy box in that mine. Everything points to my baby being at the center of this crazy conspiracy. I'm not leaving town until I know." She looked up at him. "Please."

Daniel kneaded the back of his neck. "Noah gave me a computer program that the CTC psychologist has been using to help witnesses and trauma victims remember details. If you want—"

She leaned forward, eagerness pulsing through her. "You don't even have to ask. What are we waiting for?"

Finally something to help her remember.

"Don't get your hopes up. It's experimental. It doesn't always work, and you're still physically bruised. We haven't tried this with anyone this recently injured. The concussion may affect it."

"It doesn't matter. We have to try. *I* have to try."

Daniel nodded cautiously, but for the first time since she had woken, Raven sensed possibilities.

"We need quiet, solitude, safety," he said. "The motel won't do. I'll need to find another location."

He pulled into the motel's parking lot in front of their room. "We aren't safe here?"

"You're not safe anywhere. It's a small town. They know we're nearby. It's time to go off the grid."

Daniel exited the truck, then took her by the hand. She followed him, watching him as he walked to the front of the motel, looking around, his entire body alert. This was the warrior. This was the man who made her feel like she could breathe again.

The motel's office door opened up. Daniel's hand went to his midback, where she knew he tucked his weapon. Lucy stuck her head around the side.

Raven touched Daniel's arm. "Don't scare Lucy," she whispered.

He sent Lucy a slight nod and smiled at the timid woman. "What can we do for you?"

"Hondo made a batch of peanut butter cookies," she said quietly. "Can I bring them over without you shooting me up?"

"I don't—"

Raven shoved her elbow into Daniel's side. "Sure, Lucy. We'd love some."

"I don't like peanut butter," he muttered to Raven with a frustrated glare. "But I was going to say that I don't want her to be afraid of me."

"After scaring the woman to death, peanut butter is your new favorite food," Raven said. She brightened her smile. "I can't wait to try them, Lucy."

The woman grinned and walked toward them, carrying a small wicker basket. Hondo walked protectively behind her, glowering at Daniel, as all four made their way to room six.

"I don't think this was Hondo's idea," Daniel whispered to Raven, as he pushed his key into the lock and shoved open the door. "Go into the room and stay out of sight," he said. "No lights and don't go near the windows. I don't want to attract attention. Once they leave, we'll throw our stuff in the truck and get out of here."

Raven nodded. "Agreed."

She walked in and sat across the room, away from the door, while Lucy set her basket on the small table by the motel room window. Daniel hovered in an awkward attempt to help her, but Hondo walked in with a second basket and shoved him aside. With a sigh, Daniel lowered the blinds, dimming the available light, but blocking the view from outside.

Raven covered her mouth with a smile.

"These cookies are *not* my idea," Hondo said. "Lucy felt bad she fainted."

"I'm sorry I scared you," Daniel said, leaning against the wall next to Raven. She could tell he wanted to get this over with and pack.

Lucy poured milk into two glasses and laid out a spread of cookies and fruit. She even added a small vase of flowers before stepping back and admiring her handiwork.

"It's beautiful, Lucy," Raven said. "Thank you."

Lucy glared at Hondo. "See. Told you they'd like them," she said, wrinkling her nose. "But it's so dark in here. At least turn on the light—"

"No!" Daniel shouted as Lucy's form was thrown into silhouette against the blind.

The next moment, a spray of gunfire shattered the glass. Lucy fell to the ground. Hondo leaped toward his sister, and another volley of bullets peppered the motel room.

Daniel vaulted to the door, racing into the parking lot in time to see a car screech away.

Raven grabbed a towel and dropped to her knees beside Lucy. "Oh, my God, Lucy. Daniel, call 9-1-1."

Her heart twisted with guilt as she pressed at the wounds on Lucy's chest, trying to stop the flow of blood, but it seeped through. So much blood. Too much blood.

Daniel slammed back into the room, Trouble on his heels, and her gaze snapped to him. He plastered the phone at his ear. "We need an ambulance at Copper Mine Motel. Drive-by shooting. Two down. The car was a late model white sedan. The license plate was covered in mud, but my guess is Texas plates."

"Daniel," Raven choked, the towel turning red in her hands. "I need more."

He sprinted to the bathroom and threw her a set. She grabbed one and replaced the one that had soaked through. Trouble whimpered and lay in the corner while Daniel ran to Hondo. The big man let out a low moan. Daniel pressed a cloth against Hondo's bleeding shoulder and met Raven's gaze.

Her eyes burned with emotion when she looked down at Lucy's innocent face. "You're going to be okay. The ambulance is coming."

God, please let her be okay.

"Hondo," Lucy whispered. "I'm all bloody. Am I dying?"

Her brother shoved at Daniel, groaned and rolled toward her.

"No, baby girl," he said, his voice choked. "I promised Mom I'd take care of you. And I always keep my promises. You're going to be fine."

"It hurts," she whimpered. "I don't like it." Her voice trailed off, and her eyes closed.

Hondo struggled to his hands and knees while Daniel pressed a towel against his shoulder. The big man reached out a shaking hand. "Lucy—"

Raven placed her shaking fingers at Lucy's throat. "I feel a pulse. But barely."

Hondo cried out with grief. "Who did this?"

From a distance, a siren screamed toward them.

Raven met Daniel's gaze. "This is all my fault," she whispered. "If only I could remember and stop these people.

Blood soaked the second towel. Lucy was still. Too still.

"Don't give up," Raven begged. "Please don't. Hondo needs you."

Hondo sank to the floor, holding his sister's hand. "These animals don't deserve any mercy, Adams. You make sure my Lucy gets justice."

Daniel's face went hard. "I promise we'll get them, Hondo. I keep my promises, too. I'll find out who did this, and they'll pay. No matter what it takes."

Chapter Seven

The sun had fallen too far in the sky by the time the crime-scene team had come and gone. Daniel stuffed the last few personal items into his duffel while the doctor checked out Raven in the motel room next door. They'd be hard pressed to make it to the location he'd found when he had searched the satellite images of the area for a place to hole up.

The scent of blood permeated everywhere from the stain on the floor of room six where the paramedics had worked so hard to save Lucy. Her heart had stopped twice, and when they'd carried her out, her complexion was still gray.

Daniel had seen enough bullet injuries to know her chances weren't good. He didn't know whether Hondo would survive, either, but he knew if Lucy didn't make it, the man's life would be changed forever. Hondo had lived to protect his sister.

Nothing Daniel could say would ever change the reality that his choice to return to the motel may have cost two lives. Hondo had every right to hate him. If something like this were to happen to either one of his sisters, Daniel would lose it. He yanked the duffel bag's zipper closed, his frustration boiling deep inside.

The men who were after Raven didn't care who they hurt. Anyone who got between them and their objective was fair game. Daniel hadn't lied to Hondo. Their attackers deserved to die for what they'd done.

Sheriff Galloway stood in the doorway and scowled. "I don't like you taking off into parts unknown with no backup."

"Tough. We've got to disappear. Lucy's closer to dead than alive, and Hondo's not much better. You hired me for my expertise. Well, my gut says 'get the hell out of here.' I'm holing up in a place they can't find us. And if they do luck out, I'll defend Raven with whatever it takes." Daniel tucked the Glock in the back of his jeans. "I can't protect Raven here."

The only other way he could help her was to make use of his psychology degree and try the memory therapy. For that she needed quiet and safety. Daniel could use the open spaces to think. Yet they had to be close enough to Trouble, Texas, that they could return quickly, and since the town truly was hours from anywhere, that left one option.

"Which way are you heading?" Galloway asked, his voice low.

Daniel slung his duffel over his shoulder. "Sorry, Sheriff. The fewer who know the better."

Galloway slapped his Stetson against his leg. "How will I get in touch with you? What if I discover her identity?"

"Call Blake Redmond. I'll keep in touch with him," Daniel said. "That's the best I can do." He shoved his way past Galloway, scrutinized the surroundings, then tossed their meager belongings into the back of the truck beside the small satchel Noah had given him and the whip. His entire body on high alert, he searched once again. Though the clouds to the west had darkened the horizon, two hours of daylight were left. Daniel hoped it was enough.

The streets had been cordoned off due to the crime

scene. Galloway's young deputy stood watch. So far, so good.

Daniel returned to the neighboring room and stood in the doorway as the doctor finished his check on Raven.

"She okay?" he asked.

The gray-haired man scowled. "For someone who's been in a cave-in, an explosion and a drive-by, sure, she's great."

Daniel grimaced. "Now you know why we're leaving." He held out his hand to Raven. "You ready, darlin'?"

She rose. "How are Lucy and Hondo?" she asked.

"In surgery in El Paso," Sheriff Galloway said. "It's too soon to tell."

"Would you tell Hondo…" Raven gripped Daniel's hand like she clung to a lifeline. "Would you tell him I'm so very, very sorry? I wish…" Her voice trailed off. "I hope they'll be okay. I guess there's nothing else to say, is there?"

Daniel led her to the truck and helped her inside. Trouble looked at him expectantly. "Come on, boy. You get into the front seat for this ride. I think she needs you."

Trouble hopped onto the floorboard, and Raven scratched his ears.

Daniel shut the door on them and faced Galloway. "Thanks, Sheriff. I'll be in touch to resign when this is over."

Galloway ignored the comment. "Stay safe."

Daniel paused. "If you see Hondo, tell him we're both sorry. For everything. If he ever needs anything…I won't forget what happened today."

"I'll let him know when the time is right."

With one last stiff nod, Daniel slid into the driver's side and pulled out onto the highway. Raven sat quietly next to him, her hand buried in Trouble's fur as if the animal would keep her grounded. A mountain loomed in the distance to the west, the sun barely setting over its tall peaks.

"Where are we going?" Raven asked, her voice raw with emotion.

"There's a section of desert below Guadalupe Peak with several caves where we can find shelter and quiet," Daniel said. "I have a SAT phone. Noah and Elijah can get in touch if they discover something. If the CTC psychological program works, we can call them. But we'll be safe there."

He glanced in the rearview mirror and tugged hard at the vehicle, pulling off the road and behind a small bunch of juniper trees. With a quick move, he slid out his Glock and waited.

"What are you doing? Did you see someone?"

"No, but if we're being followed, this is the only way out of town. I'm taking no chances."

A few minutes passed. Not one car went by. Daniel glanced at his map and took off down a dirt road. The holes and rock roads jarred the truck. Daniel peered over the darkening landscape. He'd have to stop soon, but he wanted to put as much distance between them and Trouble, Texas, as possible.

"I don't think anyone *could* follow us, even if they wanted to," Raven said with a quick look behind them.

"That's the point." The final rays of dusk pierced the dust, exploding in color across a sea of rock and sand. No sign of civilization peeked up for miles in any direction.

"No distractions, that's certain," Daniel said, scanning her face with a concerned gaze. "Any dizziness left?" he asked.

She shook her head, and for the first time since he'd found her in that mine, he didn't see her wince. She pressed her fingers against the cut on her temple. "My head is still a little sore, but at least it doesn't feel like someone took a hammer to it anymore."

"Good." Daniel studied the dramatic rocks thrusting up from the earth. "The place we're heading will be quiet. It'll give you a chance to rest your mind."

"I may never be able to have peace again. Too much has happened," she said softly. "I don't know if I'll ever forget Lucy's look at me after she was shot. She hurt so bad," Raven said, her hand twisting the material of the latest pair of borrowed scrubs she wore.

"If I've learned anything over the past few months, it's that you can't forget. You can only try to live with what happened." He patted her hand. "You have the strength to do that, Raven. I know it."

Uncertainty clouded her expression—and something more.

"I can see a question in your eyes, Raven. What do you want to know?"

"Horrible things were done to you," she said softly. "I can't imagine. Do you think...do you think it'll ever be over for you?"

God, what a question. Unknowingly, the woman had flailed a layer of skin off his soul with her words. "I don't know."

Her gaze met his, and she nodded. "Thank you for being honest. It's one of the many reasons I trust you."

He cleared his throat. "Look, I'm not one to trust. I'm trained to deceive. In every assignment I dealt with men and women who had no consciences, who would lie, cheat or steal for money or power or a twisted view of the world." He stuffed his free hand in his pocket and toyed with the bullet casing.

"Then why do you keep doing your job? You sound like you hate it."

"Someone has to."

Her gaze narrowed with concern. "This CTC you keep mentioning—you work for them? How can they expect you—?"

"They want me to take a job. Right now I'm…" he paused "…on a leave of absence from my regular gig."

Her questions were getting too pointed. He shifted in his seat and checked the darkening sky. An outcropping of rock caught his attention, and he recognized the lay of the land. Maybe his luck was changing. "We're almost there." He pointed to a spot halfway up the side of a low mesa.

A flash of lightning pierced the blue-gray clouds, its jagged end snapping toward earth. A rumble of thunder followed the spark.

Large raindrops hit the windshield.

Trouble whined.

"Are we climbing up?" Raven asked.

"There's a four-wheel-drive path halfway up. We can't leave the truck down here. That last turn took us into a low-lying wash." The truck's headlights flashed against a rock face. "See the water-level mark. Flash floods can happen out here in no time."

"It's not raining that hard."

"Maybe not here but who knows up in those mountains. It doesn't happen often, but at this time of year, you can't be too careful."

By the time Daniel maneuvered the truck to higher ground and parked as close to the cave as he could get, the rain had started really coming down. "Who'd think we'd end up in a rainstorm in the deserts of West Texas? But it's too dark to change plans."

He slammed on his Stetson, ducked out of the truck, and then grabbed his equipment and the small bag of toys Noah had given him. His fingertips hesitated over the whip, but with a small curse, he grabbed it.

Noah knew him well. Daniel wouldn't let the duke win. A few hundred feet later, he stood in front of a shallow cave. At least he didn't have to search for occupants; he could see to the back. Thank God. No more dark, winding passages. He returned to Raven, opened the passenger door. Trouble jumped out of the truck and headed for shelter.

"Smart dog," Raven said.

"He's a survivor." Daniel led Raven to the cave. He unpacked a sleeping bag and the provisions Galloway had provided for them.

Within minutes they'd set up camp. A small hunting lantern illuminated the earthen room. Darkness had closed around them, but the night roared with thunder, and lightning streaked between the clouds and arced like daggers to the earth. Rain pummeled the dry ground, running in torrents off the side of the mesa into the wash.

"I wasn't expecting this," he said, raising his voice over the roar.

Raven huddled against the rock wall, hugged her arms to her body and shivered slightly. The temperature had cooled. Daniel pulled off his field jacket and wrapped it around her.

"Thank you." Raven smiled up at him in gratitude. His heart did a flip inside his chest. She knelt down and pulled out a protein bar. "Dinner?"

He snagged the food and sat just inside the cave's entrance, looking out at the rain. This position was safer—in so many ways. "We won't be leaving anytime soon," he said quietly. "With this much water, the ground would collapse from under us. Even the four-wheel drive will have trouble getting through these conditions."

"Which means no one can follow us," Raven said quietly. "We're safe."

He twisted to look at her vulnerable features. "Yes, you're safe." *Even from me.*

God, he hoped so.

Raven clasped the locket. "I wish I knew if the baby was."

What could he say? Daniel rubbed the nape of his neck to ease the tension. He focused on her face, doing his damnedest to ignore the three walls encroaching on him. The fresh air helped. At least his heart wasn't racing through his chest. Small rivulets of water dripped down his back, reminding him he wasn't being especially supportive. He was sitting half outside.

Raven sat alone at the back of the cave, looking small and desolate. He couldn't deny her need. Shoving aside his demons, he ducked inside, something he would never have done a few days ago. He settled next to her and wrapped his arms around her. "You're safe now," he repeated, pressing her trembling body close to his side. "Let's look at her photograph."

The flickering lantern bathed Raven's pale skin in light, illuminating her face. God, she truly was beautiful.

She released the locket's catch and opened the necklace. Noah had taken a few strands of the baby's hair and a copy of the photograph back to Carder for analysis, but he'd left some hair and the original snapshot.

Daniel had insisted. Raven needed the connection those few strands gave her. He knew that. When everything was taken away, somehow you had to find one concrete belief to hold on to. Raven's belief was that the child in the locket was her baby.

Raven's brow furrowed in concentration, and her fingertips touched the edge of the image. "Look at those innocent eyes. They give me hope," Raven said softly, glancing up at him. "Hope. It's strange, but the word makes my heart warm. Maybe I haven't truly lost it."

Her lashes fluttered closed. She leaned against him, and he focused on the feel of her body pressing close. The walls had stopped closing him in, and a small fire of optimism kindled inside. Maybe he was healing a bit.

Raven stirred. "Something tells me I wanted her very badly," she said. "Like I waited a long time for her."

She blinked, swaying back and forth, a small hum escaping from her lips that was barely audible over the storm outside. He leaned his head closer to her lips. A lullaby, perhaps?

"Ashes, ashes," she sang. "We all fall down." Her body stilled. "I don't know how I know, but I hate that song. It gives me chills." Her shoulders sagged, and she opened her eyes. "For a moment something was there. Something bad. Then it vanished."

"Every day the flashes become more frequent," he said, pulling her even closer.

"I miss her so much. How can I when I don't even remember her? I'm so scared I won't remember in time," she said, frustration mounting. "I feel like I'm failing her."

He turned Raven into his arms. "You are not a failure." He cupped her cheek, unable to look away from her. "You are courageous and brave and caring." His voice turned hoarse at the words. "In fact, you amaze me."

Her pupils dilated, turning her cinnamon-colored eyes dark with awareness. His body tensed. Everything inside of him wanted to lean into her, to touch her, to hold her, not in comfort but in something much more dangerous.

"This probably isn't a good idea," he muttered, even as his body strained against his jeans. He couldn't resist. He leaned into her.

His thumb rubbed against her full lower lip. Her mouth parted. Raven raised her hand to his scarred cheek. "You're a good man, Daniel Adams, but I don't need you to protect me. Not from this."

Her tongue teased the pad of his thumb. His body tightened against his zipper, and he swallowed.

"Kiss me," she whispered.

He couldn't stop himself even if he'd wanted to. He lowered his mouth to hers, gingerly, gently, softly, though every part of him screamed to yank her close. He teased her lips with his mouth, dancing over them until they parted under his caress.

A groan rumbled in his throat. He brought her closer to him. Her breasts crushed against his chest, and his hands explored her back, up to her head, pressing her closer. She let out a small whimper and put a hand to her bandaged forehead.

He released her immediately. "I hurt you," he said. "I should have known." He slid away.

"My scalp's just a little tender," she said, her breathing coming fast. She leaned forward. "Don't stop."

Daniel took a shuddering breath. His hand reached behind him and encountered the whip he'd tossed into the cave. He sighed as the passion left him, and reality returned. "It's not a good idea. Whatever is happening between us, it's not real, Raven. It's just the crazy circumstances."

Her eyes cleared. "I may not know my name, Daniel, but I know what's real." She gestured between them. "This is real. You may not like it, but it's definitely real."

He shoved his hand through his hair. "Look, I can't hide that I want you, or that I crave a lot more than a kiss from you. We both know it would be easy to just let go, to escape for a while, but..." Daniel clutched the whip and held it before him. "Even if you remembered everything, I have baggage I won't saddle you with."

She stared at the coiled leather in his hand. "What's that for?" she whispered, a trace of fear in her voice.

"Therapy," Daniel said, curling his hand around the handle. "It's the whip my captor, the Duke of Sarbonne, used in Bellevaux. Noah gave it to me before he left. As a present."

"That seems cruel. Why would he do that to you?"

"Because I dream about that whip," Daniel bit out, his voice hard. "Every night. You need your memories back, Raven. I'd give anything for my memories of that time to be erased forever."

Lightning cracked outside, and Daniel winced. "Because sounds like that can send me back to that dungeon in seconds. My PTSD makes my back burn as if the bastard were whipping me right now." He shifted his shoulder and then rose until his head nearly hit the roof of the cave. "Get some rest, Raven. I'll be outside." He paused. "Maybe Noah is right. It's time to exorcise some demons."

"Let me help you. Let me comfort you like you've comforted me. I'm a good listener." She held out her hand to him. "Stay with me."

He frowned at her, then looked back at the rain pouring down. At least the thunder and lightning were moving on. "I can't stay. Not until I'm certain I'm not a demon myself."

CHRISTOPHER LEANED BACK in the driver's side of the SUV and stared at the ramshackle house on the darkened street just on the edge of the war zone in El Paso.

"You sure this is her house?" he asked Tad. "It's a dump."

His friend popped a wad of chewing tobacco into his cheek. "No mistake. I got a good friend at the phone company. She looked her up for me." Tad gripped his crotch. "She got a little extra for her effort. Good thing she likes it rough."

Christopher shook his head. "You really are a depraved SOB. Did you get rid of the body?"

"Nah. I didn't kill her. Thought about it, but women who like it my way are hard to find."

Christopher opened the SUV door. "Well, now that the bitch who tried to steal my baby sister is finally dead, I can start my life over. Wait here."

"Yeah, yeah. Hurry up. It's hot as hell still, even if it is night," Tad muttered, tugging his phone from his pocket. "I'll check some porn sites while you're gone." He smirked and kicked up a heel on the dashboard.

Christopher shook his head. Sometimes he didn't know about Tad's taste in women. None of his friend's relationships were like what he had with Chelsea. She'd saved his sanity. Christopher had hated growing up in the middle of nowhere—except for the hunting—until he'd found Chelsea. Back then she'd lived in Van Horn, only an hour away. He'd loved her the moment he saw her at a high school football game, dark hair blowing in the wind, green eyes sparkling. He should have written more, but she'd still be glad to see him.

His heart thudded against his chest, eagerness adding a spring to his step. He walked up the sidewalk, scanning right, then left. Habit from his military training. An old woman peered through her front window, then quickly closed the curtains. People knew better than to get involved in this neighborhood.

The first thing he'd do is get Chelsea out of here. They'd move into the big house with his mom and sister. Chelsea deserved a nice house. She could help take care of the baby in preparation for their own family.

He smiled at the image, placed his hand on the door-knob and tested it. The lock jiggled. Dangerous for this area.

Christopher knocked softly. Padded footsteps creaked across the floor. A curtain loosely fluttered.

He banged again.

"Chelsea, honey, it's me. Christopher. I'm home."

She didn't open the door.

His body tensed; his jaw tightened. "Chelsea. It's me. Open up," he said, his voice low and urgent.

The floor creaked near the door. What the hell was she doing? He'd imagined this day from the moment he'd been forced to redeploy. They'd cancelled his leave twice for disciplinary actions. It had been too long, and this wasn't the way homecoming worked.

He pounded on the wooden door over and over and over again. "I'm back. Just like I promised. Damn it, let me in, Chelsea." His temper erupted, and he let his fist fly. The wood cracked beneath the force.

He stood back, ready to kick it in, when the door creaked open, and Chelsea's terrified face peeked out.

"Chris…Christopher. I…I thought you were still over-seas."

"Yeah, well, things changed." In one move he shoved into the house. "Why didn't you open the door for me?" He grabbed her by the hair and tilted her head back. "Is someone here? Is that why you wouldn't answer?"

"No, of course not. I…just…" she licked her lips, and her gaze darted left "…couldn't believe it was you. There's no one here, Christopher. I promise."

Eyes darting left was a sure sign of a lie. Christopher shoved her away then slammed through the small house, checking every room.

Empty.

His heart thudded with fury that had no way to expend itself. Why did she always do this? Get him worked up when she didn't have to. He sucked in several deep breaths and walked into the living room. She cowered in the corner.

Immediately remorse washed over him. "I'm sorry, baby. The war got to me. It was ugly, and I've just missed you so much."

He grabbed her arms and pulled her close, tucking her against his chest. He needed sex, and he needed it now. Nothing else would take the edge off.

She shivered against him, and a small sob escaped.

He caressed her hair. "It's okay, honey. Everything's all right. I'm back. I'm here now. Things will be like they were before. Just you and me."

He picked her up and carried her into the bedroom. "How about a welcome home?"

Her eyes went wide. "But...but..."

He frowned. "Don't you want me?"

"I...uh...I don't have protection."

"You don't have to worry about that, sweetie. We don't need it. I want to have babies with you. I always have."

Ten minutes later he sat up, sated but irritated.

"What's wrong?" he demanded. "Why were you crying?"

"N...nothing's wrong. Just...I'm...happy you're back." She stared at the wall, at a painting of a woman alone on the beach, but tears wet her cheeks.

"You women are nuts. Tad's waiting for me, but I'll be back." He touched her face. "You'll never be alone again. We'll be together forever, Chelsea. We'll be so happy together."

He kissed her, and left her soft and warm in bed, making sure to lock the front door behind him.

He couldn't stop smiling and slid into the SUV.

"You look satisfied." Tad frowned. "Didn't take long."

"Been a while." Christopher grinned. He leaned back in his seat with a sigh. "It's been a good day. I got my girl back. I'm home and have Dad's money waiting for me. My baby sister is safe." He flipped on the radio. "Our little shootout should have made the news by now."

The newscaster's voice droned through the radio. "And big city problems have made their way into the tiny West Texas town of Trouble. A drive-by shooting left one woman clinging to life, and her brother seriously injured. More updates as information is made available, but sources close to the investigation have identified the victims as William 'Hondo' Rappaport and his sister, Lucy Rappaport Hardiman."

Christopher jerked and slammed his hand on the dash. "Damn you, Tad. You took out the wrong targets. That woman is still alive!"

WATER SOAKED DANIEL'S jeans and T-shirt, but he didn't care. He couldn't feel the rain. He stared out at the thunderstorm, waiting for another snap of lightning. It was far enough away that he might not get struck by it. If it weren't for Raven, he wasn't sure he'd care.

With the whip in his hand, every crack triggered the memories. His mind whirled between the past and the present, but he pushed the dungeon away until he knew he stood at the edge of the wash. In Texas.

Daniel tightened his grip, the seal digging into his palm. He wouldn't let the bastard win.

A flash of lightning.

The clap of thunder.

Daniel lifted his arm. He cracked the whip over the edge. The leather snapped in the air.

The roar of thunder rolled through the night. He stared into the eerie flickering of the sky. One glance over his shoulder, and the dim light from the cave glowed like a beacon. Raven was in there. Afraid, vulnerable, huddled with Trouble, and here he was, playing with a whip.

"You won't beat me, Sarbonne!" he yelled into the night. Thunder crashed, and Daniel flicked the whip. Again and again and again. "You won't control me. I won't let you."

Rain ran down his face. His eyes burned. He might have cried. He couldn't tell. He lifted his arm again, and again, and again. Each crack drove a hole into the memories choking him. He lost himself in the desperation to annihilate his past.

"You don't control me anymore, you bastard."

Hour after hour passed until Daniel could barely lift his arm, when finally, finally, he didn't wince, his back didn't burn.

He glared into the retreating storm. Rain still pelted his face, stinging his cheeks, but the worst was over. He stared at the whip in his hand. The whip was just a whip.

Thank you, Noah.

For a moment, he considered tossing the monstrosity into the wash. He turned it over and over in his hand.

Another slash of lightning lit the sky, reflected off the Sarbonne crest. Daniel tensed, but got his emotions under control.

One demon down. Daniel yelled into the night, "You won't win. I won't let you."

His body sagged. He bent over, hands on his knees, and sucked in several deep breaths, then slowly repeated, "I won't let you."

RAVEN HUDDLED IN the mouth of the small cave and stared at Daniel through the darkness. A distant flash of lightning illuminated his features. Now exhaustion replaced the stark pain carved on his face.

He stood and looked up into the sky, his shoulders shaking with a depth of release she could barely comprehend. Tears flowed undaunted down her cheeks. She couldn't get the haunted expression he'd worn out of her mind.

He stood frozen in the rain, the water sluicing over him. Every instinct urged her to go to him, to comfort him, to wrap her arms around him and give him strength.

He was so alone. So horribly, painfully alone, but she didn't move. Daniel had pushed her away once.

Did that make her a coward?

Trouble stood just inside the cave, whining forlornly. He looked ready to leap at Daniel, but even he hesitated.

"He saved us, Trouble. What do we do?" The mutt looked up at her with a sad expression. She stood.

She took off Daniel's jacket.

Her heart aching, she stepped into the storm. Within seconds her clothes were drenched and clung to her skin. Her feet slipped on the mud, and she flailed awkwardly but didn't fall. Her entire focus remained on the man standing at the edge of an abyss she couldn't fathom.

He was alone.

He wouldn't be for long.

She took a shuddering breath and stepped closer. Daniel didn't turn around. He might not even know she'd left the cave. She hesitated.

The roar of the storm circled around them, but somehow he sensed her presence.

"You shouldn't have come in the rain, Raven," he said, his voice hoarse. "Go back inside."

"No." She slipped her arms around his waist and leaned her cheek against his broad shoulders. She hugged him tight, needing him to know she was there. "I won't leave you."

At her words, a shiver ran through his body. He placed his hands on hers. At first she thought he might pry her away, but then he let out a low groan and gripped her tight.

"I don't have the will to fight you," he said, his voice harsh with grief. He turned to her. "If you don't want me to make love to you, walk away. I won't follow."

She slid her hands lower, past his belt to the proof of his desire.

"So be it." Daniel scooped her up and cradled her against his chest. "There's no turning back now."

Chapter Eight

Raven ignored the rain. She simply wrapped her hands around Daniel's neck and clung to him. His strong arms nestled her closer. She tucked her head against his chest, his steady heart thudding in time with his quick steps. Within seconds he stepped beneath the rock outcropping into a haven from the storm. Her vision blurred, she barely noticed Trouble slinking into the corner of the cave and curling up.

Slowly Daniel set her to her feet. His hands were wet but warm on her face. His gaze hypnotized her, his eyes blazing with heat and passion and something untamed and wild.

Her breath caught in her throat, and she couldn't look away. She couldn't move; she could only stare, held fast by the intensity of him. Her lips went dry, and she moistened them with her tongue.

"Last chance," he whispered, his voice deep and husky, almost a growl.

Something about the storm outside and the tempest swirling deep inside her froze her in his arms. She wanted to be with him. She wanted to feel his strength. Everywhere. Holding her, touching her, claiming her.

She said nothing, but met his gaze, unwavering in her

certainty. She closed her eyes and leaned into him, lifting her lips to his. "I want you."

Daniel growled deep in his chest, but he didn't kiss her, just encircled her with his strong arms, holding her tenderly, close, as if she were the most precious thing in the world.

"You're vulnerable," he said.

Raven leaned slightly, grabbed at his belt and anchored him close. "Daniel Adams, you are not backing out now." She wrapped her arms around his waist and stood on tiptoes to whisper in his ear. "I may not remember everything," she said softly, "but I do know I want this."

No demands. No looking for commitments later. Just you and me finding solace in the storm.

She kissed the line of his jaw, relishing the feel of its whisker-rough edge. "I want you."

Lightning split the sky. Thunder roared. "I can't resist you," he said finally.

His hands cupped her backside. Daniel lifted her off her feet, and she wrapped her legs around his hips and her arms around his neck, holding tight. He nipped her throat, and Raven tilted her head back, giving him access to the hypersensitive skin.

In two steps Daniel pressed her against the wall of the cave. She could feel the rocks through her shirt, but she didn't care. She clutched at his hair and let out a soft gasp. He took his time, wooing her skin with kisses, exploring the pulse point at her neck, then moving lower. He nibbled at the top of her breasts and shoved aside her shirt, hitching her higher, and feasted on her curves, his mouth working magic wherever he explored.

Her head dropped back against the cave wall, and she audibly sighed. "Please," she panted. "Don't make me wait."

She could barely catch her breath. She clutched his head between her hands and bent down. Finally, her lips met his.

There was nothing tentative or new in their kiss. His mouth crushed hers, invading her very being, and she welcomed him. Uncertainty had claimed everything in her life. Except for her need for the man in her arms.

She tightened her legs around him. He took her lips again, telling her without words how much he wanted her.

The world fell away as his mouth and hands seduced her body and soul. She couldn't hear or smell or feel anything. Except Daniel.

He lifted his lips from hers, then stared into her eyes. She clutched his arms, shaking with want, needing him to douse the fire burning her skin. "Please," she whispered, trembling in his arms.

His gaze unwavering, he gently lowered them both to the sleeping bag. His eyes flickered in the light of the lantern. He trailed his finger down her jaw. "You're beautiful."

"So are you." She let her touch flutter against the scar on his cheek. He flinched, but her hand remained steady. "I love your strength and courage."

He went to speak, but she stopped him with a finger to his lips. "Shh." She pushed him, and he let her roll him to his back, then she straddled him. Her wet hair framed her face, and her hips shifted on top of his.

His eyes darkened. She lifted the scrub shirt over her head and unhooked her bra. She felt brazen but powerful. He couldn't take his eyes away from her. He cupped her breasts in his hands.

Raven leaned down and let her breasts press against his chest. "Take me now." She pressed her lips against his and then explored his mouth. "Now. That's an order."

Suddenly he laughed. "I don't always follow orders well," Daniel said, flipping her onto her back. "But this time..." His teeth teased her nipple until she arched against him. "This time, nothing will stop me."

He pressed a denim-clad leg between hers and explored her naked torso with his hands and mouth. She didn't know how he removed the remainder of their clothes so quickly, but suddenly he settled on top of her, and he was touching her everywhere. With devastating thoroughness, he worked his way down one leg, then up the other until he found the center of her. She cried out as he caressed her, and her body exploded in an eruption of need. She could feel his throbbing heat, strong and hard and wanting. "Daniel," she panted. "I want you inside me."

In response, he grabbed the bag Noah had provided and dug into the side pocket. She whimpered in protest until he pulled out a foil packet.

He slipped on the condom and held himself above her. Her heart raced until she thought it might leap from her chest, then he shifted, joining them as one. She cried out in joyous relief.

His eyelids fluttered closed. For a few moments he remained unmoving, sucking in one breath, then another.

She wrapped herself around him, tilting her hips, cradling him, surrounding him. They belonged together. She wanted to whisper the words, but she didn't dare.

As if he had heard her, Daniel let out a low moan. "God, it's like coming home."

A wall seemed to crumble between them. He lowered his mouth to hers and moved against her, driving her higher and higher until she called out into the night, her mind and heart flying free for the first time since he'd found her.

CHRISTOPHER HAD WANTED to push his vehicle to the limits to return to Trouble, but he couldn't risk anyone stopping him, so he'd gone the speed limit. He and Tad set up on the outskirts of town. Now Christopher paced back and forth beside the SUV. The grumble of thunder sounded in the distance, over the mountain, making the hair on the back of his neck stand at attention.

Static crackled from the listening device he'd placed at the sheriff's office. He shoved his boot heel into the ground and let out a string of curses; then he whirled and slammed his fist into the vehicle's side. "Damn it. What's taking so long? I was sure Galloway would know, or at least get in touch with that woman. Where the hell is she?"

Tad shoved his hand through his hair. "You never did have any patience for surveillance. It's just another part of the hunt. She'll turn up sooner or later."

Christopher rounded on his friend and grabbed him by the neck. "Listen to me. I'm protecting my family, and if I have to kill someone to do it, I will. Even you. So shut up and let me think."

A sharp ring sounded through the speaker. Chris shoved Tad away and turned up the volume.

"Sheriff. This is Noah Bradford. I'm trying to reach Daniel. I have news, and I need to talk to him. I can't get through to his SAT phone."

"Sorry, Bradford, but Adams left without telling me where they were going. Didn't trust that we could protect Raven. Not that I blame him," Galloway complained. *"Lucy's still touch-and-go. Hondo's in a bad way. I'd get the hell out, too."*

Noah swore succinctly. *"I'm sorry about your friends, but I've got to talk to him. There's a tracer in his laptop so I have his coordinates. If I give them to you, can you get to him immediately?"*

"Yeah, won't be a problem."

The man named Noah read off the digits.

"Jackpot." Christopher grabbed a pen from Tad and wrote the information on his arm.

Galloway whistled. "I just checked the map. Not good. They're by the washes that lead away from the peak. There's a flash flood warning for that area. The place is unstable at the best of times, but with the unexpected rain in the mountains, the ground there won't soak up anything. There will be flash floods and mudslides all over that land. Even if I wanted to get to him, he has the four-wheel drive. I can't risk it with the vehicles I have. Maybe dirt bikes could get in."

"Forget it." Noah let out another curse. "I'm taking a chopper to get them out."

"What's going on, Bradford?" Sheriff Galloway asked, his voice suspicious.

"That's the problem, Sheriff. We have no idea, but I've got a really bad feeling this is where the whole case is about to change."

The call ended.

Christopher grinned. "Damn straight." He and Tad jumped in the SUV. "It took a few hours, but it paid off, Tad. We know where they are now, and I got an easy way to make that woman's death look like an accident."

"Now let's go steal some dirt bikes."

DANIEL'S HEART RACED like he'd just run for his life, but he felt like he'd grabbed a small piece of heaven. He didn't want to leave the warmth of Raven's body. She lay curled against him with her eyes closed, but she wasn't asleep. Her grip on him was too strong, as if she didn't want to let him go.

An unfamiliar warmth seeped through his chest, surrounding his heart. He kissed the top of her hair and stared out into the night. It felt so right to have Raven in his arms.

He tucked her head under his chin, being careful not to bump her wound.

She sighed and wriggled closer. "Thank you," she whispered, her voice low.

He smiled and tightened his hold. "That should be my line."

She laughed. "In that case, you're welcome."

She shifted in his arms and looked up at him, the flickering of the lantern illuminating her dark hair, creating a halo around her head.

He pushed back the silky locks. How he wished he could have been there to protect her from the beginning. She should never have been so vulnerable. Her bruises hadn't faded much, and she couldn't hide the circles of fatigue under her eyes, but she was the most beautiful woman he'd ever known, because her beauty came from deep inside.

"I haven't felt like a normal woman since I woke up," she whispered. "Not until now."

"Normal is overrated," Daniel teased, even as his body hardened against hers. "Your uniqueness is way better than that. I like the sounds you make when I'm inside you."

A soft blush reddened her cheeks, and he smiled, feeling halfway human for the first time since Bellevaux. A flashing image of the black bag being pulled over his head and him being dragged into that prison cell seared his mind. He didn't want to think about his past.

No.

He hated the memories. He wouldn't let them taint this moment.

Daniel let his fingertips linger against the bruise on her temple. "Head still okay?"

"Fine," she said with a small yawn.

He kissed her temple. "Try to get some sleep. I won't

leave you," he said, settling her against him. "I'll keep you safe."

Her eyelids fluttered close. "Safe," she said. "I like feeling safe."

After several minutes, her breathing grew regular.

Daniel didn't want to move. He wanted to just disappear in this cave forever with Raven, but she shifted onto her side, and the lantern's light reflected off the locket around her neck, reminding him that disappearing wasn't an option.

In fact, ignoring the past wasn't an option.

For either of them.

PAMELA STARED AT the baby in the crib, her cheeks rosy and healthy. The other baby. If Chelsea had given her this one, everything would have been fine.

Now Pamela loved Christina with an obsession that scared even her.

The little girl whimpered and let out a sneeze.

No. This baby couldn't get sick. They'd call off the procedure. That wouldn't work.

Christina was failing faster.

Pamela raced down the hall and grabbed a vaporizer. Within twenty minutes the room was bathed in healing steam. She paced back and forth, every few seconds staring down at the child.

Christopher hadn't come home, thank God. She'd seen the wild look in his eyes and recognized he hadn't changed. Somehow she had to figure out a way to get away from him without him learning the truth about the babies.

A ringing phone pierced the night. Pamela ran into the hallway and picked up the receiver. "Hello?"

Small sobs sounded through the line. "Mrs. W...Winter?"

A chill skittered down Pamela's back. "Chelsea? You

promised never to call. You promised to disappear. We had a deal."

"And you promised me Christopher would never find me after I moved this time. That the baby would be safe. I never should have let you take her. I should have given them both to…" Her voice trailed off. "He'll find out, and he'll kill me."

Pamela gritted her teeth. Quietly she shut the door to the nursery and walked into her bedroom. She stared at the photograph of her husband, a picture to remind her of one truth. A truth it had taken her thirty years to understand. Mercy didn't win. Only power won—and witnesses weren't to be left behind.

"You have to do something." Chelsea sobbed. "He came here tonight. He…he wants me back. He wants babies with me. I can't let that happen."

"Did you upset him?" Pamela asked, shifting her feet back and forth, her gaze snapping to the photo of her husband once again. "Why did you even let him in your house?"

"I didn't know he was back. I looked through the window, and he saw me. You could have warned me. You know how he can get. I had to… I let him…" Chelsea choked back another sob. "I didn't dare risk him flying into one of his rages."

Pamela tapped her chin. She probably should have warned Christopher's old girlfriend, but the woman had betrayed her, too. A sudden thought occurred to Pamela. She rose and peeked into the nursery. What if she told Christopher about the babies using Chelsea as a scapegoat? Yes. The plan might just work. If she played it smart, she could solve two problems with one small revelation. Chelsea's call may have been the answer to her prayers.

"Help me?" Chelsea said.

Pamela drummed her fingers on the phone. She couldn't reveal her intentions. She had to string Chelsea along. "What can I do? He doesn't listen to me, either." She let her voice shake, made herself sound vulnerable. She'd certainly borne the brunt of her husband's and then Christopher's anger. She had no intention of going through that again.

"You know enough to put him behind bars. The cops will believe his mother. You can tell everyone about what he's done. About his *hunting* trips. About the kid who went missing in the wash ten years ago. I want Christopher put away. I want the baby safe. I want to be free."

"You're right." Pamela took one last look at the sleeping child in the bed. "I know exactly what to do, Chelsea. You won't have to worry anymore. I'll take care of everything."

RAVEN FLOATED ABOVE the vision: a long flowing white dress. A church. A handsome man at her side—but not Daniel. Oh, God, a man she didn't know. A man with blond hair, too handsome to be real. She had to be dreaming. Rings were exchanged, then kisses.

No. This was wrong. It couldn't be a wedding. She shook her head, wanting the images to vanish. She wanted to stay warm and loved in Daniel's arms, but those strange impressions felt real. Felt true.

She cried out, devastated, even in sleep.

"Raven, wake up. You're having a nightmare. You're okay, darlin'." Daniel held her wrists, one leg thrown across her waist. "You're with me."

Daniel's calm voice shattered the images in thousands of pieces, but her heart wouldn't stop pounding.

Blinking against the glare of the morning light, Raven looked down at her nude body and then stared at her left hand. No ring. No tan lines revealing she'd even worn one. Yet she couldn't shake the certainty in her soul that the dream was real.

"I think I'm married," she whispered.

Daniel released her wrists, rolled off her and sat up. Tension emanated from his body. He tugged on his jeans and handed her a clean set of scrubs. "You're basing this on your dream?"

"It didn't feel like a dream, more like a memory." She quickly slipped into the clothes, hating that she couldn't have stayed naked in his arms, with nothing between them. She'd felt so close to him, and now a chasm wider than the wash separated them.

"We both knew this was a possibility," Daniel said. "I never should have touched you last night. God, I knew better. I'm sorry."

The words hurt, even though she expected them. "How can I feel what I do for you if I'm…?"

Her voice trailed off. She couldn't meet his gaze. "God, this is all so crazy." She rubbed her eyes with shaking hands. "I have to remember. I can't go on like this."

"You may not like what we discover," Daniel said. He raised his hand to her cheek, then dropped it before he touched her skin. "We should work on expanding some of your memories today."

"I know." She bit her lip, longing for a connection with Daniel, even though she shouldn't. "I watched you fight to control your memories. I have to fight to retrieve mine. For my baby. And for…myself."

"Okay, then." Daniel gave her a tight smile.

He opened Noah's satchel and pulled out a laptop and a smaller bag. He set the items between them.

"What's all this?"

"The CTC program I mentioned. I think it's worth a try, but I have to warn you, it may not be easy."

Daniel reached into the bag. "Sit back against the cave wall and relax. I have a number of items. Hold them, smell them, use your five senses to see if they trigger any images, any impressions." One by one he pulled out a baby's rattle, a pink blanket, baby shampoo and several toys.

She drew in a sharp breath. "My head is pounding already. Just looking at these toys makes my heart ache."

"Take it slow. You're safe here. Close your eyes. Let your mind wander."

He handed her the rattle, and she clutched it tight.

"Nothing."

"Try the shampoo. You had a reaction to the scent before," he said.

She did and her stomach heaved, her heart tripping in panic, but no new images appeared in her mind.

For over an hour, Daniel took her through the CTC program. Finally, when an image flashed on the screen for the third time with nothing to show for it but a headache, Raven jumped to her feet. "This is ridiculous. Nothing's coming back to me. I'm pushing and pushing, and my head is going to explode."

Her eyes burned with unshed tears.

She whirled around and stared at the gray sky outside. "We're wasting our time here. I'd rather sit in that clinic as bait, waiting until that maniac comes after me. *He* knows who I am. If we trap him, I have a chance of finding out, too."

She stalked out of the cave and walked to the edge of the wash. The suffocating loneliness of the desert settled over her. She wrapped her arms around her body, shaking. What if she never remembered? What if she never knew who she was or what happened to her baby? Could she live with that?

No, it would kill her.

She stared down into the wash, and a wave of despair, deep and dark, slammed against her.

Storm clouds gathered over the western mountains. Thunder sounded and lightning flashed some distance away, but the ground began to rumble, a roar coming ever closer. She peered over the wash just as a huge wall of water raced down the rock ravine.

Daniel ran out of the cave, the whip in his hand. "It's a flash flood. Get back."

She whirled around, but water splashed over the rocks and debris, slamming into the earthen ledge where she stood. The ground behind her gave way. She dove toward a mesquite tree growing out of rock and grabbed hold of one of its branches. The bark cut into her hands but she held tight, panting.

Frantic, she looked down at the swirling water. If she fell, she wouldn't survive. "Daniel!"

"Just hang on."

Without hesitation, Daniel tied one end of the long whip around the mesquite trunk and secured the other end to his belt to anchor himself. She was so close. If he could only reach her. He leaned toward her and grabbed one hand, but her wet fingers slipped from his grip.

The bark peeled off under her other hand and she closed her eyes, certain she would be swept away when Daniel managed to snag her wrist. His face strained, he began to pull her up, but to her horror, the earth beneath his feet started to crumble. He moved back and dug his heels into the dirt, but his body tilted off balance, leaning at an angle over the flood.

The churning torrent sped just below her feet now, but that could change at any second. A barbed wire fence careened through the water, its wooden stakes and wire a deadly weapon. The debris slammed against the earth. If they fell in, they were dead.

Trouble barked furiously, but the dog could do nothing.

"What are we going to do?" she shouted. Daniel tightened his hold on her wrist.

"I'm going to swing you toward the thicker branches over there. When you land, crawl up the trunk then get as far away from the edge as you can!" Daniel yelled.

She nodded.

"Okay, let go," he ordered.

With a prayer, she did, putting her life in Daniel's hand. He groaned and twisted his torso. She swung once, twice. "Now!" he shouted. He let go, and she landed on some thick branches and climbed toward the edge.

Suddenly the dirt shifted beneath Daniel's feet, and he dropped. He grabbed the whip and started hauling himself up.

Raven had crawled toward the cave but turned back. Trouble grabbed her shirt and pulled, dragging her to safety. She struggled against the dog's hold. "Daniel!"

"Stay back." Hand over hand, muscles straining, he clawed his way to the top. More ground gave way. He slid back until he was waist deep in the water. Another tree churned in the flood, heading straight for him.

"Look out!" she yelled.

He twisted just in time for a large branch to slam into his belly. His hands gripped the leather tighter, but the current pummeled him against the dirt and rock. Only the whip kept him from being swept away.

She had to do *something*.

Raven ran to the cave and dumped out Daniel's duffel. She found a climbing rope and ran outside, frantically searching for something to tie the cord on to that wasn't about to be swept away.

Suddenly the *whoop-whoop-whoop* of rotor blades sounded from above. A wave of air knocked her backwards, and she dropped the rope. A military-style helicopter swooped down toward Daniel.

A man wearing a dark cap and sunglasses leaned out with a weapon and shouted something, then raised his rifle.

"No!" Raven screamed.

Chapter Nine

The helicopter's blades forced a downdraft that threw Daniel off balance and buffeted him toward the water. Desperate, he grabbed a tree branch, using it and the whip to climb back up. The rotor blast stung his eyes. He tightened his grip, and the leather from the whip cut into his hands, the sting sharp as it bit into his palm. If he let go, he was dead.

What the hell was Noah doing here in the CTC chopper? Elijah fired a few rounds from the semiautomatic out the side door. As the helicopter turned, angling to hover near, Daniel braced himself for another gust then fought against the rush of man-made wind.

Damn idiots were going to drown him.

He couldn't let go of the whip. He'd fall. No one could survive the swirling water below. He'd be slammed against the rocks at high speed. If the blows didn't kill him, drowning would.

The helo dove again, really low, almost as if trying to skirt the water. Daniel whipped around to see what they were doing, but Elijah's attention was far from Daniel.

Elijah's line of sight led straight to the flat mesa about fifteen feet above the outcropping.

Two figures held automatic weapons pointed directly at Raven.

Daniel crawled higher, and the tree limb bent precariously lower. He had no time left. With a curse he rammed his boot into the broken branches then, hands bleeding, he pulled himself onto solid ground with the whip. His leg throbbed—hell, his whole body did—but he scrambled to Raven. He shielded her, then shoved her into the protection of the cave.

Gunfire peppered the exact spot where she'd been.

He felt Raven's heart pounding, but no faster than his own. "Stay here." He grabbed his weapon and bolted to the cave entrance.

Elijah sent off another round of gunfire toward the mesa. Two heads ducked down.

Daniel scanned the terrain for a way to get to the bastards. A small path caught his attention. It might take some climbing. He grasped a handhold, but the sandstone crumbled. With all the rain, he couldn't count on a good hold. Suddenly the chopper flew up several feet, and Elijah raised his weapon, but before he could fire, a spray of bullets pelted the helicopter. The chopper reeled away, but an arc of fluid spewed from near the tail.

Daniel's heart stopped as the chopper swiveled out of control and pitched toward the outcropping. They were going down.

Elijah hung on to a safety strap, then with fury in his eyes, sent one last burst of gunfire. A man fell from the mesa to the ground.

Trouble bolted across the terrain at the bleeding man, who crawled toward his weapon.

The man lunged for his gun, but Trouble leaped on him, growling. The dog grabbed hold of the guy's arm, clamping down. He cursed, twisting against the animal, rolling toward the edge, but Trouble wouldn't let go.

"Stop," Daniel called out. "You're going to fall." He

snagged the dropped rope from the ground at his feet and tossed it at the second gunman.

The guy ignored him, trying to break the dog's tight grip.

The man struggled to stand, but the ground gave way. He and Trouble tumbled into the rage of water.

"Trouble!" Raven ran toward the cave opening. A loud explosion rent the air, and a blast of heat seared the cave.

Oh, God, had Noah and Elijah made it out?

"Stay put. I have to check the helicopter!" Daniel shouted, waving Raven back. "There's a second gunman."

Raven's frantic gaze whipped around, taking in the horrific fireball. In the distance, a motorcycle engine revved, then faded away.

Daniel raced to the wash's edge, searching for Noah and Elijah. The only way they would have survived was if they had jumped into the floodwaters. Some choice. Burn or drown.

He caught sight of Noah's dark head bobbing, then Elijah's blond one. They fought to reach a long flat rock perched a third of the way into the wash. There was a small plateau nearby, just above water level. If Noah and Elijah could get to it, they might have a chance.

Daniel whirled around. "We need another rope..."

Raven was already digging into his duffel. She pulled out the second climbing rope.

"Hurry," he said. "They don't have much time."

Daniel and Raven raced along the crumbling edge of the wash, and he searched the chaotic maelstrom.

Trouble's body was wedged against a thick log, and he struggled to stay afloat.

"Trouble!" Raven screamed.

"I see him. He's heading for the rock."

"We have to help him," she said, then her face paled,

and her hand clamped to her mouth. "Is that Noah?" Raven asked, pointing.

Daniel followed her gaze. A dark-headed man's body bobbed facedown in the water. Noah? It couldn't be. Not after surviving four tours and countless missions.

The man's body smashed off a rock and flipped onto his back. Daniel let out a relieved sigh. "It's not him. It's the shooter who fell from the edge."

Even at thirty feet, Daniel could tell the gunman was dead. He couldn't see his eyes, but the guy had barbed wire wrapped around him and a steel rod impaling him through his chest.

"Stand on that rock. You'll have a good view. Keep Noah and Elijah in your sights and point them out," Daniel said. "I'm going to help them."

She gripped his hand. "Be careful. Please."

"Always, darlin'." He looped the rope over his shoulder. The water moved fast. If it rose much higher the cave would be flooded, as well. He watched the waves shove a log past. The way looked clear. He had about fifteen feet to get to the levee.

Daniel shoved his feet between rocks trying to get a firm grip. If he slipped, there was nothing to stop him from being swept away. Knees bent, he picked his way as fast as he could, gripping boulders, avoiding debris.

A fence post scraped his arm, but within minutes he'd reached the dry land.

"Daniel!"

Raven pointed at twelve o'clock. Trouble was headed his way. The wet dog clung to the log, but he stared at Daniel.

Daniel maneuvered himself in front of the log, and when the dog got close enough, Daniel grabbed him under his shoulders, falling backward.

Trouble's legs went out from under him. He whined and licked Daniel's face.

"You're welcome."

Daniel got up and studied the mountains. The clouds still hovered over the peak. He looked at his feet. The levee had narrowed. The water had already risen several inches. Within minutes the one rock jutting out of the wash would be underwater.

Desperate, he searched the churning rapids, then he saw Noah's dark hair. The man clung to a small rock, but his grip was slipping.

"Noah!"

He couldn't hear Daniel.

Noah's grip slipped, and he plunged under the water. Daniel gauged the distance, ready to jump in, but instead of heading toward the rock, the current carried him to the side.

"Damn it."

Daniel raced down the ten-foot rock. Noah was a few feet away. Daniel took a deep breath and plunged into the churning water. His hand gripped the collar of Noah's shirt. He grimaced at the weight.

Suddenly Noah's arm reached around and gripped Daniel's wrist. He heaved, dragging Noah to safety.

Trouble nosed Noah's hand, and the man rubbed the wet fur. "That was fun," he said, his voice full of irony. "Elijah?"

Daniel shook his head. "I don't know."

"There!" Raven yelled.

Daniel turned and recognized the man's sandy blond hair. Trouble let out a frantic bark.

"We can't reach him." Noah panted. "He's too far."

"But he can grab this." Daniel uncoiled the rope, forming a lasso. Who knew junior rodeo would come in handy in his life? He had one shot. He eyed the spot, swung the rope and let it fly. The loop landed just in front of Elijah.

If only he would see it. He looked very, very still.

Suddenly Elijah ducked underwater. A large log popped where his head had been. Then a strong tug grabbed the rope. He'd slipped his shoulder into it.

Daniel and Noah pulled on the line, veering the man toward their sinking island. He grabbed the rock and turned over, gasping for air.

"You guys always have this much fun on the job?" he gasped, coughing up some of the muddy water. "Remind me never to agree when you volunteer to pilot that flying gas can," he grumbled at Noah. "I'll take the lab any day of the week."

"Just another day at the office," Noah joked. "You make a good cowboy," he said to Daniel.

"We're not safe yet. The level's still rising." Water lapped at Daniel's feet.

Elijah couldn't hide his exhaustion.

"Can you make it?" Daniel asked Elijah. He gestured across the rapids.

Elijah nodded, his expression fierce and determined.

Daniel looped the rope around Trouble's collar, then each man secured the line between them. By the time they'd knotted themselves together, the level had reached their ankles. Trouble had become unsteady. He slipped down and nearly fell in.

"Ready?" Daniel asked.

They nodded. As quickly as possible, they maneuvered across the faster-moving flood. Finally, they reached the edge where Raven stood. Daniel sat back, his legs suddenly feeling the stress of being in thousands of square feet of roaring flood.

Raven dropped beside him and wrapped her arms

around him. "God, you scared me." She tentatively touched his cheek. "You're hurt."

"We're alive," he said.

"Barely. So let's not do that again." Noah scowled at Daniel. "You had to choose *this* godforsaken place to hide out during a flash flood?"

"It usually doesn't rain now. There's been a drought." He glanced at Raven. "We needed to be near town in case there was a breakthrough."

Noah's jaw throbbed. "How'd these guys find you?"

"I don't know. Not because they followed," Daniel said. "I made sure of it."

Elijah brushed some mud off his soaked jeans. "Maybe whoever's after Raven has a few toys. Satellite locators, listening devices."

Noah let out a curse. "I bet that's it. I gave the sheriff your coordinates because I needed to talk to you."

Raven looked stunned. "You don't think he's part of this?"

"I don't trust anyone right now," Daniel bit out, wiping his hand across his face. "If the sheriff's clean, then the perps probably bugged the phones. That would explain why they keep turning up." Daniel looked over at the raging water. "I wish we could get prints on the gunman. He handled that weapon like he's shot an automatic weapon before."

"You think he was military?" Noah asked.

"Yeah. Even hurt, the guy had a few moves." Daniel glanced down the wash. "I doubt we'll find his body anytime soon."

"What do we do now?" Raven asked, slipping her hand into Daniel's.

"Get out of here." He panned the landscape. "The second shooter could come back. I'll use the SAT phone to

call the sheriff, pray his line's not being monitored. He'll
have to arrange to pick us up. I can't get the four-wheel
drive out for days." Daniel paused. "What were you guys
doing out here anyway?"

"We couldn't get through to the SAT phone," Noah said.
"Maybe the cave blocked the signal?"

"I didn't want to risk leaving it in the weather." Daniel
cursed. "What was so important that you had to risk this
weather? Not that I'm not damn glad you did."

Elijah met Noah's gaze, and the look they shared sent
a chill of foreboding through Daniel. He tugged Raven
up against him.

Her entire body tensed. "You know something, don't
you?" What little color remained drained from her cheeks.

Elijah sucked in a deep breath. "I took the evidence we
gathered and ran some preliminary tests. The blood on the
toy box lid and the carpet was yours. So far I can't identify
the other blood sample, but we're checking databases." He
shifted. "I got curious about the hair from the locket so I
tested it. The results are…surprising."

"Tell me," Raven pleaded.

"According to the DNA, the baby in the locket is not
you, Raven. She's not your child, either. In fact, she's not
related to you at all. But she is related to your attacker."

THE HOSPITAL LOOMED on the horizon. Christopher skid the
dirt bike into the parking lot. He fought to pull the key out,
then yanked off his helmet. They'd killed Tad. His only
friend. The sole person who understood him.

The damn weapon Christopher had used had jammed.
That bitch should be dead—her and the meddling men
she'd somehow collected.

Just like a woman to ruin everything.

Christopher shoved the kickstand of his bike in place

and glared at the saddlebag where he had hid the weapon. He'd toss the thing later. A ballistics specialist could trace the bullets he'd managed to fire back to this gun. For now he had to figure out how to get rid of the woman. He had to fix this.

He stared up at the hospital. When his mother had called to tell him his sister was here, he couldn't believe it. She'd looked perfectly fine when he'd seen her. Rosy cheeks, healthy. Even better than the pictures he'd received while in Afghanistan. What had happened?

He didn't need this now. His mom could be so stupid and gullible. She'd been oblivious to his dad's lovers, his businesses, the illegals crossing their land for a fee. She wasn't capable of taking care of herself, so he was stuck with her.

He stomped into the hospital, mud clinging to his combat boots. His expression set, he ignored the fearful looks when he crossed the lobby to the elevator. Let them think what they liked. He hit the up button. The lit numbers above the doors crept down. Eight, seven...

Too slow. To hell with this. He stalked across the tiled floor and yanked the staircase door open. Then, taking two steps at a time, he rushed to the third floor and burst onto the pediatrics ward.

A nurse glared at him, then held her finger to her lips. He scowled at her, and she paled. Could she see her death in his eyes? He felt angry enough to kill anyone in his way.

Damn Tad. Why'd he have to get shot?

A floor-to-ceiling mural of giant bears with balloons grinned at him from the wall. He hated bears. If he had had his gun with him now, he would have strafed it.

He made his way down the hallway, looking for room three-fifteen. He stopped outside the oncology unit. Oncology couldn't be right. Three-fifteen was in the cancer ward? What the hell was wrong with Christina?

Bile rose in his throat, and he opened the door. His mother sat in a chair next to one of the room's cribs. Christopher looked down at the tuft of black hair and pale face of the baby in the crib.

"Who is this?"

His mother blinked through teary eyes. She kneaded her hands in her lap, refusing to meet his gaze. "I'm so, so sorry, Christopher. I wanted to tell you. Really I did, but she convinced me not to."

He stilled. "What are you talking about, Mother?"

His mother bit her lip. "This is Christina."

Christopher leaned over the pale, thin child lying so still. No. This wasn't right. "No way. Who's the other kid? Because this baby isn't Christina."

Pamela started crying.

"What's wrong with her?" He couldn't get over how sickly his adopted sister appeared, almost as if she were close to death.

Pamela choked back a sob. "She has aplastic anemia. Her body doesn't make enough new blood cells. It's like cancer."

"Can't they do something?"

"She has a severe case. Only a bone marrow transplant will cure her, and she has a rare blood type."

"Like me," he said. "But they do matches. We'll do a drive. We'll find a donor."

"I already did," Pamela said, pointing to the second crib in the room. "I found a perfect match."

Christopher looked at the second child, rosy cheeks, dark hair—the baby he'd thought was Christina. He stared at his mother, noting for the first time the intensity in her gaze, the almost manic energy. "Who is she?"

Pamela shook her head. "I promised I wouldn't tell you."

He whirled her around. "What's going on, Mother?"

Pamela stood over the sickly baby, looking down on her daughter with a tender smile, and stroked her cheek. "I missed you when you were in Afghanistan, honey. Despite everything you did and how you left, you were still my son." She turned to him. "I know I shouldn't say anything, but I've prayed about it. You have a right to know. I got a visit after you left the last time. From Chelsea."

Chelsea. "You hate her and never made it a secret," Christopher said, crossing his arms. "Why would she come to you?"

"She needed money," Pamela said, biting her lip, worry on her face.

Funny, his mother normally had a stoic expression that never revealed anything. It came from years of hiding her fear of her husband. Christopher had the same gift.

"Chelsea came to me with a…problem. You'd been forced into the military. She didn't have your number, and she was overwhelmed and embarrassed by her predicament." Pamela straightened. "I should never have agreed to keep it a secret, though. She lied to me the entire time. She's a whore, but as soon as I saw Christina, I knew—"

Pamela halted, as if terrified to go on.

Christopher could feel his brain revving with frustration, recognized the temper on the edge of an explosion. The army shrinks had tried to help him control himself. It usually worked when he wanted it to. He sucked in a breath while fighting against the urge to ram his fist through the wall. "Just *tell* me. What did you know?"

Pamela shrank away from him. "Stay calm, Christopher, please. Chelsea was pregnant. She never wanted you to know. Christina is *your* child. And my grandchild."

He clawed his scalp and let loose a loud string of curses.

Fighting against every violent instinct inside, he clutched the crib and stared down at the baby. *His* baby.

"She's mine?" He studied his daughter's features, so very familiar, then looked at the other baby. "She's a perfect bone marrow match? Weird. They even look alike. Or they would if Christina were well."

Pamela straightened. "That's because they're identical twins."

Christopher gasped. "And Chelsea didn't tell me?"

"You're not the only one Chelsea lied to," Pamela said. "These are your twin daughters, and Chelsea sold one of them to the highest bidder, to the woman on the television. I hurt her when I was trying to get your daughter back for you. I'm lucky I even found out what Chelsea did."

Christopher could feel his blood pressure mount. His temple throbbed; his hand shook. Fury like he'd never experienced erupted along his skin, raking like hot coals.

"Chelsea lied about everything," he snarled. "I would have loved her forever, and she betrayed me." He slipped a Bowie from his boot. "You don't have to worry about her anymore, Mother. She'll be dead by tonight."

"The little girl in my locket is my attacker's baby?" Raven yelled.

This couldn't be happening. Her mind searched the snippets of memory she'd recovered, but she had nothing. "She's not mine?"

The horizon swayed.

Daniel scooped her into his arms before she hit the ground.

"Way to go, genius." He glared at Elijah, as he sat with Raven on the ground.

Raven clutched the locket around her neck. "There must be some mistake. I remember a pink blanket. I remember a

baby. I've *had* a baby. The doctor said I delivered a child."
Raven grasped Daniel's arm. "Why would I be wearing a
locket of a baby that wasn't mine? It doesn't make sense.
Who is she?"

Noah cleared his throat. "We're searching the DNA
databases. It's taking a while to access the criminal and
military records, but we may know part of the answer. Elijah, overachiever that he is, used age progression software
to provide a guess of what the baby's parents might look
like. We ran the image through my new facial recognition
software. We found a 90 percent match to a woman from
El Paso. We're trying to get her DNA."

Raven opened the locket, her heart twisting in grief.
Over the past three days she'd come to love the baby's
sweet smile, the sparkling eyes, the dimple. In her heart
and mind she'd bonded with this baby. Raven's chest tightened in panic at the thought of losing her daughter, and
she started hyperventilating. She grabbed her throat, trying to suck in air.

Daniel faced her. "Okay, darlin'. Bend over, take deep
breaths. We'll figure this out."

She focused on calming her breathing. "You're saying
my baby has *another* mother?"

This entire conversation felt wrong. It couldn't be true.
And yet the nausea rising in Raven's gut was real. Some
part of her believed Elijah and Noah were right.

Noah's expression softened. "We don't know everything yet," he offered.

"I'm sure there's an explanation," Elijah interrupted.

"A mug shot in El Paso matches the profile," Noah
added. "The woman has moved since her arrest, though.
They're tracking down the address. We'll know more after
we interview her."

Daniel rubbed Raven's back, but she could barely feel

his touch. The image inside that locket had been the only touchstone in her life, besides Daniel, since she'd opened her eyes in that mine. Now she felt adrift.

"What's the possible mother's name?" Raven asked.

"Chelsea Rivera," Noah said. "She's got a string of arrests for shoplifting, a few minor drug charges, but nothing major."

Raven closed her eyes, willing her memory to explain the facts, but the name meant nothing to her. And her head had begun to throb once again.

She glanced at Daniel and could hardly stand to acknowledge the sympathy written on his face.

He hugged her closer. "We'll find out who the baby is. This could be a coincidence. Or perhaps you adopted this woman's baby."

"I wish I could remember."

Noah leaned forward. "Did the program work? Did you recall anything that will help?"

"Only that I might be married," Raven whispered.

Noah let out a low whistle. He met Daniel's gaze and raised a brow.

Raven ducked her head. What had happened between them was beautiful and special. She'd fallen for Daniel. She refused to believe that was wrong.

He turned Raven in his arms. "We *will* find the baby and the answers. I promise you that."

"Zane at CTC is running Chelsea's background, including finances," Elijah interjected. "If we get the woman's blood sample, we'll be able to confirm or disprove her identity."

"We have to talk to her. She might be able to clear everything up," Daniel said, standing, helping Raven to her feet. "We might be mere hours away from answers."

"I pray so." Raven chewed on her lower lip. "But I'm terrified I won't like the answers."

The sound of another helicopter broke through her thoughts. A rescue chopper this time.

"I'll get our supplies from the cave," Daniel said to Noah and Elijah. "You all grab the sheriff's attention."

Raven slipped her hand into Daniel's. "I'll help you," she said quietly, her fingers trembling.

He didn't argue.

Trouble followed them into the cave, close to Raven's side.

"You okay?" Daniel asked.

"Not even close," she said. "How can this be? I remember a wedding. I remember a baby who may or may not be mine. I may have adopted a child. Why would any of these things make someone want me dead? Did I steal the baby?"

Daniel brought her face within two inches of his own. "Don't be crazy. We'll figure it out."

She nodded her head and climbed up the rocks to their cave.

Standing next to him, she stared inside the rock haven, the place they'd made love, the place she'd felt so close to Daniel. She glanced over at him. "I was happy here for a few hours. At peace, if that makes sense."

"Me, too. For the first time in a long time." He bent his head and touched her lips lightly with his. "I don't regret holding you in my arms, Raven. No matter what happens, I won't ever be sorry I made love to you."

He knelt down and started stuffing items in the duffel while Raven gathered up the baby toys and packed Noah's small bag.

They were done too quickly. "I want to disappear," she said. "I don't want to be part of this craziness anymore. Does that make me a coward?"

"It makes you human," he said.

Daniel hitched the pack on his shoulder and led the way out of the cave. Raven paused for a moment. The water had slowed some, but still churned violently. She shivered, remembered dangling from the side until Daniel had rescued her. They both could have died.

The limbs on the cracked trunk they'd climbed on swayed, catching her attention. The whip was still tied to the tree and hung against the bark. She stepped toward it, and Daniel stopped her.

"I don't want it, Raven. I don't need it anymore. It's just a memory now. Not a demon."

Daniel held out his hand to her. Raven had to look back once. How ironic. Daniel had abandoned his memory on the edge of a cliff in the middle of nowhere, while she'd spent three days praying to remember.

Now all she wanted was to forget the past few hours ever happened and find her baby.

DANIEL COULDN'T SIT still. He paced in front of the window in the sheriff's office after eliminating the listening device planted on the outside phone line. Their only good news was that Lucy and Hondo had both come through surgery. While it might be a long recovery, particularly for the small woman, they would survive.

Noah and Elijah had left to trace the dead shooter's motorcycle that had been left at the top of the mesa. They'd come back with a stolen vehicle report, no leads and no prints other than the owner's. The guy must have used gloves.

Another fruitless path. Man, they needed a break.

Raven sat stiff in the wooden chair across from the sheriff's desk, her entire body tense and wired.

The sheriff tilted his Stetson back. "Raven, you *still* don't remember anything?"

Daniel crossed his arms in irritation. "She already told you she didn't, Galloway. Just let her alone."

"It's okay," Raven said with gratitude in her eyes. "He has to ask, and I wish I had answers." She turned to the sheriff. "I see flashes of scenes, but it's only bits and pieces. A wedding, a pink blanket. Nothing that helps. Certainly nothing about Chelsea Rivera. But I won't give up. I have to remember. I don't have a choice."

Damn, she was grace under pressure. Daniel couldn't help but admire her. She might have been thrown by the news that the baby in the locket wasn't hers, but she'd rallied, hounding Noah and Elijah for every detail they had. Unfortunately there was nothing more.

The fax machine in the corner whirred to life.

Raven jumped to her feet, and Galloway strode to the machine. He perused the message.

"Well?" she asked. "Is there any news for us?"

"The name Wayne Harrison mean anything to you?" the sheriff asked.

She rubbed her temple, rolling the name through her mind. "No. Maybe. I don't know," she said. "I feel like I *should* know it. This is *so* frustrating."

"Who is he?" Daniel asked.

"According to CTC, a draft was drawn on an account jointly held by Wayne Harrison and his wife, Olivia. It was made out to C.R.—Chelsea Rivera—for over fifty thousand dollars about twenty-one months ago.

"Even more interesting than the amount is the fact that within a few months of receiving the money, Ms. Rivera entered the hospital." The sheriff handed Daniel the fax. "On the maternity ward."

"And my baby might be hers?" Raven gulped. "Are you saying I might be this Olivia Harrison?"

"I don't know, but Chelsea's hospital bill was also paid by Wayne and Olivia Harrison. Could be a private adoption. Could be something else."

Sheriff Galloway stroked his chin. "No birth certificate, though. Kind of weird. And I don't believe in odd coincidences. Money for a baby doesn't usually result in a legal transaction."

Raven glanced from one man to the other and fell back in her seat. "Oh, God. Do you think the baby was bought on the black market?"

Daniel recognized the moment she understood the possibility. Her eyes widened, then she shook her head. "No. I wouldn't do such a thing. I wouldn't buy a child. I can't be this Olivia Harrison."

He knelt in front of her. "Don't jump to conclusions. The woman I know would need facts first."

Raven's hands shook, and her fingers had gone cold. "But do we even know who I am, what I was capable of before they left me for dead?" She rubbed her temple. "It doesn't matter." She opened the locket and held it up. "This baby exists. Who I am doesn't matter right now. She's out there somewhere, and I need to find her. I won't stop until I know for sure that she's safe and loved. Whether she's mine or not, we have to help her."

Noah burst through the sheriff's door. "We have a maternal DNA match," he said. "Chelsea Rivera was a witness in a felony. They did a DNA profile before they eliminated her as a suspect."

"How did you—" Sheriff Galloway started.

"Don't ask," Noah muttered. "The point is the preliminary results are a match. Chelsea Rivera is that baby's mother. And we have her address. She lives in El Paso, not two hours from here."

"Then there's only one thing to do," Daniel said. "We visit Chelsea Rivera and find out what she knows about the baby in the locket."

Chapter Ten

The midafternoon sun glared down on the loaner SUV's windshield, and Daniel cursed the fact that he had no sunglasses. The temperature had to be creeping up on eighty degrees. Trouble sat in the backseat panting. Fall hadn't hit El Paso yet, but then, most things in Texas were ornery like that.

Daniel let out a slow breath when they drove by Chelsea Rivera's current address. The house had been easy enough to find.

"Quiet neighborhood," Noah commented. "Run-down, but not a war zone."

"I'll circle the block." Daniel kept the speed steady, as if they had a destination in mind. "We'll find a secure location to park the car."

He took a quick pass around the block, eyeing potential escape routes.

"How about there?" Raven asked when they came upon an alley.

Cinder-block walls provided cover, and Daniel nodded.

"Good eye," Noah said. "Only a few houses down."

Daniel backed the SUV into the narrow space between two houses and set the vehicle to Park. With Trouble not far behind, Raven climbed out of the backseat, while Daniel opened his door and Noah followed. They stood just out of sight of Chelsea's house, but Daniel's nerves were frayed and edgy.

"Seems quiet," Noah said. "I doubt we'll need backup. Galloway and Elijah can let us know how the Harrison lead pans out, and we may solve this thing before dinner. I know this great cantina—"

Daniel raised his hand. "Don't go there. Every time the situation seems real quiet, Raven and I have almost gotten killed," Daniel said. "Noah, stay with her. I'll signal you."

"What?" Raven said. "You think you're going to just walk up to this woman's door, and she'll talk to you? I hate to tell you this, but you're big, muscular and intimidating, and you walk enough like a cop that she's going to be wary. I should go, too."

"Not happening." His gaze fell to her necklace. "Can I borrow the locket?" he asked.

Raven set her jaw, but she lifted the chain over her head. "You are the most stubborn man." He could see her desire to run across the street and question Chelsea herself, no matter the danger.

Sometimes Raven had a backbone of steel. Usually something that completely turned him on. Not right now, though. He'd gone cold with worry. He had to keep her safe, but whoever wanted her dead seemed two steps ahead of them all the time. The thought wasn't comforting.

Wary of a trap, Daniel worked his way two houses down, keeping out of sight as much as possible. Across from the target location, he paused behind a hedge and hunkered down. He glanced over his shoulder. Noah, Raven and Trouble remained hidden from view, unless you knew where to look. Daniel knew she'd be safe. Noah wouldn't hesitate to sacrifice himself for her.

Neither would Daniel.

He remembered the look he and Noah had exchanged

earlier. They understood each other. If anything happened, Noah would get Raven to CTC headquarters in Carder; then he'd come back and finish what Daniel had started.

He stepped onto the pavement, out of the direct line of sight of the front door and window, then crossed the pothole-littered street. The neighborhood was probably last on the list to get any work done. Not enough registered voters on this street to pressure the city council.

A quick glance in the backyard revealed nothing but a sad thatch of grass and a few struggling perennials in a small planter. He signaled Noah to keep alert, then walked up the broken sidewalk. Once there, he stood just to the right of the doorknob.

The neighborhood was silent. No curtains moving. This was one of those revolving rental streets where neighbors just didn't want to get involved with people who might not be around the next month. Isolation was a lot safer.

Daniel didn't like standing here in the open. His Spidey-sense was working overtime, though he had nothing to base it on. Daniel's shoulders tensed; the hair on the back of his neck stood at attention.

He shifted his shoulder and tucked his Glock within easy reach. He knocked on the door.

A wooden creak sounded through the poorly insulated walls. The curtain quivered.

"Ma'am. I know you're in there. My name is Daniel Adams. I just need to ask a few questions. It's about your baby."

"Go away. Please," a frightened voice begged.

"Not until I talk to you."

"Who...who are you?" she asked, obviously terrified. "Who sent you?"

"No one." Daniel held up the locket to the window. "I'm hoping you can tell me about this child."

The curtains pulled back, and a dark-haired woman with terrified eyes blinked at him. Her cheek was discolored, as if someone had hit her. Daniel's gut burned.

"Do you need help, Chelsea?" he asked softly.

"No, I need you to—" Her gaze honed in on the locket like a laser beam. "Where'd you get that? Mrs. H would never have given it away."

"This locket belongs to Mrs. H?"

"Yes." The woman's hand moved to her throat and lifted a gold heart from beneath her blouse. "She gave me one just like it. To remember."

A soft smile crossed Chelsea's face.

The sound of wood splintering toward the back of the house was followed by a scream. Gunfire exploded, then glass shattered the window where she stood.

Daniel heard a dull thud hit the floor.

He gripped his Glock and shoved his shoulder into the door. The jamb gave way. Chelsea Rivera lay on the floor, her face gone, blood streaming from a horrifying head wound. The bullet had entered from the back and exploded.

The back door slammed.

Knowing Raven was safe with Noah, Daniel raced through the house to the kitchen and out a side door.

Nearby, a motorcycle revved and the powerful engine roared. The shooter headed west. Daniel ran into the front yard, then into the street, his boots thudding on the pavement. The roar of the motor grew louder. Bike tires squealed. Daniel leaped toward the sound, hoping to get a glimpse of the plate.

He caught sight of a black Harley racing down the street, its license plate covered with mud and unreadable, just like the sedan from the drive-by shooting. The guy wore leathers and a very expensive helmet.

The shooter was definitely not from this neighborhood. He was rich. Panting, Daniel watched the bike speed away.

He slipped the gun into the waist of his jeans and jogged back to Noah and Raven.

She stood behind the SUV and peered around Noah, who'd placed himself between her and danger.

"You see anything useful?" Daniel asked.

Noah shook his head. "Sorry. Too far away."

Raven looked up at Daniel. "What happened?"

"Chelsea was shot right after I got there. She didn't say much, but she had a locket just like yours."

"She did?" Raven asked, her expression tentative. "Are you saying he killed her?"

Daniel nodded. "She didn't make it. I'm sorry."

He dropped the gold heart into her palm. "But Chelsea said the woman who gave her the locket had an identical necklace."

Raven stilled. "You know who I am?"

"Mrs. Harrison gave Chelsea that locket." Daniel said softly. "I think we finally know your name."

SIRENS RAGED ALL around the SUV when Daniel pulled out of the alley. Raven's heartbeat quickened, and her fingers gripped the scrub pants she wore. She held her breath when Daniel slowed and moved to the right. Three speeding police cars passed the SUV with lights flashing, but the cops just swerved into Chelsea's driveway.

"Will Noah be okay?" she asked. "What if they arrest him?"

"He can handle himself. Noah has connections. Even if they do arrest him, he'll be out in a matter of minutes," Daniel said. "It's more important that we find Wayne Harrison fast. I don't want to stay here to explain what we were doing visiting Chelsea, or why you're wearing an identical locket to hers."

"They'd never believe what's happened to me," Raven said. "If *I* heard my story, *I'd* think it was a lie."

"Amnesia's hard to believe, since you can't answer most of their questions. *If* you're Mrs. Harrison, then you paid Chelsea. Fifty thousand dollars changed hands. There's no baby and no birth certificate. Very suspicious."

"And I can't tell them why any of it happened." Raven rubbed her forehead, trying to ease the headache that had returned. "What a nightmare."

"For now Noah will have to handle the questioning. Hopefully Wayne Harrison will have enough information for us to explain your presence in Chelsea's life."

She touched the cut on the side of her forehead. "Do you think whoever killed Chelsea is the man who attacked me?"

"It's a safe bet." An edge tinged Daniel's voice. "I'm looking forward to shaking some answers out of your—" He stopped. "Out of Wayne Harrison."

Her husband. That's what he'd meant to say.

She drank in Daniel's strong profile, his hands, his fingers that had caressed her, touched her, loved her. She didn't want to remember giving herself to anyone but Daniel. Raven scratched the base of the ring finger of her left hand and voiced her greatest fear. "Do you really think he's my husband?"

"No. I think you *were* married," Daniel said. "Your dreams have been accurate as far as we know. There *is* a baby. And Wayne Harrison is our only lead." Daniel slid her a heated glance. "I don't want you to be married, Raven. I want what I can't have."

Before she could ask what he meant, his phone rang and he pressed Speaker. "Adams here."

"It's Elijah. We got a hit on Raven. I'm messaging you the info and a photo."

A quick pull of the turn signal, and Daniel stopped by the side of the road and put the SUV into Park.

Raven turned toward Daniel, praying and dreading the scan would have all the answers.

A tone sounded. Daniel tapped the message, and Raven held her breath.

A newspaper article appeared as an image on the phone's screen.

Oh, God. A wedding announcement.

One glance at the photo and caption made Raven gasp. *Mr. and Mrs. Wayne and Olivia Harrison.*

"It's me," she said sadly. "Me and the man from my dream."

PAMELA WINTER STARED at the small baby in the hospital's crib, hoping for a miracle. She couldn't remember the last time she'd slept. Grit stung her eyes each time she blinked.

Her baby girl looked so pale.

"You'll be okay, Christina." Pamela caressed the thinning hair on her beautiful daughter. "We have to disappear, but you'll get the bone marrow transplant, and everything will be better."

With care, Pamela lifted Christina out of the crib and sat with her in the rocking chair. The little girl in the adjacent crib whined, staring up at them. She held out her arms.

Pamela ignored the healthy baby. She'd have to entertain herself until Christina was well. And she would be well. Pamela had chosen their new safe house carefully. Near the Mayo Clinic. She'd hidden enough money from Christopher that she wouldn't have to work again. With Christina's sister as the donor, things should move fast at the new hospital. Everything was going to work.

All she had to do now was trigger Christopher's temper enough so he'd hang himself, and then she and her daughters would disappear. Forever.

"I'll make you all better," she whispered in Christina's ear. "He will never hurt you."

Heavy footsteps paused at the door. Pamela stilled, afraid to look around. It shouldn't be Christopher. After the lies she'd told him, surely he'd left to kill Chelsea for her. Pamela was too busy to do it herself.

The pediatric hematologist came up beside her.

She looked up and took in his solemn expression. "What's wrong?"

Panic twisted her gut, just like the day she'd learned of Christina's illness. During the horrifying search for a matching donor, Pamela had finally discovered the doctor who had revealed Chelsea had had twins. After that, it had been easy to find the other baby. The Harrisons hadn't hidden their adoption.

Pamela had thought her troubles were ending. How wrong she'd been.

The doctor frowned. "Christina's blood work doesn't look good. Since her sister is a match, we need to start the chemotherapy right away. Otherwise, if Christina's health deteriorates, it might be too late."

Pamela froze in the rocker. Time was up. She'd have to eliminate the final risks.

The forger was gone; Chelsea was gone.

All that remained were Wayne and Olivia Harrison.

And one other.

The only other.

Christopher.

She wrung her hands. Could she kill her own son? Did she have the nerve?

The baby whimpered and rolled over. She opened her beautiful eyes, dull and weak with fatigue.

Pamela melted at the sight and hugged her daughter close. She couldn't lose her. She met the doctor's gaze. "May I stay with her 24/7?"

"I'll set things up for that and the chemo," he said, and left the room.

"And by the time you do all that, we'll be gone," Pamela whispered, humming. "Mama will do anything for you, baby girl. Anything." She rose and placed her precious bundle in the crib.

"We'll leave here soon, baby. Very soon."

Ashes, ashes, we all fall down.

DANIEL STARED OUT the SUV window at the late-afternoon sun, hating Elijah for the news he was giving over the phone.

Trouble had found himself a cool spot in the cargo area of the vehicle. He'd been too quiet. Maybe the mutt sensed the high level of emotions.

"I'm married?" Raven whispered, obviously devastated. "No. It can't be."

"You're not married now," Elijah rushed to say. "You were. You and your husband divorced shortly after you adopted your daughter."

The words swirled in Daniel's head. Raven wasn't married. She'd adopted a daughter, but she wasn't married anymore.

"What's my daughter's name? Please, Elijah. Tell me you know her name," Raven pleaded.

"Hope," Elijah said, clearing his throat. "The baby's name is Hope."

Raven's face lit up in a smile. Daniel had never seen such an expression of joy on her face.

She threw her arms around his neck and hugged him. "She's real, Daniel." Raven buried her face in his shirt, her choking sobs unstoppable. "She's real. Hope's mine. She's my baby."

"Yes, darlin', she's yours." Daniel set Raven back and wiped her tears away with his thumb.

"But where is she?" Raven asked.

"Elijah?" Daniel prompted, praying there was more good news, but when silence settled over the phone, he grimaced. "Can you tell us anything else?"

The forensics expert cleared his throat. "Raven has full custody, no visitation for the ex-husband, Wayne, and there's no nanny, but, I'm sorry, Rav...Olivia, I don't know where Hope is."

"I have to find her. And, Elijah, call me Raven," she said softly, wrapping her arms around herself. "I don't know how I feel about this Olivia Harrison yet."

Daniel hugged her close, and she collapsed against his chest, the pressure of the past few days finally taking its toll. He wanted to promise her the world, but despite the progress he'd made, his demons could coming roaring back anytime. So he'd conquered the sound of a whip. His other issues would be much harder.

Daniel faced the fact that he might not be there for her forever, but he could find Raven's daughter. He ignored how his throat had closed off at the idea of letting Raven go. He shoved the regret from his mind. "Run a check on Wayne Harrison. I want to know if he owns a motorcycle, a Harley in particular, *and* if he has any connection to the mines surrounding Trouble, Texas."

"Will do," Elijah said. "We'll get back to you with the information and his address."

He signed off, and Raven took a few deep breaths. "You think my husband did this?"

Daniel shrugged. "It's a strong possibility. Most of the time when a child disappears, a family member is responsible. He never reported you missing. That could mean he didn't want your absence noticed."

"No one reported me. Don't I have *any* friends or relatives? Was I all alone?"

Daniel couldn't stop himself from touching her in an attempt to comfort her, to keep the possibilities from tearing apart her hope. With each caress she leaned into him more, and something deep within him shifted as he eased closer. How would he live without her?

"Why would he take the baby?" she asked, her voice etched with pain.

"Maybe he changed his mind. Maybe he regretted giving her up. I could never give up my daughter unless… unless I was a danger to her well-being."

She fisted the material of his shirt. "You'd never hurt someone you love."

He appreciated her faith, but it was misplaced. "My father had flashbacks like I do. He ruined my sisters' lives. He hurt them badly."

"He hurt you, too." She tightened her grip. "How did you cope with his death?"

Daniel wrapped his arms around her. "I became the man of the family after he killed himself. I did what I had to do." He tilted her head to him and stared at her lips. They parted, inviting him to lose himself in her. But he knew Raven being with him would ultimately break her heart. Not to mention his own.

Thankfully his phone trilled again. He pressed Speaker. "Adams."

"Olivia?" a man's questioning voice filtered into the truck. "I'm looking for Olivia Harrison. I was told I could reach her at this number."

Daniel squeezed the phone until his knuckles whitened. Who the hell was giving out his private line? "Who are you?"

"Wayne Harrison."

Raven bit her lip. "Wayne?"

"Yeah. You sound strange. Are you all right?"

Even though Daniel didn't know her ex, and Wayne's words were all fine, his voice was off. Very hesitant and cautious. Something was wrong.

Daniel scowled. Or else Daniel just hated the guy on principle. What kind of jerk would give up his daughter—or Raven?

She finally answered. "I'm fine..."

"Then where have you been? I've been worried. I called your house a half-dozen times." Wayne's voice broke. "I mean, I know I'm your ex, but even then—" He sounded sincere, like he really cared that she'd been missing. Daniel would give him that.

According to the article on both Olivia and her ex that Elijah had sent to Daniel's phone, the guy was an accountant with an Ivy League education, and he made a good living. Why wouldn't someone smart like Olivia want to be with someone like Wayne Harrison? They made a perfect couple. Steady, reliable.

"Umm...why were you trying to reach me?"

Wayne paused. "Look, this guy called me asking about your daughter. I told him I'd signed over full custody and don't have anything to do with her, but he doesn't believe me. He claims he's her birth father. I thought you said the woman we paid had full rights. Did you make that up?"

"Are you saying you don't have the baby?" Raven asked softly.

"Why would you ask me that?" Wayne asked, his voice

low. "Of course I don't have her. What's wrong with you, Olivia?"

Raven bowed her head. If her ex didn't have Hope, then they were back to square one—except they knew her name.

"What was the birth father's name?" she asked, taking her cue from Daniel.

"He didn't tell me. Look," Wayne said, "let me come over right now, and we can talk about this. I don't... I'm concerned. You sound really weird."

Daniel shook his head, and Raven tipped her head in agreement. "I can't. There are things happening..."

"Fine. I get it," Wayne interrupted. "I know I let you down when I didn't want to raise someone else's kid. I thought I could do it, so sue me. But, Olivia, we can still be friends."

"I don't know," Raven answered.

Wayne's voice dropped to nearly a whisper. "We need to talk. This guy. He's—" Wayne grunted. "Dangerous. If I can't come to you, then come my way. I'm at the El Paso house."

She bit her lip and sent Daniel a questioning look. He debated. Wayne could be telling the truth. Maybe, just maybe, they'd get a lead. Daniel nodded his agreement, and simultaneously sent out a text to Elijah and Noah to track down more information.

"I'll be there," she said.

"Soon?" Wayne urged. "Could you come now?"

"As soon as I can," she promised.

Daniel ended the call, then punched in Elijah's and Noah's numbers for a three-way conversation. When they were on the line, Daniel let the temper he'd been holding flare. "Which one of you boneheads gave Wayne Harrison my cell number?"

"I did." Elijah's voice was matter-of-fact, calm and non-apologetic. "Sheriff Galloway contacted him during our investigation. The guy called back, said he needed to talk to his wife. From GPS I got his location. Figured we wanted to have a conversation with him one way or another. He still a suspect?"

Daniel rubbed the back of his neck where a tension headache had started moving up his skull. Elijah was right, damn him. Daniel glanced at Raven. He was emotionally involved. He couldn't deny it, and it was affecting his judgment.

"The conversation was odd," Daniel said, clutching the phone tighter, "but I don't think he has the baby. He does have answers, but he's evasive."

"Then we go to him," Noah said.

The options kept narrowing, particularly without a birth certificate. Daniel knew they were missing a piece, something critical, something important. Something that would reveal who wanted Raven dead and who had taken her child. If it wasn't Wayne, then who? And why? There had to be a reason.

Daniel just prayed that when he figured out the truth, it wouldn't be too late.

CHRISTOPHER SHOVED THE gun into Wayne Harrison's temple. "Well done. Guess this shows you why you shouldn't leave your back door unlocked. You never know who will just walk in off the streets."

Wayne dropped the phone back on the cradle. "Please. Take anything you want, just let me go. I did what you asked. I don't know anything."

"Shut up before you piss me off. Do you have a basement?" Christopher asked.

"W-why? What are you going to do to me?" Wayne's voice shook.

"Not very brave, are you? What, you think I'm going to kill you down there, bury your body like some deranged serial killer?" Christopher chuckled. "Might be a change of pace, but I'm on a mission, my friend. A very important mission."

Christopher dragged the gun's barrel across Wayne's cheek. "You paid fifty thousand bucks for my kid, didn't you?"

"I didn't want to," Wayne protested. "It was all Olivia. She met the mother at the ob-gyn, and the woman said she couldn't take care of her baby. When Olivia lost our baby, she got in touch with her. That's all I know."

Christopher twisted around to backhand the coward. "What was the mother's name?"

Wayne rubbed the blood from his lip, his eyes wide and wary.

Christopher again pushed the gun to Wayne's head. "Her name, or you're dead."

"Chelsea Rivera." The words rushed out.

"You're dead. You know too much."

"Please," Wayne begged. "I don't know who you are. I won't tell anyone. I swear."

Christopher kicked the man in the groin. Wayne collapsed, and Christopher shoved him over onto his back. "Men like you disgust me. My father chewed people like you up and spit them out his entire career. My mother was right. We end this here. Today. My daughters will be with me from now on."

He pressed his boot into Wayne's windpipe. The guy turned red and sucked in short breaths. "Now, where's the basement?"

Gasping for air, Wayne pointed to a door just across the living room.

"Crawl," Christopher ordered. "Belly crawl like the sniveling worm you are."

Wayne made his way slowly to the door and opened it. A narrow staircase disappeared into the dark.

Christopher smiled, checking the layout. Perfect. One exit. One entrance. Like shooting targets during boot camp. Tad would've had fun with this one. A small twinge of regret nipped at Christopher's conscience. Tad had been a good friend. He shouldn't have died like that. The man watching over Raven would pay. Christopher would take his time finishing off that one.

"Get up and turn on the light, Harrison."

Wayne rose and flipped the switch.

"Down the stairs."

Suddenly Wayne whirled around and shoved his shoulder into Christopher's chest. He stumbled back.

"Idiot." Christopher raised his gun and fired a gut shot. Harrison was dead. He just didn't know it yet.

Blood seeped through his shirt. Wayne groaned and grabbed at the wound. "You're crazy!"

Christopher shook his head. "My dad taught me how to shoot. Uncle Sam taught me how to kill." He grabbed Harrison's hair and gazed into the coward's fearful eyes. "Now get down there. I'm not through with you yet."

Chapter Eleven

Raven didn't think Daniel could drive any faster. He whizzed around the curves like an Indy driver. She peered into the afternoon sun and eyed a street sign for North Mesa. If Trouble didn't have dog ears, she might just scream. Instead she clenched her fist, her nails biting into her palm.

"Not familiar?" Daniel asked.

"Not a glimmer, and I'm starting to wonder if I'll ever remember."

"It's only been a few days. You're still healing." He set his hand next to hers on the seat. "Even if you don't, you'll go on. You'll create a new life. You and your daughter—when we find her."

Her heart fluttered at the nearness of his hand. But he didn't hold it. Was he trying to tell her something? To pull away? Her heart stuttered a bit, because in her mind, she could see a picture as clearly as the landscape through this upscale neighborhood. Daniel, her, Hope. A life together. She would be his. *If* he wanted her.

She couldn't call it love, because she had no frame of reference, but if love meant your heart skipped whenever he whispered your name, if love meant trusting a man with *your* life, with your child's life, if love meant having complete faith a man would always think of you before he thought of himself, if love meant knowing a man could be counted on to protect you heart and soul, then she had to believe she loved Daniel.

She clutched at her shirt just above her heart and took a shuddering breath. My God. She loved him. Suddenly she couldn't think; her leg bounced and she tried to focus, watching his hands steer, his eyes study the surroundings and his small smile when he met her gaze.

He pulled up to a large two-story house, the white stucco gleaming and the red tile contrasting, and stopped. "Your ex has a nice place," he said, lowering the windows a bit and opening the door.

Trouble started barking frantically, turning on the seat.

"Trouble. Stay," he said. The dog jumped into the back-seat and stuck his nose out the window. "Don't worry, I'll leave the air-conditioning on for you, but this isn't the kind of neighborhood you can roam free in." He glanced around. The place oozed upper middle class. "I don't want to bail you out of the dog pound."

Raven unlocked her car door but stopped when Daniel's phone rang. He glanced down and hit Speaker. "How close are you?"

"Not too far," Noah said. He paused for a second. "Do you want the scoop on Olivia Harrison?"

Raven's back tensed. She bit her lip. Did she want to know? What if—?

Coward. They needed whatever would help them find the baby. She didn't matter. Her daughter did. She sent Daniel a quick nod.

"Give us what's relevant."

"Raven, honey? You okay with that?" Noah said softly.

"I need to know," she said, her voice barely loud enough to be heard.

"Well, you got a few facts from that bio in the wedding announcement, but you caught yourself a smart one, Daniel. Try to let some rub off on you. Olivia graduated magna cum laude in biochemistry. Figured out something about DNA sequencing that I can't understand. She's got several patents that brought in a boatload of money. That house you're standing in front of? Her ex got it in the divorce settlement."

"I'm not surprised she's smart," Daniel said. "When she started spouting off chemical formulas on day one, I knew she was something special."

Raven's cheeks heated, and she squirmed in her seat.

Noah cleared his throat. "I did find out one thing. Brace yourself, honey. You weren't wrong about having a baby. Two years ago you were pregnant. Seven months along. Something went wrong, and your baby daughter was stillborn. I'm *so* sorry."

Raven's heart started pounding. She doubled over and grabbed her belly. She could almost feel the pain gripping her stomach. Hard contractions, without hope. Flashes burned into her mind. Despair so deep she could barely breathe.

Daniel grabbed her and wrapped his arms around her, holding her tight against him. His warm breath whispered against her ear. "Listen to my voice, Raven. Don't let it take over. Come back to me."

Tears wet her eyelashes. She glanced up at him. "My baby is dead," she said.

"Yes. You named her Sarah," Noah said. "A few months later you adopted a baby girl. Chelsea Rivera was the birth mother. That fifty thousand dollars paid her expenses. About a month after the adoption was final, your husband filed for divorce."

"Jerk," Daniel muttered.

"Hope," Raven whispered, begging her mind to remember the baby's face, not from a photo, but from a memory. She opened the locket and stared at the dark-haired baby. "How old is she now?" Raven asked.

"Eighteen months."

Raven leaned against Daniel, soaking in his strength. She needed to find Hope. He rubbed her back for a moment. Finally she straightened. "Wayne Harrison said the baby's birth father wants her. Who is the father?"

"I'll keep looking. I found your pediatrician's records—don't ask how—but I can't seem to locate her birth certificate. I'm hoping Elijah can unravel the state vital statistics records."

Daniel glanced at his watch. "How far from Harrison's house are you?" he asked.

"Another half hour," Noah said.

"We're going in. Maybe we can get a description of the father from Wayne, see if he matches the jumper in the canyon. Or if he was riding a motorcycle."

"Watch your back. Elijah and I will be there as soon as we can."

Daniel stuffed his phone into his pocket and looked down at Raven. He slid his thumb under her eye and cupped her cheek. "You up for this?"

"I don't know him," she said softly. "I have nothing invested in Wayne Harrison. Hope is all I care about." Raven gripped the locket. "We have to find her. This man—whoever he is—can't have her."

"He won't get her. She belongs with you."

Raven nodded, but Daniel's words tugged at a huge fear. "If I never remember, can I be her mother? Will they take her away?"

"No way. You are passionate, determined and loving. From the moment I found you, all you've thought about is finding that little girl. You believed when everyone else doubted. That's what a mother is. Believe me, I know. I have a good one." He tucked a strand of her black hair behind her ear. "If they do question your parenting ability, I have a lot of friends in very high places."

Raven hugged him and kissed his cheek. "Let's find my daughter, Daniel."

"Let's meet the ex," Daniel groused, his eyes dark. "I still think he's a jerk for abandoning you."

"We don't know why," Raven said.

"I don't care. Any man who would abandon his child doesn't deserve sympathy."

She winced, knowing he was talking about *his* father, *his* family as much as Wayne Harrison. Together they headed down a long sidewalk to the front door. The manicured lawn was perfect. The plants and trees were perfect. Nothing looked out of place; it was as if the house belonged on the cover of a magazine.

"Not real lived-in, huh?" Daniel said.

"Sterile," Raven muttered. "I can't believe I lived here."

Daniel rang the bell. After a few moments, he knocked on the door.

"That's odd. He knew we were coming."

His posture changed. Raven recognized the awareness. She'd seen him in this stance, as if searching for danger by sight, smell and feel. He glanced around the neighborhood. "Nothing unusual." He peered in the front window. "The house looks deserted, but then again, it could be he's the ultimate anal neat freak."

"I wish I knew," Raven said. "Is Noah sure this is the right house?"

"Noah doesn't make mistakes like that, but I'll double-check." A quick text later, Daniel pressed the doorbell a second time. "This is it."

He tried the knob. It opened.

"Maybe something happened to him…"

"Mr. Harrison?" he called. "Wayne?"

"Basement," a pained voice said. "I…fell."

They rushed to an open door. Daniel flipped the light switch, but the stairwell remained dark.

"Wayne?" Raven called.

"Here," a muffled voice muttered. "I need help. I can't walk."

Daniel pulled out the small but powerful flashlight from his pocket. Raven gave him a look. He shrugged. "It's come in handy."

Daniel led the way down the tunnellike stairs, shining the light on the steep steps. She didn't want to fall. One head injury a week was plenty.

A sniffle sounded from across the room. Daniel turned at the landing, then stilled.

"Run," he hissed at her, blocking her view.

"If you want to see my daughter again, Olivia, you'll join us," a soft, threatening voice promised.

DANIEL COULDN'T BELIEVE he'd let them get into this position. Trouble had warned him. Without hesitation, Raven stepped around him and down the last couple of steps. Inside he wanted to scream at her to run, but she wouldn't. He couldn't expect her to. This guy had played the only card that would trump her own safety. Hope.

Just as Daniel wouldn't hesitate to risk his life for Raven.

He scanned the area. Two closed doors on one wall. A bathroom, maybe, and a storage closet, though what Wayne had in a room with a steel door made Daniel wonder. As to exits, several high windows lined the top of the wall, but Noah wouldn't be able to see in with the darkening blinds. The rest of the basement was a typical man cave, with video games, a big-screen television, comfortable sofas and recliners, and a bar and refrigerator.

All in all, they were stuck in another freakin' cave. He and Raven couldn't get away from them. Of course, this time they had company.

RAVEN'S EX SAT bound to a chair, his entire body stiff, his fear palpable. His face had been battered; blood stained his side, dripping down to the floor. The man's pasty complexion made Daniel curse. The guy was still losing blood. He could go into shock at any moment.

Daniel shifted, trying to ease his hand to his pocket. If he could warn Noah, or maybe reach his Glock—

"I wouldn't do that," his captor said. "I won more than my share of shooting awards in boot camp. Phone and gun on the floor. Slide them to me."

Well, hell. The guy had training. Knowing he had to take the risk, Daniel flicked the edge of the phone, sending a warning signal to Noah, then he did as instructed.

"I bet you carry a knife, too."

Daniel weighed the alternatives.

"Don't get cute with me, spook. I find you lied, I won't hesitate to kill her. That's my plan anyway."

Knowing he couldn't risk Raven's life, Daniel slipped the Bowie from his ankle sheath and tossed it on the ground. The knife didn't make any noise on the carpet.

Raven stepped forward. "Where's Hope? Let me see her."

"You think I'd involve my little girl in cleaning up this mess?" the man said. He pressed the gun's barrel to the base of Wayne's skull. "When I kill him, his brains will fly all over this room."

Wayne whimpered, and Daniel stiffened, searching for an angle to shut the bastard up.

"I've seen your work." He nodded at Daniel. He raised the gun, aiming it at Raven's chest. "Olivia, move away from him. Open the door to the wine cellar."

She looked around the room, her face panicked. She glanced back and forth between them.

Their captor let out a shout of laughter. "Holy hell. You don't remember anything, do you?" A gleam appeared in his eye. "Very interesting. I'll give you a clue. It's not the wooden door. Your ex thinks his wine collection is valuable enough to warrant protection. Maybe after this is over, I'll enjoy a few vintages."

The man chuckled, and Daniel gritted his teeth in frustration, letting out a vicious curse. The boot camp graduate kept perfect position. Daniel couldn't risk a frontal assault, not without casualties. He wouldn't be able to disarm the guy before Raven went down or her ex ate a bullet.

"If you don't want Wayne to die in front of you, I suggest you move, Olivia," their captor said.

Raven hurried across the floor. With a shaking hand, she flicked the latch. The metal door swung open with barely a wisp of sound.

"Please," she said, turning toward him. "I understand you love your daughter. We can work something out."

"You *bought* my daughter," he growled. "You stole her from us."

Raven shook her head. "No. I wouldn't have. I helped Chelsea—"

"Don't mention her name. I made her pay."

"You…you killed her?" Raven asked.

"She betrayed me." His eyes had gone crazy.

"You'll never get away with this," Daniel said, easing slowly toward their captor, working for an angle to attack.

He shook his head. "You have no idea what's going on

here, do you? You're all dead. No one's left who cares, no one to talk. We'll start over."

The guy's twitchy fingers flexed against the trigger. He was unpredictable, and that made him too dangerous.

"That's enough of your games. Olivia, come two steps toward me to give secret agent man plenty of room."

Raven moved, and Daniel cursed under his breath. A prime opportunity gone.

"Get inside that room," the man ordered Daniel.

With a deep breath, he walked through the steel door. The stone walls looked way too familiar. He paused at the entrance.

"I can shoot her right now," his captor said.

Daniel fought his own instincts not to make a mistake. He had backup. He just had to keep them both alive until Noah arrived with Elijah.

Raven met his gaze. Did she see the panic clawing up his insides?

She must have, because she nodded her head.

He took a few steps deeper into the room. Seconds later Raven stumbled inside, and the steel door slammed behind them.

With a worried expression, she gripped his hand. "Don't worry. I'll help you," she whispered. "I won't let you lose yourself."

Daniel blinked, eyeing another dungeon.

DUSK HAD FALLEN when Pamela pulled the stolen SUV in front of Wayne Harrison's house. Not a bad neighborhood...for now.

She leaned her head back against the leather seat. Her life as Pamela Winter ended here. Today. The terrified wife and mother were gone. A new woman had discovered strength enough to leave the past behind and begin again.

In a strange way, thanks to Olivia Harrison.

She picked up her cell phone and dialed her son's number.

"I have them," Christopher answered. "We've won, Mother. No one can take my girls away from me now. Not once I kill them all."

"Even her bodyguard?" Pamela asked.

Christopher lowered his voice. "Yeah. He's not so tough."

"Find out who else knows anything about our plans, then kill them. We'll save your daughters together. No one will ever steal them again." She studied the phone in her hand. This would be her last conversation with Christopher. She refused to regret it. He'd become just like his father.

Pamela glanced in the backseat. A box of dynamite sat in the floorboard. She'd hated her husband's business. She'd liked the money, but she'd hated being dirty and grimy. The only good thing about having to work with him in those early days was that she'd learned how to blow a hole in the ground.

She could blow a hole in this house.

The perfect plan. The perfect scapegoat.

"I'm going to enjoy this."

She recognized the eagerness in her son's voice. She remembered that same tone when he'd headed out for his hunting trips. She shivered. Her son was as certifiable as his father.

"We can't attract attention. I'm a half hour away, honey. Can you wait until dark? Better cover that way."

"I'll wait. You have the babies?"

"All packed up. We'll leave as soon as I get there." Pamela tossed the phone in the passenger's seat and picked up a throwaway cell she'd purchased at a drug store. She pocketed it and exited the vehicle.

A large dog stuck his nose out of a window of another SUV parked in front of Harrison's house. A deep bark escaped from him, then another.

Pamela froze. She looked around. No one seemed to be paying any attention. She stood still for several moments. Christopher didn't come to the door. They obviously couldn't hear the mutt inside the house.

She threw a rock at the car. The dog ducked down, then returned, still barking.

Damn it. She wouldn't have much time. Eventually the stupid canine would attract attention.

Ignoring the dog, she went to work. Within minutes she'd taken the box to the back of the house. Wayne Harrison had made it easy to stay hidden, with all the trees in his yard.

Within seconds she'd placed three of the four charges. She stepped back and dialed 9-1-1.

"What's your emergency?" the voice asked.

A sob escaped Pamela's throat. "Please, please. Help. He's going to kill her. I know he is."

"Who are you talking about, ma'am?"

"My son. He's crazy. He just got out of the army. He wants to kill that woman I saw on the news. The woman without a memory. Her name is Olivia Harrison. He said he was going to kill her and her husband. I know he's going to their house. You have to stop him. He's taken my husband's gun and dynamite. He's going to kill them."

"Ma'am—"

With a smile, Pamela ended the call and tossed the phone on the last explosives. She bent down and set the final charge.

Soon her family would be safe. Her real family. Hope and Christina. Everything would be fine this time.

She was starting over.

THE STEEL DOOR slammed, and a lock turned. A small sliver of light filtered on the side of the darkening blinds from the single window near the ceiling.

Raven clutched Daniel's hands. Even in the dimness, his eyes were wild, with that same look she'd seen above the wash.

"Not a dungeon," he whispered. "A wine cellar. A wine cellar."

She cupped his face between her hands, desperate for him to see her, not those nightmarish visions. "You fought this battle once, Daniel. You can do it again. Look at me."

Daniel blinked, and the faraway look in his eyes cleared. He stared down at her, his hazel eyes holding her captive. He cupped her cheek. "Thank you. I'm back."

"I know," she said. "You always come back."

He didn't respond, and she prayed he believed her, but something told her Daniel would never be satisfied until the episodes never returned. She didn't know a lot about PTSD, but she couldn't imagine it was something that just stopped one day.

"We have to get out of here." Daniel grabbed the window jamb and lifted himself up, tearing down the covering. It didn't help much with the sun setting, but at least they could see the room more clearly. Several shelves lined the stone walls with bottle after bottle of wine. A few boxes were stacked in the corner, but there wasn't much else in the room.

"I think you can fit through this window, Raven. I got a signal off to Noah. He should be here soon, but I won't take a chance with your life."

"What about Hope?" she asked, gnawing on her lower lip. "He knows where she is. He has to."

"Once we're out of here and have backup, we'll get the information out of him. No matter what it takes." Daniel jumped down. "I need something to break the glass."

The wine bottles wouldn't cut it. Raven walked the edge of the room. They could break the shelves apart and hope the noise didn't attract attention. Or…

She grabbed a fire extinguisher from the corner. "Will this work?"

He grabbed her face and kissed her. "Brilliant." He held the extinguisher and looked around. "It'll make a lot of noise." He lifted a wine bottle and swung it down against the rack, shattering the end and leaving a jagged weapon behind.

They both held their breath, but the steel door didn't open.

"It'll be ten times worse when I break the window." He handed the broken bottle to Raven. "If that bastard opens the door don't hesitate. Do as much damage as you can."

Raven wouldn't have considered herself bloodthirsty, but after what that man had done, she didn't think she'd lose sleep if she had to carve up his face. Raven crouched near the door, clutching the neck of the jagged bottle with a death grip.

Daniel cleared the bottom two shelves and rigged a stool from the wooden parts. "This is it." He stepped up and heaved the extinguisher at the glass.

It shattered.

Using his jacket to protect his skin, Daniel shoved aside the remaining shards. "Okay, darlin'. Let's get you out of here. Noah should be here soon. Call the cops from a neighbor's house and hide until they get here."

She hesitated. "What about you?" Even she could

tell Daniel couldn't get his shoulders through the small window.

"I'll be fine."

Without another word, Daniel hefted Raven up. She stuck her head out of the window and let out a strangled gasp.

Wave upon wave of memories pummeled her. Unable to bear the agony, she let go and slid back into Daniel's arms, sagging against him.

"My God, you look like you're going to faint. What happened?"

Raven could barely catch her breath. "The woman outside," she panted. "I recognize her. Pamela Winter. She's the one who tried to kill me. She's the one who buried me alive." Raven gripped Daniel's shirt. "And I saw dynamite."

Chapter Twelve

Daniel hitched himself to see out the window. Sure enough, a woman in a designer suit held the ends of four wires and a detonator in her hands. He followed one of the wires to a bundle of dynamite. "She's going to blow the place," he hissed.

Suddenly, as if sensing their presence, she raised her head and searched her surroundings, her gaze narrow and suspicious.

"Lift me up," Raven ordered. "Maybe I can make her see sense."

They didn't have anything to lose.

"Pamela!" Raven yelled. "Don't do this. We can work it out."

"It's too late," Pamela bit out. "You wouldn't help me. You wanted to find out more damned information while my baby was dying. Now I'm claiming my family and yours."

"But—"

She slammed down the ancient dynamite blaster.

In a split second, Daniel grabbed Raven by the waist and threw them both behind one of the heavy wine racks, wedging themselves between the solid wood back and the stone wall. He sent up a small prayer for Raven and covered her with his body.

An explosion erupted, shaking the earth, then a second, third and fourth followed.

Dirt rained down, but the stone walls didn't crumble. The wine rack swayed and fell back, angled against the wall, but it held, making a small canopy over their hiding place.

Soon an odd quiet settled over them. Daniel pushed aside the wine rack and looked around. He peered outside the window. Black smoke poured from the house.

He stared around the small stone room. "The dungeon saved us," he muttered. The irony of it all. Christopher may have saved their lives by locking them away. But they weren't safe yet.

Daniel rushed to the steel door and placed his hand onto it. Heat burned his palm, and he snatched his hand away. "We have to get out of here."

He looked down. Smoke filtered in under the door.

"What about Wayne?" Raven asked.

Daniel pointed to the foggy tendrils. "The fire's already here. We can't open the door. If Wayne survived, they're already out."

Her eyes widened. She gave a sharp nod. She knew. Both men were probably dead.

Daniel bent down below the window and folded his hands together. "Come on. Climb through that window."

He heaved her up, and she squeezed her torso through the window. The smoke formed a wall behind Daniel, like a death call. He coughed. They were out of time.

"Hurry," he said as the smoke rose, pushing her hips through the small opening. Suddenly Raven slipped from his hands.

"Daniel, are you in there?"

At Noah's shout, Daniel sent up a prayer of thanks. He hefted himself up. "Get her out of here," he said, coughing.

"She's fine," Noah said. Daniel's shoulders struck against the window jamb. He sucked in a breath of air. "Get a crowbar."

Noah took off. Smoke billowed into the room on either side of him. He blinked back the stinging from his eyes.

"Hold your breath and move out of the way," Noah said. "I'll be as fast as I can. I only need a few inches."

Daniel released his hold and fell back into the wine cellar. The smoke had gotten so thick he couldn't see anything. He kept one hand on the jamb. If he let go, he could die in here.

"Back away, Daniel! We have a sledgehammer."

Keeping his hand against the stone wall, Daniel eased away. His lungs burned. He couldn't hold his breath much longer.

The wall shook. Two strikes later, stone crumbled over him. "That's it!" Noah yelled. "Get out here!" he shouted through a series of coughs.

Spots in front of his eyes, Daniel followed his touch to the opening. His hands curved over the window's edge and two hands grabbed him, dragging him out of the burning building.

Noah didn't stop until he'd dragged Daniel ten feet away, then he fell back onto his butt.

Daniel sucked in a lungful of air, and a coughing fit hit.

"Damn, you almost ended up as barbecue," Noah said. "How did you avoid that?"

Blinking the smoke out of his eyes, Daniel stared at the inferno Wayne Harrison's house had become. Fire spewed into the sky; black smoke billowed upward. "Stone wine cellar. Strongest room in the house," he said, still coughing as his gaze swept through the rescue personnel, looking for one dark-haired woman. "Where's Raven?"

"Paramedics have her."

Daniel stumbled to his feet. "Is she going to be all right?"

He scanned the chaotic scene and headed to the emergency vehicles. His heart raced, and then he saw her, face smudged, an oxygen mask on, Trouble at her feet—but she was safe.

Daniel's knees buckled in relief, and Noah grabbed his arm.

A fireman ran up to them. "Anyone left in there?"

Noah nodded. "Two. In the basement adjacent to the room where you found us. The door was hot."

The man nodded and ran toward his teammates, and Daniel lurched toward Raven. He knelt in front of her. "You're okay?"

"You saved me. Again."

Daniel hugged close the woman who'd once more almost died because of him. "Thank God you're all right."

"Do you know who did this?" Noah asked.

"Her name is Pamela Winter," Raven said. She met Daniel's gaze, her eyelashes wet with tears. "I remember. The moment I saw Pamela, I remembered everything."

PAMELA RUBBED HER face with her hands. She should have used a timer. Stupid mistake. The explosion had sent debris flying, shattering her windshield. She'd wasted precious minutes taking back streets so she wouldn't get stopped by the cops.

Finally she'd reached the exchange point, dumping the stolen SUV for the car Hector had set up. The car she'd take north to her new life.

Pamela didn't bother parking in long-term. She had to get her daughters and leave.

Now that everyone who could steal her life was dead, everything would be okay. Christina would get well. She and her daughters would live the good life. Away from Trouble, Texas.

She tapped her foot waiting for the elevator. Finally the metal doors slid open. She pressed the number for the pediatric floor. This would be the hardest part, getting the girls out without anyone seeing.

She might have to put them in a laundry cart. She'd attract attention with two babies in her arms.

The doors slid open, and she walked past the nurses' station.

"Mrs. Winter?" A solemn-faced nurse flagged her down. "I need you to come with me."

Pamela's throat closed. They couldn't possibly know anything. Olivia and Wayne Harrison were dead. Christopher was dead. She was home free. She struggled to tamp down the panic.

"After I make sure my daughters are all right." Pamela quickened her pace down the hall.

The nurse followed. "That's what I need to talk to you about."

When Pamela reached the small room with two cribs, she skidded to a halt. One was empty.

"Where's Christina?" Pamela whirled around at the nurse, wanting to strike out. *"Where's my daughter?"*

The nurse stepped back warily. "She's in the Pediatric Intensive Care Unit. She developed a heart arrhythmia. They're doing everything they can to stabilize her."

THE FIRE HOSES sent several arcs of water onto the burning house, and the sky filled with hissing steam. Despite the firefighters' efforts, the conflagration continued to crackle and burn. Smoke stung Raven's eyes. She still couldn't believe Pamela Winter had done this.

Daniel stood at the edge of the emergency vehicles talking urgently to one of the cops. They shook hands, and Daniel strode over to her. "They've put out an APB on Pamela, but I had to tell him I didn't know the identity of the man who locked us in the wine cellar. They'll want to talk to you."

She tapped her temple. "I've seen him before…or I've seen his picture, but where?" She grabbed her head. "Why won't my memory work?"

Daniel squatted down in front of her. "It'll come to you, but for now, do you have any idea where Pamela went?"

Raven bit her lip. "Try the hospitals. Search for Christina Winter."

"Who is that?"

"Chelsea's daughter." Raven rose and paced back and forth. "Pamela called me and told me that Chelsea had given birth to twins. I never knew, Daniel. If there had been two, I would have taken both of them. She told me that her daughter was ill and that Hope might be able to help. I agreed to a blood test so they could determine if the girls matched. They more than matched. They're identical."

Two firefighters let out a shout and raced away from Wayne's house. A wall fell, and the flames licked at least twenty feet in the air. The lot had turned to hell.

"Pamela invited me to her house to meet her daughter. I brought Hope." She shook her head. "If only I hadn't taken her with me."

"You couldn't have known," Daniel interrupted.

"When I got there, Pamela started talking about surgery and anesthesia. I wanted to help, but I couldn't sign a consent form without getting an opinion. Hope was only eighteen months old. I needed to understand the risks."

Raven clutched the locket. "She went crazy, starting screaming and yelling about how I was killing her daughter. I got upset and tried to leave, but she screamed, 'No!'

Then she shoved me." Raven pressed her hand to her forehead. "That's the last thing I remember until I awoke trapped in the mine. I'm so lucky you found me."

Daniel motioned to the cop and gave him Christina's name. Raven's eyes widened. "I just remembered where I saw the guy from the basement. His picture was on Pamela's wall."

"Really?" Daniel tugged out his phone and tapped in a few lines. Within seconds he turned the phone around, showing her a graduation photo. "Christopher Winter. He was Pamela's son."

"She killed her own son? Oh, God, she really is crazy. And she has Hope. And Christina."

Noah raced over to them, his expression grim.

Raven bit her lip. "What's wrong?"

"They found Hope," Noah said. "She's in the hospital." He frowned. "Unfortunately Christina is in intensive care."

Daniel grasped Raven's elbow and guided her toward the SUV. "Then that's where we're going. Tell the cops. I hope they intercept Pamela before she gets to the twins."

"CHRISTINA CAN'T BE in ICU," Pamela insisted, her desperation mounting. "She was doing fine earlier."

"I'm sorry." The nurse gave Pamela's back a comforting pat, and Pamela fought to keep herself from shoving the stupid woman away.

"The doctor wants to make sure she's stable enough for the procedure tomorrow. She was definitely struggling for a while. He wants her in ICU so she'll have constant monitoring and extra care to prepare for the bone marrow transplant. It's not her first arrhythmia, but this bout took a lot out of her."

Pamela rubbed her arms to ward off the chill of the nurse's words. "But Christina is stable now?"

"Yes. For the past hour. I just checked on her progress."

Pamela clenched her fists. Damn it, she'd been *so* close to getting the babies away. She paused. If Christina wasn't in immediate danger, then maybe the plan would still work. *If* Pamela could get her daughter out of the ICU. Of course, the unit had ridiculously tight controls and constant monitoring, but Pamela had a gun.

No contest on who would win that one.

"Can I see her?"

The nurse smiled. "I'll take you."

Pamela glanced over at Hope, the girl's bone marrow the cure for her deathly ill daughter. Taking the eighteen-month-old into ICU wasn't an option. Pamela would have to come back for Hope.

Pamela followed the nurse down the hall. She buzzed into ICU, and they stepped inside.

"I'd like to see Christina Winter."

"You'll have to put on scrubs and a mask first."

After dressing, Pamela walked to the sixth crib. They'd attached Christina to a heart monitor and an IV. "Can I be alone with her?"

"You have five minutes. That's it until next hour."

After the nurse left, Pamela glanced down at her gown. She'd grabbed the largest one possible. Was it big enough to hide a too-small baby? It had to be.

Pamela leaned down to Christina. "Mommy's going to get you out of here."

Her daughter's eyes blinked, and she smiled at her mother, a weak smile, but the baby reached out her hand and gripped Pamela's finger.

Her adrenaline was racing. "Mommy can do this, baby girl." Pamela had to time everything perfectly. If they turned their backs, she could rush out.

Her own heart pounding, she twisted one of the EKG

wires until it snapped. A monitor screeched, and Pamela threw open the curtain. "Something's wrong. Please, help her."

The nurse rushed into the room and silenced the machine.

"She was thrashing a bit, and then the monitor went off," Pamela said.

"One of the wires is damaged. I'll find another set and be right back." The nurse smiled. "She should be okay. It will only take a few minutes to hook her up."

"Thank you," Pamela said.

The nurse closed the curtain behind her.

Pamela unhooked the IV. Christina cried a bit, but Pamela tucked the baby against her chest, wrapping her in a blanket. Most people wouldn't stop someone in hospital clothes if they were in a hurry. She thought she heard the sound of sirens in the distance and panicked for a minute, then realized it was probably an ambulance heading for the E.R.

She held the baby close and grabbed the fabric curtain, wondering if the nurse had returned yet.

Suddenly a speaker squawked above her. "Code Black. This is not a drill. Code Black."

A vise clamped around her chest. What did that mean? Was someone dying?

She peeked around the curtain.

Two policemen entered ICU, and the nurse pointed at Pamela.

No. This couldn't be happening.

Pamela lunged through the curtain, clasping the baby to her. She bolted for the elevator.

One of the cops veered to the left to head her off. "Ma'am. You have to stop."

The nurse picked up the phone. "Security. Pamela Winter is in PICU. She has taken her daughter."

"Leave me alone!" Pamela screamed. "She's *my* daughter. I have the right to take her out of here."

The policeman stepped closer. "Just hand me the baby. Everything will be fine."

Pamela shook her head. "Nothing is fine. Everything is wrong. We're supposed to be gone."

"You're not leaving here with that baby."

The other cop snapped, "She's not going anywhere but a jail cell."

Pamela's entire body stilled. *They knew.* Somehow they knew what she'd done. They would take Christina away from her.

"No. No one can take care of Christina but me."

She whipped her husband's gun from her pocket. "Stay back!" She aimed the weapon at the nurse, and the cops froze. "My daughter and I are leaving. Try to stop me, even make a move toward your weapons, and you're dead."

Pamela backed up until she reached the ICU door's entrance, pushed through, then raced down the hall. She skidded to a halt when two security guards rounded the corner.

"Stop!"

The baby started screaming. *Oh, God, don't let her have a heart attack.* Frantic, Pamela whirled around and bolted toward the door to the stairs. She shoved through, and the metal door slammed off the wall.

Thundering footsteps pounded toward her from behind and from below.

A security guard yelled, "You can't escape now! You're trapped."

"No! Get away from me! She's mine!" Tears blurred her vision, but she fired two shots down into the stairwell.

The men ducked momentarily, but then started coming after her again.

Hysteria had her feeling like her mind was going to explode.

"Leave me alone! You're scaring her."

She fired off two more bullets, and heard the pained cry of one of her pursuers.

Clutching the terrified baby tighter, Pamela turned and ran higher, tripping over the stairs in her fatigue. There was only one floor left. Would the door be open?

If not, could she reach the roof?

Maybe she could bolt the door? Or there might be a fire escape? Didn't all buildings have to have one?

A man grabbed her ankle, and she whirled and shot him point blank in the head. He fell back and tumbled down the stairs, dead. One more obstacle behind her.

"Don't follow me. I will kill you all," she yelled into the emptiness.

She stumbled her way onto the top floor landing, ragged breaths sawing in and out of her chest, and yanked on the door but it was locked. "No!"

Sobbing now, she headed to the next door, marked Exit, probably to the roof, so she burst through and slammed the door, then shot at it until there were no bullets left in the gun. She jammed the door with her revolver.

Her mind inundated by crazy thoughts, she couldn't think, she could only clutch Christina tight. Pamela staggered out onto the wide expanse. Far below, sirens and lights flashed. Dozens of police cars and fire engines surrounded the hospital. A SWAT team vehicle pulled up, and soon snipers poured out of the back.

Oh, God, they were going to kill her.

She sank to her knees, rocking the baby to and fro. "All I wanted was for you and me to be happy. I won't give you up, baby girl. I can't."

FIFTEEN MINUTES COULD be an eternity. Daniel swerved into the hospital parking lot and the SUV screeched to a halt, Noah and Elijah on his tail. He grabbed Raven's hand, and they raced to the entrance.

Two cops blocked them. "I'm sorry, sir. The hospital is on lockdown."

"Frank Detry, the SWAT negotiator, requested us," Daniel said, his voice firm. They didn't have time for this. "We have information about Pamela Winter."

Expression skeptical, the cop muttered a few words into his radio. His eyes widened. "Follow me."

The cop led them to the elevator, and he punched the top floor button. They exited, and a solemn-looking man with a military haircut walked over to them. "I'm Detry. Thank you for coming." His gaze pinned Raven. "Pamela Winter wants to see you. She's threatened to jump off the roof with her baby if she can't talk to you."

Raven blanched. "What about the little girl called Hope Harrison? Maybe she's been listed as Hope Winter? She's my daughter."

"She's fine. She's on the pediatric floor, in no danger. I'd like to tell you that you can see her now, but I need your help. I don't know how much longer my team can keep Pamela talking."

Daniel cut him off. "No way in hell are you going up there, Raven. This woman's already tried to kill you twice. Hell, she blew up her own son."

"I have to go," Raven insisted. "That poor frightened baby never did anything to anyone. Her mother is dead. So is her father. She's Hope's sister. Her twin. Who's going to look out for Christina if not me?"

Daniel couldn't fight her. He'd have done the same thing. But he also knew she wouldn't be out there alone. No way. No how. "I'm going with you."

"I checked you and CTC out," Detry said. "We could use you. Come with me."

In the stairwell leading to the roof, the SWAT team fit Raven with a bulletproof vest. "She has a gun, and she shot a few security guards and killed a cop, but she hasn't fired it in the past half hour. We're hoping she's out of ammo, but we don't know that for certain. The door is barricaded. If you can get her away from the roof's edge, we can take her out."

"You can't attack. She's holding a baby."

"We'll try to stop her other ways, but if she starts shooting again, all bets are off."

Daniel walked Raven to the door and turned her in his arms. "You really want to do this?"

"No. I'm petrified, but I'm the only chance that child has."

"You'll stay safe. No crazy chances. Promise?" He touched her cheek. "Come back to me?"

"Now?" she said incredulously. "Now you get mushy on me?"

"Come back to me, and I'll work on my timing."

She went up on tiptoe and kissed him on the lips. "I'll be back. You've given me another incentive."

The SWAT negotiator hammered on the door to the roof. "Mrs. Winter, we've met your demands. Olivia is here."

They heard scraping at the door, then it swung part of the way open.

"Send her out alone, or Christina dies." Pamela's voice became more distant with every word.

When Raven looked around the door, she saw Pamela had returned to her spot on the ledge. The baby looked very ill. Her weak cries broke Raven's heart.

"Pamela?" Raven called. "Your baby is sick and needs care. Please let me help you."

The woman whirled. "Help me? My baby is *dying,* and it's all your fault. You wanted to wait. Get another opinion before the transplant. Christina didn't have time to wait. *You did this to her!*"

Fear struck Raven's heart. "Please, Pamela, come away from the edge. We can work this out."

"Sure. You'd like that," Pamela raved. "You know they're going to take Christina away from me. I bet you wanted them both all the time."

A grappling hook flew over the edge of the roof. She stiffened, desperate not to give anything away. *Daniel?* She had to make certain Pamela didn't look his way. She shifted positions. "I was happy with Hope. I wanted to help you. *I intended to help you.*"

Pamela paced on the ledge, her movements erratic.

"But you had to wait. Then you had to hit your head. I only pushed you a little. You tripped on a toy. You messed up everything."

DANIEL HELD ON to the rope, slowly inching his way up from the top floor window to the roof. Elijah and Noah were climbing up the opposite side. Hopefully Winter didn't have three bullets left, or the surprise would be theirs instead. Daniel hauled himself quietly over the roof ledge, ignoring the agony in the hand and leg that had been shattered in Bellevaux.

An air-conditioning duct blocked him from Winter's view, and a lot of space separated him from the two women. Pamela looked at Raven with such hatred that a chill invaded Daniel.

"Get on the ledge with me." Pamela aimed the gun at Raven's head. "Now."

She'd *promised* him she'd stay safe. When they made it off this roof, he'd...he'd kiss her until he forgot this moment ever happened. Daniel's heart stuck in his throat as Raven stepped onto the narrow lip of the building.

Wind buffeted both women, but Raven had the added disadvantage of the recent concussion, and she wobbled precariously on the thin concrete shelf.

"Please," Raven begged, holding out her arms. "Let me take the baby inside."

Pamela waved the gun at Raven.

"She's mine. No one else can have her," Pamela raged. "If you'd just done what you were told, Christina would have gotten her treatment already. She'd be cured."

Raven took a step forward. "The doctors can still help her, Pamela. Don't give up on your daughter."

Daniel caught Noah's profile in the corner of his eye and spotted two SWAT snipers on the roof across the way. If Pamela would only give Raven the baby.

Raven was way too close to her, though. If Pamela went over, she could take Raven down with her.

"Christopher is dead. I killed my own son. You really think they're ever going to let me see her again? What do I have left?"

"Christina isn't going to die if you let her go back inside the hospital now," Raven argued. She took one step closer, and Pamela turned to face her, her back toward Daniel.

He leaned forward then ran silently ahead. He couldn't cry out a warning, not without making things worse. His fists clenched, he crouched in position, waiting for an opportunity.

Pamela peered over the side, and a cry went up from the crowd. "They want me to jump, those animals." Christina whimpered, and Pamela hugged the baby closer. "That's the kind of world I'd be leaving her in. She's better off dead. We both are.

"Ashes, ashes, we all fall down..."

Pamela bent over, staring at the street below. "It's time to end this."

Raven reached toward Pamela. "Don't. Please."

"I'm not going alone. You're coming with me." Pamela grabbed Raven's arm and headed over the side.

Daniel lunged for Raven, arms outstretched. He barely grasped her wrist before she fell. His entire body tensed, and he yanked her to safety.

Elijah and Noah came in from the other side and snagged hold of Pamela, but she was already dangling off the roof, fighting them violently. "Let me go!"

Daniel raced back to the edge. The crowd below shouted and pointed. The firemen had a large trampoline set up to catch anyone who fell, but Daniel knew the baby would never survive a fall from that height by herself.

Pamela jerked against Elijah and Noah, and the baby slipped from her arms.

Pamela had lost her hold on the baby.

Daniel dove off the roof and grabbed the baby as she fell. The ground came up fast, and just before he landed, he twisted, landing on his back on the trampoline, Christina cradled in his arms.

Pamela screamed, berserk now, biting Elijah's hand and breaking his hold. Noah still had her, but he was dragged halfway over the ledge, scrambling for a foothold and struggling to keep his grip on her. Elijah lay on his belly, grabbing for her again, but she slammed her gun hard against Noah's head and pushed away from him.

She aimed at Raven, who had come up behind Noah to help.

"I saved one for you," Pamela said and pulled the trigger just as Noah shoved her aside.

Daniel watched from down below, frozen, as Pamela whirled around, lost her balance and plummeted to the ground. The firemen who were helping Daniel and the baby from the trampoline had no time to move it to save her.

Daniel clutched the baby protectively to his chest, shielding her from the sight. His heart filled with the most incredible tenderness as the tiny little one sobbed weakly and curled in closer to him.

Raven exited the hospital and ran into Daniel's arms. "Is it over?"

"It's over, and this precious girl needs a doctor."

Raven looked at the possessive way he was holding Christina and smiled. "It looks like she's already worked some of her own medicine."

Daniel felt the cold, dark places inside him start to fill with a healing warmth as he thought of the future. "You may be right."

THE EIGHT DAYS that had passed after the events on the roof could have easily been eighty. Dressed in an isolation suit, Raven rocked Christina, her slight weight barely registering. The chemo had taken its toll, but Christina was holding her own. The little girl let out a small yawn, then settled in for a nap. Her pale face remained wan, and every night Raven hit her knees in prayer that the transplant would work. She'd fallen in love with Hope's twin, who looked so much like her daughter. And yet they were very different. Hope had a light about her. Christina was an old soul. Quiet, a follower, but always watching.

At first the hospital wouldn't let Raven see Christina, but Daniel had come to their rescue once again. When social services had sent in a caseworker, he'd called CTC. She didn't know who Ransom Grainger was, besides head of CTC, but the man had major connections. He'd provided her with an attorney, and now Raven had temporary custody of Christina, hoping to make it permanent. The lawyer thought they had a good chance because of Hope.

Raven prayed he was right.

She pushed the rocker back and forth until Christina's breathing became slow and regular, then she placed her in her ICU crib. With a last look at the little girl who had been through so much, she quietly exited the isolation ward.

Outside, she removed the protective clothing and mask and leaned back against the door. Her eyes burned with unshed tears. What if Christina didn't make it? She didn't want to lose her now.

She felt an arm pull her close. She didn't have to open her eyes to know his touch, his scent. She leaned into Daniel.

"How is she?" he whispered.

"She's so weak, so tired. I'm scared."

"She's a fighter, too. I've seen those determined eyes." Raven smiled. "She is that. Where's Hope?"

"Your daughter is now trying to keep up with Ethan, the son of my sheriff buddy, Blake, and his wife, Amanda, from Carder. They took her for pizza. Ethan has decided he's going to marry her someday."

"Let's get her out of diapers first," Raven said. She rested her head against Daniel's chest. "I hope I did the right thing in okaying the transplant."

"If it had been Hope—"

"I would have done the same thing." She gave him a tired smile. "Thank you."

"For what?"

"For being here. Most wouldn't want to be bothered."

Daniel rubbed the nape of his neck. "You needed me. I told you that I'd be here as long as you needed me." He held out his hand. "How about some fresh air?"

She nodded, and they left the hospital. Trouble trotted right beside Daniel, following them into an open area before settling in the grass and watching them.

Ignoring their canine voyeur, she breathed in and stared at the man beside her. She wanted to ask him a question, but she was afraid of the answer. However, her heart needed to know. "How long are you staying?"

He dropped her hand and stepped back. "Do you want me to leave?"

"I never want you to leave." Raven couldn't meet his gaze. "If you'd asked me a few weeks ago if I would or could fall in love in a few days, I would have called you crazy. Daniel, I fell in love with you."

He stared at her, open-mouthed.

Heat rose in her cheeks. "Yeah, that's what I thought you'd say. I need someone in my life who wants a family. I have two girls to look after. I can't—" Her voice broke. "If you don't want the same, I…I can't be around you anymore. It makes me want…more than you can give."

"What do you want?" His eyes burned into her, holding her captive.

"I've seen you with Hope. You're always here, always caring. You make my heart race when you touch me. I love you, Daniel Adams, but I don't think you feel the same."

"You're wrong." He pressed his lips softly to hers. Raven's entire body collapsed against him. "I love you, Raven. You gave me stillness and peace that I never thought I'd find. You touched me in that wine cellar and drove away my demons. But more than that, I've watched you with Christina. I've watched you love that little girl you didn't know. You gave her the strength to fight. How could I not love you?"

With a shudder, Daniel held her close.

She shivered against him, and Daniel closed his eyes. "I want to be there for you. Forever. Always. I want to love you, the girls and any children we may want in the future. But it's a risk, honey. Those demons will always be there for me. All I can promise is that I'll fight them for you, for the children."

She leaned away and cupped Daniel's cheek. "If you'll fight, I'll be there by your side, Daniel. I will never give up on you. I'll never give up on Christina or Hope."

"Then I have just one question, my love." Daniel knelt on the grass. Raven stared down at him; her breath caught. He pulled a box from his pocket. A bullet casing tumbled out with it, landing on the grass.

Daniel stared at the bit of brass, but didn't pick it up. Instead he held out her ring. "Will you marry me? Can you love me, despite my flaws and my fears?"

She knelt next to him. "I will marry you, Daniel."

He slipped the diamond on her hand. "I promise you, Raven, to never give up. On life, on love, or on you."

Epilogue

Darkness surrounded Daniel. Above him, below him, around him, he could feel the walls against his shoulders.

The nylon play tunnel rippled along him. A joyful giggle tinkled through the darkness, then another joined in the chorus. Finally two small figures collapsed onto his chest and hugged him.

"You captured me, my little princesses." He laughed softly. "What am I going to do?"

A light flicked on, and Daniel looked behind him through one of the open ends of the tunnel. Raven stood in the doorway with her hands on her hips, Trouble sitting at her feet. "You're all going to wash your hands for dinner, that's what you're going to do. Daddy has to study for his big exam."

His two girls ran to their mother and wrapped their arms around her legs. She knelt down and kissed each nose. "I'll be checking those hands, ladies."

"Okay, Mommy!"

Hope grabbed her sister's hand and dragged her off to the bathroom. Hope was such a little mother to her twin, probably because Chrissy had been so sick for so long.

Trouble wagged his tail and followed the girls.

At four years of age, they'd grown so much since those dark days.

220   *The Cradle Conspiracy*

"Chrissy's color is good." Daniel crossed the room to his wife.

His wife.

His heart flooded with satisfaction. He'd never thought he would be here. Never imagined, after everything that had happened with his father and Daniel's captivity, that he would find any kind of peace. Now he was over a year into getting a doctorate in psychology to specialize in helping victims of PTSD.

Not only had Raven quieted his soul, she'd filled his heart.

She burrowed her face into Daniel's chest and wrapped her arms around his waist, leaning into him. "The doctor was supposed to call today. He hasn't called. That can't be good."

"We'll deal with whatever comes our way." Daniel lowered his mouth to hers, tasting her lips with a promise. "Never give up. On life, on love, on each other. Wasn't that our vow?"

"Always." Her eyes held a tinge of fear. Neither one of them had allowed themselves to think beyond the bone marrow transplant. They couldn't. He wrapped his arm around Raven, and together they walked down the stairs.

The girls stood on the landing, wet hands outstretched, identical grins on their faces. Just as Raven bent over to inspect the job, the phone rang.

She froze. Daniel plucked the receiver from the base unit. "Hello?"

He strode over to her and leaned her back against him, tilting the phone so she could hear. His body tensed, bracing himself for the worse.

"We received Christina's tests results, Mr. Adams. Her blood work is as normal as it can be."

Raven's knees gave way, and Daniel took her full weight. He couldn't stop grinning.

"We'll run the test periodically," the doctor added, "but I think we're out of the woods. Congratulations."

Their daughters, sensing something had happened, stopped their playing. Chrissy looked up at her parents. "What's wrong, Mommy?"

Hope gripped her sister's hand. "Is Chrissy sick again, Mama?" The girl's eyes grew wet with unshed tears.

Daniel raced across the room and grabbed one daughter in each arm. "Everybody's well." He whirled them around. "We're having a celebration. Ice cream all around."

"Yea!" The twins escaped his embrace, skidded to the kitchen and stared intently up at the freezer.

Daniel held out his hand, and Raven linked her fingers with his. He kissed the tips one by one, and she shivered.

"How about a date tonight? We could make some more memories," Daniel said, his voice low and full of promise.

Raven's eyes flared with passion, and Daniel smiled at the love shining just for him.

She leaned into him, her weight trusting and true. "Memories we'll never forget."

* * * * *

Merry Christmas
& A Happy New Year!

Thank you for a wonderful
2013...

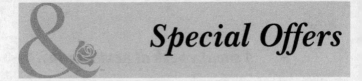

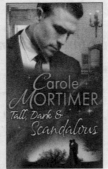
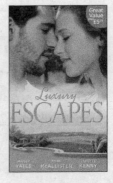

Come in from the cold this Christmas with two of our favourite authors. Whether you're jetting off to Vermont with Sarah Morgan or settling down for Christmas dinner with Fiona Harper, the smiles won't stop this festive season.

Visit:
www.millsandboon.co.uk

0114/MB452

MILLS & BOON®
Book Club

Join the Mills & Boon Book Club

Want to read more **Intrigue** books?
We're offering you **2 more** absolutely **FREE!**

We'll also treat you to these fabulous extras:

- 🌹 Exclusive offers and much more!

- 🌹 FREE home delivery

- 🌹 FREE books and gifts with our special rewards scheme

Get your free books now!

visit www.millsandboon.co.uk/bookclub
or call Customer Relations on 020 8288 2888